THE
GORDIAN
KNOT

KEVIN MARSH

Published by Paragon Publishing
© 2014 Kevin Marsh

ISBN 978-1-78222-265-1

Book design, layout and production management by Into Print
www.intoprint.net
+44 (0)1604 832149

Printed and bound in UK and USA by Lightning Source

Other books by Kevin Marsh:
The Belgae Torc
The Witness

www.kevinmarshnovels.co.uk

'A friend is someone who knows about you and still loves you'.
Elbert Hubbard

For Maria my best friend

PREFACE

The Gordian knot is a legend of Phrygian Gordian associated with Alexander the Great and is often used as a metaphor for an intractable problem.

I thought this an appropriate title because of the challenges facing my characters. The mystery and power surrounding the Belgae Torc has an effect on them all and this forms the basis of The Torc Trilogy.

As the plot is linked with both Germanic Paganism and Celtic mythology, I chose the Triquetra, a three cornered shape and symbol used by both Christians and Polytheists, as a foundation for some of the druidic rituals in the story. It is also an appropriate image for the cover of the book.

This particular design is influenced by an illustration in the Lindisfarne Gospels and although it's a Celtic or 'trinity knot', I think it symbolises the metaphor perfectly. The colour green and the Celtic element is for Orlagh and her Irish roots.

Every aspect of my novel is influenced by this magical design, and the title; The Gordian knot, leads nicely into the final part of The Torc Trilogy, but that is of course, another story.

Kevin Marsh
March 2014

Part One
Fountain of Life

Thou shalt have no other gods before Me

Exodus 20:3

PROLOGUE

A beautifully restored Junkers JU52, nicknamed 'Iron Annie' lifted her wheels from the tarmac and rose gracefully into the air. Olga Zindel and her brother Ernst were at the controls, they were both wearing wide grins across their faces.

'Iron Annie' was heavy and slow to react, but she was a pleasure to fly. Her cockpit contained none of the refinements of a modern aircraft, but that was her charm. Constructed in the 1930s, she had been designed using flowing lines and curves that were not just aesthetically pleasing but aerodynamically sound. Her three BMW Hornet A2 liquid cooled radial engines were original but had been extensively overhauled and it was not just her engines that had been refurbished, her airframe had received a thorough examination and now the aircraft was once again fully operational.

Olga eased the control column gently forward as the aircraft reached its operational height and at 4000 metres, they settled into level flight. With the engines set for economic cruising, the vibrations running through the airframe subsided and now both Olga and Ernst could begin to relax and enjoy the ride.

From the windows on the flight deck, they had a clear view over the mountain range that stretched out ahead of them; it reminded Olga of a wrinkled duvet. The colour of the terrain was as varied as a patchwork quilt; rich greens indicating thick forest and vegetation interspersed with shades of brown and grey where the rocks and sandy soil formed mountaintops and valleys.

With Olga in the pilot's seat, Ernst sat at the little navigation table situated just after the flight deck. One of them would have to remain at the controls at all times; 'Iron Annie' was high maintenance, she had no autopilot or satellite navigation systems.

Speaking into the intercom microphone attached to his earphones, Ernst gave his sister a direction heading and she made the necessary changes to their course. The noise inside the cockpit made communication impossible; the only way they could make themselves heard was by using the intercom system.

'Iron Annie's' nose was now pointing due east and her controls were set for level flight, her trim was good and she required less muscle to hold her steady. Glancing over her shoulder at her brother, Olga nodded her

appreciation and a wide grin split her face, she would have it no other way. She loved to fly vintage aircraft and had logged up many hours. Ernst preferred to fly modern aeroplanes especially jets but he too had hundreds of hours logged flying old piston engined aircraft.

"Well that's it." Ernst spoke into the microphone. "I'm going to get us some coffee."

Easing his long legs from the cramped space, he made his way back into the cargo hold and grasping at the overhead rail, ducked under a bulkhead rib before straightening up in the larger space beyond. The fuselage resembled a long corrugated tube, the walls made from thin aluminium sheet vibrated and rattled especially when flying through turbulence, but this was nothing unusual.

There was only one crate strapped into the hold and reaching down beside it, he unstrapped his satchel containing a thermos flask and neat packs of sandwiches.

Ernst and Olga were a team, business partners struggling to make ends meet. They were in the airfreight business but their ageing cargo jet would never pass another bill of health. Their enterprise was sadly coming to an end as was their relationship with their financiers, so it was an opportunity that neither of them could have imagined when an organisation calling themselves the Phoenix Legion contacted them. The job on offer was too good to miss; it was hardly a difficult decision to make. On closer inspection, they discovered that a group of executives devoted to everything German ran the Phoenix Legion and both Olga and Ernst were patriotic enough to appreciate this.

Glancing around the hold, Ernst had to pinch himself; he still couldn't believe that he was actually flying a Junkers 52. The level of restoration was breathtaking, it was as if the old aircraft had just rolled off the production line, but 'Iron Annie' was in fact older than he and his sisters combined age.

He eyed the packing case. Fabricated from wood, it stood waist high with dimensions that made it a perfect cube, but strangely, it looked a little out of proportion. He wondered what it contained, they had docu-ments relating to its passage, but the contents remained a mystery, the inventory simply stated archaeological artefacts.

He was aware that the German high command during World War Two were fascinated by ancient treasures, he also knew that priceless items were stolen from Europe during the German advance. Maybe this case contained such treasures; he frowned as his imagination threatened to run wild.

Their destination was also a mystery; an abandoned airfield in northern Turkey, but he was professional enough not to ask questions, it was simply his job to deliver the goods.

Squeezing back into the cockpit, he sat in the co-pilots seat next to his sister and poured two mugs of coffee. Handing her one he then turned his attention to unwrapping the packs of sandwiches.

"What do you think we are carrying?" Olga glanced at him as she took the mug.

"I've no idea." He replied.

Usually she didn't care about such things but today was different and as Olga chewed thoughtfully on her sandwich she had no idea why her curiosity was aroused, she simply had a burning desire to know what was inside that packing crate. Earlier she had watched from the edge of the runway as men loaded it into the aircraft and it was then that something strange happened. The hairs on the back of her neck had stood up and she had an overwhelming desire to look inside the crate.

Curiosity was an infectious thing; she was going to have to satisfy it before long. Olga shuddered as she checked the instrument panel. One of the engine temperature gauges was a little high and watching it intently, she realised that the needle was climbing slowly beyond the normal operating range. There was not yet cause for concern but instinctively she reached for the throttle and reduced the revs to that engine. This would make little difference to their progress and with a slight adjustment to the trim wheel she nodded with satisfaction.

"Just keep an eye on that Ernst, we don't want to break it." She grinned before handing control over to her brother.

They had been in the air for almost two hours and were flying over a barren mountain range with peaks reaching to just over 3000 metres. It was not a particularly hazardous journey, there were no high winds or pockets of turbulence to send them jerking across the sky. The aircraft rose and fell gently in the Mediterranean air, the only thing to rattle the fuselage was the vibrations of the engines. Olga left her seat and stretched her long legs out before disappearing into the cargo hold. She was not as big as Ernst and was able to move around much easier in the cramped space. Once she had used the tiny chemical cubicle, which had been added especially for their convenience, she eyed the packing case with interest. Reaching out she rested her hand on the warm wooden top and could feel the vibrations of the aircraft running through her fingers. Pulling her hand away sharply it was as if the case was alive and looking around she mumbled something under her breath, embarrassed by her childish reaction.

She had to know what was inside. No one would know if she lifted the lid, she would of course replace it once her curiosity was satisfied.

Moving towards the maintenance locker, she found a small crowbar and used it to prise off the lid. The nails came out easily and placing it to one side, she began to feel around with her fingers. Pushing her hands into the packaging, the shredded paper was like straw protecting the items from a hazardous journey.

Her fingers touched something solid and lifting it carefully from its resting place, she pulled out a silver flask. There was no indication to its contents and once she had scrutinised it she put it down carefully beside the crate. Going in again, she found a package wrapped in greaseproof paper. Unwrapping it carefully her eyes widened as soon as she saw the light glittering from its twisted golden surface. A beautifully crafted neck ring appeared in her hands and lifting it higher she knew it was priceless. It was old; she had seen such things in museums, but never before had she held an object of such ancient beauty. She recognised it as a Celtic torc crafted from finely twisted white gold and she revelled in its magnificence. Looking closer she could see gold threads woven together to form a rope thicker than her thumb, the quality of the work-manship was exquisite; she had never seen anything so beautifully worked. Finials of solid gold had been crafted into the shape of horses' heads; these adorned the ends and a chain so fine she could hardly see the links. Although delicately made it was strong even after all these centuries and moving closer to one of the windows set into the fuselage, Olga held it up until it caught the light. She studied the symbols carved into the gold with interest, she had no idea what they meant; its message from the past was beyond her understanding.

After the initial shock of her discovery, a wide grin settled on her face and she experienced an overwhelming urge to try it on. It would do no harm to slip it around her neck. As soon as the idea flashed into her head, her fingers were unfastening the golden chain, and lifting it up she slipped it over her head.

The weight of it against her neck was satisfying, its significance as an object of power was re-assuring and it made her feel like a queen. Wearing such a magnificent object, she could now begin to understand how a chief must have felt. The torc represented the wealth of a nation and she was proud to be wearing it even if it was for just a fleeting moment, besides it could have been her own ancestors worshipping the bearer of such a torc. Turning towards the cockpit, she wanted to show her brother, the power of the torc was intoxicating, she must share it with Ernst. She could feel its force running throughout her body, it was like a weak electrical current or a vibration against her skin then suddenly from the corner of her eye, she thought she saw movement. Turning towards the tail section, she knew it was unlikely, there could not possibly be anyone there, but her eyes widened and she drew in a sharp breath. Standing at the end of the fuselage was a red haired woman dressed in a long white robe. Olga blinked, it couldn't be true, in her heightened state of excitement she realised that her imagination must be running wild, but the woman continued to stare. Vibrations running through the metal at her throat became stronger and the torc began to feel hot. It was as if it was alive, like a serpent encircling her neck, it drew tighter and the first glimmer of fear touched her soul. Moving her hands to her throat, Olga tried to lift the torc over her head. She wanted rid of it, her breath was coming in quick gasps, and as the torc wound tighter around her neck she cried out in panic, but the sound of her terror was lost in the noise of the aircraft.

The red haired woman moved slowly towards her and with every step, the illusion became more realistic. Reaching out, her ice-cold fingertips stung Olga's cheeks and moving backwards Olga almost stumbled. She couldn't pull her eyes away from the woman's stare, her rich green eyes seemed to burn into her very soul and Olga shuddered as evil thoughts filled her head. She had no idea where they came from but they occupied her mind until she could think of nothing else.

Suddenly as if unable to support the overwhelming burden, her legs gave way and she struggled for breath. The woman looming over her reached out and placed her hands on top of Olga's head. She could no longer move and as her eyesight began to fade the red haired woman seemed to enter her head, her evil grin devouring her soul and unable to resist, Olga took her final breath.

In the cockpit, Ernst felt the aircraft lurch and his eyes flew to the instrument panel. The gauge registering the nose engine's temperature was dangerously high and it no longer sounded smooth. Gripping the throttle handle, he eased it back reducing power to the engine and immediately the noise began to subside as the engine responded. Nudging the two remaining throttles forward, he increased the revs to both wing engines and resumed level flight, he then adjusted the trim wheel to compensate for the distribution of power before shutting down the ailing engine. As soon as this was done, he opened the cowling flaps to allow cool air to rush into the engine compartment; this would help cool the overheated engine before any more damage could be done. Slowly the needle on the temperature gauge edged away from the danger zone and Ernst sighed with relief, but then another shudder ran through the aircraft. Suddenly the port wing rose as it rode an invisible cloud of turbulence and gripping the control yoke tightly, Ernst was experienced enough not to fight the aircraft. Feeling for its movements, he coaxed it gently until the airframe settled down.

"Olga," he called over the intercom, "I need you here sister." His voice was edged with urgency but there was no response. Ernst frowned, and thinking the worst wondered if the sudden movement had unbalanced his sister, maybe she had fallen. If she was injured, there was nothing he could do to help her, he had to remain at the controls his hands were full with flying the aircraft.

Glancing worriedly over his shoulder, he could see nothing beyond the bulkhead separating the cockpit from the cargo hold.

"Where are you Olga?" He spoke into the intercom again more urgently this time.

Suddenly the starboard engine began to clatter and glancing at the control panel Ernst turned his head to look out over the wing. Smoke was billowing from the engine cowling, curling back in dirty black clouds over the wing and he could hardly believe what he saw. There had been no indication that the engine was about to fail. Instinctively he reached for the fire extinguisher switch and once activated he watched as black smoke turned to grey. Ernst held his breath, the next few seconds were critical but with a sigh of relief, there were no flames, the extinguisher had done its job. The temperature gauge was reading normal and the engine was still running, but he would have to close the cowling louvres. If there were sparks around the engine the blast of air moving over it may fan them into something more serious, however by doing this the engine would soon overheat just like the first one. All this ran through his head in a second. Ernst reduced power to that engine and immediately the propeller began to lose momentum. He checked his altitude, it was holding at just under 4000 metres, the peaks below fluctuated between 2000 and 3000 metres, this gave him an operational height of just a 1000 metres. It was a slim margin but if the situation did not become any worse, he was prepared to live with it. He knew that at some point he might have to trade altitude for airspeed, but with the engines in their condition increasing power and trying to climb was out of the question.

He adjusted the inner flap section of the wings, this effectively lowered the stalling speed and now the aircraft should remain airborne even if it lost more momentum then, easing forward on the throttle, he coaxed a little more power out of the remaining good engine. The nose began to creep round so he applied pressure to the rudder bar to counter the yaw.

He had no idea what was going on, what had caused the engines to overheat was a mystery; there must be some mechanical anomaly because none of them were running at full power.

"Olga, I really need you now." He shouted into the intercom. His heart was hammering inside his chest and his mouth had gone dry. Tightening his grip on the yoke, he could feel every vibration running through the aircraft, then without warning the starboard engine coughed and its propeller seized. Pushing the emergency stop button he shut the engine down before it could destroy itself and damage the aircraft, then pushing the throttle on the remaining engine all the way forward the nose slewed sideways. Using all of his strength, he fought against the pull and applying more rudder the aircraft began to side slip. Frantically he searched for somewhere to land, they would not remain in the air for long, the strain on one engine alone especially at full power was too much.

The terrain below was mountainous and barren, nothing was level and he realised there was little hope of getting down in one piece. Turning the dial on the radio, he selected an emergency channel and began to send out a mayday.

I

BERLIN 1943

Pale autumnal sunlight bathed the façade of the Institute of Anthropology, Human Genetics and Eugenics and as Dr Harald Von Brandt stood in the street, he stared up at the building and smiled. This was going to be his place of work for the foreseeable future and the prospect of living in Berlin pleased him immensely.

Harald was a scientist, his field of study Human Genetics. He was involved in a project to study the effects of poisonous substances on human beings and his principle aim was to discover antidotes to an increasing number of poisons emerging from laboratories all over Europe. His work had taken him to numerous concentration camps throughout Germany and Poland, where 'volunteers' from all walks of life had been made available for his experiments. Joseph Mengele was at the head of the organisation responsible for carrying out these tests, and Harald was appalled by the suffering that people in his care had been subjected to under the umbrella of advancing the good of science.

Harald had been transferred from his university in Hamburg twelve months previously because he was the most senior and respected scientist in his field, but now under orders from Mengele, his work in Human Genetics was taking him in a very different direction from the one he had started out on.

His time at the concentration camps had filled him with dismay but he had learnt to keep his opinions to himself. He had always known of such places but the suffering and distress of the people incarcerated there went beyond his comprehension.

Whilst working in Poland, Harald had met Adolf Hitler. Hitler had given a talk to a group of scientists on the racial and eugenic policies of Nazi Germany, and when the presentation had finished Hitler had singled him out. During their strange conversation, the Führer told him of his admiration for the Greek city of ancient Sparta. He made references to his second book, which had not yet been published, giving Harald an insight into its contents. In it was a section dedicated to selective infanticide. Hitler regarded Sparta to have been the first 'Volkisch State', and this he looked upon as a model for Germany. He was convinced that by identifying the sick, weak and deformed children, their destruction was more decent and in truth, a thousand times more humane than allowing them to reach maturity and pass on their defective genes by breeding. The cost of sterilising undesirable degenerates was a drain on the treasury so why not remove the problem at the beginning?

Hitler was committed to the idea of breeding a race of pure blood Aryans and had charged Heinrich Himmler, the S.S. leader, to form a selective breeding program. He wanted women of 'pure blood' to bear fair haired, blue eyed children, so across Germany and Norway an organisation called Lebensborn came in to existence. This was a program that allowed the support of genetically valuable women to have children without the stigma of being outside of marriage.

Hitler had invited Harald to be part of the Lebensborn breeding program. As a selected member, he was considered to be genetically sound and this was another reason for his transfer to Berlin.

Picking his way through the crowds that filled the pavements, Harald strode up the steps leading to the entrance of the Institute and once inside went straight to his laboratory. He was in charge of dozens of technicians who were involved in delicate experiments analysing samples taken from the local population in order to determine who was 'genetically sick'. Reports and additional information had been collected from doctors and welfare departments from all over the districts and it was this paperwork that had to be carefully checked against the results of his experiments. Once his reports were complete it was the job of the S.S. Medical board to decide who was worthy of life. Those selected for sterilisation would be sent to a specially commissioned centre and those who were to be exterminated under Action T4, a 'euthanasia' program, went to an extermination camp.

Harald did his best to subdue his feelings of guilt and revulsion; he was involved in actions that went against his moral principles but what interested him most was his study of poisonous gasses, toxins and hazardous substances. He realised that his discoveries could possibly enhance medical treatments, or could be used on the land in the form of pesticides, but he was under no illusions, the military regime were desperate to develop weapons of mass destruction.

Part of his work involved searching for vaccines and antidotes that would combat the effects of such poisons and he was on the verge of a breakthrough. Work that he had begun almost eighteen months earlier was about to come to fruition. He had discovered a vaccination that would counter the effects of the powerful nerve gas Sarin. Sarin had been discovered in the early 1930s and was initially developed as a pesticide, but now it was about to be used as a weapon far more deadly than anything seen in the trenches of the Great War.

It was his belief that once his vaccine had been administered the body would become immune to the effects of the poisonous gas. He had no idea how long the drug would last once in the system or the side effects if any, but his experiments would help him to understand the limitations of his discovery. He had not yet made his work public, he would keep it to himself until he had proof that it was effective, only then would he inform his superiors.

"Good morning Von Brandt." A tall middle aged man greeted him as he entered the building.

"Dr Ziegler, it is indeed a good morning." Harald eyed the man suspiciously. He loathed Ziegler, he considered him a coldblooded psychopath.

"I have the patient you require in the testing room."

"Thank you. Make her comfortable and I'll be there in a moment."

The testing room was a gas chamber, an airtight sterile room where experiments were carried out. Gas was pumped in and contained for a controlled period of time before being extracted by pipe work and collected in tanks where it was then safely disposed of.

Harald, shrugging off his jacket, slipped into a white lab coat and made his way to the testing room where a dark haired young woman was sitting nervously on a metal chair. The first thing he noticed as he entered the room was that she looked terrified.

"My name is Dr Von Brandt," he said trying to sound calm and reassuring. "I don't want you to be afraid; I'm not going to hurt you."

They were alone; Ziegler would be joining them shortly. He was in the laboratory preparing the drug that Harald would inject into his patient.

"In a few minutes I am going to give you an injection, you shouldn't feel any effects. Have you had your breakfast this morning?"

The pale faced girl nodded.

"Good," Harald listened to her heart through his stethoscope before checking her airways and lungs. He read her notes carefully then he said. "So, you are Christina and you are seventeen years old."

She nodded again but remained silent.

"Good," Harald smiled. "Once I have given you the drug I will leave you alone and observe through that window. After about twenty minutes, I will come back in and carry out some simple tests. I will check your heart, breathing and temperature; I will ask you for a urine sample and take some blood. Do you understand?"

The girl glanced up at him and Harald saw dark smudges beneath her eyes. She looked exhausted and incredibly vulnerable and he couldn't help feeling sorry for her.

"You must drink plenty of water." He said indicating to the jug sitting on the metal table.

Ziegler entered the room and put the tray he was carrying down noisily on the table next to the water jug. Picking up the syringe, he made a point of waving it towards the girl. He knew that Harald liked to pamper his patients with kindly talk, but sub humans like this deserved no such treatment.

"Give it to me." Harald snapped. "I will administer the drug."

Ziegler frowned and almost snarled, he was looking forward to sticking the needle into the girl, he would make her squirm, she deserved all the pain he could give.

Harald was gentle with the needle and although Christina closed her eyes and tensed her muscles, she felt nothing as he injected the drug into her arm.

"There we are, now that wasn't so bad." He looked at her and smiled.

Ziegler had no idea what Harald was experimenting with and because of this he despised him even more. He could discover nothing about Harald's work; he merely did what he was told. This was not an arrangement he was happy with but he carried out his duties regardless of his feelings.

"Just try to relax," Harald told the girl. "No harm will come of you." He was fairly sure of the outcome of this test, but there was always a risk.

Leaving Christina alone in the room, Harald sealed the door and went into the adjoining laboratory where he paused to look through the observation window. She was staring back at him, her eyes huge and black, were filled with tears. She was holding herself rigid, her trembling hands clasped tightly in her lap, the sleeve on her left arm still rolled up where he had given her the injection.

He paused before reaching for the lever that would send gas into the room, then sliding it forward he activated the valve. The only indication that the system was working were the dials on the control panel slowly turning.

Christina could hear the hiss of gas coming through the pipes and instinctively she held her breath. She stared fearfully around, her heart hammering inside her chest, but nothing happened. The air remained clear; there was no discolouration or fog as the room filled up. When her lungs were about to burst, she could stand it no longer and let out a gasp of frustration. The precious air inside her rushed out and she sobbed, she could do nothing to halt the breath that expanded her chest. Fully expecting to be overcome by poison, tears spilled from the corner of her eyes but she remained conscious. The air was tainted with a sour odour that stung at the back of her throat but her head remained clear and all the while, her hands were clasped tightly in her lap.

Harald watched from behind the protective glass. He knew that it would take about three minutes for the room to become saturated with gas; he also knew that if it wasn't for the vaccine, Christina would be dead already. The gas mixture he was using was lethal and would have killed her in seconds.

Three minutes passed but Harald waited another sixty seconds before pulling another lever that activated a pump and the gas was purged from the room. At the same time, fresh air flooded in and five minutes later, it was safe for him to enter.

"How are you feeling my dear?" He asked the moment he stepped through the door.

Christina was unable to answer, her throat was constricted by sobs and tears soaked her chalk white face.

"Take your time." He told her softly, and resting his hand lightly on her shoulder, he could feel her body trembling through the thin material of her blouse. The shock of the experiment must have been terrifying and he truly felt sorry for her.

Ziegler was watching from the window. He knew that Harald's experiments were sanctioned by the very top, he had seen documentation bearing Mengele's signature, but still he was desperate to know what was going on. He was however wise enough not to ask too many questions.

Harald scribbled in his notebook as he waited for the girl to recover. Once she had regained her composure she told him that she was feeling okay, just a little light headed. She was still trembling, the experience had almost been too much for her to bear, she was convinced that she was about to die. Many of her friends had been taken away and subjected to experiments and most of them were never seen again.

"I told you that everything would be alright," Harald smiled. "We will continue to monitor you for the next few hours. Now," he said giving her a bowl and pointing towards a cubicle. "I would like you to provide me with a urine sample then I will need to take some blood."

She nodded and made her way slowly across the room. Harald, turning his back, busied himself with the equipment that he would need to take a blood sample, and when they were finished, he led her to the door.

"Ziegler, take Christina back to her quarters and have her monitored for the next twenty four hours, if there are any changes report to me immediately."

Ziegler nodded and led Christina away.

Harald was pleased with the outcome of his tests. He had expected the girl to survive, she was young and fit but he would have to carry out similar experiments on subjects of different ages before he would be satisfied that his drug worked.

In the early days before his breakthrough, he was experimenting with atropine and pralidoxime, but these antidotes were ineffective when using a concentrated form of Sarin. Unfortunately, all of his subjects had died from the effects of exposure to the gas.

He had worked tirelessly in his laboratory in Poland searching for a solution to the problem then suddenly all his hard work began to pay off. Now after many months he was in possession of a viable vaccination that would protect people against the effects of concentrated Sarin.

The men in government wanted answers but he realised that if he gave into them many thousands of people would die. Harald was no fool; he knew they were going to use Sarin nerve gas as a weapon of mass destruction. Releasing the concentrated gas over a city would wipe out the population leaving the buildings and belongings untouched. Unlike conventional weapons, this method would be hugely effective but cause no damage to property. An invading army could be vaccinated this would protect them from the effects of any lingering pockets of gas.

Harald finished writing up his notes then dropped his notebook into the wall safe behind the desk in his office before sealing the heavy steel door.

II

Bombs had fallen during the night, the RAF was on the offensive, the bombing of Berlin had begun.

Harald made his way along the path towards the Institute and was shocked by the devastation. Fires still burned in parts of the city and the air was thick with smoke. The sharp acid smell of cordite from high explosives still lingered and it stung the back of his throat. Where once buildings had stood all that remained was burned out ruins and now work parties toiled to clear away debris that littered the streets. Essential services such as water and gas had to be shut off as men went about their dangerous work if further death and injury was to be avoided. Things were bad enough with bodies buried under piles of rubble. These were innocent families, civilians killed in their own homes by the enemy.

When will this madness end? Harald wondered as he stepped over bricks and masonry littering the footpath. Further from the city, the devastation was minimal, stray bombs had damaged properties and started fires but on the whole the suburbs had escaped the maelstrom that swept through the centre.

Eventually he caught sight of his destination, the building looked unscathed and he was relieved to see that nothing had changed. Harald arrived amongst a throng of excitement and expectation and the moment he pushed through the entrance of the Institute he was caught up in the confusion that reigned within. People he had never seen before filled the corridors each carrying armloads of files and equipment. They appeared to be emptying the offices and he had no idea why this was happening. The energy of the place was infectious and as he pushed against the crowds, he frowned. He had received no orders instructing him to pack up and move out. Perhaps this was a precautionary measure, if the bombing was going to continue then it made sense to remove important papers to somewhere safe.

"Have you seen Ziegler?" Harald asked a technician.

"I think he is with the patients." The man answered as he rushed past.

Why would Ziegler be with the patients? The thought filled Harald with a sense of foreboding and as he made his way further into the building, he became increasingly uneasy.

The long corridor took him past various offices and testing laboratories then finally he arrived at the wards where the patients slept.

Suddenly from the left hand side of the corridor two men appeared dragging a woman between them.

"What is the meaning of this?" Harald bellowed.

The men stopped and looked up in surprise. "Dr Von Brandt," one of them stammered uncertainly.

Harald looked at the girl they were supporting and her head lolled sideways. She was dead; a small calibre pistol had been used as a murder weapon and his blood ran cold. He pushed past them and the muffled sound of a pistol being fired filled him with rage.

The ward housed twenty women and iron framed beds were arranged in rows down the length of the room. Many of the women were barely out of their teenage years and most of them were pairs of twins.

Glancing to his right, Harald could see the beds on this side of the room were occupied but something was wrong. It took him a moment to realise the women were dead, each one with a small hole drilled into the side of her head.

"What is the meaning of this?" he shouted.

Ziegler looked up as a group of uniformed officers surrounded him.

"Ah, Dr Von Brandt." One of the men stepped forward. "My name is Wolfgang Eismann and I have orders to close down this facility."

The man was wearing the uniform of an S.S. Officer and his face showed no emotion. Harald shuddered; he disliked Eismann the moment he spoke. He had encountered men like him before, that was in the days when he was forced to work with Joseph Mengele.

Glancing to his left Harald was appalled. Leather straps used to secure the women when uncomfortable procedures were being carried out were now holding them down to their beds. At least these women were still alive, each one shocked into silence by the horrific events that were unfolding around them. Occasionally one would utter a prayer or moan softly, terrified by the prospect of death.

"Close us down?" Harald stared at the man. "I don't understand." He took a step closer. "Why do you find it necessary to murder my patients?"

"Patients?" Eismann mocked. "I see no patients."

"I will not allow you to murder these innocent and defenceless women."

"Dr Von Brandt, you have little choice in the matter, besides, I see no innocent and defenceless women here. These are merely by-products of a foul sub-human species who have no right to remain alive therefore it is my duty to ensure that they are exterminated." He nodded and the pistol popped again, the woman in the nearest bed shuddered then lay still.

"This is outrageous," Harald shouted. "On whose authority are you acting?"

"Ah, you will find that my orders come from the very top." Eismann looked satisfied and it seemed to Harald that he was enjoying every moment of his devilish work.

"By the way Dr Von Brandt," he sneered. "When we are finished here I will require you to hand over the results of your experiments. I want your notes regarding the Sarin gas and the vaccinations that you have developed."

Herald could hardly take it all in, the murder of his patients was horrendous enough but the thought of handing over his notes was something that he could not allow.

The next woman in line was Christina and Ziegler grinned as he approached her bed. He was enjoying himself as much as Eismann, he knew that Harald had become fond of this particular young woman. Slowly and deliberately, he raised his pistol until it was level with the side of her head but it disappointed him when she remained still. She refused to shudder as the warm muzzle touched her skin.

Christina stared up at Harald, her huge dark eyes filled with sadness. He promised to keep her safe, had told her that she would come to no harm, that she was important to his work and he would never hurt her. There was nothing he could do to stop the slaughter and when Ziegler finally squeezed the trigger, she didn't even blink. Harald turned smartly on his heel and marched out of the ward. It was essential that he got to his office before Eismann, he was not going to allow the man to remove any of his papers.

Christina's expression haunted him, the look of utter despair that filled her huge dark eyes overwhelmed him with sadness. He had let her down and he knew he would never be free of her incriminating stare. He wanted to vomit and his head was reeling, but there was no time for self-pity.

Going directly to his office, he opened the wall safe and with trembling hands seized the notebook and stuffed it into his pocket, then turning towards his desk, he gathered up his papers and in a futile attempt to delay Eismann, he stuffed them into the safe and slammed the door. He knew it wouldn't take the man long to get at them, but at least he had the satisfaction of knowing that he had not handed over his work willingly. He would never give his notebook up, it was his prized possession, here were recorded the real results of his tests. His theories were correct, Christina had been living proof of that, his vaccination worked and now he had to get away before it was too late. Eismann and his men would come after him as soon as they realised the notes in his safe were incomplete.

Hannah Stempfle was making her way home after working a shift at the clothing factory. The destruction was appalling, luckily, it had not been sufficient to halt production, but she had never seen anything like it before. The god of war had called and left his visiting card.

The citizens of Berlin were left in shock; they had been assured by the Führer that this could never happen, they were safe, the enemy would not dare wreak havoc on Germany's principal city.

Hannah was still shaken by the terrifying experience. During the night, she had been forced to take shelter in the cellar beneath her house and had remained there until it was daylight. She had been asleep, safe in her bed, the war nothing more than worrying reports on the wireless, it made prices soar in the marketplace, and took young men away from their families, but suddenly it had arrived on their doorstep. The noise of sirens going off in the middle of the night had woken her instantly and she knew what she had to do, but the thought of going into the darkened cellar alone was her worst nightmare come true.

Gripped by fear Hannah could do nothing but listen to the drone of aircraft overhead and then the terrifying sound of bombs as they fell on the city just a few kilometres away was almost too much for her to bear. Some of the bombs had fallen short of their targets, the explosions rattling her house and filling the cellar with dust. The thought of being buried alive had almost driven her insane and squeezing her eyes tightly together, she had whispered a prayer. The raid seemed to go on forever, one fearful hour after another, and in the total darkness of the cellar, she had never felt so alone.

Dodging around a group of men who were piling up bricks on the side of the road, she stumbled and dropped one of the packages that she was carrying. Strong hands reached out to support her, this unexpected act of kindness prevented her from falling and she was able to recover her balance.

"Let me help you," a rich, deep voice heavy with accent sounded close beside her.

Hannah gasped as she turned to look at the man. His dark eyes were striking, his features sharp and lean, a legacy of slave labour and malnutrition. He had once been a handsome man but was now reduced to a shadow of his former self. She shuddered and sensed hopelessness then her eyes were drawn to the star pinned to his chest.

"Thank you but I'm fine." Forcing a smile, she stepped away from him.

He stooped to pick up her fallen package. The wrapping had torn revealing its contents and for the briefest of moments the man looked longingly at the cut of meat, then moving quickly, he folded the flap before holding it out to her.

"Thank you, you are so kind."

His smile was warm and under very different circumstances, Hannah was certain they could have been friends. She held nothing against the Jewish community, she even refused to believe what was being said about these people, but she was painfully aware of the dangers surrounding them.

Glancing away she saw the guards patrolling the street, they were overseeing the work party and it would not do to be seen talking to this man. With a nod of gratitude, she took her package and hurried away.

Once inside the house Hannah stood for a moment with her back pressed up against the door. Her heart was hammering inside her chest, and closing her eyes, she breathed deeply in an effort to calm her nerves. She was trembling, the stress of the last twelve hours was beginning to tell, she was exhausted and all she wanted to do was to lie down and rest, but unfortunately, there was no time for that. Counting slowly down from ten she arranged her troubled mind and allowing herself a few moments longer, she thought about how lucky she was to be living in such a nice house. Here she felt safe from a world that was falling apart around her. Up until now the ravages of war was something that happened to others, but in the dark hours of night, everything had changed. The bombing of Berlin by British and American bombers had begun and she had a feeling that her neatly ordered life was about to become very difficult.

Hers was a middle class neighbourhood where decent professional people lived, but if it were not for Harald she would never have been able to live here. He alone was responsible for her luxurious surroundings; her meagre income was hardly able to keep up with inflation. The most basic of supplies were becoming ever more difficult to find and now the bombing had started the situation would only become worse.

Slowly Hannah moved away from the door and shrugging off her coat, made her way towards the kitchen. She dumped her packages on the table before going to the vegetable rack where she selected items for their meal. Later she was going to see Harald and she smiled at the thought.

Being selected for the Aryan breeding program had changed her life, if it wasn't for Lebensborn she would never have met him, he made the selection process seem worthwhile. Now the humiliating tests were over and no genetic deformities had been found, she was free to breed with a 'racially pure' man.

The Lebensborn project was designed to create the perfect Aryan race and she was proud to be part of it. Hannah came from a good middle class family, which enabled her to be partnered with Harald Von Brandt. He had proved to be an honourable man who was more than happy to look after her as best he could. Hannah was relieved; she had heard terrible things, women being forced to live in institutions where they were treated no better than prostitutes. These places had been set up specifically as breeding centres where high-ranking officers would go regularly to mate with women. She would never have agreed to take part if she was to be treated like a baby making machine. Children produced this way could never be certain of their lineage, at least with Harald she knew who the father of her baby was going to be.

One of the advantages of being a member of Lebensborn was the financial assistance she was going to receive from the government, this would be in place the moment she became pregnant and all the help she would need would be on hand. Until then Harald had seen fit to set her up in a comfortable neighbourhood and with his support, she was able to make ends meet.

Hannah lifted vegetables from the rack and set about preparing them. Harald was due to arrive at seven thirty and he would be on time, he was always punctual, she would have to be ready.

As she worked, Hannah pushed her exhaustion aside and keeping her fears at arm's length, thought about Harald. He was becoming much more than simply a breeding partner. This was not supposed to happen, he was after all a married man, but this did not stop her from dreaming, there was no harm in that. Indulging herself in her fantasy, she imagined being his wife, but it was not long before reality overwhelmed her and she realised that this could never be. Theirs was a relationship based on a mutual understanding. They were to produce a perfect baby, an Aryan child who would help lead Germany to continued greatness. Hannah smiled again, she was happy in the knowledge that she was doing something important for her country, but she was afraid. The enormity of the task was sometimes overwhelming, but with Harald by her side, she was able to draw comfort from his strength. With him, anything was possible and she could feel her bosom begin to swell with pride. Harald remained a mystery that she found fascinating. Seldom did he talk about himself, she knew that he was a scientist and was aware he had recently come to Berlin. He was engaged in an important task, but beyond that, she knew nothing more.

They had been together now for just over three months. At first, their relationship was strained, she did not think it would be possible to overcome her inhibitions and perform the task they had been set. She was not the kind of woman who would go with a man easily, she knew what she had to do but when the time came, she was unprepared. Fortunately, Harald had been the perfect gentleman, he was kind and understanding and their relationship developed until the time was right. Once they began, nothing could hold them back, now their lovemaking seemed as natural as drawing breath and she could not get enough of him. Tonight she was going to present him with a lovely meal; all she ever wanted to do was please him.

She had no idea what would become of them once she became pregnant. Naturally, she wanted their relationship to continue, but their future was as vague as a landscape on a misty morning. The fact that Harald might be expected to service another woman was something that she cared not to dwell on.

As soon as she was finished in the kitchen, Hannah ran a bath and for the first time that day devoted some time to herself. At last, she could begin to unwind, ease the stiffness from her tired muscles, and lowering herself slowly into the perfumed water she lay back and closed her eyes.

After what seemed no time at all she woke with a start, the water was turning cold and her skin had begun to wrinkle. Quickly she rinsed the soap from her hair then standing up reached for a towel from the rack. Wrapping herself in its soft warmth she stepped from the bath and rubbed vigorously before allowing herself time to shiver.

She wanted to look her best for Harald, her plan was to encourage what they already shared and develop it into something more permanent. Looking at herself in the mirror, she was confident that she could do that, then, shaking the thought from her head glanced at the clock. It was almost seven thirty and hurrying to finish her make-up, she heard him knock at the front door.

The moment she saw him Hannah knew that something was wrong; he looked pale, his face haggard and drawn. There were dark smudges beneath his eyes and for the first time she noticed worry lines at the corners of his mouth.

"Come in." She said and drawing him into the house showered him with love and comforting words.

"Here," holding out a glass to him she smiled encouragingly, "drink this."

Taking it from her with shaking hands, he drained the glass. His face distorted as the liquid burned at the back of his throat and his eyes became moist as he drew in a breath.

"What is the matter, has something terrible happened?" She studied him closely she had never seen him like this before.

Harald, staring back at her was unable to say a word, all he could see was the sad face of Christina and he shuddered. He couldn't possibly tell Hannah about what had happened at the Institute, so drawing in a deep breath he pushed away the terrible image and allowed Hannah's lovely face to fill his vision. Only then did the colour return to his face and he smiled.

"I'm just tired," he began, "the bombing last night kept me awake."

"The rest of the city too." she said, relieved to hear the sound of his voice.

They talked about the damage caused by the bombs and he gave her an account of events further afield. It was not good news, the enemy was fighting back in France and their army no longer enjoyed the foothold they once had.

"Let's not dwell on the horrors of war," Harald said, "something smells good." This time he spoke more softly.

Hannah sighed with relief as the mood lightened between them and she watched with pleasure as he glanced appreciatively at the perfectly laid table. Coming up beside him, she slipped her arms around his neck and standing on tiptoe kissed his lips. She could feel the warmth of his body close to hers and closing her eyes she breathed in his scent.

"Tell me Hannah," he whispered, "how was your day?"

Their conversation flowed easily and Hannah watched as Harald lit the candles that were standing in holders on the table, then, turning away she went into the kitchen and began to pile mouth watering food onto plates. It was at times like this she was happiest, Harald appeared relaxed and her heart skipped with relief as he became more like his old self.

"Are you happy here?" he asked as soon as she re-appeared.

Taking their places at the table, they lifted their wine glasses in a toast to each other, their movements natural as if they had been rehearsed a hundred times before.

"Yes very much," she nodded, "especially now you are here with me."

She studied him over the rim of her glass and he grinned as he saw

26

her looking. In companionable silence, they enjoyed their meal, Harald doing his best to push the horrors that haunted him away. He appreciated the effort she had made and he could think of no other place he would rather be. She did not have to go to all this trouble; they could have conducted their business very differently, but he admired and respected her, it would not do to reduce what they shared to just sex.

He was aware of their developing relationship and he also realised that she would like it to become more permanent, but his situation was complicated; he had a wife to consider. Sadly, he had not seen her for almost two years, the camps in Poland where he had been sent to work were not suitable for his wife, so they were forced to remain apart, this was not a situation he enjoyed.

"As soon as I become pregnant will you be sent away?"

Her question took him by surprise and he wondered if somehow she had managed to read his thoughts.

"I have a job to do here in the city," he replied, wondering if that were still the case.

Hannah smiled, she was content with his reply but at the same time was under no illusions; she would have to go into one of the birthing clinics set up by the welfare institution. Here women like her could give birth safely in the knowledge that they and their babies would be properly cared for. Unmarried women who were either pregnant or who had given birth could remain there and receive aid. The program would allow her to have her baby anonymously, away from where she lived and without the stigma of bringing a baby into the world outside of wedlock. Even though the birthing program had the full backing of the government, there remained members of the community who were against single women becoming pregnant.

Hannah knew that her child would be taken away the moment it was born. Nurses and midwives would care for it until adoptive parents could be found. It would be the task of some high-ranking S.S. officer and his wife to provide a home for a newly arrived member of the Aryan race. Hannah was fully aware of this; she had agreed to the terms with the doctor in charge of the project at the outset and had willingly signed papers, which effectively meant that she had sold her baby to the state. In return for her services, she would receive a healthy allowance and ongoing support until she was in a position to support herself again. At first, this agreement had seemed quite acceptable, the benefits far outweighing the disadvantages, but as time went by, she began to doubt her decision. How would she cope with the emotional wrench of giving

27

up her baby? She had underestimated the part she was expected to play and had not contemplated falling in love with her breeding partner.

Harald was becoming uncomfortable; he could sense her changing mood and the last thing he wanted was to dwell upon the uncertainty of their future.

"To us and to the moment," he said lifting his glass.

Once they had finished their meal, Harald led her to the bedroom where he began to caress her softly. His movements were a little uncoordinated and when it came to the buttons on her dress he fumbled dismally. It was quite unlike him to have consumed so much alcohol, so pushing his hands gently away Hannah giggled and slowly began to undress in front of him. As soon as she was naked, she leaned against him and helping him to undress, her fears that he was perhaps a little too drunk to make love evaporated under a cloud of urgency. Never before had she experienced anything quite like this, the intensity of their love making left her breathless and she cried out in pleasure over and over again.

Eventually she lay cocooned in a state of euphoria and listened to his deep even breathing. Something had changed, she felt calm and somehow complete, it was then she knew with certainty that she had conceived and snuggling up close to him, she thought her heart was about to burst. She was so happy and as soon as Harald was awake, she would confide in him, but for now she would enjoy the moment, keep her secret to herself for just a little longer.

Sometime later, she awoke and the place in the bed beside her was empty and cold. She lay silently in the darkness struggling to make sense of the sounds around her. The atmosphere in the room had changed, no longer was it warm and filled with love, it was then she heard him sob.

"Harald," she called out softly, "what is it?"

Sitting up she pulled the cover up to her chin and shivered as she searched the gloom in an effort to locate him. He was slumped on the floor against the wall and she sensed that he was holding something in his hand.

"Harald," she called out again more urgently this time.

The continued silence frightened her and all she wanted to do was to go to him, hold him in her arms and tell him that he was going to be a father, but something terrifying held her back.

"Please Harald, tell me what's wrong."

The sound of her voice made him cry out and it was a while before he could speak. When finally he opened his mouth, the effort robbed him of his dignity and his strength.

"I have been forced to work with the devil himself," he cried, his voice shaking with emotion. "Joseph Mengele, that steely hearted angel of death."

The depth of his despair was overwhelming and Hannah gasped. It seemed an age before he could continue; perhaps he wanted to spare her the agony of his wretched life. There were things he had seen, things he had done, his guilt like chains that bound him. His conscience could no longer spare him; it consumed him and sent him to hell.

"What good can be salvaged from the ashes?" Images of Christina filled his head. Her huge dark eyes staring back at him pierced his soul and he knew that he could never be forgiven for what he had done.

Suddenly a flash lit up the room and thunder engulfed the air. Harald was thrown back against the wall by the force of the bullet tearing into his brain and as the pistol flew from his grip it skittering across the floor. It was then that Hannah began to scream.

Part Two

Demons rise up to strike at the Eagle and the Lion

*Watch therefore, for you know neither the day nor
the hour*
Matthew 25:13

⫼ⵜⵜ

DUBLIN

MODERN DAY

Orlagh stopped in the street and glanced up at the tall Georgian town house. She never grew tired of admiring it especially now the web of scaffold poles had gone revealing the fresh paintwork. She was particularly fond of the small square windows set into huge sashes either side of the door. These were the eyes of the house observing the world as it passed by and in the glass was reflected a kaleidoscope of colour like rainbows from the sky.

Pushing against the heavy iron gate, she made her way up the short flight of steps and slipped her key into a polished brass escutcheon plate set into the original front door. This had once been a sad, weather beaten entrance but now it stood sentinel, a proud gateway to the house. Restored by local craftsmen, it wore a new coat of paint and standing back Orlagh admired it immensely.

As a student she had lived here, renting rooms from a landlord who had no interest in the building beyond collecting a monthly income. Rarely did he maintain the property. This had saddened Orlagh, she hated the way the building was left to deteriorate and she realised the only way to save it was to buy her part of the house. It had taken years to convince the landlord to sell, but with her grandmothers help the man was finally persuaded to go along with their plans and between them Orlagh and her grandmother turned her small maisonette into a magnificent home. One by one, they refurbished the rooms bringing them back to their former glory and it was by studying books and collecting brochures of the period that they were able to complete their task.

Unfortunately, her grandmother passed away before the project was completed but it was her legacy that enabled Orlagh to buy the rest of the house. In memory of her beloved grandmother, Orlagh continued with the restoration and now with the builders gone her home was complete. Of course, it was much too big for her alone, but that did not bother her, she loved the house, it was a lasting monument to her grandmother.

Orlagh maintained a deep respect for history and now surrounded by many beautiful things she had inherited her grandmother's impeccable taste. The only modern equipment to find its way into the house was in the kitchen. Up to date appliances lessened the burden of domestic chores, but here Orlagh was a disaster. Rarely did she cook for herself, when she did it was to prepare the simplest of meals, whenever she needed more she would call upon friends or employ someone to work their culinary magic.

Pushing open the front door, she stepped into the hallway and her grin widened.

"Jerry." She called as she hung her coat on the stand. She knew he was there; the aroma of fresh coffee permeating throughout the house was a sure sign.

Jerry Knowles appeared and wrapping her up in his arms, he lifted her off her feet and placed a kiss on her cheek.

"I could murder a cup of that," she nodded towards kitchen. As soon as he'd put her down Jerry took her by the hand and led her along the hallway.

"Hard day?" he smiled, watching her as she slumped down into a wooden backed chair.

"No not really, I'm just exhausted."

Jerry offered her a steaming mug of coffee and as she took it, she closed her eyes allowing the rich aroma to drift up over her face.

"This is heavenly," she said savouring the moment. "How was your day?"

Their relationship had blossomed during the last twelve months and although he did not officially live there, Jerry spent most of his time with her. He was a mature student in his final year at Trinity College and when he was busy writing up his notes he would return to his own flat in town near to the university.

They had met at the National Museum eighteen months previously when Orlagh was delivering a lecture on Celtic Ireland. She was employed by the museum trust as an archaeologist and sometimes gave talks about her work.

"I've just completed the final draft of my thesis on Gog and Magog, the descendants of Noah," he told her. "I used a comparison linking them to the rivalry between the superpowers."

She stared at him and raised her eyebrows. Since their adventure searching for the Belgae Torc, his studies had taken him in quite a different direction. His interests lay in German mythology and Neo-Nazi Paganism, but his experiences had left him with some radical new ideas, which some academics found fascinating. He was actively encouraged to explore his ideas and expand his theories; his papers were openly welcomed and often debated by the professors of the college.

This had also re-kindled an interest in his great grandfather's work. The famous Sir Geoffrey Knowles had been a gentleman archaeologist who in 1912 had discovered the Belgae Man; a perfectly preserved body of an Iron Age man found in an ancient peat marsh in Somerset. The man had been the victim of human sacrifice and surprisingly was wearing a magnificent gold torc.

The torc itself remains a mystery surrounded by intrigue. Some say it has ancient mystical powers, people who have handled it report feeling strange vibrations running through the metal and since its discovery, many have died suddenly whilst wearing it. The torc has been coveted for this reason, some even trying to harness its powers. During the Second World War, the Nazi's owned many ancient artefacts, using them as symbols to generate unity amongst their people and the Belgae Torc was one of their prized possessions.

"That's sure to get tongues wagging." Orlagh smiled before sipping some more of her coffee.

"I've been thinking." Coming round the table, he stood behind her and placed his hands on her shoulders before resting his chin on top of her head. "As you've been so exhausted lately, what say you we take a holiday?"

Lifting her hand, her long delicate fingers explored his knuckles before curling around them and she frowned as thoughts of her busy schedule threatened to influence her reply. Thinking of an excuse to turn down his offer she realised that there was nothing needing her immediate attention. Besides, she had holiday owing so was convinced that her boss Peter O'Reilly would rubber stamp the idea. Nothing could stop them from getting away for a couple of weeks.

"Okay," she nodded, cautiously wondering what he had in mind.

"I was thinking maybe Turkey, somewhere along the Black Sea coast or perhaps the Aegean."

She remained silent whilst going over his proposal in her head then she said. "Sardis was an ancient city of Asia Minor or Turkey as it's known today. In the 7th century B.C. it was the capital of the kingdom of Lydia and was the first city to mint silver and gold coins." Turning in her seat, she looked up at him. "You do realise that I won't be able to sit on a beach all day with my nose stuck in a book. We must explore the Hermos valley, so it will have to be the Aegean region."

IV

For the next few days, Orlagh's mind was in a whirl, her schedule was not particularly busy but she found a thousand things that needed to be done. At first, O'Reilly had not been happy about her sudden request for a holiday.

"Peter, it's nothing like last time, it's not as if you're sending me away on some assignment. Jerry and I are simply taking a holiday." She did her best to reassure him.

He was more than a little concerned; he was worried for her safety. The last time he sent her on an assignment she had been kidnapped by terrorists and almost died. That was twelve months ago, but still the psychological torment haunted him mercilessly.

"Besides," she continued, "I'm sure Jerry will take good care of me," she smiled at him sweetly. "Not that I need looking after." She added.

Peter winced. He thought very highly of Orlagh, in fact he regarded her more like a daughter and would do anything to keep her safe. He realised that his misgivings were unfounded, she was after all an independent young woman and finally he agreed to her taking her holiday, but there were conditions. He insisted that she send him at least two postcards and telephone Janet, his secretary, regularly just to let him know that she was safe.

Orlagh reluctantly agreed to his proposal but wanted to tell him that he was being ridiculous, but she respected him too much so decided to keep quiet. She realised that his overprotective feelings towards her were based on the guilt he harboured after sending her on an assignment that almost got her killed. It couldn't be easy for him having to live with those kinds of thoughts, but he must realise, she was not his little girl who needed wrapping up in cotton wool, she was one of the leading archaeologists on his team.

Janet had arranged to meet Orlagh for lunch. There were things they needed to discuss so rather than do it in an office somewhere in the museum, Janet seized on the opportunity to get out from behind her desk. The chance was too good to miss; she would make sure that Peter paid for their lunch. She hardly had an expense account but she was willing to try.

"He acts as if he's your father sometimes," Janet said when Orlagh told her about their boss. "He's far too protective towards you and it's getting worse. Don't you think that's a bit weird?"

"He's just worried," Orlagh said studying Janet. "It's sweet of him to care as much as he does, but this time it will be different, I'll be on holiday. Jerry will be there too and we'll be just like any other tourists having a wonderful time."

"Ah, you don't have to worry." Janet tossed her head. "He's away with the fairies!"

Orlagh grinned, Janet had a way of coming out with the strangest phrases. "Are we talking about Peter here or Jerry?"

"Peter of course, now would I be saying such a thing about the lovely Jerry?"

Orlagh laughed, she knew just how much Janet fancied Jerry and she made it her business to tease him about it at every opportunity.

Tucking into her tuna salad, Orlagh was enjoying her lunch especially as Peter was picking up the bill. She had no doubts that Janet would claim back every euro spent.

"Now," Janet began, settling a serious expression on her face. "The Archaeological Trust sent through an e-mail this morning." She glanced up to make sure she had Orlagh's full attention before going on. "It seems that some metal detector enthusiasts have discovered something near Newgrange, it could be an Iron Age hoard of some description." She went on quickly giving Orlagh no chance to respond. "Initial investigations have thrown up a number of finds but they have reached the point where they need experts to go in and open the site. Peter wants you to head up the team."

Orlagh nodded her head thoughtfully as she finished a mouthful of tuna. "When will it start?"

"They want someone over there immediately but with you going away on holiday we'll have to put them off."

Orlagh's green eyes flashed as she ran the problem through in her head. She rarely missed an opportunity to be in on a dig at the outset. Usually archaeologists would be called in only when things became interesting, but Orlagh liked to get her hands dirty from the start. She could not resist pushing the first spade into the earth, get stuck in with the heavy work, but this time things would have to be different.

"Don't delay opening up the site. Can't one of the others do it, or at least make a start then when I get back I could take over if required."

Janet thought for a moment, going over in her mind the list of up and coming student archaeologists who might be capable of running the dig.

"Adam could do it." She said tapping the side of her nose with her fingertip. She always did this when making decisions.

Adam Lawrence was one of Orlagh's students; he was a very capable and dedicated young man, who if slightly eccentric at times was a brilliant historian.

"Yes," Orlagh nodded, "Adam will do a great job, I'll be more than happy to work with him when I get back."

"Well that's settled then," Janet smiled happily. "I'll let the Trust know."

Picking up the menu, she studied it for a moment. "Shall we order a sweet?" She glanced at Orlagh, her face full of mischief.

"You're pushing your luck, we've had wine already! She indicated towards the almost empty bottle standing on the edge of their table.

"We might as well push the boat out; it's not every day we get to go out for lunch, besides Peter's paying."

J ack Harrington was standing on the bridge of his new survey ship *Ocean Pride*. A multi-purpose service vessel, or MPSV for short, the *Ocean Pride* was the largest ship in his fleet. At a hundred and thirty metres long, she was capable of carrying one hundred and ten passengers along with ten officers and twenty crew. Jack could never envisage filling the ship with so many people but the extra space would be useful for storage.

On the forward deck, where the heli-platform was situated, stood a Sikorsky S-92 helicopter. This was one of his favourite toys; he had a passion for flying especially helicopters.

The S-92 was a four bladed, twin engine, medium lift helicopter built for both military and civilian markets; it was capable of carrying twenty two people or a heavy cargo. Jack looked down from the bridge and admired the Sikorsky, although it was a big bird, its lines were pleasingly sleek and dressed resplendent in bright orange and white paintwork, the helicopter displayed the same livery as his ships.

Men were fussing around on the decks, tidying away bits of equipment or simply enjoying the cool sea breeze under a cloudless Mediterranean sky. On the after decks stood two huge cranes, the crew had named them Hengist and Hawsa. Working together, they were capable of lifting 45 tons. Situated further along the sides of the ship were a number of lighter hoists and flanking the workshops stood the service cranes. The aft end was an area of open deck where items salvaged from the seabed could be safely worked on and stabilised before being moved into the work- shops. The ship also boasted two state of the art laboratories, a hospital with a fully functioning operating theatre, a well stocked pharmacy and for the enjoyment of the crew a library containing computers, hundreds of books and magazines. There was also a shop and a gymnasium.

Captain Paul Seymour was standing beside Jack looking as smug as the Lord of the Manor surveying all that he owned.

"Sure is a great ship." He glanced at Jack, his face split by a huge grin.

"I'm glad you think so." Jack replied straining to maintain a straight face.

They were both like kids on Christmas morning and although would never admit it, both men were excited to be in charge of such a splendid ship.

"Captain," a voice sounded over the communications system. "You should hear this."

Moving swiftly towards the panel mounted on the bridge Paul flicked a switch and made some adjustments with the computer keyboard. The ships radio had picked up a faint distress signal and the officer on watch had recorded it. Both Paul and Jack listened in silence.

"Where did it come from?" Paul spoke into the microphone linking him to the communications centre located several decks below. "Was it transmitted from another ship?"

"No sir, I don't think so. It's coming from inland and the best position I can give you is somewhere over the Kackar mountains."

They were currently sailing in the Black Sea off the coast of northern Turkey.

"The Kackars are a mountain range rising above eastern Turkey," Paul said turning towards Jack. "It must have been sent from an aircraft."

Jack was thinking the same thing.

"What do we know about the area?" Paul spoke into the microphone. He knew that the Comms officer had access to the internet and would probably have already been searching for information.

"Well sir, it's a National Park, so I guess it should be run by Rangers with rescue teams on hand for such emergencies. The mountains rise to almost 13,000 feet."

Paul listened intently as the man read facts from his computer screen.

"If it's as barren as I imagine it could take a rescue team days to locate the crash site," Jack wiped his hand over his face. "Don't suppose a stricken aircraft would stand much chance against those mountains."

They both knew that it would be impossible to land safely in a mountainous region; neither of them needed reminding of the dangers.

"We could take the Sikorsky up, do a little prospecting." Jack grinned, itching to get into the air.

Just over a year ago, they had narrowly escaped death whilst flying over a mountainous region in northern Spain on the border with Portugal, their mission, to search for kidnapped archaeologist Dr Orlagh Gairne and Roz Stacey, one of their crew members. The terrorists holding the women had fired a missile, bringing them down in a devastating fireball and destroying part of a Portuguese vineyard. Although injured, both Jack and Paul survived the crash.

"Do you have a fix on their position?" Paul asked.

"No sir, all I have is a DF signal and a bearing."

Their direction finding equipment had given them a compass bearing, a course along which they should find the crash site. They had no idea how far along that line they would need to travel, all they could do was to fly along it and keep a sharp lookout.

"Not much to go on," Paul said. "Will be like searching for a man overboard in a rough sea."

Jack looked at him and grinned. "Well I'm willing to give it a go. What are the weather conditions inland?"

There was a pause before the Comms Officer made his report. "Good at the moment sir, not much cloud over the mountains but that could change as quick as you like."

Paul was already studying the chart. They were currently holding a westerly course heading towards the Bosphorus strait and Istanbul. They would need to change course, head southeasterly, find a suitable seaport close to the Kackar Mountains. From his chart, he could see that the nearest port was several hours away.

"Let's do it." Jack urged, making a decision that would change their mission completely.

This trip was supposed to be a leisurely cruise, an opportunity to learn about the handling characteristics of the ship, a chance to complete the sea trials that began a few months earlier.

As the new co-ordinates were fed into the navigation computer Jack left the bridge and went forward to ready the helicopter. Ordinarily Paul would have accompanied him, he never missed a chance to fly as co-pilot but on this occasion, he was more than happy to remain aboard the *Ocean Pride*. His last ship; the *Sea Quest*, had been unbelievably sunk by a U-boat when salvaging the wreck of the *Hudson Bay*. At the end of the Second World War, this ship had gone down in the north Atlantic on the edge of the Bay of Biscay. She was carrying a cargo of Nazi gold and treasure stolen from museums across Europe. The Belgae Torc was one of the treasures listed on the ships inventory and that was the reason Dr Orlagh Gairne had been assigned to the salvage operation. It was her job to identify antique treasures as they emerged from the wreck but a group of fanatical terrorists also wanted the contents of the *Hudson Bay*. A fully restored U-boat complete with torpedoes had put an end to their mission. Paul was greatly affected by the loss of his ship and now he felt even more responsible for the *Ocean Pride* and the safety of her crew.

Jack knew how his old friend felt and as he made his way across the deck, he realised he would have to find himself another co-pilot. Pushing open the heavy steel door leading to the hanger, Jack found Wings Wallace, a softly spoken twenty seven year old pilot from Baltimore. He was standing at a workbench brandishing a spanner and he looked up as Jack appeared.

"Wings, we'll be going airborne in twenty minutes, get your stuff together and meet me on the Sikorsky in ten."

"Roger that boss." Wings replied without question.

Jack, climbing into the cockpit, breathed in deeply. The smell reminded him of a new car. The aircraft had only a few hours of flying on the clock, just enough time in the air to check out the systems. Jack grinned and his heart beat faster, like a bloodhound he was onto the scent and could hardly wait to get this bird into the air.

VI

Orlagh and Jerry left Dublin on a flight, which took them to Izmir International Airport via Frankfurt. They finally reached their hotel in the small seaside town of Kusadasi on the Aegean coast well after sundown and once they had booked in and were shown to their room, Orlagh was delighted to discover a huge sliding glass door leading onto a balcony. The door was open and a warm sea breeze was drifting into the room, it was pleasant so the air conditioning remained silent.

Going straight onto the balcony, Orlagh leaned against the railings and sighed contentedly. Jerry dropped their bags beside the bed before going out to join her. Coming up behind her, he slipped his arms around her waist and she leaned back against him.

"This is gorgeous," she whispered, not wanting to spoil the magic.

The only sound was the sighing of waves washing up on the beach just a short distance away. They could see very little, the sea was a huge black mass stretching all the way to the horizon and occasionally in the distance; a small light would flash from a fishing boat or coaster. Gradually as their eyes became accustomed to the dark, more was revealed. The sea was alive with movement, a light swell turned into small white caps as waves rolled onto the sand, and when the moon became brighter a finger of silver pointed all the way to the horizon.

The appearance of the moon stirred something deep down within Orlagh and she remembered the time when she had been kidnapped. Memories of the druids and their ceremonies clouded her mind and she shuddered. Jerry felt her change of mood and tightened his hold around her. His presence gave her the confidence to confront her nightmares and she was comforted knowing that she was not alone.

Over the last twelve months, she had struggled to come to terms with her ordeal, occasionally a suppressed memory would rise up to ravish her mind. Jerry had worked tirelessly giving her the love and support that she needed to overcome these heartrending moments and she adored him even more for his understanding. They had worked together with a counsellor on a positive strategy that would allow her to accept what had happened and gradually conquer her fears.

Eventually they turned and went back into their room, there were cases to unpack and they were both exhausted from their journey.

The following day sunlight flooded their room filling it with a warm golden glow. Hopping out of bed, Jerry threw open the sliding doors and went out onto the balcony. He was surprised to see that the beach was literally just across the road, a wide strip of white sand giving way to an ocean of deep blue was just a few minutes away. Taking in the view, he watched as jewels sparkling on the surface rode white horses up the beach, smoothing out the wrinkles in the sand.

"It's a pity you hate lazing on beaches." He called out over his shoulder as Orlagh began to stir.

"I just burn under the sun; it's not much fun going the colour of a ripe tomato, no amount of sun block is sufficient to fully protect my skin."

Jerry grinned as he watched her climb out of bed.

"I'm going to have a shower," she told him and disappeared into the bathroom.

He continued to watch the lazy morning as it slipped by beneath his balcony, this is what he liked about being on holiday, times when there was absolutely nothing else to do. The sun was warm against his skin and he knew it would soon become much hotter, but for the moment there was a welcome breeze drifting into the bay.

Orlagh emerged from the bathroom wrapped in a huge towel, and stepping back from the window she loosened it and began to dry her damp body. It was now Jerry's turn to freshen up, if he remained watching her for much longer he would have to take her back to bed. Grinning at the thought, he crossed the room and disappeared into the bathroom.

"So," he called out from behind the closed door. "What's on the agenda for today?"

"We'll have a quick look around the town, get our bearings and see what's going on." Reaching for a brochure, she began to read out aloud. "'Kusadasi is a beautiful seaside town by the Aegean Sea. It is mainly catered for tourists, so like all seaside towns it doesn't have much of a culture.' What a strange thing to write in a brochure don't you think?"

"Something has obviously been lost in translation." Jerry replied.

"We must visit Ephesus, the ancient ruins of the Roman Provincial Capital."

He knew she was still reading from the brochure, her knowledge of this part of the world was limited. Of course as an historian, she knew about the ancient ruins and the architectural marvels left by the ancestors of this land, but her kind of archaeology was very different to what went on here.

43

"We also have to catch up with Takat, he will be surprised to see us here."

Takat Demir was curator of the Ephesus museum, he would have the answers to all her questions and they could rely on him for local knowledge, he would also be useful as a translator.

"Didn't you tell him we were on our way?"

"Of course not, I want to surprise him. I was working it out the other day, I haven't seen him in almost six years, can you believe that?"

Takat had visited Ireland on a cultural and historical exchange trip, an arrangement between the National Museum of Ireland and the Ephesus Museum. At the time, Orlagh had just become a member of the organisation and was tasked with playing host to the Turkish visitors. From their first meeting they became firm friends sharing many common interests. Orlagh had been fascinated by his knowledge of the ancient kingdom of Lydia that was now western Turkey. They remained in touch, often sharing professional opinions and although Jerry had never met Takat, he felt as if they were old friends.

By the time he had showered and shaved Orlagh had dried her hair and was dressed in a bright lemon tee shirt and white shorts. She was wearing comfortable flat-soled gladiator sandals and was now applying a small amount of make-up to her face.

"Come on slow coach, I'm just about ready for my breakfast."

VII

In a valley where steep rock faces soar upwards to meet the sky a grove of druids were engaged in a sacred ceremony. Their voices rang out in a monotone chant resembling a Buddhist Mantra and the sound echoing from the sheer walls merged as one to form a loud and chilling moan. This was a welcome for generations of spirits to join with them in the circle and as the delicate light became stronger, shadows were chased from the valley. The druids tightened their circle and standing on an ancient site where water once flowed, could feel the vibrations bubbling up through the rocks beneath their feet. Deep underground the river raged, no longer on the surface it defied time by following its original course and as one with the elements, it reverberated through the earth drawing the druids to this spot.

Here the spirits were strongest and as the chanting rose in intensity, they poured through the gates from the Underworld. Now the mantra was even louder, a hypnotic sound as old as time itself, binding the souls of men together, galvanising those who were gone with those still living. The gates of Anwyn were open and spirits came up from the earth. This was strong magic, never before had the druids invited so many of their ancestors to join them. They realised the consequences of such an act but united in solidarity they made a powerful force.

The ritual was underway the paradox had begun. Druids dressed in white robes appeared, their strange words and movements provoking the gods and goddesses. These were the high priests, revered amongst their ranks. As senior members, their voices could be heard above the rest and one by one, the others became silent until all that remained was the pure sound of the high priests. Their voices rising up, an eerie echo against the rock face soaring above their heads.

The air became charged as they waited, the living holding their breaths as the dead joined them and the ritual reached its climax.

"When we honour our sacred ancestors," one of the priests cried out, "we are acknowledging those of our own blood. Those who have come before us, those who have tilled the land where now we live, those of our heritage whose teachings we seek, come forth so that we shall understand." The priest raised his arms above his head and turned his face towards the sun.

"The dead are in the wind, they speak in whispered tones. They are in the water, which flows beneath our feet, and in the land, which holds much wisdom. Now they feed the earth that nourished them. Feel our ancestors, feel their force, their souls walk amongst us. They are in the earth and in the trees; they are in the birds and the bees. They shine in the morning light and in the stars of night. We beseech thee, come join us once again in this land of the living and together we shall not fail."

The druids cheered, their voices rising to meet the sun, the sound of unity filling the valley, as once did the river that flowed so many years ago.

VIII

Jack allowed the nose of the helicopter to drift upwards as he steered over another jutting peak, the mountain landscape both beautiful and unforgiving as it spread out beneath them. Green meadows filled with jewel-like flowers were a delight to the eye, and dotted around the pastures they could see goats and occasionally a cow, but as they climbed the environment changed, it became inhospitable but undeniably dramatic.

The glaciated mountains were alpine in character with steep rocky peaks formed when the earth was still young. Here there were numerous mountain lakes, each reflecting the sky like glass windows. Some were incredibly deep with water as black as night itself, the clear blue sky overhead could do nothing to penetrate these cold, murky waters. Jack, peering down, wondered what kind of life could survive in the depths, during winter months the lakes froze over until they were thick with ice.

The Kackar Mountains are as old as the earth, their name taken from the Armenian *Khachkar* literally means 'cross stone' and may be used in various senses. It can describe the whole range, including many mountain groups, or just the Kackar-Kauron group with its highest peak, or only the peak itself.

Wings remained alert in the co-pilots seat; it was his job to watch over the helicopters systems. He was also expected to take over the controls at a moment's notice, so he constantly scanned the instruments and checked the navigation system until he was satisfied that they were on course.

Jack was doing a sterling job keeping strictly to the flight path and guided by the DF, he followed the most direct route towards their target.

From time to time Wings glanced out of the side window; only a fool would ignore the dramatic landscape below. Occasionally he would spot a village clinging precariously to the crags. It amazed him to think that anyone could eke out an existence in such an unforgiving environment. He wondered what kind of life the people in this remote area led; he was certain it would be very different from his own. What he took for granted would be a luxury here, simple things like fresh running water, hot showers, electricity at the flick of a switch. He came from a land of plenty, a rich environment where he could get whatever he desired any time of day or night. Were these people content he wondered,

47

their simple lives seemingly idyllic must be difficult at times. Free from debt and commercialism their way of life appealed to him for all of two minutes, then he realised that it would not do for him. He began to think about the hard times, cut off for months on end from the outside world by bad weather conditions. He had never experienced having to huddle together with his family in one frozen room in order to keep warm or go without hot food. In Baltimore, he had everything he wished for and more.

"What do we have here?"

The sound of Jack's voice coming over the intercom startled him out of his reverie. The nose of the Sikorsky swung round in a tight turn and as it lost speed, Jack side slipped along a narrow strip of vegetation growing between the rocks.

There on the ground beneath them lay a tail section from an aircraft complete with rudder.

"Must have been a big aircraft," Wings said as he stared out of the side window.

Easing the Sikorsky forward Jack followed the debris trail, which began to form a hundred metres further along the slope.

"Looks like it came in hard," Wings continued. "No chance of completing a safe landing here though."

Jack remained silent as he concentrated on flying lower over the crash site. Rocks thrusting up towards them were like fingers pointing towards the sky and using all his skills he squeezed the helicopter through an outcrop that curled above them. There was something strangely familiar about what he could see lying on the mountain beneath them, a chill swept over him and a feeling of déjà vu left his skin covered in pimples.

"Looks like a vintage aircraft." Wings said as he craned his neck for a better look. "That corrugated section reminds me of an old German Junkers. They used corrugated duralumin to form the bodies of their JU 52's"

"A tri-motor." Jack said confirming the young man's suspicions.

Part of a wide cantilever wing section came into view, then they found one of the large BMW engines, which had been torn off on impact.

"Just look at that radial," Wings said, his eyes becoming huge as he stared in disbelief. "We gotta get down there for a closer look."

Jack grinned as he glanced across the cockpit. He could see a lot of himself in the young co-pilot. He would have reacted in the same way twenty years ago but life's experiences had taught him to be a little more cautious.

"Let's just see what we have here first."

Easing the helicopter further along the narrow slope, they discovered the remains of a smashed fuselage, confirmation that it was indeed a Junkers JU 52. This was a vintage aircraft, a German tri-motor used extensively during the Second World War. Designed as an airliner in the early 1930s, it had some unique flying characteristics and because of this was put to work as a bomber, troop carrier and parachute platform. It remained in service until the 1980s, carrying cargo with many of the world's airforces and civil aviation companies.

The main fuselage lay on its side wedged between two huge rocks; both wings were missing, as was the tail section. The cockpit had disappeared completely, destroyed when the huge nose mounted engine was driven backwards into the aircraft by the force of the impact. The aircraft was coloured drab grey and olive green, there were no obvious identification marks or other logos, but then Jack found what he was looking for. On a section of corrugated duralumin torn from the fuselage, he could make out the image of a bird rising from the flames.

"The Phoenix Legion," he muttered softly.

A cold shadow passed over Jack and as he shuddered, the blood drained from his face leaving him pale and chilled.

"We'll do another sweep," he said trying to sound calm. "Run the cameras, I want to record every detail."

"Roger that." Wings nodded as he activated the equipment.

Surveillance cameras located under the nose of the helicopter were the same type used by the police and military. The Sikorsky also carried a Forward Looking Infrared System, or FLIR. This equipment could detect heat signatures and was particularly useful when flying at night.

"What have we here?" Jack murmured just before making his turn.

A red shape huddled beside a rock caught his attention and hovering for a moment longer, side slipped closer for a better look.

"It's a body." Wings said as he identified the shape.

"Use the camera to see if you can pick up any body heat."

Jack nudged the helicopter even closer and turning the nose slightly he brought the FLIR onto target as Wings activated the system. A computer screen on the flight deck blinked into life as it synchronised with the camera.

"No sign of life." Wings reported as he scanned the image.

"Look there's another one." Further down the slope they could see a second body.

"Do you think they came from the aircraft?" Wings glanced across at Jack.

"I doubt it, look at their clothes. They must have hiked up here, besides its unlikely anyone survived the crash."

"Maybe they were unlucky enough to be caught out when the aircraft crashed; it could have come down on top of them." He glanced at Jack, not really believing what he had just said.

The helicopter made another slow pass over the scene and they recorded the images. As soon as the manoeuvre was complete, Wings pressed a series of buttons on a keyboard and sent the file to the *Ocean Pride.*

"We'll have to put down somewhere and have a closer look." Jack said as he searched for a suitable landing zone. It was at times like this he wished he had a smaller helicopter, he could see a dozen places where he could have landed but the Sikorsky was a large aircraft, which required a lot more space.

Half a mile down the slope he spotted what he was looking for and a few moments later, the wheels touched down and Wings unbuckled his safety harness. Jack shut down the various systems and the rotor blades began to power down then he opened the door and jumped to the ground.

Wings was already half way up the slope, going at a blistering pace he weaved his way around the rocks. The going was much harder than it looked but Jack set off not allowing the younger man to outdo him.

The first body they came across was a young man, his pale skin and fair hair told them that he was not a local; he must have been one of the many visitors walking and climbing these peaks. Wings crouched down beside him and began searching his pockets for clues.

"He's been down for some time," he made his report. "He's stone cold and rigor has set in."

The other body was the same, a man of similar age. Again, there were no visible causes of death so Jack and Wings made their way up towards the remains of the aircraft. As they got closer they could smell aviation fuel, the fumes were not strong so did not cause an immediate hazard. There had been no visible fire; the engines they had seen earlier were clean and seemingly in good condition. Jack looked at the perfectly restored remains and could not help making a comparison with the equipment he had seen used by the Phoenix Legion. Much of what they owned seemed to be genuine relics from the Second World War, meticulously restored and in some cases modified to suit a specific purpose.

The fuselage was lying over on its side, and the damage caused by the crash was extensive. The cockpit was completely destroyed and with the tail section missing the remains looked out of proportion. Jack studied it searching for the safest way in.

"We'll go in through the gap where the tail section should be and do a sweep along the fuselage."

Carefully they picked their way over the debris and once inside, razor sharp edges of aluminium and splintered wooden spars threatened to snag their flying suits. Shards of glass littered the floor along with fragments of wooden insulation board. Jack was impressed, it had withstood the crash remarkably well, but there were a tangle of electrical wires and hydraulic pipe work that must be avoided so they moved cautiously along the fuselage.

A wooden crate, once strapped to the deck was now upturned, wedged against the forward bulkhead. Moving towards it, Jack held onto a piece of hanging pipe and using it for support worked his way over a rock, which had penetrated the aluminium skin. Planting his feet either side of the crate he pulled it upright. Straw and paper packing materials made up the bulk of the contents, but pushing his hands into the box he rummaged around searching for whatever was left inside.

Wings wriggled his way into the cockpit, forcing himself between crumpled sheet metal and smashed instruments. On impact, the engine had smashed its way into the cockpit crushing instruments and the pilot, whose remains were not recognisable as human. The poor man must have been killed instantly, Wings thought, at least he wouldn't have suffered.

Backing out of the confined space, he began to sort through the debris strewn across the navigation desk. There was no evidence of a flight plan and he could find no other documentation so carefully stepping over buckled aluminium panels he returned to the cargo hold.

"Jack." He called out suddenly as he made a grim discovery. Under the pile of debris lay the body of a woman.

"Any sign of life?" Jack asked as he moved up beside Wings.

"No, there are no obvious injuries; I can't see any broken bones or other trauma." Running his hands over her body, he checked the pockets of her flight suit and found an identity card.

"Olga Honig." He said reading the name on the card. He glanced at the picture of Olga; she had been a pretty thirty something with the purest blue eyes he had ever seen. Now her face was far from pretty, her

51

expression a mask of shock and horror. "She must have been terrified," he whispered. "I wonder what she was doing back here."

Jack was thinking the same thing.

"We had better get out of here; we have to report this to the authorities."

Something caught Jack's eye as he stood up, and making his way back along the aircraft he found a small silver coloured flask wedged in between some broken spars. At first, he thought it was a thermos but on closer inspection, he realised that it was something else. It was the kind of container used for transporting dangerous substances. Weighing it in his hand he thought it too light to be containing liquid, perhaps it was empty. He wasn't going to open the top to find out, that job needed to be done under the right conditions, he had seen things like this before so stuffing it into his flight suit pocket he followed Wings out.

The sun had disappeared behind the ridge and the air was a few degrees cooler. Jack knew the air temperature would continue to plummet quickly at this altitude once the sun went down.

Wings was already making his way back towards the bodies along the path so Jack hurried after him and as they passed the first victim he dropped down beside him. Something was weighing heavily on his mind, he was not comfortable leaving these unfortunate people without knowing how they had died. Taking hold of the man's arm he rolled him over onto his side and it was then that he found it. An identical flask to the one he had picked up in the wreck, this one however was open. Jack moved away quickly not wanting to touch it, he had seen enough. Whatever was inside that flask could have been responsible for their deaths. The other victim was about one hundred metres away, what could have been deadly enough to bring a man down at that distance?

Jack shuddered, his imagination running wild. There was no evidence to suggest the second man had staggered away after being incapacitated. Moving to where he lay, Jack lifted him carefully to see if he could find another flask but there was nothing.

When he got back to the helicopter, Wings already had the engine running and was about to power up the rotors.

"Before we go I want to talk to Linda on the ship."

For Jack the nightmare was beginning all over again, the restored Junkers JU52, the Phoenix Legion logo on the side panel and the mysterious flasks. There were too many coincidences and he did not like it one bit.

Linda Pritchard was one of the doctors serving on board the *Ocean Pride,* her background was in research and as a scientist, she was second to none. As soon as Jack heard her voice on the radio, he outlined the details of his findings.

"On board the Sikorsky you should have a first aid kit," she told him. "I want you to get me blood samples from all three victims. It is important that you get blood from the woman in the airplane. You should also have protective sterilised suits."

"Yes we carry spare suits." Jack said.

"Don't forget to wear face masks too; I don't want you contaminating my blood samples."

Jack grinned; she did not remind him to take care of himself.

Orlagh and Jerry booked their seats on a tour bus that would take them from the port of Kasadasi to Ephesus, one of the world's most magnificent archaeological sites of antiquity.

They were hoping to catch Takar at his museum sometime during the afternoon but their schedule was a bit sketchy. Although their tour guide had given them a timetable, things were not going exactly to plan. The philosophy of the company running the tour was 'everything will happen in its own time and everyone will be happy'.

From Kasadasi the bus took them north to St. John's Basilica, passing the Byzantine fortress of Selcuk and the ruins of the Temple of Artemis. They were assured there would be time to stop there on the way back.

The bus was packed with middle aged tourists mostly from Europe but a few were Japanese. The age range reminded Jerry of typical cruise ship, he was by far the youngest traveller on the bus with Orlagh a close second. He found this a little sad, history after all was for every generation and he could not help thinking there should have been younger people on the trip. He wondered if schools in Turkey encouraged their children to engage in such rich history or was living amongst these ruins merely a common experience.

"Wow, just look at that," Orlagh said, delighted by what she saw. "Everything is so well preserved in this dry climate." She was completely overwhelmed by the magnificence of it all.

"You would love Egypt," Jerry grinned. "The Valley of the Kings would simply blow you away."

"Have you really been there?" She asked wide-eyed with excitement, but unable to wait for his answer, something else caught her attention and she looked away.

"There is so much to see, I couldn't possibly do it all in one day."

Jerry smiled, Orlagh looked magnificent, her face was flushed with excitement and he adored her. She meant everything to him, although she radiated confidence and poise, he loved the way she sometimes appeared vulnerable and uncertain, it was at times like this he was compelled to wrap her up in his arms and keep her safe from the world.

Ephesus was one of the best and most complete Roman towns or cities in Turkey. Jerry had read the brochure earlier that day but nothing could prepare him for the wondrous sights that met them as they stepped off the bus.

"Wow, would you just look at that, it's truly amazing," Orlagh said, confirming his thoughts.

It was not too hot, the sun was yet to reach its zenith, but the air was dry, so pacing themselves they let the tourists from the bus go on ahead. Their tour guide had given them information packs so they could please themselves. All the others had chosen guided tours, but Orlagh and Jerry planned to spend some time exploring on their own before going to find Takat.

They entered the ancient city through the Magnesia Gate then making their way slowly down the hill, their minds reeled as they took in the wonders that waited to greet them. The Roman provincial capital was arranged in a neat grid formation and was laid out like a huge building site. Orlagh could hardly believe her eyes, she had seen pictures and diagrams of the city before but still the shock of seeing such marvels for herself was almost overwhelming. She saw the Odeum, the Celsus Library and the Temple of Hadrian, and staggering under the sheer weight of history, she allowed her imagination run wild. She fancied she could see people from 2000 years ago going about their business amongst these fine monuments, but the sights and sounds assaulting her senses disappeared as quickly as they had come once Jerry slipped his hand into hers. This simple act of affection grounded her in the present.

There were perfectly preserved mosaics laid out like gigantic puzzles on the ground and stepping carefully around them it didn't need much imagination to see how they would have looked in their prime. Columns rising up out of the ground stood proud like sentinels guarding this sacred place. For over 2000 years these stones had bathed in the light from the sun, she found it hard to comprehend that this place, seemingly timeless, had stood under the clear blue sky for generations. Like wise old men, these columns must have many secrets to tell.

Turning to her left, she moved slowly towards the Library of Celsus. Only the façade remained, but this was her most favourite structure of all. Jerry was reading from the notes he carried.

"The Library is built on a platform which has nine steps, the full width of the building."

Making their way up the steps, they paused under the columns at the top. This was the front entrance and once inside they were amazed by what they saw.

"The central columns were larger than those at the ends." Jerry continued as they went slowly across the floor space. Orlagh was always humbled when walking in a place where people had walked so many years ago, and stepping over foundations that once supported walls she could not help thinking about the conversations that must have gone on here.

"This made the building seem much larger than it really was," he said. "The library once held thousands of scrolls around its walls in specially created niches."

Orlagh looked up at the gap between the inner and outer walls, and Jerry seeing where she was looking explained.

"The gap between the walls helped to protect the scrolls from the temperature and humidity."

"What I wouldn't give to be transported back in time, experience being here in its heyday, to mingle with the people who visited and worked in this place." She looked at him wistfully before continuing. "I would have been a librarian in Roman times, a scholar. Just think about the research possibilities, the knowledge from all those thousands of scrolls."

Jerry smiled; she was an academic through and through.

They lost all sense of time as they wandered around the ruins, connected by a common interest, they bounced ideas and facts off each other, testing their historical knowledge to the extreme. Although enjoyable, the experience was exhausting both physically and mentally and now the heat was beginning to rise from the ruins.

It was Jerry's turn to be amazed as they came across the Great Theatre. It was typically curved in Roman design with high backed staging that could seat over 25,000 people.

"Would you believe it," he said reading from the brochure. "This theatre is still used for performances today."

"We had better get a move on," Orlagh glanced at her watch. "Takat will have locked up and gone home before we get there." Her face blossomed into a cheeky grin.

Jerry knew she was right, but he found it difficult to drag himself away from the theatre. Taking her by the hand, they set off along Harbour Street, the grandest street in Ephesus that once boasted street lamps and shop fronts.

X

As the ceremony drew to a close the druids were charged with the energy of their ancestors. The air around them was vibrant, alive with spirits from the Otherworld and as they made their way along the valley, they chanted their appreciation.

Two men had exchanged ceremonial robes for conventional western clothing; they wore gortex jackets, heavy-duty trousers and hiking boots.

They had already been given their orders and were aware of the penalty for failure. Nodding respectfully towards the high priest, they were honoured to have been chosen for this mission, and having already received a blessing from the spirits, made their way out of the camp and disappeared into the wilderness.

Linda Pritchard was working in one of the laboratories on board the *Ocean Pride*. Dressed in a white biohazard suit with sealed surgical boots on her feet, she stood at a fume cupboard her arms extending into protective gloves secured to the front panel. She was using tools from a specially designed toolkit to probe the flask that Jack had recovered from the wrecked aircraft.

She had already examined the blood samples taken from the victims of the crash but her findings were inconclusive. Of one thing she was certain, the sample taken from the woman found inside the aircraft proved that she had not been killed by whatever it was that struck down the men on the mountainside. Linda had a feeling that the woman had already been dead when the aircraft crashed, but this would of course be almost impossible to confirm.

As a precaution she had moved everyone out of the lab and secured the door, she was now breathing air from a filter system that was independent to the rest of the ship. The fume cupboard also had its own system feeding directly into a cylinder, nothing inside the cupboard could escape into the lab or infect the rest of the crew, but still she was taking no chances.

"Can you hear me boys?" she said, testing the communication system.

Jack and Paul were in the control room watching their computer screen where they could see Linda working in her lab. She looked into the camera and winked at them.

"We can see and hear you clearly Linda." Paul reported.

"Good, then let the games begin." Slowly and methodically, she manipulated the tools that she was using to open the flask.

"We have here a type of Dewar flask," she told them as she worked, it was important to record every detail on the digital audio recorder. "The flask has a double layer construction, like two thin walled bottles, one inside the other. Between the walls is a vacuum; this ensures an effective insulation which minimises the convection of heat."

She continued in silence for a few moments, working at the stopper whilst holding the flask in a metal stand. Once the seal had been broken, she picked up a long hollow glass tube and fed it into the neck of the flask, but when she withdrew it, it looked empty.

"I have captured a sample, now transferring it to the microscope for analysis."

Inside the cupboard was a small platform where samples were laid before the computerised microscope could zoom in. Sensors linked to the computer picked up and analysed minute changes inside the cupboard, any findings were automatically compared with a vast database stored in the computer memory.

"Bingo!" Linda said as she used the keyboard to send commands to the microscope. After making a few adjustments, an array of coloured dots appeared on the screen.

"Are you getting this?" she asked.

Jack and Paul could see the image on the computer screen.

"Sure can, what the hell is that stuff?" Paul asked.

"What we have here gentlemen unless I am very much mistaken is a type of phosphorus-containing organic chemical, an organophosphate of some kind."

Jack looked at Paul and frowned.

"Care to enlighten us further Dr Pritchard?" Paul said.

"Well," Linda began. "It's a chemical agent but it's nothing like I've seen before," she paused before going on. "It resembles Sarin, a chemical that was discovered by German scientists whilst developing pesticides during the 1930s."

"A nerve agent?" Jack said glancing at Paul again.

"Yes, it was developed for use as a weapon of mass destruction."

"But you said you have never seen anything like this before. Is that sample Sarin?" Paul asked.

"Yes but not as we know it," she replied. "This chemical agent has been modified. The changes made are modest I grant you that, but what

58

effect this has I can't say. I will have to do some tests."

"Okay Linda," Paul said calmly. "You do whatever you need to do then report directly to us, just be careful with that stuff."

"Before we go," Jack interrupted. "Is the content of that flask sufficient to cause the deaths of those men we found on the mountain?"

"Oh yes without doubt. Once airborne this agent will spread out with minimal dilution over a vast area, it's lethal to any living thing in its path."

"But we didn't find any symptoms on the individuals, no vomit or any other indications to say they had been poisoned."

"Maybe the modifications have turned it into a rapid killer. Normally exposure to Sarin will be fatal in a few minutes, but of course, it will leave clues. If it has been modified to kill in seconds, the body won't have time to respond in the normal way."

"You didn't find anything unusual in the blood samples," he reminded her.

"True but then I didn't know what I was looking for; I'll check them again later and get back to you."

"Okay Linda, you take care now," Paul said as they turned away from the screen.

"We know the Phoenix Legion is behind this," Jack said. "We saw their logo on the wreckage. Have we got any information on Olga Honig?"

Paul spoke into the intercom system to the Officer tasked with finding out more about the dead woman.

"Just completed my report sir, the file is now on the computer hard drive."

Paul touched a series of buttons on the keyboard and the screen changed, then, double clicking on a command button, he opened the file.

'Erik and Olga Honig, brother and sister, ran an airbus and cargo ferry business flying out of Hamburg in Germany. Their company, *LuftHonig*, closed down six months ago when the pair disappeared off the radar. Rumour has it that they fled the country leaving business debts of just over 500,000 euros. Erik, 38 and Olga, 32 are said to have been recruited as pilots by an unknown organisation operating in the Middle East.'

"Not much to go on," Jack said. "We do know however, that this unknown organisation is the Phoenix Legion."

"Could be they sub-contracted to the Legion as pilots for that one flight."

"Maybe," Jack frowned, "it's more likely to be the Legion who employed

59

them. They have all the credentials, young German professionals with substantial debts and a good reason to disappear."

"Guess you're right." Paul scratched his chin.

"I'm going to do some research of my own," Jack said.

He left the control room and headed for his cabin.

XI

The museum was tucked away beside the entrance to the ancient city and from the look of the building Jerry could see that it had been added to more than once over time.

Orlagh leading the way, was filled with excitement as she rushed into the museum, she spotted Takat immediately.

"Dr Gairne," he said coolly as if he had been expecting her to drop by at any moment. "What a surprise."

"Takat, how are you?" They embraced before the man stood back to appraise her, after a moment he turned towards Jerry.

"This is Jerry Knowles," Orlagh said stepping back so the men could shake hands.

"Mr Knowles, I'm very pleased to meet you."

"How do you do."

"You are English," Takat said. "I can tell from your accent."

Naturally, he expected a companion of Orlagh's to be Irish.

"Jerry is the great grandson of the very prominent Edwardian archaeologist Sir Geoffrey Knowles."

Takat frowned as he recalled his knowledge of British history.

"Ah yes," he exclaimed, "the infamous Belgae Torc."

It was hard to tell how old Takat was, his hair had receded over the top of his head but it hung down around his shoulders and was the colour of dark toffee. His face was heavily lined and tanned by the sun and as Jerry looked closer, he could see traces of Arab in the man's features.

Takat's intelligent dark eyes surveyed them both with a glimmer of humour then turning towards Orlagh he took both her hands in his.

"Has something happened to you?" he asked, his voice full of concern, but the smile never left his face. "You are surrounded by light, your life force is strong, you are simply glowing."

"I'm not pregnant if that's what you mean," she laughed.

"No not at all," Takat, amused by her blunt but humorous reply, grinned. "It's just that you appear so much more vibrant than I remember."

She glanced at Jerry and Takat could see the love flowing between them. He smiled his understanding but knew there was more to it. Jerry was not at the centre of the glow, which surrounded her.

"So," he said, "what do you make of my domain?" Waving his arms about expansively, he was immensely proud of his museum and the artefacts of which he was custodian. "Welcome to Turkey, the world's largest museum." Takat's grin was infectious.

He showed them around describing every item on display. He told them stories of his own archaeological digs and they marvelled at the treasures that filled every room.

"The Ephesus Museum is a rich and important museum," he said proudly. "Artefacts come from digs at Ephesus, St. John Church, the Beevi Mausoleum and other important local ruins. They are displayed here for visitors to see and to admire, academics are welcome to access information from our extensive library."

Both Orlagh and Jerry were impressed, they delighted him with their questions and Takat was overjoyed to have the opportunity to discuss historical matters with such distinguished guests.

He adored Orlagh, he had never forgotten the kindness she had shown him during his visit to Ireland and his knowledge of European history had been fuelled by her enthusiasm. She taught him so much about Irish culture.

The time they spent with Takat sped by quickly and it was almost time for them to return to their tour bus.

"Are you continuing your visit to Sirince village?" Takat asked.

"Yes," Orlagh replied, "we are going to browse amongst the tented stalls and shops." She smiled, quoting a line from the brochure she had read earlier.

"You must also visit the Byzantine church there." Takat said looking thoughtful. "Would you mind if I came along with you. Will there be room for me on your tour bus?"

"What an excellent idea," Orlagh beamed. "I'm sure there will be a seat for you."

Orlagh found the tented stalls at the little village of Sirince a delight and she discovered that she was skilled at the art of bargaining for goods. Not once did she pay the asking price for anything but managed to knock the seller down until she was convinced she had a bargain. Jerry and Takat trailed behind carrying the bundles and packages that she accumulated on her tour around the market square.

After a while, they managed to draw her away from the shops and found seats in a shaded spot where they ordered thick Turkish coffee.

"Tell me more about your adventure regarding the Belgae Torc." Takat said the moment they had settled.

Orlagh told him about the survey ship she had been working on and how it was sunk by a torpedo fired from a restored German U-Boat. She recounted her dramatic escape with Roz Stacey, one of the ship's engineers, through the moon pool in the bottom of the ship moments before it sank, and as she talked both men listened intently. Jerry had heard it all before but he loved to listen to her melodious Irish lilt, it was like music to his ears, he would never grow tired of the sound.

"Your experience seems to have strengthened your resolve, perhaps that's why you appear different. An adventure like that must have left its mark."

"This coffee is very good." Orlagh said wanting to change the subject.

A local fortune teller was making her way around the tables. She was entertaining the tourists by reading coffee grounds in the bottom of cups and they adored her. She was an attractive young woman whose dark skin was not yet ravaged by time.

Jerry studied her as she moved, he loved her traditional costume but there was something endearing about the way she flirted unashamedly with all the men. She flattered them all, telling them in a mellow voice what they wanted to hear.

Although she looked like a simple country girl, Jerry was not fooled he could tell it was all an act. The tourists did not seem to care, she was what she appeared to be, an attractive, mysterious young woman who was both entertaining and informative.

Jerry noticed that she avoided anyone who looked local, she targeted the westerners and Takat, sitting at their table, was a good enough reason for her to keep her distance.

With only one table left before theirs, she eyed them suspiciously, but could not resist coming over. Takat said something and she seemed to relax; she smiled at Jerry before beginning her speech. Takat had to translate as she reached for Orlagh's cup. She stared at it silently then after a while, her eyes became wide and a frown creased the smooth skin between her eyes.

A magnificent golden Torc filled her vision and she gasped as she felt its power. Words that she did not understand tumbled from her mouth heavy with accent.

"The Belgae Torc," she said, gasping as she saw the image of a strange woman coming towards her from out of the mist. Beside her was a wolf and she knew the woman's name was Madb, she and the animal were connected.

"Madadh-allaigh." She said hardly able to pronounce the strange word.

This was the name of Madb's animal ally, and behind them, she saw the stag. He was a magnificent creature exuding warmth and wisdom. His eyes were bright and could have been stars. Before she could utter a word, she sensed this beast was connected to Orlagh. She had no idea what an animal ally was or why she was seeing such things, it terrified her but curiously, she realised they would do her no harm.

She shuddered and glancing at Orlagh talked swiftly, Takat did not understand some of the words but he translated as best as he could.

Suddenly a red haired woman filled her vision. Her eyes burning fiercely, she resembled the woman sitting at the table but that is where the similarity ended. The woman in front of her was gentle and kind, she could feel it in her spirit, unlike the face in the bottom of the coffee cup.

"You must beware of the goddess," she said. Her eyes rolling up into her head, she began to tremble. "They are waiting for you, bad men are there."

Suddenly she cried out and fell to the pavement. Jerry was beside her in an instant but she recovered immediately. The look she gave them was murderous, and scrambling away continued in an ancient tongue that none of them could understand. Her voice rising in pitch, she began screaming obscenities and as she rounded the corner of the nearest building, she disappeared from view.

"Well, what do you make of that?" Orlagh said, clearly shaken.

"Whatever she saw was obviously unpleasant." Jerry replied.

The girl had said things that made sense to him. She spoke of Madb and called the animal allies by name.

"Take no notice," Takat said. "She is nothing but a charlatan, no more than an act for the tourists. Did you see how she was flirting with all the men?" He knew there was more to it than that, but he did not want to admit it to Orlagh. He realised it was all to do with the Belgae torc and it seemed there was unfinished business with the goddess; staring at Orlagh, he feared for her.

Jerry slipped his arm protectively around her shoulders, and moving closer could feel her trembling.

XII

The following day Takat received some disturbing news from one of his colleagues who was visiting relations in a small mountain village. The moment he realised the significance of the news he telephoned the hotel where Orlagh and Jerry were staying, but he was too late, they had already gone out for the day.

"Do you know where they might have gone?" he asked the receptionist.

"No sir, they have with them a number of brochures, but I'm sure they haven't taken a tour bus trip."

Takat grunted and thought for a moment. "Did they leave a contact number for a cell phone perhaps?"

"No sir, we have nothing like that in our records."

He thanked her before adding. "Please let Dr Gairne know that I have been trying to contact her, it's a matter of some urgency."

He cursed himself for not having been more careful with the business card she had given him six years earlier; the cell phone number might still be the same. He considered contacting The National Museum of Ireland, where she worked, but they were unlikely to pass on such personal information. He would just have to be patient.

Orlagh and Jerry were sitting at one of the small tables set up on a pavement overlooking the harbour and as they talked quietly, they watched the ships coming and going.

The morning was beginning to heat up, a clear Mediterranean blue filled the heavens and stretched from horizon to horizon, there was not a single cloud in the sky. The sea was calm and sparkled like a turquoise carpet studded with jewels and Orlagh smiled as the warm breeze played gently with her hair.

"I don't really fancy visiting another ancient city today," she said. "My head is still trying to cope with all the wonders we saw yesterday."

Jerry knew exactly what she meant, he was also finding it difficult to digest everything they had seen. She looked tired, he knew she had not slept well the night before, the events of the previous day were obviously still too raw. Although they had discussed it the evening before, Jerry thought there was still more to be said.

"So what do you think happened yesterday?"

She knew exactly what he meant but did not answer immediately; instead, she stared at him over the rim of her coffee cup.

"It's strange how that woman knew so much," she began, "there's no reason for it, she couldn't possibly have known what happened to me."

"True," Jerry nodded, "her knowledge of Celtic animal allies was certainly impressive."

"Well not really," she looked at him thoughtfully, putting her cup down on the table before going on. "There was a strong Celtic influence in these parts in ancient times. This whole area of eastern Turkey, as you know, was the Kingdom of Lydia. The people who lived here were not much different from our own Iron Age people. Of course their culture and lifestyle was not the same but countries all across south eastern Europe have Celtic links." She paused for a moment to ensure that she had his undivided attention. There were more people about now, many of whom were females heading for the beach wearing nothing more than skimpy bikinis.

"It makes sense that these ancient people followed some kind of basic rule and beliefs. We know that Celtic artwork in this area was the same as in Ireland, Scotland and France. Tombs were of a similar design so there must have been interaction and shared beliefs amongst these ancient cultures. It also follows that animal allies and other such beliefs were universal."

"I agree," Jerry nodded, "but why did she target you in particular and why the theatrics?"

"I guess she saw in me a strong Celtic link, red hair and pale skin, I do rather stand out here," she grinned.

"Okay, that's true, but I don't believe that was the reason for her attention. Everything she said was spot on, it was exactly as you told me, Madb and her ally; Madadh-alluidh and of course the stag."

Orlagh giggled. "I just love the way you say that, your pronunciation is priceless."

"Well, you know what I mean, Gallic isn't my natural tongue."

He looked hurt so Orlagh reached across the table and stroked his arm gently, her expression forgiving she treated him to one of her most endearing smiles.

"Anyway," she continued, "there's no logical reason for it. Let's just say for a moment that she is truly gifted and, guided by spirits, was drawn towards me."

Jerry glanced at her and his expression hardened. Orlagh knew he was a disbeliever, but he allowed her to continue.

"The spirits drove her to reveal my animal ally, she knew all about Madb and the wolf. I believe she actually saw the Goddess of Hibernia and despite all that gave me a clear warning. You heard what she said, *'You must be aware of the goddess, they are waiting for you, bad men are there.'* We can't ignore what she told us."

"But you've already confronted the goddess, Madb took care of her whilst the animal allies spirited you away or whatever it was they did."

She could see he was becoming uncomfortable speaking about this. Jerry dealt in logic and facts; he was an academic, where spirits and animal allies were concerned he remained unconvinced. His philosophy dictated that archaic human beliefs had no place in modern day reasoning.

"Well I think it would be wise to be vigilant, just in case there's some merit in her warning." Orlagh tossed her head and looked around.

People surrounded them, men were sitting at tables drinking and smoking, any one of them could be a potential threat. Pushing aside her thoughts of paranoia, she realised these were simply innocent people going about their business, none of them had any interest in her. She sighed and folded her arms across her chest.

"More coffee?" She asked.

On the northern coast of Turkey, a few miles off shore, the *Ocean Pride* was cutting smoothly through the Black Sea at her most economic speed, her destination; the Bosphorus Straits.

Dr Linda Pritchard had completed her initial examination of the contents of the Dewar flask and had looked again at the blood samples Jack had collected. She was ready to present her findings and was now making her way through the ship towards Jack's office. Under her arm, she carried a laptop computer and a buff coloured file.

Jack was already in his office when she appeared.

"Linda, come in," he held the door open for her. "Paul is on his way, he'll be a couple of minutes."

She nodded and put the laptop on his desk. Once it was set up, she turned her attention to her file, arranging papers neatly in some kind of order.

"Coffee?" Jack called out over his shoulder. He was filling a mug from a dispenser built into the wall.

"Yes please," she replied and turning to watch what he was doing, said. "I can't believe you managed to get your own coffee machine plumbed into your office."

"Perks of the job," he grinned.

"Perks, what perks?" Paul asked as he strode into the office.

"I was just asking Jack to explain how he managed to get an industrial sized coffee machine as a fixture in his office."

"Don't you have one?" Paul asked in mock surprise.

Linda looked at him, she was not sure if he was being serious, he was implying that he had one too. She decided to let the matter drop and taking the mug Jack was holding out to her, turned towards the huge monitor fixed to the wall. Reaching for a lead, she slipped the jack plug into a socket on her laptop then the screen came alive. There was only one icon flashing on the screen so double clicking on it, she opened the file.

"Well gentlemen," she began, "I re-checked the blood samples. The sample from the woman was clear of toxins, so it wasn't the substance from the flask that killed her. I still think she was dead before the aircraft impacted into the mountain, but I've failed to confirm the cause of death. There was an increased level of adrenalin in her blood, so something must have excited her moments before she died." She paused to check her notes and took a mouthful of coffee.

"Now, as far as the samples from the men are concerned, they are something else." She flashed a diagram up on the screen and began to explain how it worked.

"As you can see from the toxicology results there is a raised level of …." She paused to study the men. "Well let's just say it's a particularly nasty nerve agent."

"A potential weapon of mass destruction," Jack made a comment.

"I didn't actually say that, but it's a possibility, we have no evidence to back up that claim." Linda was a little surprised by Jack's reaction.

"Where did it originate from," Paul asked. "Is it something newly developed?"

"As I suspected earlier, it's basically Sarin, a nerve agent developed in the 1930s."

"Production and stockpiling of Sarin was outlawed by the Chemical Weapons Convention of 1993, when it was classified as a Schedule 1 substance."

"That's right," Linda said turning to Jack. "I didn't realise you were so knowledgeable regarding chemical weapons."

"I'm not," he admitted, "I looked it up on the internet last night."

"So let me get this straight," Paul, sounded serious. "Are you telling me that someone has a pile of this stuff?"

"We can't say for sure," Linda glanced at him, "but what we do know from my research is that this is no ordinary type of Sarin. It's been modified significantly." She was trying to keep her report simple but was failing miserably.

"Sarin is a chiral molecule, typically racemic," she pointed to a three dimensional illustration that appeared on the screen. "It has four substituents attached to the tetrahedral phosphorus centre. Now, the Sp form," she pointed to the screen again, "is the more active enantiomer due to its greater binding to acetylcholinesterase. It is prepared from methylphosphonyl diflouride and a mixture of isopropyl alcohol."

Jack and Paul looked at each other. As far as they were concerned Linda was speaking a foreign language, but they tried to look intelligent and focussed on the screen.

"Isopropylamine is added to neutralise the hydrogen fluoride generated during this alcoholysis reaction," she continued. "As a binary chemical weapon, it can be generated in situ by this same reaction."

"Okay," Paul said with a frown, "let's get this straight. The chemical weapon is made up of constituent parts which are then mixed together like a cocktail to form the nerve agent."

"That's right. For example, a shell fired from a large field gun would have within it separate compartments containing the binary precursors for Sarin. Once it's been fired the shell spins through the air and the chemicals get mixed together then on impact the shell casing splits open releasing the nerve agent."

"How effective is the gas?"

"Sarin is estimated to be over five hundred times more toxic than cyanide."

Paul hissed through his teeth and glanced at Jack.

"So what's different about this sample?" Jack asked. He knew there had to be more.

Linda reduced the size of the diagram on the screen and flashed another one up beside it so they could make a comparison.

"As you can see, this model differs from the conventional set up."

They studied both slides noting the differences.

"So in layman's terms Doc, what does all this mean?" Paul asked turning towards Linda.

"Well, for a start this strain has a much longer shelf life. Sarin degrades after a few weeks depending on the purity of the precursor materials. The sample you found Jack is far more powerful than regular Sarin."

"Heck!" Paul could hardly believe what he was hearing.

"This means that it's far more reliable when released in an airborne attack. Now," Linda paused, "the really interesting part is that our nerve agent is fully self contained. It doesn't require mixing to become effective, basically what you see is what you get." She glanced up at the screen as if the diagram made perfect sense.

"How much agent did you get from the Dewar flask?" Jack asked.

"Enough to kill those men on the mountain, luckily there was only two of them. Did you say the second victim was a hundred metres away?"

"Yes that's right." Jack nodded.

"Death would have been immediate, even in pure mountain air and over that distance. You found no symptoms because of the agent's fast acting nature. Normally there would be signs, once the agent is ingested or absorbed through the skin, the victim undergoes a series of stages, for example, a runny nose, tight chest resulting in breathing difficulties, nausea. Eventually there is a loss of bodily functions, the victim vomits, defecates and urinates. Twitching and jerking finally takes place and death occurs during a series of convulsive spasms."

"This would take some time." Paul said, his face turning pale.

"Yes it would, depending on the victim of course."

"But our sample delivers death immediately." Jack reminded them.

"Yes it does." Linda nodded.

Jack realised that the Phoenix Legion must be back up to strength and planning their next atrocity. So many questions were raging through his head. He must find out how much of this agent they had, where it was being manufactured and stored and more importantly what they were planning to do with it. He wondered how much time they had.

XIII

Orlagh and Jerry spent the day like any other tourists exploring the little seaside town, learning about the people who lived there and generally soaking up the atmosphere. When they were tired of the shops and museums, they strolled along the shore where they admired the palm trees growing alongside the coastal road. The buildings facing the beach were an interesting mix of architecture, old and new they provided hotels and holiday lets for the visitors.

With sand on their feet and a warm breeze on their faces, they were carefree and happy in each other's company. They chose not to discuss further the events of the previous day.

When the sea air and the brilliance of the sun exhausted them, they returned to their hotel. It was mid afternoon and time to relax by the pool with a book and a long cool drink.

"Ah, good afternoon Dr Gairne." The receptionist said as soon as they appeared.

Orlagh frowned, something was wrong. She had not given her professional title when signing into the hotel.

"I have a message for you." The receptionist behind the counter continued before slipping a sealed envelope across the polished top and smiling at Jerry.

"Thank you." Orlagh said as she picked up the note then they made their way towards the stairs.

Once inside their room she tore open the envelope and pulled out the card.

"It's from Takat," she said glancing up at Jerry. "He wants me to telephone him the moment I get this message. This number must be for the museum, I wonder what he wants."

Rummaging through her bag, she found her mobile phone but typically, there was not much signal so sitting on the bed she reached for the telephone on the little bedside table.

"Hiya Takat, its Orlagh." She spoke into the handset.

Jerry listened to the one sided conversation and Orlagh nodded a couple of times.

"Okay, we'll see you then." She returned the handset to its cradle then looked up at Jerry. "He has something important to discuss with us, he wouldn't give me the details over the phone but wants to meet up later."

"Okay," Jerry nodded, "I wonder what can be so important."

Orlagh shrugged her shoulders and standing up, went to the mirror where she checked her face before running a brush through her hair. She gathered up another bottle of suntan lotion and her book and pushed them both into her bag before going into the bathroom. Quickly she changed into a swimsuit then pulling on a light linen shirt, she reached for her floppy hat.

Erich Schiffer, commander of the Phoenix legion was sitting at his desk in an office situated deep underground in a secret bunker. He was staring thoughtfully at a handwritten note that he placed carefully on his antique desk. The coded message alerted him to the fact that an old adversary was patrolling off the coast of northern Turkey. Jack Harrington's ship had been spotted in the Black sea and was currently at anchor off Trabzon, the principle city of north eastern Turkey.

Schiffer had also been informed that a Sikorsky S-92 helicopter had left the ship and was currently somewhere over the Kackar mountains. He rubbed his hand wearily over his face and sighed. This was the second piece of bad news he had received that day. If Harrington had located the wreckage of the Junkers 52, then it was reasonable to assume that he was now in possession of the chemical samples and even the Belgae Torc. If only he could have got to the crash site first, he thought. The loss of his transport aircraft had come as a shock, it had never occurred to him that something could go wrong. The Junkers was a reliable aircraft; it was hardly a hazardous journey across the Kackar mountains especially in daylight and in good weather. It also did not seem possible that Harrington could have known about the flight or the cargo the Junkers was carrying, his being in the area must have been a lucky coincidence. Still Schiffer had to consider that he might have had something to do with the disaster.

Suddenly he reached for the telephone on his desk and issued an order.

"Heidenrech, come in here now."

He hardly had time to replace the receiver before a man wearing the uniform of an S.S.Officer appeared.

"I want two men dispatched to the Aegean immediately." He said, staring at the man whose gaze was fixed on a point just above his head.

"Dr Gairne is reported to be holidaying in the seaside town of," he consulted his notes, "Kusadasi. I want her and her companion detained and brought here for questioning."

"Yes Herr Schiffer." The man snapped his heels smartly together before affecting a perfect about turn then he disappeared quickly along the corridor.

Schiffer grinned, if Harrington had the chemical and the Torc, then Dr Gairne may well be a useful bargaining tool. He tapped the corner of his desk with his fingertips and frowned. It seemed a coincidence that both she and Harrington were in this part of the world at the same time. His contacts had assured him that there had been little passing between them these past twelve months. He was certain they were not operating together but perhaps his information was wrong. A nerve twitched at the corner of his mouth and his fingers drummed harder on the desktop. If Harrington were responsible for the loss of his aircraft, then he would be made to pay.

Takat arrived at the hotel just after seven thirty and going through to reception announced his arrival by telephoning Orlagh's room.

"We'll join you shortly," Jerry told him. "Go into the bar and make yourself comfortable."

Takat chose a quiet corner where they would not be disturbed, he arranged comfortable chairs around a small table then sat with his back against the wall. He preferred it this way, he liked to face into the room, see what was going on.

Orlagh and Jerry appeared moments later and Takat stood up as they approached. Orlagh was wearing a green blouse of finest silk that she had purchased from the market at Syrince the previous day. Around her neck, she had wound a string of amber beads, the colours perfect against her skin and red hair.

"You look beautiful." Takat told her as he kissed her cheeks.

She beamed at him and sat down in one of the chairs. Crossing her legs elegantly, she looked up at both men.

"What can I get you to drink?" Jerry asked.

"A crisp dry white wine for me." Orlagh said and Takat asked for a beer.

Jerry went to the bar to order their drinks and the moment he returned to the table, Takat began to outline the reason for his visit.

"One of my colleagues has gone to visit his family in a small mountain village in eastern Anatolia and he contacted me earlier today with some very disturbing news." He looked at them both gravely. "Describe to me what happens when someone wears the Belgae Torc." Reaching for his beer, he sat back in his chair.

Orlagh was taken aback by his request and it took her a few moments to gather her thoughts. She eyed him suspiciously before telling him what she knew.

"It's true that most people who put the Torc around their neck will die soon after," she began. "Death comes in many forms and can in many cases be attributed to natural causes, for example a stroke or fatal heart attack whilst in others it remains a complete mystery."

"Call them acts of god if you will." Takat nodded and studied Orlagh carefully before going on. "You wore the Torc and survived."

"Yes I did, but so did my friend Roz." She shuddered at the memory and leaning forward picked up her glass.

"How do you explain that?" Takat asked.

"Perhaps it was because of Madb, we had the protection of the spirits." She shot a look at Jerry before explaining about the animal allies.

"The fortune teller mentioned these things yesterday," Takat nodded thoughtfully.

Orlagh remained silent; she was reluctant to tell him more. It annoyed Jerry that she could take these things seriously.

"So it's true then, the Belgae Torc has the power to take a life."

"Yes, I'm afraid it does." Orlagh nodded. She wondered why he was so interested in the subject.

"There was a young girl from the village where my colleague's family live," he began, "who died recently. It is said that she was wearing a golden torc around her neck when they found her. I'm sure it was the Belgae Torc, my colleague described it to me in detail."

For a moment Orlagh remained speechless, she stared at him in utter disbelief. Gradually as she recovered, questions began to form in her head and she wanted to know more.

"But that's impossible, how do you know it's the Belgae Torc?"

"From what you have just told me and the description my colleague gave, it seems likely to be the same torc."

"I don't understand, how did it come to be there in such a remote place?"

"I'm afraid I don't have all the answers," Takat said, "but one thing is clear, if that's where the torc is then we must go there and get it."

XIV

Early the following morning Takat drove them out along a rough road leading to a small airfield where his cousin kept a light aircraft. Orlagh saw it warming up at the end of a short grass runway and as they drove through the open gates, a hand came out of the cabin window and waved. Takat flashed the cars headlights and headed towards the empty hangar situated to one side of the runway.

"It's going to be a long day my friends." He told them as they climbed out of the car. He had already briefed them on the journey. The flight itself would last for about seven hours then they would have to drive to the village.

The Cessna 172 Skyhawk was a four seat, single engine light aircraft that had a cruising speed of a little under 240km/h. The mountain village was just under its maximum operational height and providing there was no bad weather or high winds the aircraft would get them there safely, but it didn't have the fuel capacity to complete the journey in one go so they would have to land and take on fuel.

"At least we'll be able to stretch our legs, seven hours is a long time to be stuck in such a small aircraft." Orlagh worried about the practicalities of such a long journey.

They walked the short distance to where the aircraft was standing and approaching it from the rear avoided the spinning propeller. Takat opened the door and Orlagh climbed in. It was just like a car inside and as Jerry slipped in beside her Takat introduced them to his cousin.

The aircraft was idling but still they had to shout to make themselves heard above the noise of the engine. With the introductions over, they buckled themselves in then the aircraft lurched forward and began its run along the grass strip. The noise from the engine increased rising in pitch as the propeller spun even faster, one minute they were bumping madly along the runway and the next, as the aircraft rose into the air, a smooth sensation left Orlagh's stomach sinking. Her fingers gripped Jerry's hand tightly and he looked at her and grinned. She had never been in an aircraft as small as this before and her heart was beating rapidly against her ribs.

After what seemed an age the engine revs subsided and the aircraft drifted into level flight. Through the windscreen, Orlagh could see the horizon; it was nothing more than a distant haze, a vague colour against the clear blue of the sky. Glancing out of the side window she looked down on the sights of Turkey, everything was moving in slow motion and with the ground so far below, it seemed that they were nothing more than an insignificant speck against the vastness of the sky.

Cramped inside the cabin Orlagh was reminded of the helicopter ride she and Roz had been forced to take when abducted by Schiffer. There had not been much to see then, the whole terrifying experience had been filled with uncertainty and apprehension, but at least now, she had Jerry to keep her safe.

A few miles from the mountain village in the Kacker mountains two men exited the rear of a helicopter that was hovering a few feet above the ground. Their destination should have been the Aegean coast almost nine hundred miles away, but they had been diverted. A message had come through on the radio whilst they were in the air and the pilot was forced to change course.

The helicopter, now free of passengers gained height rapidly and flew away leaving the men to make their own way to the village. Their target was the third house on the main street heading in a westerly direction. There was only one street going through the village and the men had already pinpointed the house using a small hand held computer and a satellite link.

The villagers were gathered around a grave in a small cemetery along the mountain path. They were there to pay their final respects to a young girl who had died mysteriously a few days earlier and united in grief they wept with the family for their terrible loss.

The parents had thought their luck had changed when the girl presented them with a golden torc. She told them she had found the treasure on a grassy slope at the base of a rock face. She had no idea where it had come from or what it was doing there but she had picked it up and pushed it into her backpack. Forgetting about the strange object she enjoyed herself, spending an adventurous day climbing with her friends, but it was not until later that her luck began to change.

Standing before her parents with the torc in her hands, she was compelled to put it around her neck. It made her feel like a princess, the golden torc glittering like a royal jewel against her smooth skin, but it wasn't long before she began to feel a powerful force flowing through it. At first, it was a pleasantly warm sensation, but it soon began to vibrate and tighten against her throat. Strange visions filled her head and she struggled to rid herself of it but the force was too strong. She had never

76

experienced energy like this before; it permeated through her skin and into her bones until engulfing her completely, then the Goddess of Hibernia appeared and stole away her soul.

Two strangers entered the village just as the last shovelful of earth went into the grave. Flowers were arranged neatly on the loose earth, turning the little barren place into a sea of bright colour then finally the group of mourners turned away. With their eyes full of tears and their hearts heavy with sadness, they made their way silently along the path towards the village.

It did not take the men long to identify the house, and forcing their way in they discovered the atmosphere inside was cold and cheerless. Undeterred, they began their search giving no thought to personal belongings. Everything in their way they smashed needlessly, going through the neat little house until they found what they were looking for. Wrapped in a cloth and pushed to the back of a drawer, they found the Belgae Torc.

The family returned home to discover the intruders. Gathering her children to her, their mother cried out in alarm as she wrapped herself protectively around them. Their father entered the house alone leaving them standing in the doorway, and stumbling over the ruins of their furniture, he disappeared into the back room.

One of the intruders reacted the moment he appeared, lifting his arm he fired his pistol at point blank range, the impact of the 9mm bullet splitting his skull, lifted the man off his feet and slammed him into the back wall, he was dead before he hit the floor. The sound of a woman screaming did nothing to deter them and moving back into the front room, they fired their weapons indiscriminately. Bullets skimmed over the heads of the children huddled in the doorway but tore into the woman. She staggered backwards onto the path but managed to remain on her feet, her face twisting into a mask of terror and confusion as her eyesight began to fade. The last thing she saw were the faces of her terrified children.

The little blue and white Cessna Skyhawk having completed the first leg of its journey was standing at the edge of a grass runway being re-fuelled by a small tanker.

"How far do we have to go now?" Orlagh asked as she shrugged on her jacket. The terrain had been rising gradually as they travelled north east and now several thousand feet above sea level the temperature had dropped a few degrees.

"It's only about an hour flying time but when we arrive we have to go by road for about half an hour," Takat replied. "We should arrive before dusk."

They had arranged to stay in the village overnight and return the following day.

"It will be strange to hold the Belgae Torc again." Orlagh said.

"Just don't be tempted to put it around your neck." Jerry grinned, but she could tell by the tone of his voice that he was not joking.

"Peter will be overjoyed when he finds out I have it."

Peter O'Reilly, her boss, had long wanted the torc as part of their collection in Dublin.

"How do we stand with the law? We have no idea who the torc belongs to or how it came to be here." Orlagh looked up at Takat.

"From what you told me about the druids and the Nazis who almost killed you last year, I wouldn't be concerned about such things. It's an ancient artefact that should be in a museum on display for the enjoyment of everyone."

She realised that what he said was true, besides the torc had been lost for so long that ownership must surely have been relinquished by now.

"Whatever compensation you offer the family will be beyond their wildest dreams; you must remember they are mountain people who live simple lives. There is very little money in their village," Takat continued.

"So we can negotiate on behalf of the museum and be within the law?"

Takat nodded in response.

The rest of their journey was uneventful and almost two hours later, the old land rover in which they were travelling bumped along the mountain road and came to a stop just outside the village.

"That's my colleague." Takat nodded towards a man who was standing on the side of the track.

"You can't go any further." The man said gravely as he approached the land rover.

"What do you mean?" Takat asked as he opened the door.

"There have been deaths in the village." The man continued in English so they could all understand. "Two gunmen came to the house of the dead girl and when the funeral was taking place searched it looking for the torc. Unfortunately they were still there when the family returned from the cemetery." He paused for a moment, his throat working with grief.

"The men killed both husband and wife before making off with the torc."

Takat swore under his breath and turned away. He needed a moment before he could face Orlagh and the others.

"So the torc is gone." He said turning to his colleague. "Who were these men?" No one had an answer.

Orlagh covered her mouth with her hand and choked on the dreadful news. She was still inside the land rover and winding down the window, leaned out and spoke.

"How many children have been left?"

"Seven." The man whispered.

"Holy Mary, Mother of Christ." She crossed herself and tears coursed unchecked over her cheeks.

XV

The *Ocean Pride* was anchored not far from the city of Bodrum, an ancient city, which stood proudly overlooking the Aegean Sea.

A tender from the ship was lowered into the water and Jack prepared to go ashore. He had a meeting with an expert at the Institute of Nautical Archaeology; it was there he hoped to find the answers to some of his questions.

Captain Paul Seymour appeared beside him at the top of the boarding stairs.

"You coming too buddy?" Jack asked.

"If you don't mind, I'd rather like to stretch these old sea legs of mine."

Paul was obviously ready to relinquish command of his new toy to one of the officers, and Jack's smile widened. He was beginning to think that Paul would never leave this ship; he thought he would have to adopt Wings Wallace as his new sidekick.

"What?" Paul saw the look on his friends face.

"Didn't think you'd ever leave this baby," he nudged his friend with his elbow. "You sure you don't have a woman in this port?"

Paul shook his head and laughed, he had nothing to say in his defence, so leading the way he went down the boarding stairs and stepped onto the deck of the tender.

The buildings housing the Institute of Nautical Archaeology were spectacular. They resembled a complex of Roman influenced architecture surrounded by beautifully tended gardens. The main set of buildings housed the offices used by permanent staff and off to one side was a series of dormitories.

Jack and Paul approached along the main pathway and as they drew closer, a door suddenly opened revealing a man wearing a crumpled linen suit.

"Jack Harrington, how the devil are you, you old sea dog?" His crisp English accent was pleasant to hear.

"Lewis, not bad. Yourself?"

Both men beamed at each other.

"This is my old friend Paul Seymour, Paul this is Lewis Philpot."

They shook hands.

"Listen, would you chaps care for a spot of tea?"

"Yeah, that'll be real nice."

They followed him into the building and along an air-conditioned corridor to a well appointed but empty rest room.

"Sit where you like," Lewis told them, "it seems we have the place to ourselves."

Whilst he made tea in a tiny kitchenette, Jack and Paul studied the pictures arranged around the walls. High quality underwater photographs had been enlarged and framed, these were studies of projects that INA had been involved in over the years.

"Welcome to TINA." Lewis said with a grin as he placed a tray of tea in front of them.

"TINA?" Paul frowned.

"Turkish Institute of Nautical Archaeology one of my little jokes." Lewis told him.

Paul glanced sideways at Jack and raised his eyebrows.

"Right," Lewis said becoming serious. "Let's get down to business."

From a box file, he produced a sheaf of papers and studied them for a moment before going on. "I assume that you are both familiar with the sinking of the *M.V. Wilhelm Gustloff.*" He fixed them both with a stare.

Jack nodded but Paul looked confused.

"Here," Lewis passed them both a collection of papers that were stapled together. "A little bit of background information." He said.

Paul read the title; '*The sinking of the M.S. Wilhelm Gustloff*, then he began scanning what appeared to be an old newspaper report.

For the first time in four years, the former Nazi pleasure cruiser started her engines. Fleeing from the brutal Soviet Red Army onslaught, the M.S. Wilhelm Gustloff is ready to leave port. Every available space onboard is jammed with over ten thousand German refugees, naval personnel and wounded soldiers. The vessel is designed to hold a maximum of eighteen hundred and eighty eight passengers and crew.

Paul sucked in his breath as he studied the figures.

"There were four thousand children and youths onboard, on their way to the west," Lewis told them. "As you can see, they were leaving Oxhoft Pier in Gotenhafen, Gdynia in Poland. The date was Tuesday 30th January 1945."

"Not a good time of the year to be in that neck of the woods." Jack said.

"Quite, the temperature was well below freezing, the ship had to be escorted from its berth by icebreakers."

"Can you imagine what it must have been like, all those people crammed into the ship." Paul shuddered as he looked at the photograph.

"Yeah, despite the cold it must have soon have become pretty humid below deck." Jack said.

"You're right," Lewis agreed. "Reports tell us that it was so uncomfortable that people removed their bulky lifejackets, going against the orders of those in charge."

"So once they were at sea, the captain of the Gustloff ordered his ship to show running lights." Paul said as he read the paragraph highlighting that fact. "Even though they were sailing through hostile waters."

"Yes," Lewis nodded. "Apparently they received word that a convoy of minesweepers were in the vicinity and rather than risk collision he showed his running lights."

"I guess with the weather so bad the captain had to do something, the ship wouldn't have had the benefit of modern electronics like we have today."

"That's correct," Lewis said. "What they did have was frozen solid so they had to rely on lookouts. The report tells us that the ship was covered in ice and they were passing through some heavy snow storms."

"So the lookouts would have been virtually blind." Paul said. "I take it there is something significant with the sinking of this ship."

Jack looked at him. "Apart from the fact that it remains the worst maritime disaster of all time, the loss of life was far greater than that of the Titanic. Over nine thousand people died, murdered when the ship was torpedoed by a Soviet submarine. Only about twelve hundred were plucked from the water alive."

They were silent for a few moments as Paul contemplated the horrors of his friend's statement.

"The point of all this of course is that we think the Gustloff was carrying a hoard of treasure, artefacts plundered from across Europe by the Nazis during the war," he glanced at Jack. "We also think that one of those treasures is the fabled 'Amber Chamber.'" Lewis passed Paul another set of papers.

He studied the photograph in silence. It was of a magnificent room decorated with amber panels, which looked as if they were made from solid gold.

The Amber Chamber was dubbed the 'Eighth Wonder of the World', he read.

"This 18th century work of art disappeared during the war, looted by the Nazis." Jack began filling in the details. "It's said to have contained over six tons of amber, and although knowledge of its whereabouts was lost in the chaos at the end of the war, many believe that it was loaded onto the Gustloff. The Russians thought so too, they took the wreck apart searching for it but came up with nothing, or so they said."

"There are many theories surrounding its disappearance," Lewis took up the story. "You will see in the report that over many years and countless investigations it's thought that component parts from the room may be hidden in an underground bunker or disused mine shaft. Treasure hunters have devoted their lives to searching likely locations across Eastern Europe." He paused to study the men and wondered if Jack would rather continue, but obviously, he was content to remain silent.

"New evidence has come to light recently. It seems the Soviets may indeed have found it on the Gustloff and transferred it to a sealed container, but the ship carrying it was lost mysteriously off the coast of Ukraine in the Sea of Azov. It was only recently that the wreck has been discovered."

"So that's why Ed and the *Nautical Explorer* have been in the Sea of Azov for the past few weeks." Paul said, everything now slotting into place. "And why we've been fooling around in the Black Sea."

"I didn't want to say anything until my suspicions were confirmed," Jack said glancing uneasily at Paul. "Ed thinks he may have located the container but he needs us to go in and check it out. His ship has been at sea for three months and is pretty low on supplies, they need to go into port and re-stock."

Paul nodded but remained silent. He continued to read up on the Amber Chamber.

"If the Soviets hear about what we've found we could have a potential threat on our hands." Jack told them. "You can bet your bottom dollar the *Nautical Explorer* has been on top of their suspicion list, especially being so long in that part of the world."

Lewis pulled out another pile of papers from his box and passed them across the table.

"Here's all the information you need, there are also official documents giving you the backing of the Institute of Nautical Archaeology to undertake an underwater salvage operation."

Paul looked up, he realised that all the fancy documentation in the world would not stop the Soviets from getting their hands on the treasure given half a chance.

XVI

The sun rose majestically into the sky gilding the eastern horizon as it went. It was going to be another beautiful day.

Orlagh was awake, having slept badly she could no longer remain in bed, so slipping her legs from under the lightweight duvet, she stood up and pulled a silk robe around her shoulders before sliding open the balcony doors. Outside the air was freshly perfumed by plants growing beneath the window, and as the cool sea breeze washed over her the view across the bay almost took her breath away. The haze that usually hugged the horizon had not yet appeared and she had an uninterrupted view of the sunrise. Jewels sparkled like golden coins on the surface of the water and as the tiny fishing boats left the harbour their hulls flashed like silver fish. Orlagh smiled, she could not remember seeing a view as magical as this before and hugging herself, she tried to forget the memory of her haunting dreams.

Glancing back into their room, she could see Jerry asleep in the tangle of bedclothes. He appeared so child-like and her heart skipped a beat as she remembered the intensity of their lovemaking. It had been a long time since she had felt as happy as this, he made her feel complete and she realised how lucky she was to have found him. The death of her grandmother had been a devastating blow, and although no one could replace her, Orlagh believed that she would never feel happy again, but all that changed the moment she met Jerry. She believed he was heaven sent, but she would never admit to that. She had been giving a talk about Celtic Ireland at the museum where she worked and the last thing she expected to find was the man of her dreams. Jerry was everything that she was looking for and it did not take her long to realise that it was true and now their lives were so intertwined they were inseparable.

Orlagh was still deeply upset by the events of the previous few days. They had flown back to Kusadasi after spending an uncomfortable night in temporary accommodation beside the airstrip on the mountain.

"You should get some rest," Takat had told them. "Forget about all this and enjoy the rest of your holiday."

She knew she could never do that, people had died because of the Belgae Torc and somehow she felt responsible. She wanted to know why it had suddenly turned up in Turkey.

Jerry stirred and opened his eyes. For a moment, he looked startled as he hovered on the threshold of reality, then he saw her standing in the doorway bathed in a golden aura from the rising sun.

"I thought I'd died and gone to heaven," he grinned happily. "You look so angelic standing there."

"Good morning sleepy head!"

Slipping out of bed he came to her and folding his arms around her waist, kissed her neck then buried his face in her hair. She smelled as fresh as the morning air and was as warm as the sun on his back. Searching for her lips, he kissed her again and slowly slipping her robe over her shoulders, he pushed her gently down onto the bed.

Their tour bus, winding its way along the narrow coastal road, took them towards Bodrum and Orlagh had her face pressed up against the window. The view across the bay was stunning, the sea shimmering turquoise under a hot Mediterranean sky delighted her and everywhere she looked, she found a gem. Small boats working their way around the coast reminded her that crafts like these had been trading in the Aegean for thousands of years. All kinds of treasures lay undiscovered beneath the water; ancient trading vessels had been found with cargos of obsidian from Milos, Milian vases and even gold from Egypt. These wrecks helped archaeologists to understand how people lived around the Mediterranean, how developing cultures emerged and how they influenced each other.

Allowing her mind to wander she immersed herself in history, but it was not long before the horrors surrounding the torc came back to haunt her.

Jerry sensed her change of mood and searching for her hand wound his fingers around hers. Orlagh leaned back against him, he was solid and warm and she fitted perfectly into the curves of his body. She had to remind herself that they were on holiday and the mystery surrounding the torc was no business of theirs.

A little way behind the bus, a dark blue hire car was following at a discreet distance. Orlagh had not noticed it earlier when it was parked near to their hotel.

"Look at that." Orlagh exclaimed suddenly. She had spotted something out in the bay.

Jerry looked to see where she was pointing and could see an orange and white survey ship laying at anchor about a mile offshore.

"I'm sure that's one of Jack Harrington's ships." She told him.

Jerry pushed his face up against the window and spotted a helicopter standing on a raised platform over the bow; it was painted the same colour as the ship.

"Surely Jack can't be here too," she continued. "That would be too much of a coincidence."

Jerry nodded then said. "I suppose it could be possible, with all that underwater surveying going on around these shores he could be involved. I was reading about the Institute of National Archaeology in Bodrum earlier, maybe he has something to do with them."

They watched the ship in silence until receding into the distance, it grew too small to see then their thoughts turned to Bodrum and they began to think about the day ahead.

By the time the tour bus dropped them off at the harbour they had come up with a plan. First, they were going to visit the castle that was situated on the peninsula. It was a magnificent medieval stronghold built by the Knights of the Hospital of St.John of Rhodes. The castle had been turned into a museum, its 'romantic ruins' having undergone restoration in the late 1950s. It officially opened its doors in 1961, displaying objects retrieved from wrecks on the seabed, now it housed a vast collection of exhibits from all over the region. Orlagh had already studied an article about the castle that she had found in a magazine.

The dark blue car cruised slowly past the bus as it parked at a designated dispersal point beside the harbour wall, then a short distance away it stopped and two men got out. Standing beside the car they watched as tourists got off and as Orlagh and Jerry appeared two men pushed past almost knocking her off her feet. Jerry called out but they ignored him and disappeared into the crowd.

"Are you okay?" he asked, stepping up close beside her.

She nodded. "Let's get a cool drink." She had already spotted a collection of small tables and chairs arranged beneath a huge sunshade.

"This is nice," she said the moment they settled. "Wouldn't it be great to have your own boat here?" She glanced at the small yachts tied up to a pontoon.

Jerry eyed her suspiciously; she had never expressed an interest in sailing boats before.

They ordered long glasses of cool fruit juice and enjoyed the warm breeze coming in off the sea. The harbour was busy with market traders and tourists and Jerry watched as the crowds passed them by. It wasn't long before he spotted the two men who had pushed past them; they were sitting at a table close by and every now and again one of them would glance their way.

He wondered who they could be, it was obvious that they were not local men, but they did not look like tourists either. He frowned and picking up his glass took another sip. Orlagh was telling him about the castle so he forgot about the men and focussed on what she was saying.

They finished their drinks and made their way leisurely around the harbour looking at the colourful market stalls and dreaming about life on a sailing boat.

The two men sitting at the table watched them go and then they got to their feet.

"What's going on here?" One of the men standing beside the blue car said. "Surely they can't have bodyguards."

"No I shouldn't think so." The other replied, his eyes narrowing as he watched the two men disappear into the crowd. "Up ahead is a narrow street leading up to the castle, if it's clear that's where we shall take the girl."

His colleague nodded and instinctively reached for the place under his shirt where he kept his pistol.

"We'll dispose of the Englishman and deal with the goons if necessary."

They crossed the road and split up, making their way separately around the marina before going up the hill to where the street narrowed at the base of the castle.

Jack and Paul had concluded their business with Lewis Philpot and were now heading back towards the harbour.

"Do you really think the Amber Chamber is in the Sea of Azov?" Paul glanced at Jack.

"It seems so. Lewis has some pretty sound evidence."

"If it had been loaded onto the *Wilhelm Gustloff* surely the Soviets would have salvaged it when the subs went down to check out the wreck." Paul continued.

"Don't get too excited," Jack said. "There are so many stories surrounding the whereabouts of the Amber Room, no one really knows what happened to it. People have died searching for it, there's even a curse attached to the mystery."

"How can tons of amber simply vanish?" Paul frowned. "It's not as if it's a pocket size artefact, the containers it was stored in must have been huge."

"Which makes me wonder; what is on that wreck in the Sea of Azov. From the pictures I've seen, the container doesn't seem large enough, besides if it's full of water what state are the panels going to be in after all these years?"

"You're right," Paul nodded. "Amber lasts forever but the panels that made up the room must be in pieces by now, it will be the biggest jigsaw puzzle ever."

"We won't know for sure until we go down for a look see. Ed seemed pretty excited about the find." Jack reminded him.

Paul remained sceptical he would need convincing.

"Are you sure there won't be any trouble with the Soviets? We will after all be prospecting in their own back yard."

"You worry too much." Jack grinned. "I promise I won't scratch the paint on your new ship."

"Well you know what happened to the last one. The *Sea Quest* was also on a simple salvage operation."

Jack hardly needed reminding but he chose to keep his thoughts to himself.

They entered the narrow street and shadows from the tall buildings drew in around them. Their footsteps echoed loudly from the stonework and Jack instinctively became alert. In the shadow of a doorway, he saw movement, it could easily have been residents preparing to leave their home but something didn't feel right. For a fleeting moment, he caught sight of two men and knew they were not local, their colouring too pale, the natives of Bodrum were dark haired with olive coloured skin.

Jack quickened his pace, all was not well, he had learnt from bitter experience to listen to his gut feelings and today was no exception.

At the end of the street, two more men appeared but suspiciously, they dissolved into the shadows.

"We may be in for a spot of trouble." Jack whispered.

Paul nodded; they were unarmed but more than able to handle themselves in a brawl. It was then that Orlagh and Jerry appeared. At first, Jack did not recognise them, his attention drawn to the place where the men were hiding.

"Glory be, it can't be true!" Paul said loudly. He knew it was Orlagh the moment he set eyes on her.

Jack realised that Orlagh and Jerry must be the intended targets. There were four attackers spaced out along the narrow street, they had to be working together. Orlagh and Jerry were walking into a trap.

"Jack, Paul," Orlagh called out. "Is it really you?" She could hardly believe her eyes.

Jack quickened his pace once more, eager to get to her before the thugs.

"I don't believe it," she continued.

Jack and Paul remained watchful and as soon as they drew level with Orlagh and Jerry, they marched them quickly out of the narrow street and into the sunlight.

"What's going on?" She asked nervously.

As soon as they were safely back on the quay and surrounded by tourists Jack could relax.

"Who are those men following you?"

"What do you mean?" Orlagh replied.

"There were two men on the tour bus this morning," Jerry said. "They were acting a little suspiciously."

"Two men," Jack frowned. "Are you sure there was just two?"

Orlagh glanced from Jack to Jerry. "What are you two talking about?"

Ignoring her Jack listened carefully to what Jerry had to say.

"What did they look like?" he asked as soon as he was finished

"They were just like any other tourist," Jerry shrugged. "They both had longish hair and one of them had a beard." That was all he could remember.

Jack shot a glance at Orlagh who was looking anxious.

She had heard enough about strange men and unable to hold back any longer said. "It's so lovely to see you both, you look so well."

"Too much good food and high living I'm afraid." Paul grinned patting his belly. "You don't look so bad yourself." He stepped forward and wrapped her up in his arms before shaking hands with Jerry.

Turning to Jack, she kissed his cheek.

"We were on our way to the castle," she told them, "there's a great museum there. What are you doing here yourselves?"

"We had a meeting at the Institute of Nautical Archaeology." Jack replied.

"Are you surveying ancient wrecks?"

"No, nothing like that," Jack glanced sideways at Paul. "Just visiting an old friend." He relaxed a little as no one appeared from the narrow street.

"We are on our way back to our ship," Paul said. "She's a replacement for the *Sea Quest*. Would you like to have a look, take the opportunity to see the coastline from off shore?"

Jerry looked at Orlagh, he could tell from her expression that she would like nothing more.

"That's settled then," Jerry agreed. "It's probably not a good idea to remain around here on our own."

They made their way through the marina towards the floating pontoon where the tender was waiting to take them back to the ship and it was not long before they were stepping onto the deck of the *Ocean Pride.*

The ship was riding at anchor about a mile and a half off shore and from her elevated position on the forward deck; Orlagh had a splendid view of Bodrum. The castle looked magnificent standing sentinel on the peninsula overlooking the harbour, and the buildings clustered around it gave the impression of a safe haven. She could understand why ships throughout history had used this as a place to unload their cargos. The garrison stationed at the castle would have been a deterrent for pirates thinking about attacking trading vessels in the harbour.

Jerry was off with Jack somewhere in the depths of the ship, he wanted to see the moon pool and the engineering workshops, these were places that Orlagh had seen before and she had no wish to go near them again. She was disappointed to discover that Roz Stacey was not a member of the crew; Roz was involved in a restoration project at their headquarters in New York.

"So," Paul said as he came up beside her at the rail. "How long have you been in this part of the world?"

"Four days," she replied. "We arrived last Saturday evening and are staying in a lovely little hotel in Kusadasi."

"Why Turkey?" he asked as he leaned casually against the rail.

"Why not, Turkey is a huge open air museum, so what better place for a couple of historians to spend their holiday."

Paul grinned and as he looked at her, his wide set, amber coloured eyes narrowed against the glare from the sun.

"So you've had yourselves a good time so far?"

"Oh yes, this place is marvellous, there's so much to see. Everything is steeped in history and culture; I don't know which way to look half the time." She gave a little laugh. "I've even managed to meet up with an old friend who lives here."

"Well that's good," Paul nodded.

"This is a lovely ship," Jerry said as he appeared from one of the steel doorways. "The technology is simply mind blowing."

"I'm glad you like it," Paul said turning towards him. "Orlagh tells me you are staying in Kusadasi."

"Yes, that's right."

"Well, what say we give you guys a ride home?"

"We are heading that way," Jack said. "We can contact harbour control, see if we can tie up there for tonight."

Paul nodded. "How about we get together later, have dinner onboard?"

"What a splendid idea," Jerry said glancing at Orlagh who was smiling enthusiastically.

He glanced at his watch and was appalled at the time; it was mid afternoon already.

"How long will it take to get to Kusadasi?" Orlagh asked.

"Not long," Paul reassured her. "You'll have plenty of time to get to your hotel, freshen up and return to the ship. In the mean time let's get you comfortably settled with some cocktails."

Both Jack and Paul wanted to know more about the men who were following them, but clearly, Orlagh had no idea that she may be in danger. Not wanting to upset her, they decided to avoid the subject.

The breeze on the afterdeck was a welcome relief after the heat of the day and once they had settled, they talked about things they had done since they last saw each other. A couple of hours later the ship gently nudged the wall of the harbour at Kusadasi.

"Do you need me to organise a cab?" Paul asked.

"There's no need, our hotel is just a short distance away along the promenade," Jerry replied. "What time do you want us back this evening?"

"Dinner will be served at 20:00 hours."

Leaving the ship, they made their way happily along the beach and fifteen minutes later arrived at their hotel. Arm in arm they crossed the road oblivious to the blue car and occupants watching them.

Jerry avoided talking about the events of the day; he did not want to spoil her joyful mood. He had discussed it with Jack briefly during the tour of the ship and he got the impression that Jack knew more than he was letting on. Strangely, he seemed reluctant to talk about the subject of abduction. Orlagh had been kidnapped along with Roz Stacey twelve months previously by the Phoenix Legion, and Jack had lost good men in a rescue operation that had foiled an attempt to bomb London and Washington using atomic weapons.

"What a coincidence meeting up with Jack and Paul just like that." She called from the bathroom.

"Yes indeed it is." Jerry replied. He wondered what they were really doing here in Turkey.

Two hours later, they were refreshed and had changed for dinner. Leaving the hotel, they retraced their steps along the promenade and looking towards the harbour, they could see the *Ocean Pride*. She was a magnificent ship, her bright orange and white paintwork gleaming proudly in the evening sunlight.

The blue car drove slowly past then stopped by the roadside. The passenger got out and pretended to look at the front wheel but as they drew level, he stood up and opened the rear door.

"Get in," he growled.

"I beg your pardon," Jerry stared at him.

"Get in the car, I won't tell you again."

"Who are you, what do you want?"

The man pulled a pistol from his jacket pocket and pointed it menacingly at them. He kept the weapon low ensuring that it was hidden behind the door.

Jerry stiffened and his fingers tightened around Orlagh's hand. He saw movement from the corner of his eye and suddenly a hole appeared in the door panel. The car rocked under the impact and a dull thud split the air, then the rear tyre exploded and Orlagh cried out as Jerry forced her back against the low wall lining the promenade. Using his body as a shield, he stood over her as the windscreen blew out, showering them with glass.

The man standing beside the door threw himself into the passenger seat and the car sped away dragging the deflated tyre along the tarmac road.

"What's happening?" Orlagh cried out as she held onto him tightly.

"Not sure yet, best stay down for now."

She had no intention of showing her head above the wall.

Suddenly men appeared beside them. "Mr Knowles I presume?" one of them grinned. "Captain's compliments sir, we are here to escort you to the ship."

Jack was waiting for them on deck when they arrived and surrounded by their troop of bodyguards, they were ushered up the boarding ramp.

"Care to tell me what's going on?" Orlagh said the moment she saw him. "We could have been killed."

"No, I don't think so," he said, "they were hell bent on kidnapping you. I had you under surveillance the whole time. We saw the car outside your hotel and ran a check on its licence plate, turns out it belongs to a hire company. It was hired three days ago by men who paid with cash, so unfortunately there's no trail to follow. I had a sniper up there." He glanced up towards the bridge.

"We didn't hear any shots," Orlagh said looking at him strangely.

"That's because we used a silencer, couldn't have noise ringing out around the harbour, we may have frightened the natives."

"Do you know who those men in the car were?" she asked.

"No, but I have my suspicions. We need to sit down and talk about that, there are also a few things you should know."

XVII

The druids gathered in the evening as the sun was setting. The sky was alive with flaming orange and pale salmon hues and shadows were feeling their way down into the valley. The sacred grove was bathed in light and as the druids entered, they formed three interlocking circles and began to chant. The ancestors had named this place Gorseddau when the earth was still young and it had remained a site of great importance.

The chanting continued as drops splashed from the cauldron of Cerridwen. Three drops fell from the sky as the ancient symbol of Awen appeared, then the ceremony of re-birth began.

Nine virgin priestesses paraded for the druids' approval before they entered the inner circle. They danced around the cauldron in which a brew of barley, flowers, herbs and sea foam was stirred, before breathing into the mix their pure life force.

One by one, the druids came forward, each drinking three drops; these were the Drops of Inspiration, three drops stolen from his mother cauldron by Gwion. This was powerful magic and when the drinking was over the remaining brew was poured away. This was the ceremony used to breathe life back into the Goddess of Hibernia.

The goddess had been struck down by the spear of Madb, the spiritual ally of Orlagh Gairne, also the creator of the Belgae Torc.

The druids called on Brighid, the triple aspect Goddess of the sun and fire, and as the sun burned low in the western sky, her spirit filled the horizon.

The druids chanted low at first, their voices rising and falling in intensity until the grove was filled with sound. Positioning themselves, they formed a triple circle, this was to represent the Earth, Sea and Sky and calling upon the Goddess of Hibernia they invited her to join them in the inner circle.

Brighid hung her cloak on the sun wheel that could be seen clearly in the sky, at the same time Cerridwen, lifting her cauldron began pouring the essence of pure gold and a rivulet of yellow light swirled as the druids began to sing.

The priestesses continued to dance, their feet skipping lightly over the ground, and into the very centre they moved until they reached the sacred ground that was enriched by gold from the cauldron of Cerridwen.

The Earth Mother stirred beneath their feet and volcanic forces as old as time awakened, then the world held its breath. The druids, sucking in the golden light, held it in their lungs and exhaled gently through their noses as all the while the sky darkened above their heads. The fading light cast shadows amongst them and the priestesses continued to dance.

The energy became intense and the inner circle belonged to the Goddess of Hibernia. All those within could feel her presence and slowly she gained in strength, and drawing on those around her, listened to the druids calling out the Awens in three then six then nine monotones, the sound filling the surrounding woodland with ascending and descending scales.

The nine dancing priestesses were intoxicated with ritualistic elixir, and with their hearts pounding they became breathless. They were waiting for the goddess to appear, each one ready to give up their life, and as they drew tighter into the inner circle, they stopped and became still as the earth began to vibrate beneath their feet.

Turning to the west, they raised their arms in praise of Brighid and gave thanks to the drops of Awen that spilled from the cauldron.

Suddenly the goddess appeared; her hair a mass of golden flames, which faded until it became as dark as blood, and drawing near to one of the priestesses, she moaned in ecstasy and was re-born into the light.

As soon as she was able, the goddess began to speak, her voice rising clearly above the sound of chanting. The druids stopped to listen and through the priestess, she told them her secrets. They focussed on her words and were left in no doubt of her will.

When she had finished, the goddess withdrew, and refreshed with life that was pure she shuddered with delight.

The priestess rolled her eyes skyward as the last rays of sunlight touched her face then slipping silently to the ground, she paid the ultimate price.

Orlagh shuddered as she felt her soul stir. She glanced at the glorious sunset over the western horizon and could hear her grandmother's voice. At moments like this, she used to say, 'someone must have walked over your grave'. Pushing the thought from her mind, she focussed on Jack's face in an effort to listen to what he was saying.

"I believe that the Phoenix Legion is once again operational."

"Why do you say that?" Jerry asked as he studied him.

"We found the wreckage of a restored Junkers JU52, it came down over the Kackar mountains."

"How can you be sure it belongs to the Phoenix Legion?" Orlagh asked.

She was still upset by the events of the day, twice they had managed to avoid being attacked or worse, and now she was beginning to think their holiday was blighted. It was turning into a disaster, people had been killed because of the Belgae Torc and now Jack was telling them the Phoenix Legion were behind it all.

"There was a logo painted on a panel, it was unmistakable, besides, we did some checks and it's confirmed, the crew have been linked with the Legion."

"Were there any survivors?"

"No," Jack shook his head.

"What else did you find?" Jerry had a feeling there was more.

Jack told them about the two unfortunate mountain climbers.

"We are pretty sure they were killed by coming into contact with a deadly substance." He went on to tell them about the flasks containing Sarin.

"Were these containers left over from the war?" Jerry asked, toying with the stem of his glass. He was fully aware of the experiments carried out during the Second World War.

"No, I'm afraid not, it's more serious than that. These flasks contained a modified version of the gas; it was much more concentrated, kills in seconds and leaves barely a trace. It's virtually impossible to identify the cause of death."

"What would the Phoenix Legion want with something so toxic?" Orlagh was horrified by what he had just said and now, feeling frightened, her eyes flashed nervously between Jack and Jerry.

"We can only guess at that. Before it was atomic missiles, this time it's a potentially deadly biological weapon."

"A biological super weapon from the sound of it." Jerry said, a frown creasing his face and reaching for Orlagh's hand, he squeezed her fingers gently.

"I wonder what they want it for." She shuddered.

"Now that I would like to know." Jack looked at Jerry before continuing. "Have you maintained contact on the internet with the 'Brothers of the Sacred Whisper', Max Meyer wasn't that his name?"

"Yes," Jerry nodded, "we have remained in touch. Why do you ask?"

"He might know something about this. If the Phoenix Legion are up to their old tricks then someone must have some information."

"I could ask him," Jerry nodded.

"Is that where the Belgae Torc came from?" Orlagh said suddenly and both men looked up, surprised by her outburst. "We know the Belgae Torc found its way to the mountain village," she continued, "could it have been on that aircraft?"

Jerry told Jack about the village and the family murdered by gunmen.

"A young girl found the Torc whilst out in the mountains; it brought bad luck on her family and her community."

"Where exactly is this village situated?" Paul asked as he appeared from a doorway. He had been away on some errand and had missed most of their conversation.

Jerry told them where it was located and Paul flashed up a computer. He pulled up some charts of the area and studied them before making his selection then the screen filled with an ordnance survey map.

"Not far from the crash site," he nodded, "here's your village."

They all looked to where he was pointing.

"This is where we found the Junkers," he zoomed in so they could get a better view. "It's about ten kilometres, six miles from the village as the crow flies."

"Nothing more than a casual stroll for someone who had been brought up on the mountains."

"But she couldn't have gone up to the crash site," Orlagh said, "there was no mention of that, in fact, no-one in the village seemed to be aware of an air crash on their mountain."

"So the torc must have been found somewhere between the village and the summit." Paul said rubbing his fingers over his chin thoughtfully.

"We don't have to know where it was found," Jerry admitted, "but it's quite possible that the torc came from the aircraft."

"I agree," Jack nodded, "it does sound plausible. We know the Phoenix Legion were in possession of it."

"Have you any idea where the Junkers was flying from?" Jerry asked.

"I'm afraid not, it wasn't fitted with a flight recorder, the mountain area it was flying over is so barren that it's unlikely there were any witnesses, besides the only people near enough to see where it came down were killed by Sarin gas."

"Surely an old aircraft like that couldn't have much range," Orlagh said, "so it must have been based close by."

"It had an operational range of about six hundred miles," Jack told them. "I agree with Orlagh, it must have come from a neighbouring country. There was no evidence that the aircraft was fitted with extra fuel tanks and the engines were standard BMW radials, Second World War issue."

"You don't think the Phoenix Legion went up there to search for the wreckage?" Orlagh looked at Jack.

"No, the authorities would have been there soon after we left. We were the first on the scene having responded to the distress signal sent out by the pilot moments before he lost control."

"How did you manage to get there so quickly?" she asked.

"We were close by in the Black Sea; our Comms officer recorded the message and managed to get a fix from their radio transmission."

"I don't suppose you know what caused it to crash?"

"No, the weather was good at the time. Of course we had no idea it was the Phoenix Legion, all we knew was that we were responding to an emergency." He drained his glass before going on. "We got there a couple of hours after the aircraft came down."

"We come back to the same questions," Jerry began, "what made the aircraft crash, was it transporting the Belgae Torc and what was it doing with flasks of a deadly modified super gas?"

They were silent for a moment.

"Listen," Jack began suddenly, "I don't think it's safe for you to remain here, you know what happened earlier. We are about to take the ship out, do a little prospecting in the Azov Sea, we should be gone for about six days. How about you join us for a little cruise, give us some time to work out what's going on."

Jerry glanced at Orlagh. "I don't mind," he said shrugging his shoulders.

"You might find it interesting," Jack continued. "We have permission from the Institute of Nautical Archaeology to check out a wreck off the Ukraine coast." He told them nothing about the container that he thought might contain the Amber Chamber.

XVIII

The druids were waiting in the shadows on the quayside. They had tracked the progress of the *Ocean Pride* from Bodrum and were now hoping to abduct Orlagh from the harbour at Kasadasi. They realised it would not be easy, they had seen the way Jack Harrington's men foiled the attempt made by Schiffers men earlier. The druids' objective was simple, they were charged with returning to their grove with Dr Orlagh Gairne, failure was not an option.

"If we are staying we'll need to pick up some things from our hotel." Orlagh said as practical as ever. They had agreed to Jack's proposal, a short cruise and the prospect of underwater archaeology had whetted her appetite.

"I must insist on sending some men to accompany you."

"Do you really think that's necessary Jack?" Jerry asked. "I don't expect to see the thugs you scared off any time soon."

"Don't forget there were four men following you in Bodrum today, we've only seen two of them so far."

"Do you think they are members of the Phoenix Legion?" Orlagh asked. Fixing her huge green eyes on Jack, she waited patiently for his reply.

"Yeah, I'm afraid I do, besides, who else could they be?"

Orlagh shrugged her shoulders and glanced at Jerry.

"It's no use looking at me," he said, "why should anyone want to kidnap me?"

"Don't underestimate your value," Paul spoke for the first time. "By association you have been put in the frame, Orlagh may well be their target, but to get to her they may find it necessary to go through you."

Jerry nodded, what Paul said made sense.

"If it is the Phoenix Legion, what would they want with me after all this time?" Orlagh tossed her head and looked at each of them in turn, then sitting back in her chair she crossed her legs.

"Well I can't answer that," Paul said. "Maybe it's a case of unfinished business." He shuddered as he thought about the giant atomic missiles he and Jack had found on the remote islands in the Mediterranean. The druids had named the missiles Gog and Magog, after the two biblical warring giants, and he couldn't bear to think about what would have happened if they had not been destroyed.

"I would like to know what their intentions are," Jack muttered, "I have the feeling that nothing good will come of this. The Sarin gas we found in the Dewar flasks must have been samples." He sounded grim and as he spoke, a cool breeze broke over the deck chilling them all.

"It's getting late," Orlagh said breaking the spell. "We had better go and get our things."

Paul used the telephone stored in a tiny alcove on the bulkhead and sixty seconds later two security guards appeared.

"Please escort Dr Gairne and Mr Knowles to their hotel. They need to collect some bags, when they are done bring them safely back to the ship."

"Aye aye sir." One of the men said. They didn't need to ask questions, they had both been involved in the incident earlier and were aware of what was expected of them.

The druids became alert as soon as Orlagh appeared and remaining hidden they watched as she left the ship accompanied by two guards. Ten minutes later they were standing on the beach opposite the hotel and from the shadows, they had a clear view of the entrance.

Orlagh and the others disappeared into the building, but the druids did not have to wait long before they reappeared. Retracing their steps, they made their way back along the promenade.

There were no opportunities for the druids to make their move, all they could do was remain in the shadows and wait their chance. The men flanking Orlagh and her companion would certainly be armed and skilled in the art of self-defence. There was also a chance that like before a sharp shooter would be stationed on the ship observing their every move.

With Orlagh and Jerry safely back on board they were shown to their cabin. It was very late and they were exhausted, so falling into bed they left their bags unpacked on the floor.

On the deck, a steward was clearing away the table where they had their meal and once the rubbish sack was full, he made his way down the ramp towards the huge bins on the quayside. Lifting the lid of the nearest bin, he tossed the sack in and let the lid fall shut, but as he turned back towards the ship, the druids struck. They were swift and he did not realise he had been stabbed until he saw the handle of the knife sticking out of his chest. Pain gripped him and with failing strength, he fell to the ground. His eyes widen with shock as his attackers moved into view and he opened his mouth in an attempt to shout a warning but it was too late, his final breath sighed from his throat and darkness overcame him.

Between them, the druids heaved his body up and tossed it into a rubbish bin. One of them loosely resembled the man, height, build and colouring, so casually he walked up the boarding ramp and once on deck he looked around. There was sure to be security cameras covering that part of the ship and there was no way that his colleague could come aboard without being seen. Keeping to the shadows, he moved along the deck and after a moment found what he was looking for. A coil of rope had been stowed neatly in a storage box beside a lifeboat and lowering one end over the side, the druid on the quayside caught it and began to climb. Hauling himself up, he rolled lightly over the rail and landed silently onto the deck, then together they made their way towards a doorway and like stowaways disappeared into the depths of the ship.

Early the following morning the *Ocean Pride* slipped her moorings and made her way majestically out of the harbour and into the bay. An hour later Orlagh and Jerry were awake.

"What say you we take a shower?" Jerry said mischievously, and rolling over he looked at Orlagh who was lying beside him in the huge double bed.

"Do you think there's enough hot water?" She eyed him sleepily through a curtain of red hair that covered her face.

"I should think so, but with the thoughts I'm having I think a cold shower would be more appropriate."

Orlagh giggled and tried playfully to push away but his exploring hands were insistent.

"Didn't you get enough last night?" she gasped between bouts of laughter.

"I can never get enough of you my love," he grinned, "besides, I didn't do you justice. I was exhausted last night."

Pulling her towards him, he kissed her passionately on the mouth and instantly she felt her body begin respond.

The next couple of days passed as if they were living in a dream. The sea resembled a calm blue carpet that was kind to them and all they could do was lay back and enjoy the sun. They spent most of their time on the upper deck where their privacy was respected, the only time they saw members of the crew was at meal times.

The ship was in pristine condition, clutter free and everywhere they went was the scent of fresh paint. They fell in love with the ship, neither of them had cruised before but they were both resolved to consider a cruising holiday at some time in the near future.

Orlagh glanced across at Jerry; he was slumped in a deck chair with his sun hat pulled down over his face. She knew he was asleep and smiled as she reminded herself just how much she loved him. Theirs was an honest and natural relationship, they adored each other in equal measure and there was never a moment of disquiet between them. She was so happy and had to pinch herself constantly just to be sure that it was real and not just a dream.

This was a lazy time, they had not stopped since arriving in Turkey and the stress of unexpected events had almost soured their holiday. They had seen some amazing things and meeting up with Takat had been marvellous, but running into Jack had changed all that. From experience, she knew that wherever he went adventure was sure to follow, but for now they could enjoy some quality time together and still look forward to a little historical intrigue. It would be interesting to discover what excited Jack, the mystery surrounding the sunken ship had drawn her in and she was looking forward to learning more about it.

The following day the *Ocean Pride* arrived over the spot where the ship lay. In the relatively shallow water of the Sea of Azov, they had to manoeuvre carefully, there wouldn't be much water between the keel and the superstructure of the wreck below. Vibrations ran through the decks as the side thrusters made tiny adjustments to the ships position, and using GPS to maintain station, the atmosphere on board changed.

The Sea of Azov is the shallowest sea on the earth, depth of water ranges from one metre to about fifteen and as the water is rich with silt and plankton many varieties of fish thrive in these ideal conditions. From above, the algae rich water appears green, but in very hot dry spells the water can turn as red as blood. Considered an internal sea of Russia and Ukraine, it is governed by both countries.

Excitement filled the air as workmen scurried around an eyeball ROV supported in its cradle on the service deck. The tiny remotely operated vehicle was about to be sent down to take a look at the wreck. The water here was shallow enough for divers but Jack, as cautious as ever, would not risk the lives of his men. Diving on a wreck could be hazardous so sending down the ROV was the most sensible thing to do.

Hawsa, one of the service cranes, was being readied to lower the ROV into the water and a crewman was hooking up the umbilical cord that was the ROV's lifeline.

Orlagh and Jerry were in the Wardroom, having just finished a late breakfast and as they drained their cups of coffee, an officer approached their table.

"Good morning Dr Gairne, Mr Knowles," he nodded to them both. "Captains compliments, would you care to join him in the control room in fifteen minutes?"

"Good morning to you," Orlagh said smiling up at him. "Please tell Captain Seymour that we would be delighted to join him."

"Very good Ma'am." He executed a perfect about turn and briskly left the room.

"I guess they are going to send a ROV down to take a look," Orlagh told Jerry. She had seen this all before whilst on board the *Sea Quest*, that had been in the Bay of Biscay twelve months previously when they had dived on the *Hudson Bay*.

Jerry nodded; he could see she was thinking about the time before.

"I suppose they have to decide how to proceed, find out what it is they are dealing with." He had never dived on a wreck before. Scuba diving did not interest him in fact; he disliked the idea of swimming under water especially near sunken ships.

"We had better get ourselves organised and find the control room."

"I just need to pop back to the room first," she said, getting up from the table.

As they made their way to their cabin, they passed a man in the corridor. He mumbled a greeting but kept his head down avoiding eye contact. Orlagh had to move to one side as they passed and the air crackled with static as her skin reacted to his touch. Drawing in her breath sharply she glanced at him as he disappeared along the corridor.

"What is it?" Jerry frowned. He noticed the way she had reacted.

"Nothing," she told him and moved faster.

Once inside their room Orlagh disappeared into the bathroom and a few minutes later, she re-appeared.

"Have you seen my head scarf?" she glanced at Jerry who was staring out of the window. The sea was an unbroken carpet stretching all the way to the horizon, they were completely alone, not another ship in sight.

"I want to tie my hair back," she continued as she searched through the cupboards.

"Where did you have it last?" Jerry turned towards her.

Ignoring his question, she moved to the chest of drawers that served as a dressing table. An array of make-up and small bottles containing creams and potions were lined up on top and they rattled as she pulled open one of the drawers.

Jerry was so annoyingly organised, he never lost or misplaced anything, everything he owned had its place and she wished that she could be as tidy.

"What's this?" she pulled her hand from the drawer.

She was holding a small piece of smooth wood; it was as long as her little finger and covered in intricate carvings. Turning it over, she studied it carefully.

"It reminds me of an Ogham charm." Orlagh whispered, pronouncing it Owam. "Look at the characters carved into the wood."

Jerry knew that Ogham was an early druidic alphabet and according to academics, was a method used for sacred divinatory purposes.

"Staves of wood carved with Ogham characters, a practice similar to Rune magic used in the north." He said, quoting from a text that he had once read.

"What's it doing here, it doesn't belong to me." Oragh looked up at him.

"Perhaps it was already in the drawer before you put your stuff in there."

She thought that unlikely and was convinced she had checked before using them, but what other answer could there be?

"The man we passed just now," she said.

Jerry studied her face, her complexion had turned pale and her green eyes burned like a fever, he could see that her mind was working.

"He is a druid," she went on before he had time to respond. "I could feel it; there was something very odd about him." She shuddered and looked away as an icy breeze touched her skin.

Jerry thought for a moment, what she said was true he had felt it too. "What's a druid doing on the *Ocean Pride*?"

"We had better get to the control room, Paul is waiting for us." Orlagh did her best to sound calm but inside she was in turmoil. "We need to talk to Jack, tell him there's a druid on board."

Pushing the charm into her pocket, she moved towards the door and opening it carefully peered along the corridor before leaving the room.

Further along the corridor in a storage room used for linen, two druids looked at each other triumphantly. One of them was holding a silk scarf and a sweet delicate perfume rose from its folds as he waved it in the air, then he ran his fingers over the soft material. Shivering with delight he could feel Orlagh's life force radiating from its brightly coloured folds and closing his eyes, he smiled with delight as he absorbed the gentle feminine vibrations.

In the control room, Paul and the ROV pilot sat in seats facing an array of instruments built into a flight deck like panel. Pushing open the door, Orlagh and Jerry stepped into the darkened room. Jerry was impressed the moment he saw the technology filled space.

"Mark?" Orlagh cried with delight as she recognised the man sitting beside Paul.

"Dr Gairne, it's been a while." His grin was infectious.

"I didn't know you were on board." Orlagh, standing close beside him, pressed into the narrow space.

"Been a bit busy," he grinned as he took her outstretched hand.

Jerry squeezed closer and shook Mark's hand before taking their seats facing the screen on the console. Mark reminded him of a busy flight controller surrounded by digital outputs, dials and gauges of every description.

"We are just about to send Kitty II down to do a little prospecting."

Kitty was the name he had given the eyeball ROV, he liked to christen all the remotely operated vehicles. The original Kitty was destroyed when a fully restored World War II German submarine she was investigating exploded in the Bay of Biscay.

Suddenly Orlagh was struck by a strange sensation and her skin crawled as her heart rate increased. At first, she thought it was an adrenalin rush, a prelude to the excitement of discovering something of great historical value, but she realised this was not the case. She knew it had something to do with the druids; she had experienced emotions like this before.

Jerry was aware of the sudden frisson that passed through her and searching for her hand, took it in his and gave it an encouraging squeeze.

"Cut Kitty free." Mark said speaking into his microphone and engineers on the deck above responded to his requests. After a moment, he turned to Paul. "Kitty is ready to go captain."

"She's yours to fly." Paul grinned. They always went through this ritual. It was like a lucky charm, a kind of superstitious performance before the prospecting began.

Orlagh smiled; she had heard this before in the control room of the *Sea Quest*.

Bubbles erupted like champagne from a bottle as Kitty submerged beneath the waves and all they could see on the screen was a maelstrom of grey and white froth.

Kitty began her descent; it would not take long to reach the wreck as it was lying in shallow water. The screen on the control panel lit up as Mark activated the powerful searchlights situated beside the camera, the high-resolution lens served as Kitty's eyes. In the top right hand corner of the screen digital numbers appeared, recording depth, direction and an array of other binary displayed conditions. This information was invaluable and Mark checked his instruments constantly as he steered Kitty towards her goal.

On the deck, an engineer played out the umbilical cord; this was Kitty's lifeline, a digital highway through which information was relayed. If the umbilical cord became detached, Kitty would effectively be on her own. She was programmed to retrace her steps and surface before sending out a distress signal, which would enable her to be recovered.

"Coming up on the wreck now." Mark sounded calm, although Orlagh knew he was as excited as everyone involved in the salvage operation.

Probing lights began to reveal shadows and Jerry moved forward in his seat. He was fascinated by what he saw on the screen. The wreck was not as big as he had imagined, covered in silt, it was laying on its side half buried on the seabed. Small fish darted away from Kitty as she inched closer and with her lights playing over the wreck and beyond Jerry was amazed at how flat and sandy the bottom was. He expected to see rocks and underwater plants but here there was nothing; the bottom reminded him of a sandy beach. The wreck was covered in green algae, and as Kitty moved closer, he began to recognise parts of the ship.

Orlagh had no idea what she was looking at, there was nothing on the screen that she could identify, even the flashing numbers and controls were a mystery to her. She watched as Mark moved the little joystick forward and the picture on the screen began to change.

Kitty glided over a rail and made her way along the deck, her thrusters kicking up a cloud of silt as she went. She had not gone far when an open hatch appeared ahead and slowly Mark guided her towards the dark chasm that led into the ship.

Unlike the *Hudson Bay*, this ship had no hole blasted in its side, the only way in was down one of the hatches.

Memories of the Bay of Biscay came back to her. A lot had happened in the twelve months since that adventure, and there was much about that trip she would rather forget.

"Entering hold number one." The sound of Mark's voice cut through her thoughts.

Kitty slipped silently into the darkness of the interior and as her lights illuminated the hold, Jerry watched with fascination.

"Ed Potterton has already surveyed this wreck," Paul explained quietly, anticipating Jerry's questions. "We know the container is in this part of the ship."

"Can I use one of the computers?" Orlagh asked suddenly. She had become bored by the images on the screen. There was something more pressing that she wanted to explore besides, she had seen all this before.

"Sure, use this one." Paul indicated to a keyboard beside her elbow.

Turning in her seat, she booted up the computer and logged onto the worldwide web. Her fingers dancing over the keys, she looked up at the screen as she typed 'Ogham divination and charms.'

Options appeared and using the mouse, she scrolled down until she found what she was looking for. Orlagh knew that the Ogham alphabet was sacred, it was used by druids in some form of ritual, but little is known about how they actually used it. Unfortunately, nothing was written down, the only records in existence had been those passed down by word of mouth or interpreted by Roman scholars at the time. *'We are left to guess how Ogham divination may have been accomplished'*, she read.

'Reconstructions of the practice are largely based on Roman descriptions of the northern practice. Norsemen used runes in a similar way so taking this as the standard, druids used meanings for Ogham characters derived from beliefs about sacred woods.'

Reaching into her pocket Orlagh drew out the stave of wood and rubbed her fingers lightly over the strange symbols, she knew these to be letters of the Ogham alphabet, but as yet was unable to define their meaning. Turning her attention back to the screen she continued to read the text.

'Modern Ogham divination is carried out by means of a set of twenty or twenty five staves, or twigs, each carved with one of the Ogham letters.'

Hers contained more than one symbol or letters.

'The especially ambitious will assure that each twig is of the correct tree or plant, but often a simple set of birch twigs will be used.'

She glanced at the wooden stave and wondered what type of wood it was made from.

'To perform a divination, a set of twigs is scattered onto a specially inscribed diagram or onto a mat or canvas on which a diagram has been drawn. This is usually a series of concentric circles marked for the past, present and future, however, in this practice there are many variations, some of which are quite complex. The staves are scattered on the mat and interpreted accordingly to where they fall.'

There was a list of woods with their associated spiritual connection and as she scanned down the list, her fingers fiddled with her stave. Suddenly one of the descriptions stood out above the others, Ido (yew):- Death, renewal, Otherworld affairs.

"Captain Seymour sir, Comms officer Jefferson here." The voice coming over the intercom distracted her thoughts.

"Go ahead Jefferson."

"We have a radar fix on six inbound contacts," he began, "we have been tracking them for fifteen minutes and there has been no change in course or speed."

"What type of contact are we talking about here Jefferson?"

"Aircraft sir, we calculate their speed to be just under two hundred miles per hour."

"That's slow for combat jets." Paul said imagining the worst. The Soviets may have put up a frightener.

"The contacts appear to be too small for jet fighters, besides, they are flying considerably slower than we would expect. They are also currently over Ukraine, not Russia."

Paul frowned as he considered what Jefferson had told him. Soviet jets could very easily have been flying over Ukraine, was this just a devious and harmless ploy or did he have something to worry about?

"How soon before we have visual contact?" he asked.

"They are approximately one hundred and fifty miles west of our position, at their current speed they will be over us in forty five minutes."

"Roger that Jefferson, update me on the situation every fifteen minutes." Paul rubbed his hand over the back of his neck as his muscles began to tighten. He wondered if Jack was aware of the situation.

"We have contact sir."

The sound of Mark's voice jolted his thoughts and in front of him on the computer screen, he could make out the murky picture of a huge storage container.

"Take Kitty in for a closer look," he told Mark. "Circle round, let's see if there are any obstructions before we decide how to raise it."

They would have to lift the container out of the hold; that would mean cutting a hole in the deck. It would be impossible to open the huge loading doors, the ship was lying over on an angle and with the passage of time, it would prove impossible to go in through the conventional way.

Orlagh focussed her attention on the screen in front of her and blocking out the sound of rising excitement she typed quickly, her fingers skipping over the keyboard. She wanted to know more about the yew tree and its significance. The text on the screen changed and as she began to read, something caught her eye.

'The yew; sacred tree of transformation and re-birth.' She scanned the words, all the time adding to her knowledge of the yew tree and its connection with Celtic ritual. She knew of course that yew trees traditionally grew in churchyards. It's generally thought that as the yew tree is poisonous, it was grown in churchyards as a precaution. Animals were not grazed in these places so were unlikely to come into contact with the poisonous plant. She continued to read.

'The dangerous aspects of the tree were used in medicines; the seeds collected and processed. Arrowheads were dipped in the juice from the crushed seeds, coating them with poison. The wood was also used for making spears, spikes, staves, hunting bows and eventually the famous longbow of the Middle Ages.

The yew, also known as the death tree was often planted to encircle churches or churchyards; this was probably a legacy of the druid's sacred groves.'

Most of this she knew already, but she had very little knowledge of identifying ancient carvings and different types of wood. Sitting back in her chair Orlagh studied the wooden stave again. She was certain that it was yew, but could hardly believe the warm, golden orange wood was poisonous.

The intercom crackled again as Jefferson delivered his report. Nothing had changed, the aircraft were still inbound and flying at a constant speed and altitude.

'The yew can be used to assist journeys into the Otherworld and to increase openness of communication with spirits from the Otherworld.' Orlagh thought of the Goddess of Hibernia, the red haired goddess in her own likeness. Suddenly she felt uneasy, it was as if the goddess was there beside her and she shuddered. Pushing these thoughts away, she focussed her attention on the screen and continued to read the text.

'Magically the yew is used for summoning spirits and any other

Otherworld communication.' Orlagh had been subjected to a terrifying experience a year ago when the Belgae Torc was placed around her neck in a ritual that had almost taken her life. Spirits from the Otherworld had accompanied the Goddess of Hibernia, who had attempted to steal her soul. Fortunately, Madb and her animal allies had been on hand to save her. They continued to keep her safe, but now once again the spirits were becoming stronger and the druids were doing everything in their power to restore equilibrium to the spirit world.

In order to become whole again, the goddess would have to collect Orlagh's soul. She had been denied this before and the only way to wield real power was to install Orlagh beside her on the spiritual throne of the Otherworld.

Fifteen minutes later Jefferson's report was unchanged.

"Get the eyeball out of there," Paul said with some urgency. He had a bad feeling, the incoming aircraft must be hostile and it would take Mark longer than fifteen minutes to recover the ROV.

Paul was taking no chances, he had already lost one ship. A World War Two U-Boat, carefully restored by the Phoenix Legion, had sunk the *Sea Quest* and he would do everything in his power to avoid losing another ship.

"Get the armoury open and deploy .50 cal's to the upper deck." He spoke quickly into the intercom instructing an officer on the bridge. "I want as many men and weapons as we can get out on deck."

"Aye, aye sir," came the crisp reply.

With that done, Paul called Jack. "We have a situation here Jack. There are six unidentified aircraft inbound, ETA fifteen minutes and I'm damned sure they are hostile."

"Roger that Buddy. Have you alerted the armoury?"

Paul told him about the firepower he had deployed then he made his way up to the bridge.

"Which direction are they coming from?" Jack asked as soon as he joined him.

"West," Paul told him.

Grabbing a pair of binoculars, he dashed out onto the port side wing and peered through the glasses, then he let out an audible whistle.

"Would you just look at those beauties?"

Six World War Two German Focke-Wulf FW190's were flying in perfect formation at about five thousand feet.

The single seat fighter had been a formidable adversary of the RAF during the 1940's and Jack was more than aware of their firepower. Each aircraft carried two 13mm MG131 machine guns and two 20mm MG151 cannons. Luckily, none were carrying bombs.

As he watched, they circled overhead then two broke formation and began to dive towards the ship. The manoeuvre was faultless and as the aircraft lost altitude, the pitch of their twelve cylinder engines rose as their airspeed increased. Sun glinted off the wings and fuselage and Jack stood rooted to the spot.

Suddenly the sea began to boil around them and Jack realised it was not the sun glinting off the wings but muzzle flashes. Hot metal smashed into the deck sending vibrations through the soles of his boots and for a moment both Jack and Paul could hardly believe what was happening.

"They are firing at us!" Paul shouted above the noise.

A window shattered sending glass flying across the deck then they heard the thunder of engines as the fighters roared just a few feet above the radar and communication masts.

Seconds later they were gone leaving Paul ashen faced. His beautiful new ship was being attacked and he could hardly believe it was happening all over again.

"Here come another pair." Jack warned as he dashed for cover. Slipping on shards of glass he skidded to a halt and grabbing the intercom sent out an order.

"Return fire!" He doubted his men would need encouragement but it made him feel better to issue the order.

The FW190s came howling out of the perfectly blue sky. Like harbingers of death, they spat their fire at the *Ocean Pride* and destruction rained down. The .50 cal's lining the upper deck returned fire and the noise was deafening. The weapons were set to rapid fire and the concentration of shells was quite formidable. The pilots did not expect to be shot at and were careless, immediately one of the aircraft began to trail smoke and had to break off its attack. Two more came in to take their place and as they watched the stricken aircraft speed across the waves, this pair were more cautious. They concentrated their fire at the groups of weapons on the deck, turning the area around the men into a living hell. Shells slammed into the ship sending pieces of antenna and radar dish raining down amongst them. The sound was deafening and the ship seemed to buck with every strike. Noise rang like a bell through the superstructure and inside the control room Orlagh and Jerry clung onto each other. This deep inside the ship they were safe from exploding shells but if the ship suddenly began to sink, they would have to evacuate quickly. Surrounded by all the electrical equipment the other danger of course was fire.

"Concentrate your fire on one aircraft at a time." Jack shouted into the intercom. Each man was wearing a communication earpiece and could hear his command. Luckily, none of them had been hit, but there were some superficial wounds from flying shrapnel.

The aircraft that had carried out the first attack were now lining up for another go, but this time things would not be so easy for them. Rolling into their dive, they howled down like avenging angels, spitting hot lead as they came. The men on the deck focused their return fire with devastating results.

"Take out the one on the left." Jack commanded and the men concentrated their fire.

Suddenly the aircraft slewed sideways as the canopy exploded under a hail of lead. The pilot was killed instantly and for a moment, it seemed as if the stricken aircraft would crash into the deck, but at the last minute if rolled onto its back and plunged into the sea. A huge explosion threw a huge wave over the men on the deck, but they cheered as the other aircraft zoomed harmlessly overhead.

Paul looked out from the bridge towards the hanger where the Sikorsky was parked. Thick smoke was rising up from the roof and as he watched, small explosions began to go off inside the workshop. The helipad on the forward deck leading up to the hangar was full of holes and the non-slip surface was smouldering in places. A body lay crumpled to one side of the pad, and from where he was standing, Paul could see a puddle of blood spilling from the unfortunate casualty.

Glancing back at the hangar he realised that Jack would not be pleased, if his helicopter was damaged he would be worse than a wild man.

Two more aircraft began their attacking run, this time the .50 cal's damaged one and the pair broke off their attack. They had seen what had happened to their colleague and none were keen to follow him into the sea.

Jack appeared beside Paul and staring at the flames licking up from the hangar roof said, "I'd better get over there."

Fuel for the helicopter was stored deep inside the ship, it was safely out of reach of the flames, but any of the oils and solvents used in the workshop could go up causing an explosion. Fire on board a ship was the worst possible scenario.

There was a lull in the attack, the remaining aircraft were circling high above the ship, two were trailing smoke and one had crashed into the sea. Jack suspected the pilots were thinking twice about launching another attack so he used this time to slip across the battered deck.

Inside the hangar, the devastation was unbelievable. Twisted glass, carbon fibre and splinters of metal littered the floor and black smoke was pouring from a workstation. Holes in the roof and walls where the shells had punched through let in shafts of light around which smoke curled as the air became thicker. Jack could feel his throat begin to tighten as he glanced towards the Sikorsky. It seemed undamaged, but the doors on the front of the hanger were broken and twisted so were unlikely to open. If he didn't get the fire under control the helicopter would be lost along with the ship.

Pulling an extinguisher from a wall bracket, he began to fight the flames but it was useless, fire was spreading at an alarming rate, fuelled by flammable materials in its path then suddenly men began to appear.

"Move those drums from the path of the fire." He shouted an order.

Wings Wallace moved up beside him dressed in a silver fire fighter's suit. He wrestled with a heavy hosepipe, unwinding it from an emergency fire fighting point built into the wall, then aiming for the base of the fire, he activated the water jet and almost fell backwards. Like a rugby player in a scrum, Jack pushed his shoulder into the young man's back propping him up as the water jet sprayed out like an umbrella. It sent out a curtain of spray designed to protect them as much as it was to extinguish the fire and in seconds, clouds of steam began to rise from the flames.

The hosepipe snaked wildly, but after a while, they were doing better and controlling the stream of water, they walked slowly forward beating the fire back and away from the men working to clear a firebreak.

Jack began to choke on the deadly combination of smoke and fumes and he could hardly hold on to Wings any longer, so retreating backwards he left the lad to snuff out the remaining flames. The fire-fighting suit he was wearing had its own air supply so the fumes filling the workshop were not a problem.

Other men arrived, carrying fire-fighting equipment. They stationed themselves around the Sikorsky ready to attack any flames that might escape Wings onslaught.

Outside the men on the upper deck had reloaded their weapons and were waiting for the next attack. The FW190s were now tiny specks in the sky and as they approached the horizon they disappeared so Paul had the men stand down. The radar operator kept a close watch, the five contacts were moving away at a much slower pace than they had set on their approach.

"Damage report." Paul spoke into the intercom. His voice was heard all over the ship and one by one the various compartments replied.

"Control room all okay," Mark said glancing at Orlagh and Jerry.

A red light was flashing on his control panel, it was Kitty, her umbilical cord had become disconnected and now she was making her way back to the surface. Mark prayed the eyeball ROV wouldn't become stuck in the hold of the wreck.

Once the reports came in Paul had a good idea of the state of his ship, and studying the instrument panel on the bridge, he counted at least a dozen emergency lights flashing out their warning. Glass from the toughened glass window on the bridge littered the deck but luckily, the officer at the controls had not been seriously injured. Looking towards the helipad, his heart sank. Here the devastation was at its worse; it would take some heavy repairs to get it back into ship shape. Smoke was still billowing from the hangar but it was no longer thick and black, diluted by steam, Paul realised that the fire fighting team must be winning their battle, at least now the flames were not licking up through the roof.

"Captain," a voice sounded urgently over the intercom system. "Water is flooding into the moon pool chamber."

Turning away from the carnage on deck Paul spoke into the microphone.

"Can you give me a status report?"

"Yes sir, power is down, there must be an electrical short somewhere in the system, we have an engineer working to get the generators up and running. The moon pool is completely full and water is overflowing into the chamber."

Paul checked the control panel in front of him, the system indicated that the moon pool doors in the hull were closed and sealed, but there was no indication as to where the water was entering the ship.

"Can you operate the watertight doors by hand?"

"Yes sir, we are about to secure the chamber."

"Very good, as soon as you have power operate the pumps, I want that flow of water arrested."

"Aye aye sir."

Once the watertight doors were sealed the risk of sinking would be reduced, but it would take hours to stop the leak and pump out the chamber. With the hull damaged, it would be impossible to make headway, it was imperative that repairs were carried out immediately. At least the weather was good; a heavy sea would be the end of them.

The *Ocean Pride* remained stationary in the water, Paul would not give the order to make way until he was satisfied it was safe to do so. The immediate danger was over, the fire in the hangar had been extinguished and now a team of men were clearing up the mess. Divers were being prepared to go over the side to look at the damaged hull and until he had their report, Paul could not make a decision on what action to take. Engineers were standing by to go into the chamber, but although the pumps had stopped the flow of water, the chamber was still flooded.

In the hospital on the lower deck, Linda Pritchard was busy with casualties. There had been three fatalities and several nasty wounds, these were mostly lacerations caused by flying shrapnel and concussion caused by exploding shells. One of the injured men required surgery to repair internal injuries but his condition was not life threatening and once stabilised he would have to wait until the initial rush was over.

Jack arrived on the bridge looking worse for wear; he was blackened and singed and in need of some of Linda's TLC.

"The fire in the hanger has been put out and miraculously the Sikiorsky is undamaged." He began his report.

"Well that's good news." Paul nodded. "Just look at my ship," he eyed Jack angrily. "You promised me you wouldn't so much as scratch her paint."

Jack hung his head and looked suitably chastised. He could see that Paul was angry, the last time a ship under his command had suffered damage it was sunk, so he could understand how his friend was feeling.

Paul told him about the flooding in the moon pool chamber.

"Dave Fox is down there now, he's more than capable of sorting out the problem."

Dave was chief engineer on board the *Ocean Pride*.

Jack nodded, he knew Paul was right, Fox was a competent engineer, one of the best.

"So let's see what happened." Jack said turning to one of the computers.

Feeding commands, he clicked on an icon and the screen changed as a film began to run. Cameras, situated around the ship had captured the Focke-Wulfs making their first attacking run.

They watched as the first pair of fighters broke away from the group and in perfect formation rolled onto their backs and swooped down in a steep dive. Jack and Paul were held in awe as this outrageous manoeuvre played out in front of them. It was impossible to believe that it was real and not just some Hollywood movie; no one could have imagined a squadron of World War II fighter planes attacking a modern survey ship.

"This is spectacular footage," Jack said as they watched the downed fighter crash into the sea. He programmed the computer to show that part again and with the film running slowly, they could make out every detail of the aircraft. Sun was glinting off the canopy just moments before it disintegrated and they could see strikes as shells from the .50 cals smashed into it. The pilot was killed instantly by the first exploding impact and from that moment, the majestic aircraft turned into junk. The engine cowling seemed to shudder as hundreds of rounds struck it, holes appeared in its skin until there was nothing left and sparks flew from the engine. The onslaught was awesome; the 190 didn't stand a chance. Parts became loose and fell away and moments before it disappeared, one of the wings folded as the airframe collapsed under the tremendous force of hitting the water.

Jack froze the frame just before the sea consumed the aircraft and focussing in on a panel situated just behind the cockpit, he could make out a design.

"Look what we have here."

"The Phoenix Legion," Paul groaned.

It was the same design they had found on the crashed Junkers tri-plane.

"There's confirmation, we are dealing with the Phoenix Legion, so now we know what we're up against."

"Do we just?" Jack looked at Paul. "I'm not so sure about that, there are too many questions for my liking and not enough answers."

"Jack." Mark's voice came over the intercom.

"Go ahead Mark."

"Kitty has just surfaced; she cut free from her umbilical so we need divers over there to make a recovery."

"Roger that Mark, we're onto it."

"Once we've recovered the eyeball, we'll make our best possible speed to Istanbul. We have some holes to get plugged."

Paul began issuing orders.

XIX

Orlagh was terrified, the sound of shells exploding against the ship was more than she could bear and crouching low in the control room, she forced herself into a tiny space between the panels and whimpered each time the ship took a hit.

"We should be safe down here," Mark said confidently. "We are three decks down in the heart of the ship."

Nothing he could say however would calm her overwrought nerves. Memories of being trapped inside the *Sea Quest* as it sank filled her with fear and her heart raced madly. If it had not been for Roz Stacey, she would have died that day. It had taken months of counselling and support from Jerry to banish the dark thoughts and depression that threatened to consume her. The good work that had been done was being unravelled and all Jerry could do was watch as she became ever more agitated. Slipping his arms around her, he held on tight in an effort to chase away her demons; the warmth of contact and soothing words were his sword against the monsters.

'I'm made of sterner stuff, I must pull myself together.' The sound of her own voice reasoning inside her head made her stop and listen. This was part of the self-help regime that she had developed with her psychologist and now she used it to construct a barrier against her fear.

'May your blessings outnumber the shamrocks that grow, and may trouble avoid you wherever you go.' This was the sound of her grandmother's voice as childhood memories came flooding in.

'May the good saints protect you and bless you today, and may troubles ignore you each step of the way.' This was another of her favourite sayings and as the words washed over her, Orlagh smiled. The sound of her grandmother's voice never failed to comfort her.

Once the onslaught was over Jerry coaxed her from their hiding place and almost carried her up the stairs to the afterdeck and the moment they were out in the open, she gasped greedily for air. It was as if she had been underwater and had just surfaced and pushing blindly towards the rail she vomited over the side, then her legs gave way.

Jerry was beside her whispering calming words into her ear and they remained this way until her strength returned.

"It's okay," he said rubbing her back gently, "its over."

"I'm sorry," she sobbed. "I completely lost it, what must you think of me?"

"Don't be silly." He hugged her tenderly.

"You won't ever leave me will you?" She looked up at him her face as white as porcelain.

"Of course I won't leave you," he said, looking into her tear-filled eyes. "Whatever brought that on?"

"There was a moment back there when all I could hear was that terrible noise. I thought I was alone, I don't know why but I was convinced you had gone or had been killed. I felt so empty, it was horrible."

"Don't be silly," he whispered again and holding onto her fiercely said. "You've had a shock, that's all."

It wasn't long before men began to appear. Members of the crew had been organised to clear away the debris that littered the deck, assess the damage and make emergency repairs.

They watched as divers went into the water, one pair swam out towards the eyeball ROV while others disappeared beneath the waves to inspect the damaged hull.

Mark remained in the control room, first he checked the equipment to satisfy himself that there really was no damage then he turned his attention to Kitty. The computer system was tracking the ROV and at no time was Kitty's signal lost. Without the physical connection of the umbilical cord, Mark had no control over the ROV, but using telemetry, he was able to download the information that Kitty had stored on her computer. Her onboard cameras had continued to function, recording the progress that she made on her return journey through the hold and back towards the surface, now it took Mark only a few moments to retrieve that information.

The container lay in the hold of the sunken vessel. This he found strange, he expected to find it secured to one of the decks, there seemed no reason to house a sealed container in the hold. He watched as the spotlights mounted on Kitty's framework picked out the shape of the silt covered container. Algae grew on the metal skin; it looked as if it had been exposed to the elements for years, but as he studied the screen, Mark had a feeling that something was not right. He had no idea why he thought this but it fuelled his interest, making him even more observant than he might have been.

Fish darted away as Kitty disturbed their world, her propulsion jets sending up clouds of silt that curled like whirlpools in the water around her. The picture began to clear as Kitty moved away and Mark got a good view of the interior of the hold. It was a world tinged with green and he had never seen so many fish inside a wreck before. It must be the algae, he thought, a perpetual source of food.

Suddenly the picture wavered and lines scrolled over the screen, this was the moment the umbilical cord became severed and after a few seconds, it cleared as the auxiliary power kicked in. The onboard computer was now in the driving seat and Mark became a passenger. The cameras were still rolling as Kitty turned to back track out of the hold, it was then he noticed something unusual.

"What the hell!" He exclaimed as he reached for the intercom button.

The druids hiding in the sanctuary of the linen cupboard had escaped the madness of the attack. They had set up a temporary altar dedicated to the God Bel of the Underworld. He was a powerful deity whose influence was strengthened by the arrival of the souls of the dead. Together with the Goddess of Hibernia, who was slowly gaining in strength, they made formidable allies.

The scarf they had taken from Orlagh's cabin lay over the altar and as the druids focussed their energy on the Ogham charm, they began to exert their influence. The moment the sacred object was in place it became a beacon for their powers, a focal point for the gods, and together they worked their magic, preparing Orlagh for the journey.

Orlagh was much calmer now; she lay curled up in bed in her cabin, safe from the dangers that lurked in the recesses of her mind. The ship was a solid mass around her and she could feel its force, although it was wounded, there was no immediate danger.

"I have a splitting headache," she complained.

Jerry, who was standing over her, placed his hand gently against her head and held it there as if to draw out the pain. "You just need to rest, close your eyes and sleep for a while. I'll be here when you wake up, I promise."

She smiled and doing as he said the throbbing inside her head eased and she drifted into a deep sleep.

Jerry remained watching over her for a while longer and as she slept, he began to go over the events in his mind. Their holiday had taken an expected turn and running into Jack in Bodrum seemed to be a fate that went beyond coincidence. He could hardly believe they were in the same place at the same time and with the appearance of the torc, it seemed as if some higher power was at work. Shaking his head, he rubbed his hand over his face and moved away from the bed. He did not believe in things like that, Orlagh might consider these events linked in some magical way, but she was welcome to her own opinions.

Standing by the door, he glanced back over his shoulder. She would be out for a couple of hours; her panic attack had been particularly violent. She had not had one like this for a long time, but it was understandable given the circumstances. All she needed now was rest and she would be fine. With this in mind, he decided to leave her and go to find out what was happening

Jack was making his way along the corridor towards the control room when Jerry left his cabin. He was responding to Mark's urgent message and as Paul was unable to leave the bridge, it was left to him to deal with the problem. Paul was far too busy coordinating the repair teams, he would remain in overall charge until he was satisfied that everything had been done to safeguard the men and women under his command.

"Jack," Jerry said the moment he saw him. "What's going on?"

"Jerry, are you and Orlagh okay?"

Jerry told him that Orlagh was upset and was resting in their cabin. "She'll be fine in a couple of hours."

"Will she be okay left alone?"

"Yes don't worry she just needs to lie down for a while."

"Mark has discovered something on the film that Kitty sent back," Jack told him. "Let's go find out what all the fuss is about."

As Jack led him along the corridor, he told Jerry about the FW190s.

"We have it all recorded, you can see it later. It's just like watching an old movie only this time we were their target."

Jerry could not believe how calm Jack sounded, his ship had almost been destroyed but still he could think straight. He was full of admiration for the American.

As soon as they arrived at the control room Mark ran the film.

"Watch for the moment Kitty turns to make her way back. I can't believe we missed it before."

They watched in silence as the film ran in slow motion, the spotlight running along the side of the container until they spotted what appeared to be a doorway.

"Stop it right there," Jack said. "Zoom in a bit will you."

Mark made the adjustments and Jack murmured in surprise.

"Looks like some kind of docking portal."

"What, for underwater divers?" Jerry frowned. He had seen nothing like this before.

"It's far too big for divers alone, looks more like an airlock for submersibles."

"Submarines?" Jerry frowned.

"Could be," Jack nodded, "although we are not in deep water here, it's only about forty feet." He thought for a moment as he studied the screen. "This is some kind of service hatch," he continued. "So why is a simple storage container fitted with an underwater service hatch?"

"I don't think it's just sitting on the deck," Mark began. "Looks like it's been grafted on look at that sealed fitting." He zoomed in closer.

Where Kitty had disturbed the layer of silt that had built up around the base of the container they could see a seal running around the bottom edge.

"What do we have here?" Jack said thinking aloud.

"Well whatever it is someone clearly doesn't want us to find out." Mark replied.

Jerry and Jack turned to look at him.

XX

Orlagh found herself standing alone on the shore of a gently moving river. A thin mist hung damp on the air, the legacy of a thick fog that had covered the valley like a shroud during the hours of darkness.

A Celtic boat appeared midstream and as if guided by an invisible hand it floated gently with the current. An unlit lamp was fastened to the bow and furs were laid out over the wooden bench. The boat was empty but as it drifted towards her, it stopped where water met the land and unable to stop herself Orlagh climbed in.

Once she had settled, the boat drifted away from the bank and before long, it was approaching a cave. The river disappeared into it and carrying the boat on its current, it took her in. Suddenly the lamp burst into flames as darkness settled around her, but Orlagh remained calm, she sensed no danger. The water continued to whisper softly against the side of the boat and occasionally it sang as it tumbled around and over rocks.

Orlagh thought she could see figures perched on the rocks but as she drew near there was nothing there. She did not understand the significance of these spiritual shadows so they passed her by, oblivious to her ignorance.

Soon a light appeared ahead and gently the boat drifted out into sunlight. She had crossed the boundary from the physical world to the land where spirits ruled. This was part of the Otherworld, it was much like the world she knew but here there were significant differences. This was a land where animals could speak, birds, fish and beasts of all kinds had voices, even plants were the same, every living thing had the ability to communicate.

Here it was possible to find your animal ally and Orlagh waited as the boat came to rest beside the bank. She felt welcome here, it was as if the grass and the trees were smiling, willing her to join them. Urged to leave the boat, she walked the path that wound its way from the water's edge.

It was a beautiful day, sunlight streamed down through the canopy of leaves above her head and tiny flowers at her feet released their scent as she passed filling the air with sweetness. She was at peace with herself and everything; it was here she would choose to spend eternity.

Moving silently she strayed from the path and walking amongst the trees, she opened her heart and began calling for Sailetheach the white stag who was her animal ally and protector. The deer was regarded as a messenger and guide from the Otherworld, and following such an animal led humans into contact with supernatural beings.

Orlagh realised that she must not stray far from the river, it was the thread linking her to the real world and distance would weaken the bond. There was a danger that she might not find her way back.

She did not have to wait long for between the trees in the Celtic rainforest, she could see movement. It was not clear at first who was there but then she saw antlers and a figure appeared moving proudly amongst the low-slung branches.

She smiled, her animal ally was near and her heart was thumping hard against her chest. In her mind's eye, she could see him, a magnificent stag, regal and tall, a powerful reminder of the fact that he was monarch of the forest. It was Sailetheach, who with the help of Madb and Madadh-allaidh, the wolf, had saved her from the clutches of the ruthless Goddess of Hibernia. Her eyes widened, it was not the stag that appeared before her.

An antlered shaman wrapped in the skin of a white deer stepped into view and the whole forest held its breath. The bearded creature appeared as half man, half beast and as he stood in silent contemplation, Orlagh had an opportunity to study him up close. In his right hand, he carried a gold torc and a horned serpent curled curiously around his left arm. She was not afraid as they locked eyes, it was clear that he posed her no harm, but still her breath came in short nervous gasps.

After what seemed an age he began to communicate. It was not clear how he did this, his lips did not appear to move, it was as if his voice was already there inside her head.

"There are ways of reaching your goals other than by force," he began.

"Sometimes the world, seen on a journey, will lead you to a spiritual teacher and guide," he continued. "I am Cernunnos, Lord of the forest and I come to offer you wisdom. You may well meet other shamans or spiritual seekers, some have much knowledge to share, but beware many will not be what they appear to be. Druids from your own world have much power, and they seek to do you harm." He became silent as he studied her.

"Many paths lead from the river through the trees, beyond are clearings and little lakes, different groves of trees, meadows and canyons. You may go where you please, take as much time as you need to explore. Be alert for animals, birds and fish that may approach you as Allies and helpers. Do not feel foolish or be afraid to communicate with various plants and trees, there are no barriers here in the Otherworld. When you are ready to leave, return to the riverbank, step into the boat and let it carry you gently down the river and into the light that is your own world. Use your time wisely because when you leave you will not be permitted to return."

Jack led Jerry to the Wardroom where they could talk in comfort over a cup of coffee.

"We found something strange in our cabin," Jerry began as soon as they had settled. "Someone left a wooden charm covered in letters from the Ogham alphabet."

"What the hell's that?" Jack stared at him.

Jerry explained the meaning of such a charm, and when he had finished Jack was surprised.

"Surely you don't believe a member of the crew put it there, Orlagh must have had it in her things. Perhaps it was an item left over from one of her presentations."

"I don't think so," Jerry shook his head. "She believes there are druids on board this ship."

"That's not possible," Jack laughed at the suggestion. "Did these druids take anything?"

"Yes, as a matter of fact they did." Jerry did not like the way Jack refused to take him seriously. "It might sound a little crazy, but I know Orlagh, she wouldn't make a fuss over nothing, besides, her scarf is missing and I'm sure it was there earlier." He had not realised it before but now he knew it was true. He cursed himself for having doubted Orlagh but at least now, he was prepared to defend her suspicions.

"She didn't take it out on deck and leave it somewhere?"

"No Jack, she didn't have it with her today."

"Okay," Jack held up his hands in a gesture of submission. "There have been casualties today because of the attack on the ship so we have to check out the crew. I'll have the men keep an eye out for suspicious looking personnel."

"They are not likely to show themselves Jack, stowaways generally keep themselves to themselves."

"Very well Jerry, I'll brief the men myself, get them to keep a sharp lookout, check all the out of the way places."

"Thanks Jack, I appreciate that."

Jack nodded. "Now, there is something I need you to do for me," he said changing the subject. "Contact your friends on the internet; find out what you can about the Phoenix Legion. They are up to something and I need to know what it is."

"Okay," Jerry smiled, "I'll have a word with Max from the Brothers of the Sacred Whisper, if anyone knows what's going on he'll be your man."

Jack stood up abruptly. "I've gotta go Jerry, find out what you can and I'll do something about your druids. We'll be heading back to Istanbul, the ship has sustained damage and we need help with the repairs. There's nothing to worry about so I'd appreciate it if you wouldn't say too much to Orlagh."

Jerry realised what he was saying and given her experiences on board the *Sea Quest,* it was probably best not to worry her with the details.

When Jack had gone, Jerry remained in his seat. He finished his coffee and thought about Orlagh, she would probably still be asleep. He needed somewhere quiet to work; if he were going to contact Max, he would need a computer. His laptop was in their cabin, and not wanting to disturb Orlagh, he decided to check out the library. With the men involved in the clear up operation, it was likely to be quiet there.

When Orlagh woke, she was disorientated and for a moment had no idea where she was. Slowly as the remains of her dream evaporated, she realised what was going on. The gentle movements of the ship was conformation of reality and she smiled, then stretching her arms luxuriously above her head she slipped her legs over the edge of the bed.

She was alone in their cabin, Jerry had gone so using these solitary moments to collect her thoughts she tried to make sense of what she could remember of her dream. Her rapid return to reality was a shock that left her mind reeling. Parts of her dream were still there inside her head, the scenes too vivid to be part of her imagination, and the more she thought about it the more she realised that she had experienced a Vision Quest. She had travelled to the Otherworld where the ancient spirits had communicated with her. Sitting down on the bed, she breathed deeply, hardly able to believe it could have been anything else. Never before had she experienced anything as significant as this. She realised that she could never tell Jerry; he would not believe her. Although he believed in Animal Allies, he was convinced they belonged to an earlier time; people today were too far removed from their pagan roots to be able to experience such things.

Curnunnos had been real enough but the knowledge she had gained from the spirits was stored away, just out of reach, somewhere safe in her mind. This frustrated her; the fact that she could not recall every detail meant there was much more to it than simple fantasy. Of one thing she was certain, it had been more than a dream.

Rising from the edge of the bed, she went into the wet room where she splashed cold water onto her face and glancing at herself in the mirror, she was appalled. Her pale complexion shocked her, her hair was all over the place and her eyes remained swollen from tears, then the terror she had experienced when the ship was under attack came flooding back.

Suddenly she hated herself for her weakness; she should never have behaved in such a way, so pushing these unwelcome emotions aside, she began to prioritise her thoughts. First she had to do something about her appearance, it was one thing allowing Jerry to see her like this, but the thought of Jack, Paul or any other member of the crew setting eyes on her was something that she just could not allow. The thought of it made her shudder and reaching for her make-up bag, she used the contents to good effect, then running a brush through her hair; she began to feel much better.

The library was as Jerry expected, deserted apart from one man who was reading a magazine about astronomy. Jerry nodded but didn't say anything as he entered the room, moving towards a bank of computer screens, he sat down and logged on. Typing in *Brothers of the Sacred Whisper* the screen came to life, then after a few moments he entered his password and as soon as the site opened up, he typed in Caradoc, his username.

He studied the screen, scanning the options before making his selection then he entered the forum. Running through the list of names he could not see who he was looking for, Mad Max was not there. He could of course be in a side room having a private conversation, but there was no way of confirming that, so with a disappointed sigh he was about to log off when suddenly the screen changed.

'Hi Caradoc.'

'Pixie-Lee, how are you? It's been a long while since we last spoke.'

Pixie-Lee was someone he had never met but had spoken to before. He knew that she lived in Ireland but beyond that, she remained a mystery.

'Oh not so bad. Yourself?'

'I'm on holiday.' He typed.

'Where?'

'Turkey, I'm visiting ancient monuments but at the moment I'm onboard a ship in the Black Sea.'

'What, cruising as well?'

'No, it's a long story. Have you heard from Max lately?' The screen remained blank for a few moments before she replied.

'Yes, he's around.'

'I really need to speak with him. When is he usually on?'

'Two or three evenings a week, usually after nine pm.'

Pixie-Lee was not usually very forthcoming with information, in the past he had struggled to get anything out of her. He thought she seemed a little paranoid about things generally, but then he couldn't blame her. The subjects they had discussed before had been very sensitive and one never knew who might be listening, so he could understand her caution.

'I need some information about the Phoenix Legion.' By revealing the purpose of his visit, he hoped to cause a response. The problem was she might become even more reluctant to continue, but it was a risk he was prepared to take.

'That's one hot potato.' She typed. 'Why, what's the matter this time?'

'Nothing that I'm aware of in particular,' he lied. 'I just have a feeling that something is going on and I just wanted to know if my hunch was correct.'

'Are you in some kind of trouble?'

'No, not as such.' Pixie-Lee was very perceptive, but he did not want to say too much, frighten her off before he had time to learn anything.

'The Legion does seem to be recovering some of its influence.' She told him. 'After what happened last year I'm surprised they are regaining their popularity so quickly.'

A year ago, the Phoenix Legion had been pretty much crushed. Their plan was to use atomic weapons to subdue the power of Washington and London, but Jack and his organisation had thwarted them. Since then no one had heard much of the Phoenix Legion.

'I'm working on something at the moment, researching for a paper I'm writing at university.' He hated having to tell an untruth but he could think of no other way to get her to open up. He was not prepared to tell her about the container they had found on the seabed, the attack from vintage aircraft or indeed mention the Sarin gas. He decided to keep the appearance of the Belgae torc to himself as well.

'They still have considerable influence and support in Europe,' she began, 'and from what I hear their popularity is growing.'

'Really?' He feigned surprise.

'Oh yes, in particular the southern reaches of Europe, countries like Romania, Bulgaria and the Ukraine.'

Jerry frowned; his current position put him in close proximity with all those places. If he could discover from which country the attacking aircraft had been launched, then maybe he would solve the problem of the Phoenix Legion's whereabouts.

'Does the Legion have a headquarters in this area?'

'Word has it they are operating from a medieval fortress somewhere in the Ukraine.'

'Do they have a website?'

'I guess so, probably like before, I imagine it would operate in the same way with layered security systems requiring complicated code words'.

She had helped him before when he had penetrated the Sonnenrad site. Her help had been invaluable, without her he would never have been able to solve the 'sun wheel' mystery, which helped lead Jack and his team to the island where the druids were holding Orlagh and Roz Stacey.

'Can you give me any clues?' He crossed his fingers as he waited for her to reply.

'No Caradoc, I'm not getting involved this time.'

Jerry could only guess at how scared she must have been before, not knowing if her giving away secrets would bring retribution down on her or Mad Max. Her input had a direct and negative effect on the Phoenix Legion and so far, she had managed to put up a smoke screen and avoid any unpleasantness that might have come her way.   She wanted to do nothing that might upset the status quo, especially if the Phoenix Legion were gaining in strength.

'Okay,' Jerry typed, 'perhaps Max will be able to help.'

'Maybe, you know how keen he is to hear about German Ideology, regardless of how dangerous it might be.'

With that, she was gone and Jerry was left staring at an empty screen. From their conversation, he was now convinced that something was going on. The wreck they had discovered and the container it was carrying was not what they appeared to be, he felt sure there was something sinister hidden under the Sea of Azov.

He logged off and frowned at his reflection in the darkened screen before going off to find Orlagh.

The druids were kneeling in front of their make shift altar, chanting softly to the image of Bel. The scarf they had stolen from Orlagh's cabin was still on the altar serving as a link between them. They knew she had been on a journey to the Otherworld; there were clear indications that the spirit world had been disturbed and it was left to them to restore equilibrium. They were surprised to discover that she was so receptive; they had not expected Orlagh to possess such powers. They realised that she probably had no idea just how much influence she might wield over their world, she was after all a goddess in the making.

They would have to remain vigilant, cover themselves with protective spells, not only must they be aware of the forces surrounding this woman; they must also remain in favour with the goddess.

When Jerry returned to their cabin, he found Orlagh sitting at the small table reading notes from his laptop.

"Hello," Jerry said as he opened the door. "How are you feeling?"

Turning her head away from the screen, she smiled up at him. "Much better thank you." She got to her feet and took a step towards him. "I'm so sorry I made such a fuss."

"Don't be silly," he whispered gently as he wrapped her up in his arms. "You've nothing to reproach yourself for."

She wanted to ask him what he had discovered about the attack on the ship but she did not want to spoil the moment. She felt safe in his arms, so closing her eyes she savoured the moment.

So much had happened since their arriving in Turkey and now she was beginning to think they should return home. Their holiday was turning into a nightmare and she could not stand the thought of anything else going wrong.

She couldn't tell him about her dream, he would not understand, besides, he would think her insane if she were to mention her vision quest.

"So what are you researching?" He looked at the computer screen.

"Jack told us he was looking for the Amber Chamber so I thought I'd find out something about it." She continued eagerly. "Before it was lost, the Amber Chamber or Amber Room as it was sometimes called was said to be the Eighth Wonder of the World."

"Wasn't it of Russian origin?"

"It seems to have been a joint effort by both German and Russian craftsmen." Jerry smiled as he listened to her; she was now in lecture mode.

"Construction began in Prussia in 1701. Andreas Schluter, a German sculptor was the designer and when it was finished, it remained at the Berlin City Palace until 1716 when it was given to Tsar Friedrich Wilhelm I. Over the years, it went through several renovations. It was huge, covering more than fifty five square metres and it was made from more than six tonnes of Amber." She flashed up an image of the room before going on. "During World War Two it was looted by the Nazis and brought to Konigsburg. After that its whereabouts was lost in the chaos at the end of the war."

"I remember seeing pictures of it, I'm sure it was a reconstruction though." Jerry told her.

"Yes I found something about a reconstruction project on the internet." She scrolled through the text on the screen until she found what she was looking for.

"Here it is." She began reading from the text. "In 1979 efforts began to rebuild the Amber Chamber at Tsarskoye Selo. In 2003, after decades of work by Russian craftsmen, financed by donations from Germany, the reconstructed Amber Room was inaugurated in the Catherine Palace in Saint Petersburg in Russia."

"So what happened to the original after the war?"

Orlagh frowned and scrolling further down the screen she began to skim read the rolling text.

"There are many rumours and theories." Jerry said pointing at a paragraph that confirmed what he was saying. "Some say it was destroyed by bombing while others insist it's hidden in a lost subterranean bunker in Konigsburg or buried in mines in the Ore Mountains. Jack seems to think it was taken onto a ship that was sunk by a Soviet submarine in the Baltic Sea."

"Yes," Orlagh nodded. "That would seem the most likely outcome. Once the Germans had disassembled it, the most sensible way to transport all that Amber was by sea."

Jerry thought about the container they had seen on the sunken ship. It seemed unlikely that it would contain the Amber Chamber; there was something more sinister about it. Jack would have to think again if he wanted to discover the location of the hidden treasure.

"Let's go and get some coffee," Orlagh pleaded. "I needed one at least an hour ago, if I leave it any longer I'm going to get withdrawal symptoms."

Jerry grinned, she was sounding much more like her old self.

"The Institute of National Archaeology in Bodrum seems to think that Jack is onto something." She told him as they made their way towards the Wardroom.

"Yes," Jerry nodded. "I'm sure they wouldn't have given their backing if they were not convinced."

She glanced at him curiously.

In the Wardroom, they helped themselves to coffee and sat at a table facing each other. They were on their own, the room was deserted, yet they did not have to wait long before Jack arrived.

"Hello," he said, surprised to see them. "How are you feeling?"

"I'm fine, really Jack."

She looked great, a little tired maybe the strain showing around her eyes, but apart from that, he was willing to believe her.

"We are making our way back to Istanbul," he told them. "We have to make some repairs, but I aim to return here, take a closer look at that container."

"How do you plan to do that Jack?" she asked. "Someone went to a lot of trouble to make sure you didn't get close enough in the first place. There must be something down there they don't want you to see."

"True," he nodded, "but be assured, no one will know I have returned."

She had no idea they had shot one of the aircraft down, that alone was a good enough reason for Jack to return. The remains of the FW190 might hold some clues as to where he might find the Phoenix Legion.

They stared at him in silence for a moment then Orlagh asked. "How long will it take us to get to Istanbul?"

"About two days," Jack sat down at their table. "We are cruising pretty steadily so providing we don't hit bad weather it shouldn't take any longer."

"Once we are back on shore we should think about returning home." She looked at Jerry. "Our two weeks will almost be up by then anyway, besides, I really don't want to return to our hotel."

"Just try to relax, enjoy the next couple of days." Jack glanced at them both before getting to his feet. "We'll meet up later."

XXI

The *Sea Quest* arrived in Istanbul during the early hours of the morning and slipped unnoticed alongside the harbour wall. The pilot who had come out to meet them was now standing on the shattered bridge as the helmsman nudged the ship into place. His brow furrowed as he studied the damage to the forward deck but he said nothing. He knew that bandits operated in the waters around the coast but he was surprised to see so many scars on a ship of this size.

Captain Paul Seymour was standing beside him silently overseeing the operation. Glancing sideways, he regarded the pilot. He was middle aged and as knurled as a fisherman. He had obviously spent all of his working life at sea and perhaps even his childhood too. He did not seem like a man who would be spooked easily and Paul was thankful that he asked no questions.

Paul was exhausted; he had been on the bridge since the attack and was far too tired for lengthy explanations. He was responsible for his ship and crew so would not leave his post until the ship was safely tied up alongside.

Suddenly the hull nudged up against fenders slung like huge balloons over the harbour wall, these stopped the ship from crashing into the stonework. There was a scurry of movement from the deck as men secured the ship with heavy ropes to steel bollards, and although it was nighttime, powerful spotlights lit up the area so the men could work in safety.

A tugboat was standing by to offer assistance if necessary but as soon as the men were done a signal was sent and a cloud of black diesel fumes rose into the air as it backed away. It manoeuvred in the harbour as white water rose from its bow and coursed along its flanks before it disappeared into the darkness.

Paul moved towards the control panel and systematically shut down the ships systems. Once that was done, he accompanied the pilot from the bridge leaving an officer in charge. He could now begin to relax, there was nothing more to do and as they climbed down the ramp and onto the harbour wall, he shook hands with the man. They exchanged a few words before he climbed back on board then he went to his cabin for a well-earned rest.

Over breakfast, Orlagh and Jerry discussed their travel arrangements. They had enjoyed the first part of their holiday. Visiting museums and meeting up with Takat had been the highlight of their trip. Events had overtaken them and the notion of relaxing in the sunshine with the man she loved had been shattered, but there was one thing she wanted to do before leaving Istanbul, they must visit the Grand Bazaar in the walled part of the old city.

Jack had arranged for a car to pick them up from the ship and take them to the airport, and as they stood waiting for it to arrive Orlagh was filled with mixed emotions. She was sorry they had not been able to spend more time with Jack and Paul and she was going to miss them both. Since the attack on the ship, both men had been kept busy, but now as Paul stood beside her she was conscious of him. He was a big man with an even bigger personality and as he drew her into his arms, he whispered. "You have a safe journey home."

"Now you be sure to keep in touch," she told him. "I want to hear about all your adventures."

Looking up into his dark eyes, she smiled before pulling away, then, turning towards Jack, she could see that his face remained expressionless. She would have liked their parting to be a happier affair.

"You look after yourself," he said and leaning forward he kissed her cheeks in the continental style. "Let me know the moment you arrive back in Ireland." It was then he embraced her and she could feel the warmth from his body.

"I will," she promised, hugging him affectionately. She had to force her voice to work because a lump had formed in her throat, and wrestling with her emotions, she was annoyed with herself. She was determined to hold back her tears and could not believe where all this sadness was coming from, so standing up straighter she moved towards Jerry, unconsciously seeking comfort.

Their taxi arrived, and pulling up beside the ship, the driver got out. Two security guards stepped forward with their bags and loaded them into the luggage compartment, then they held the doors open as Orlagh and Jerry climbed in.

"Are you sure you want to go to the Grand Bazaar?" Jerry said, turning his head towards her as she settled into the seat beside him.

"We can't not go into the Medieval City," she replied. "We shouldn't miss an opportunity like this, besides, we didn't plan to come here so this is a wonderful bonus, anyway, I want to do some shopping."

Jerry realised that was the real reason for her enthusiasm, she could not resist the idea of a huge market with hundreds of shops. He was in for a busy day, but even Orlagh could not visit every shop.

The security guards climbed into the car, one beside Orlagh and the other settling in front with the driver. Jack insisted they accompanied them for the day, but although they did not show it, Jerry was certain the prospect of a shopping trip appalled them as much as it did him.

Orlagh waved to Jack and Paul as the car pulled away, and she could feel her tears welling up again. She had been so pleased by their unexpected meeting in Bodrum, but her enthusiasm had been crushed when the ship was attacked in the Sea of Azov. She knew that Jack would never have exposed her to unnecessary danger and if the ship was about to sink, he would have made sure she was one of the first off, either in the helicopter or on a lifeboat.

"I think we had a lucky escape." Jerry whispered in her ear. It was as if he could read her thoughts.

"Why do you say that?" she looked at him enquiringly.

"Didn't you notice the men stationed beside the lifeboats? They remained there for the entire return journey and the helicopter was kept at constant readiness."

"Jack would never take avoidable risks, what you saw were probably precautions, besides, we were never in any real danger."

Jerry knew she was not entirely convinced and just to confirm his suspicions a shudder ran through her as she pressed up against him.

Orlagh knew that what he said was true, she had no idea of the state of the ship; Jack had deliberately kept the details to himself.

"What do you think will happen now?"

"Well," Jerry whispered. "Once the ship has undergone repairs, I guess Jack will return to the container on the seabed."

"But that's madness," Orlagh said loudly. Lowering her voice, she continued. "It's quite clear that someone doesn't want him sniffing around out there. Why do you think our ship was attacked?"

Jerry was convinced it had something to do with the Phoenix Legion. Pixie-Lee had not said as much on the website forum, but reading between the lines, he felt sure they were at the bottom of it.

The security guard sitting next to Orlagh looked up, they were approaching the walled medieval city, and he was as interested as any other tourist. He wanted to take it all in, it was his job to see everything and keep them safe.

Their flight was not until early evening so they had a good few hours before heading off towards the airport.

"I'm sure we don't have to worry about Jack," Jerry told her. "He's the most capable man I know, besides, he has every resource available to him."

Orlagh smiled, she knew he was right, Jack would do as he saw fit, once he had made up his mind nothing anyone could say would stop him.

The druids left the ship soon after the car carrying Orlagh pulled away and once Jack and his men had disappeared, they made their way down the loading ramp. Other crewmembers were going ashore, so pushing in amongst them, they remained anonymous.

They knew Orlagh was heading for the airport so it was not necessary to follow her car closely. They were sure to make contact with her once they arrived at their destination and all they had to do was to confirm what flight she was booked on.

As soon as they were away from the harbour, they located a taxi and piled into the back seat. It was their first time in Istanbul, and although on a mission, they were determined to make the most of it.

"Schiffers men are close," one of the druids muttered. "They may be dangerous."

He could sense the gunmen, but had no idea where they were located. Using his powers, he focussed on Orlagh and discovered that she was not going directly to the airport.

"The car carrying the girl is heading for the old city."

His colleague closed his eyes and frowned, he would have to consider their options. He had chosen not to use his powers, he remained fully aware of their surroundings, anchored to the present, his mind clear of spirits. It was left to the other druid to pursue Orlagh through the spirit world; he was the one in possession of her scarf and was responsible for planting the stave in her cabin. He had also carved the Ogham symbols into the wood and had performed the spells on their makeshift altar.

"We have a choice," he said. "The woman we seek has gone to the old city, we could go there or we can wait until she arrives at the airport."

His colleague opened his eyes, he had made up his mind but before sharing his thoughts, he leaned forward to speak with the driver.

"What is there to see in the old city?"

"The Grand Bazaar is most popular with tourists," he began. "There are also Mosques and many other beautiful things."

"It must be the Bazaar." The druids said in tandem. "There are many visitors?"

135

"Oh yes, in abundance," the driver continued, convinced they were tourists." "In fact nearly half a million people visit the Bazaar each day, it is a very big place."

The druids looked at each other in disbelief, and a plan began to formulate in their heads. With so many people going about their business, it might prove easy to kidnap her and lose themselves in the crowd.

"Take us there."

Their driver was proving to be very knowledgeable and his English was perfect, this encouraged Orlagh to ask all kinds of questions.

"The market in Istanbul is one of the largest in the world," he boasted. "It has over three thousand shops and is completely covered." He stopped talking as he dodged around a vehicle that had appeared from a narrow side street.

"Sultan Mehmet, the Conqueror, began construction in 1455, in those days it was mainly a bazaar of cloth sellers. Trading textiles was very popular during that time so the Bezzazistan-i-cedid was created."

Orlagh frowned and looked at him enquiringly.

"The meaning in English," he continued, "is New Bedesten. The word 'bedesten' is an alteration of the Persian word 'bezestan', derived from 'bezi', which means cloth. As you see, it means 'bazaar of the cloth sellers'." He grinned into the rear view mirror.

"Over the years," he continued, "there have been many changes." Swinging the car violently into an impossibly narrow side street, he crunched the gears and accelerated hard. "There have been fires which destroyed much of the bazaar; also an earthquake in 1894 did much damage. This was a major catastrophe and repairs took almost four years to complete."

Orlagh listened intently and wondered how many times he had repeated these stories.

"Surely today with modern shopping malls close by, the bazaar is just a tourist trap?"

"No, not at all," the driver replied. "The Grand Bazaar is a thriving complex employing twenty six thousand people."

"Are you sure? That's a lot of people." Orlagh could hardly imagine the size of the place. "It must be huge."

"Indeed, it covers a vast area. You must understand, the bazaar attracts hundreds of thousands of visitors every day."

Orlagh thought he must be exaggerating, but going on the coach-loads of tourists they had seen around the city he was probably right.

"The bazaar celebrated its five hundredth birthday in 2011 and is the most visited monument in the world."

Orlagh made up her mind; she was going to investigate his claims as soon as she had access to a computer. It seemed unbelievable that so many people would come to the old city in Istanbul every single day. If it were true, how much money changed hands both in the bazaar and in the surrounding cafés and bars. It had to be the wealthiest city in this part of the Mediterranean.

The car stopped and the security guards got out. After a quick look around, they opened the doors then Orlagh and Jerry climbed out. Once their car had moved away, the men told them that it would return to pick them up in four hours time. Orlagh was dismayed, that did not leave her much time to explore three thousand shops.

Schiffer's men followed them from the harbour. Driving their new hire car, they entered the medieval city and it was as much as they could do to keep up with the taxi ahead. Finally, it stopped in a queue of traffic waiting at the side of the road and they had no choice but to edge past and pull up a few hundred metres ahead.

They watched as Orlagh and her companion appeared, but they soon disappeared in the crowd. It would be impossible to find them again, so they abandoned their plan to follow them into the city but just as they were about to drive away, another taxi drew up. Two men jumped out and went in the same direction as Orlagh.

"Those men are the same as we saw in Bodrum."

"Get out and stay with them, use your cell phone to let me know where you are and once I have dumped the car I will catch up with you."

Without a word, the man got out and went after the druids.

Orlagh was amazed; the Grand Bazaar was everything she imagined and more. She had to decide which way to go because everywhere she looked was an assault on her senses. Little shops and market stalls stretched as far as she could see, and bright colours and sounds filled her with excitement and anticipation. The noise of so many people drawn to the same spot was incredible; traders were calling out, competing with each other and the sound of Arabic music rising up from somewhere in the crowd just seemed to add to the confusion.

Bodies crowding in around her did not deter her in the slightest; she was completely bewitched by the magic of the bazaar and just like Alice stepping through the looking glass, she was drawn towards the colours and the smells.

"This is fantastic," she exclaimed turning towards Jerry. "Would you just look at all this stuff?"

She lingered briefly beside a stall selling silk scarves, and running her fingers through the display hanging from hooks above her head, the sensation against her skin was deliciously cool and soft.

"There is every colour of the rainbow," she marvelled. "It's all so vibrant."

Orlagh moved on dragging Jerry behind her and he realised that nothing short of a miracle could stop her.

The narrow lane they were moving along was decorated with what appeared to be marble. Individual tiles of exquisite detail stunned Jerry and he was sure that some were medieval. He did not have time to study them because Orlagh, dragging him from shop to shop, was now heading towards an area selling leather goods.

The sharp smell of tanning fluid filled the air, it overpowered every other scent and catching at the back of his throat, Jerry held his breath, waiting for the sensation to pass. Orlagh did not seem to notice and plunging in began rooting through the display. Bags of all shapes and sizes delighted her with their brilliance, the colours like the scarves, were of the whole spectrum. She surprised Jerry by making a quick decision, she spotted the bag she wanted and was soon haggling the price with the shop owner. She revelled in her newfound talent and in no time at all had agreed a price. Slinging it over her shoulder, she turned to face him and her smile delighted him, he had not seen her so happy in days and looking at the gaudy colour of her new purchase he wondered if it would find a place on her shoulder in Dublin.

Following her closely, he was afraid of losing her in the crowd, and the security men trailed along behind, careful to keep them both in sight.

Jerry was impressed with the bazaar, what seemed at first to be chaos in an overcrowded place turned out to be an organised trading centre that had been in operation for hundreds of years. He was not keen to admit this to Orlagh, but he was strangely enjoying this shopping experience. Ordinarily it was something he did his best to avoid. Shopping was Orlagh's weakness and a trip into Dublin on a Saturday afternoon was his idea of a nightmare, but there was something infectious about the Grand Bazaar. History was oozing from the walls and the air seemed as charged as an electrical current. It was all around him and wherever he looked, he could see evidence of the past.

The tiles underfoot excited him, in places it was obvious that some of them had been replaced, but mixed in amongst them were tiles from an older time. Plaques on the street corners told stories that were steeped in history and he furthered his knowledge by soaking up everything around him. The vaulted ceiling high above his head was decorated with Byzantine reliefs, the details covered in gold leaf, and he was completely taken in by a 17th century kiosk that apparently was once used as a cafe. This was where the Sultan Mahmut II often came in disguise to eat his pudding, and as Jerry read from the information board, he discovered more about the Ottoman age. The Bazaar was used by the *Istanbulla,* the inhabitants of the city and was a place where people could mix freely. The market was the only place at that time where women could go in relative safety; they had to be accompanied in other parts of the city.

Orlagh had disappeared and as Jerry looked up, he could no longer see her. Standing on tiptoe, he glanced over a sea of heads before spotting her looking at some shoes. She had entered part of the market where every stall sold shoes, there were thousands of pairs of all shapes and sizes, and as Jerry made his way towards her, he could see that she was enthralled.

"I can hardly believe this Jerry," she exclaimed the moment he appeared. "Would you just look at this, have you ever seen so many pairs of shoes?"

She did not wait for his answer, and he sighed loudly as he thought about all the other pairs she had stuffed into cupboards at home.

Looking up he noticed a sign on the wall written in English. 'Turks wear yellow shoes, Greeks blue, Jews black and Armenian red.' He smiled and wondered what colour shoes the Irish were supposed to wear. In Orlagh's case, it was every colour there was.

She had already bought two pairs and was now searching through a pile of sandals. Ignoring his frown, she chose a pair and went off to do her bartering.

Jerry's attention was drawn to the next lane. Every shop in that direction was a jeweller, and the air seemed to glow with so much gold and sparkling stones. It seemed strange to him that shops selling the same stock should be found together, it must be something to do with the trader's guilds, he mused. Years ago, guilds had been set up and traders selling similar stock had stuck together, it seemed that this tradition was still observed.

In another direction, he could see armourers selling all kinds of weapons. There were beautifully curved bladed swords and hundreds of knives, some with intricate designs etched into the ironwork. Along another little alley, he spotted dozens of booksellers. Here the air was heavy with scents associated with musty books and parchment. He looked longingly in their direction but there was little chance of him browsing over the ancient volumes.

It was then that he noticed two men watching Orlagh. He thought he recognised them so jostling for position he strained his neck for a better look. He felt sure they were the same men who had pushed past them on the tour bus in Bodrum, but shaking his head, he doubted himself; it was too much of a coincidence.

He made his way to where Orlagh was standing, but she was engrossed in her shopping and had no idea that he had arrived beside her. Jerry glanced over his shoulder, but the men had gone. He smiled, he would have to loosen up a little; there was no threat in amongst all these people.

They moved on along the street, Orlagh delighting in the colourful designs of the market stalls, but Jerry was not listening, he had spotted the two men again and still they seemed to have an interest in Orlagh. Sidestepping into a covered bookstall he pretended to show interest in an old volume. The sensation of being watched intensified, but still he harboured doubts. Perhaps he was being paranoid, a little over protective towards Orlagh, but given recent events, he felt justified in being cautious so listened to his instincts.

Peering from behind a curtain that hung across the improvised doorway, he watched as the men quickened their pace. Perhaps Orlagh had been right; she was convinced that druids had been aboard the *Ocean Pride* and perhaps these were those men.

Suddenly a strong feeling of guilt washed over him and he realised that he should have taken her more seriously, especially when she had discovered the Stave of Yew in their cabin. He should have insisted that Jack make a thorough search of the ship.

Orlagh had wandered quite a way along the avenue and there were crowds of people between them. He had to get to her before the men; he must also warn the guards of the potential danger. Pushing through the shoppers, he managed to get to Orlagh and grabbing her by the arm, he turned her so she was facing him.

"We must get closer to the security guards."

She could hear the urgency in his voice so allowed herself to be led away.

"There are some suspicious looking men following us," he explained.

"Oh come on Jerry," she grinned, "you've just had enough of shopping."

"No seriously, I'm sure they are the men who pushed past us in Bodrum."

"The druids," she said and shuddered. Becoming serious, she peered at the crowd in an attempt to locate the guards.

The gunman entered the market, he could see the men he was following a little way ahead and dodging around the shoppers, closed the gap between them. His cell phone rang; it was his colleague. The car had been parked and now he wanted an update.

With his phone clamped to his ear, he realised the men he was watching had become alert. Something was happening up ahead, but he was too far away to see, there were just too many people, so pushing to one side he cut down between some stalls and made his way along a narrow service alley. When he reached the other end, he turned into the main thoroughfare and was just in time to see three men surround the red haired woman. Keeping her between them, it seemed they were shielding her from something or someone and it was not long before he realised they had seen the druids following them.

The druids were making no effort to conceal themselves and were making headway by barging shoppers aside. Speaking into his cell phone, he updated his colleague with what was happening and could do no more; the woman and her guardians were heading for the exit. They would have to come up with a plan and quickly if they were going to complete their mission successfully.

Falling in behind the druids, the hunters became the hunted as the gunman closed in. They had a common objective but if he could reduce the opposition then he would be more likely to succeed. Passing close by a weapons stall, he spotted a box of wicked looking knives, and without breaking stride, snatched one up and concealed it against the inside of his arm. No one noticed the theft or his evil intent and drawing closer he began to calculate his chances.

The druids increased their pace and closing the gap, had their target in view. The gunman, deciding that now was his chance moved in swiftly and aiming for the druid on the left, he struck a deadly blow.

The force of the long thin blade entering his body astounded the druid and winded, he was unable to cry out. Someone shoved past him and his world began to spin as he staggered to a halt, pain shot through his chest in waves and his eyesight began to fade. He was in shock and could not believe what was happening. His colleague had no idea what was going either and because of the crowd it was impossible for him to react.

Collapsing to his knees, his strength failed completely and spirits from

141

the Otherworld began to crowd in, it was then his eyesight dimmed completely.

At first, his colleague failed to see the weapon protruding from his body but as blood began to pool on the ground around him, he saw the hilt of the knife and his eyes narrowed.

Suddenly a woman began to scream and fear rippled through the crowd. A gap opened up around them as people moved away in an attempt to distance themselves from danger. It was not clear what had happened, confusion hung in the stifling air and it was impossible to see where the attack had come from, the remaining druid realised that it would be unwise to hang around. He could not afford to be detained, caught up in a lengthy police investigation, so before he lost sight of Orlagh he slipped away into the crowd.

Orlagh realised that something was going on as soon as she heard the woman scream, but the men around her refused to stop. They kept her moving, steering her away from danger and towards an exit. It did not stop her from peering over her shoulder and she could see the mayhem playing out in the street behind them. Suddenly they were out in the bright sunlight and it took her eyes a moment to adjust.

Keeping close beside her, the men hustled her over the wide pathway and down a flight of roughcast steps.

"This way." One of them said and they hurried between a wall of a building and a high wooden fence.

There was no one in sight, the pathway was deserted, so racing over the uneven surface they moved quickly putting distance between them and the Grand Bazaar.

Suddenly something stung her face and Orlagh cried out.

"Down." One of the guards shouted and grasping her roughly, pulled her into a doorway.

A shot rang out and this time there was no mistaking the sound. More dust and brick particles exploded into their faces and Orlagh cried out. The guard beside her turned and fired his pistol and the noise bouncing from the walls hurt her ears.

Jerry was crouched beside the other guard just across the alleyway. They had taken shelter behind some flimsy looking rubbish bins and Orlagh was terrified that he would be shot. The man with him was yet to fire his gun so had not drawn attention to their position, but it was only a matter of time.

"Move." Came the sharp command and she was pushed out into the alley.

More shots sounded but this time it was from across the way, the other guard was laying down covering fire to enable Orlagh to escape. She reached the end of the alley and stumbled out onto a busy main street where she fell into the road.

A car horn sounded and an angry voice shouted obscenities as a vehicle drove around her. Climbing to her feet, she limped across to the other side of the road and pushed herself up against a wall. The guard who was behind her had not appeared so she was alone.

Her heart was hammering against her ribs and fighting to regain control she glanced back the way she had come. She could no longer hear gunshots and wondered what was happening with the men, but she couldn't worry about that now. She had to keep moving, so going up a flight of steps leading to a raised footpath she discovered there was only one way to go, and heading towards a crowd of sightseers she joined the back of the group. They were making their way slowly towards the Hagia Sophia, the Church of the Divine Wisdom; she should be safe in there.

Orlagh looked up at the huge flat dome that dominated the view ahead, it was a feat of engineering that took place in the 6th century, she remembered reading about it in a magazine. The building stood on the site of Byzantium's acropolis and architects still marvelled at its many innovations. She knew that it was no longer used as a place of worship; it was now a museum and was hugely popular with tourists. Pushing these thoughts from her mind she checked over her shoulder again but the footpath behind her was clear.

She joined a group of Americans whose guided tour was about to start, so doing her best to blend in, she attempted to calm her racing heart.

The guide ushered them into the interior, and standing beneath the dome, Orlagh looked up at the thirty million gold tesserae, tiny mosaic tiles, that covered the walls.

"These have recently been restored to the brilliance they once enjoyed fifteen hundred years ago." Their guide informed them in heavily accented English.

She went on to tell them that sadly access was restricted because scaffolding had returned to enable the conservation program to continue.

Orlagh glanced back over her shoulder for the hundredth time; thankfully, the gunmen had not followed her. She had not seen them in the first place so would hardly recognise them if they did.

Her situation seemed hopeless, she had no idea who was after her and now she was alone in a strange city. The only thing she could do was to try to make her way back to the ship. Her taxi was not due for several hours, besides it was probably not a good idea to wait around for it, the gunmen were probably aware of her plans. She worried about Jerry but knew he would make it back to the ship, so making up her mind; she slipped away from the group and headed towards the main entrance. Snatching up a leaflet as she went, she opened it and studied the little map printed inside. She located the Hagia Sophia and triangulating her position with the Grand Bazaar, was able to work out which way to go. Kennedy Avenue was the main coastal route, it would lead her to the harbour which did not appear to be that far away.

Fifteen minutes later, she was running along the quay in the direction of the *Ocean Pride*. Jack spotted her from the bridge and hurrying down to the lower deck, met her as she ran up the boarding ramp.

"What happened?" He demanded, scanning the quayside behind her.

"Have you heard from the others?" she managed, gasping for breath. "I'm so worried about Jerry, there were men with guns."

"Yeah, I had a call from one of my men; he told me you were running so I sent out reinforcements to find you."

"I must have come a different way, I've seen no one."

The pain in her side began to ease now she had stopped running and as soon as she was on board ship, she breathed deeply in an effort to catch her breath.

"Have you news of Jerry?"

"No," Jack shook his head. "I'll try to find out as soon as I have you safely inside."

Paul appeared from the upper deck, he was carrying a bottle of water and handing it to Orlagh, she took it gratefully and gulped down a few mouthfuls.

"You must tell us what happened from the moment you left here," he said.

Orlagh told him everything as they made their way towards the bridge and leaving nothing out she repeated her suspicions about the druids.

"Jerry told me you thought there were druids aboard," Jack nodded. "I'm afraid I thought it unlikely so didn't take him seriously, but it seems you were right."

Paul stared at him and was about to make a comment, but then the short wave radio transmitter he was holding began to report. Orlagh could make nothing of the garbled message but Paul, holding it close to his face, understood every word.

144

Reaching for the telephone on the console unit in front of them, he dialled an internal number and began speaking to Linda in the lab.

"We have casualties inbound so make the med centre ready." He glanced at Orlagh before continuing. "There are two men injured but the third will go straight to the morgue."

The colour drained from her face as she listened to his report and her stomach tightened as her legs went weak. Jack moved closer ready to catch her if she collapsed.

"It's not Jerry." Paul reassured her the moment he had finished with Linda.

"But you said they are injured, how bad is he?"

"I've not yet had a full report, but as soon as he's on board I assure you Jerry will receive the best possible treatment."

This did little to ease her concern, Orlagh was devastated, when was this nightmare going to end?

"We'll know in about fifteen minutes." She hardly heard what he said, but Paul continued. "Go get yourself some strong coffee and wait awhile before going down to the hospital. Let Linda do what she has to do first, and in the mean time I'll cancel your cab. It seems you'll be staying with us for a while longer."

Jack was no longer standing beside her; she had not seen him leave.

"In fact, I think I'll join you for that coffee." Paul said.

He didn't think it right to leave her alone, she looked so pale and miserable. Clearly she was exhausted and he reasoned that she may be in need of company especially as Jerry was about to undergo emergency treatment in their hospital. He knew how serious his injuries were, but for the moment chose to keep them to himself. There was no point in worrying her unnecessarily, besides there was nothing either of them could do for him.

The moment they sat down together in the Wardroom Paul's cell phone began to ring and Orlagh jumped, spilling coffee from her cup.

Paul answered it and after a few moments nodded. "Thanks Linda," he said before disconnecting the call.

Turning his attention to Orlagh he watched as she mopped up the mess with a tissue.

"Jerry is seriously injured," he began and she stopped what she was doing.

"His wounds are no longer life threatening. Linda has managed to stabilise him and now her team are monitoring him. In a little while they will take him into the theatre for surgery, Linda is preparing for that now."

He continued talking slowly and calmly, his rich southern drawl thickening under stress.

#

Several months earlier, the druids had settled in a complex of ancient caves situated on the remote southern coast of Greece. Tribes had occupied these caves during the Neolithic Age and still their spirits could be heard, pockets of energy lingered, especially around their sacred places.

In the 1950s archaeologists came to this area and discovered evidence of mass inhabitation, the ancient people had left clues to their daily lives and routines and there was much excitement amongst the expedition. The cave known as Alepotrypa or 'foxhole' was thought to have been the entrance to the underworld. Local legend insisted that it was here the Greek God Hades ruled.

The druids cave remained undiscovered and until now, only the spirit world and the gods knew of its existence. It was by far the most impressive, its deepest caverns reserved only for the highest priests amongst their order.

A druid stood naked and alone surrounded by darkness, he was chanting a melody known only by those who were closest to the gods. To reach this level of spiritual quest the druid had endured many weeks of hardship.

His voice rose and fell rhythmically, as did the tension in this cathedral like place. Part of this cavern was decorated with plants and small trees in an attempt to create an area of green, a subterranean sacred grove, but although there was plenty of moisture to sustain life, the lack of sunlight soon began to take its toll.

Half crazed with hunger the druid purged himself of every comfort and only when clinging perilously close to the edge of existence was he able to use his heightened powers.

On a carved stone that served as an altar was the symbol of the triquetre. This was a complicated knot of interconnecting circles, three curves forming an alliance and used to symbolise a variety of mythological figures. On this occasion, it was being used to summon the triple Goddess of The Morrigan. This was a powerful deity representing battle, strife and sovereignty. She is often depicted as a trio of goddesses, all sisters and although membership of the triad varies, the most common combinations are Badb, Macha and Nemain.

The Morrigan has been associated with many things, including revenge, the night, magic and prophecy. She has frequently been depicted as standing on a battlefield holding two spears, and it is a well known belief that she will use her magic to gain victory rather than fight battles to win a war.

"The Morrigan, Goddess of War, hear me as I speak." The druid, holding his arms aloft threw his head back and with feverish eyes peered into the darkness. He could feel her presence, but as yet the goddess had not appeared, when she did it would be in the form of a crow.

Orlagh perched nervously on the edge of his bed; she could not take her eyes off him. Held in an induced coma, Jerry was in the ships hospital having undergone emergency surgery and the high tech equipment surrounding him was as intimidating as the thought of almost losing him. The machines were designed to keep him deeply sedated, giving him the best possible chance of surviving his injuries.

Linda had told her there was nothing to worry about, but seeing him like this Orlagh was swept into a vortex of unwelcome emotions. She would be unable to rest until she heard the sound of his voice.

Jerry had suffered a gunshot wound to his chest; the bullet ripping through his lung had deflected from a rib and did not stop until it shattered his scapula. The force of it entering his body had flung him backwards and when he landed; his skull was fractured against some blunt object. This injury was most concerning, but the equipment monitoring his recovery sent a message of hope.

It was too soon to speculate how badly he was injured, an intracranial bleed had been eased by surgery, and now the pressure inside his head was back to normal. Jerry was stabilised, but the next few hours would be critical.

Jack called a meeting. Sitting with Paul and a handful of officers, he outlined his plan.

"I propose we call in Theo Grimaldi, he is more than qualified to help with repairs to the ship." He paused to look around the table. "We have some excellent engineers but with Theo's expertise and equipment it will make the task a whole lot easier."

Paul agreed, as did the officers.

"Do you know where Theo is, Jack?" Paul asked. "How long will it take him to get here?" He was eager to begin work on the repairs.

Theo Grimaldi was a good friend who had helped them out on more than one occasion with specialist equipment and labour. He was one of the best marine engineers in the States and had vast resources at his fingertips.

"He's currently in California but can get here by the day after tomorrow. He assures me that as soon as he's carried out a survey and assessed the damage, repairs can begin."

"It sure will be good to see him again." Paul said and a huge smile split his face. "I had better warn the Quarter Master to stock up on single malt."

The men around the table grinned; Theo's appetite for scotch was legendary.

Jack ticked one item from his agenda and waited for the men to come to order.

"I want Razor and his team out here now," he became serious. "Include Mac as well. I will need him to head up the technical unit, I have a feeling we are going to need their services pretty soon."

"What do you have in mind Jack?" Paul asked with a groan.

"Well old buddy, you know I'm planning to return to the sunken ship in the Sea of Azov." He paused to look at the silent faces around the table. "I'm not convinced the container on that ship holds the Amber Chamber, but there is certainly something of interest there. Mark agrees we must investigate. Kitty picked up some interesting anomalies and having studied the data, I think there is a strong case for us returning to do a spot of prospecting."

He touched a series of keys on the laptop in front of him.

"If you gentlemen would care to watch your screens I'm sure you'll agree."

The monitors set up around the table came to life and each man sat up straighter in their chairs and leaned forward.

The footage was incomplete, only a couple of minutes long it showed Kitty's escape from the hold. The moment the umbilical cord connecting the ROV to the control room in the *Ocean Pride* was cut Mark lost control, but her cameras continued recording and as they watched, all they could see at first was the inside of a rusting hulk. Green algae covered every surface but as soon as Kitty moved close to the container the quality of the film sharpened.

"As you can see," Jack began his commentary. "The container clearly is not as old as the ship; I would have expected to see the same level of corrosion. We are led to believe that it was loaded onto the ship towards the end of World War Two."

Everyone looked up from their monitors waiting for him to continue.

149

"I think someone has gone to a great deal of trouble to make it appear as old as the ship."

"But why would they want to do that?" One of the officers asked.

"Why indeed," Jack replied. "In a moment you will see clear evidence that backs up my claim. Most of the algae covering it is false, a clever camouflage trick to deter the casual observer. Look at the bottom edge of your screen, in a few moments you will see where it has been cleverly grafted to the inside of the ship."

Jack paused allowing the programme time to catch up and as they watched, they could see where Kitty's propulsion system disturbed the layer of sand surrounding the base of the container.

"Well I'll be damned," Paul said. "It sure looks like a watertight seal. Why would anyone want to graft a thing like that to the deck of a ship?" He stared around the table searching for answers.

"It must be a portal of some kind, a watertight hatch system." One of the officers observed.

"Some doorway, just look at the size of that thing."

"It could be a diving chamber, a place for divers to rest." One of the others said.

"Why would they do that?" Paul asked. "The wreck is barely forty feet down."

"Whatever's inside that box, someone wants to keep it dry."

"If it's a hatch or chamber, how much more of the ship is dry?"

"You think it could be an underwater lab or storage facility?"

"Storage for what?" The men looked mystified.

Ideas went around the table and Jack listened to them all.

"Gentlemen," he said after a while. "The only way we are going to find out is by returning to take a look."

The men became silent as they digested what he had just said.

"It may be a Soviet facility left over from the Cold War, but I think it unlikely. It's my belief that it belongs to the Phoenix Legion."

Paul had to agree. "They were sure spooked when we got too close." The memory of the attacking FW190s was still fresh in his mind.

"How do you propose getting close enough to the wreck without rousing suspicion?"

"I've been giving that some thought," Jack admitted. "What we need is a submersible."

"A submersible would need a surface support vessel." One of the men said.

"How do you expect to get it into position without the Phoenix Legion sending out fighter planes or a submarine?" Paul asked and sitting back folded his arms across his chest and waited for an answer.

"Stealth is the key," Jack began. "I say we use an innocent looking fishing boat to get us over the wreck."

Paul and the others frowned but remained silent as they waited for more.

"The Sea of Azov is not very deep in places so a submersible strung beneath a conventional hulled fishing boat would not work. If we used a twin hulled vessel then the sub could be positioned between them, it would be accessible from the deck but remain hidden from the air. I'm sure the Phoenix Legion would keep a close watch on anything in the vicinity."

"We would have to make extensive modifications to a fishing boat and find the right kind of submersible." One of the men said.

"Well," Jack began. "We know fishing boats operate in that area because of the abundance of fish, so that is perfect cover for this operation."

"Where are we going to get the hardware?" Paul was not satisfied with his answer.

"Theo has a submersible and Lewis from The Institute of Nautical Archaeology has offered us the use of a boat. All the mods will be carried out here in Istanbul. Theo assures me it can be done within a few days."

"You seem to have all the bases covered." Paul said but he remained sceptical.

Jack nodded, wondering if it would be as simple as he thought.

Orlagh remained at Jerry's bedside, she could not bear the thought of leaving him whilst he remained in a coma. There was little she could do, intensive care equipment was all he needed, it supplied him with the drug to keep him asleep and all the nourishment his battered body required. She had to be content watching the monitors and listening to the sound of him breathing.

Linda had warned her that it would be like this, time would stand still and she would worry herself silly about how he would be when eventually he woke up.

The extent of his injuries could not fully be determined until he was conscious, there was just no way of knowing how he would react. The pressure inside his head had returned to normal and the scanning equipment registered no abnormal readings. Orlagh would have to remain content, there was no point in worrying every second of the day. She was exhausted, but her overactive mind would give her no peace.

She could not help thinking about the men who had attacked them at the Bazaar. More people could easily have been injured or killed; it was bad enough that one of Jack's men had received a fatal wound. Orlagh felt that it was her fault, and she found it impossible to forgive herself. If only she had not insisted on visiting the Grand Bazaar, perhaps if they had gone straight to the airport then none of this would have happened.

Linda assured her that it had nothing to do with her decision to go shopping. The gunmen would probably have shown up at the airport and caused even more trouble there. Orlagh, pushing these unwanted thoughts aside, thought about the strange dream she had experienced just a few days earlier. She was still trying to work out what it had all been about. Each time she was close to knowing, the realisation was snatched away leaving her frustrated. Perhaps it was nothing more than a crazy dream, but deep down inside she knew that was not true. There had to be more to it, spirits from the Otherworld had made contact with her, she was certain of that, but what she needed to know was why.

Sometimes she could feel the druids close by and the Stave of Yew in her pocket burned as if it were alive. She could feel its power but it was not as strong as the forces that surrounded the Belgae Torc. She could not bear to discard the beautifully carved piece of wood, it seemed the wrong thing to do, but at the same time, she feared what it stood for. Of one thing she was certain, she had to keep it close but she had no idea why.

"How are you feeling?" Linda appeared at the door.

She was no longer wearing her white lab coat and her long dark hair had been shaken loose, now it was hanging neatly around her shoulders. She was dressed in cotton shorts and a pink tee shirt and Orlagh noticed her tan. Linda's long legs and arms were nut brown and she wondered how she managed that after spending so much time shut away below deck in her laboratory.

"I'm okay," she managed a smile.

"You sure?" Linda settled on a chair beside her and crossed her legs. "We'll probably lighten the coma tomorrow." She glanced towards the panel of flashing lights beside the bed.

"I'm sure there will be no issues with bringing him back. I'm pleased with the way he's responding to the treatment."

"How long is he likely to be in here?" Orlagh asked turning towards Linda.

"Probably a week, we don't really know for sure, everyone is different. I like to get my patients moving about as soon as possible once they come out of a coma."

"What about his other injuries, the gunshot wound and broken bones?"

"His chest is clear, there's no sign of infection or internal bleeding and I'm certain his lung will make a full recovery. He will of course be a little short of breath for a while but we'll monitor him very closely. The complication of course is his shattered scapula, he may require surgery to put that right but we'll have to wait and see how effectively he responds to physio."

Linda remained silent for a moment and frowned as if collecting her thoughts, then, she smiled.

"You will have to take care of yourself, when did you last sleep?"

"Oh I'm grand," Orlagh said. "I doze occasionally here in the chair. I don't need a lot of sleep it's not as if I'm running around."

"When did you last have a proper meal?"

"I can't be thinking about food, not with Jerry like this." Her Irish accent became more intense.

"Promise me you'll get some rest, at least have a decent breakfast in the morning. You don't want Jerry to see you like this when he opens his eyes."

Orlagh knew she was right. She would go to her cabin, shower and sleep then eat something before returning in the morning.

The druid stared blindly into the darkness. The magic inside the cave was strong, he could feel it in the air around him and as he stood on the cold damp rock, he shivered. His intonations had become automatic; he no longer needed to think about what he was doing. The Morrigan was near, he was certain of that. She would appear soon and he would need to be prepared.

The Goddess of Hibernia will be pleased. Female energy was pulsating from the rocks and surging forth in waves, it embraced him. Drawing on his inner strength, he turned to face it and he knew he was not alone. Spirits from the Otherworld were waiting patiently for him to join them and soon he would cross over, continue his vigil from the other side, but for now, he would not pass through the thin veil that separated the dead from the living, not until he had seen The Morrigan. She was close he could smell her scent. Spiritual allies had begun to gather, their whispers were becoming more intense and he shuddered.

The following day before the sun had risen fully from beyond the horizon Theo Grimaldi walked up the ramp and stepped on the deck of the *Ocean Pride*.

His first impressions were favourable, the atmosphere surrounding the ship left him feeling good but he was surprised at how easy it was to gain access to the harbour then walk unnoticed onto the ship. Making his way forward, he headed towards the bridge and was shocked to see the scars of battle. It seemed strange that an innocent survey ship had suffered so much savagery.

On the dimly lit bridge, he discovered one whole glass panel missing from the huge windscreen, there were scratches and chips in the paintwork surrounding the digital hardware and some of the systems appeared to be damaged.

Amongst the decreasing shadows, he found his old friend Paul Seymour.

"You must be getting old Captain Seymour!" Theo growled with pleasure.

Paul, startled at first did not recognise the voice or see the man standing in the semi darkness of dawn.

"Your security stinks."

"Theo?" Paul grunted as he became fully awake.

"Sleeping on duty is a punishable offence."

"Theo you old dog," Paul said choosing to ignore his comment. "Where did you spring from?"

Stepping forward Theo embraced his old friend in a bear like grip.

"What have you gotten yourself into?" he said. "And don't tell me it's all Jack's fault."

"You happen to be right there old pal. He promised me he wouldn't so much as scratch the paintwork on my new ship."

"And you believed him." Theo chuckled.

Turning towards the damage on the bridge Paul sighed. "Just look at it."

"We'll soon have it all ship shape, you worry too much."

Paul grinned, he was overjoyed to see Theo.

"Where's all your stuff?"

"That's arriving later." Theo explained. "I have a car at the gate; my driver is dealing with the authorities. I got bored and thought I might as well stroll in, so as you see, I did."

"You'll get yourself arrested one of these days. Could you use some coffee?"

"No thanks, my caffeine levels are sufficient for the moment, besides if I have any more I won't be able to control my ageing bladder."

"Welcome to the club." Paul laughed. "We'll hold off until breakfast time then. Jack sure will be pleased to see you."

"Well before he lifts his weary head from his pillow, fill me in on what's been going on."

Paul told him everything and Theo did not interrupt. When he was finished, a long silence dragged out between them. This gave Theo time to digest what he had been told then he began asking questions.

"You're holed beneath the waterline?"

Paul nodded. "We have pumps running in the moon pool chamber and one of the forward compartments remains sealed. The rest of the damage is to the upper decks, the heli-pad area and the service hangar. We had a fire but most of that's been repaired. Our men have been working round the clock checking out the Sikorsky and ensuring the systems are in order. You know what Jack is like; he loves to get the Sikorsky airborne."

Theo grinned at some happy memory. "I have access to a dry dock just around the coast; it's not far from here and I intend to make use of it. Can we sail as soon as we've had breakfast? I assume the tide is right."

Paul nodded certain that Theo would have studied the logistics of moving the ship.

They talked easily for a while longer and as the sun came up the harbour began to stir. The light intensified and chased away the shadows, this allowed Theo to see the damage more clearly, he was shocked but hid it well.

Orlagh was in the Wardroom loading up a breakfast tray. The aroma of eggs and bacon filled the air and she was surprised at how hungry she suddenly was. Filling a mug with strong coffee, she placed it on her tray before turning to look around. Only one table was occupied but she felt certain the room would soon become crowded and lively. Two men, who had finished eating, were now sharing a joke and it lifted her spirit to hear their cheery voices.

Moving to a table, she sat down before loading up a piece of toast with egg yolk and popping it into her mouth. She savoured the flavour before reaching for her coffee then suddenly Paul appeared with a man she had never seen before. Eyeing him suspiciously, she wondered who he was. He was middle aged and stocky; his skin the colour of burnished leather and a web of creases aged his face. He looked like a man who had spent his life at sea.

The moment Paul saw Orlagh his face was split by a wide grin and he held up his hand in a gesture of friendship.

"Dr Gairne," he said formally, "this is Theo Grimaldi"

They moved quickly towards her table and Theo held out his hand. His grip was powerful and his skin rough.

"Pleased to meet you Dr Gairne, it's always nice to know a pretty looking medic."

"I'm not that kind of doctor." Orlagh grimaced as she recovered her hand.

"Dr Gairne is an archaeologist," Paul explained. He sensed her annoyance but smiled widely.

"Okay," Theo said unaware of her discomfort. "What brings an historian to the *Ocean Pride*?"

"It's a long story."

Paul began to feel awkward; Orlagh looked as if she would rather be alone.

"Let's get some chow before we start gossiping," he suggested and leading Theo away, shot Orlagh an apologetic glance.

They ordered their breakfasts and Paul did his best to steer Theo to another table but he was having none of it.

"Dr Gairne, do you mind if we join you?"

He didn't wait for an answer and pulling out a chair sat down opposite her.

"Please do," she said staring at him.

"So," Theo began, "what period of history is your specialism?"

She got the impression that he was not really interested, this was merely some chat up line.

"The Iron Age," she replied. "You would know it as the Celtic period, but that was a label coined by the Victorians to neatly group a whole host of European tribes and events."

"Interesting," Theo lied. He had no idea what she was talking about but he adored the sound of her voice. Her Irish accent was sending him wild. "Not really my thing, it might be big with you Brits, but to us Americans..." He shrugged his shoulders and grinned.

She wanted to remind him that she was Irish, but chose to forgive his ignorance.

"Dr Gairne is one of Ireland's leading authorities on this period of history." Paul said in an attempt to lighten the atmosphere.

"Is that so?"

"As it happens, it's a fascinating period in our history." Orlagh told him. She was furious at his attitude and was determined to bore him some more. "Technical advances were made throughout the Iron Age, the standard of living improved significantly allowing life expectancy to rise considerably. This was as a result of better living conditions and developing farming techniques." She was satisfied with the effect she was having so she continued. "There was even time for art and culture." She couldn't imagine that he was cultured in any way.

"I can see you are passionate about your subject."

"Dr Gairne was involved with us last year aboard the *Sea Quest*." Paul told him in an effort to change the subject.

"Well I'll be damned, so you're the historian associated with the Belgae Torc."

Orlagh was surprised that he had even heard of the torc.

"I do have some knowledge regarding the Belgae Torc." She told him. Looking at Paul, she smiled. "Look gentlemen, it's been grand meeting you but I really must be going."

As she got up, the men rose to their feet and Paul was sorry to see her go. Theo had not made a positive impression and it disturbed him to think they may have upset her. Theo didn't seem to notice and was soon shovelling food into his mouth. Orlagh had left most of her breakfast on the tray.

Paul wished he could have asked about Jerry but he felt it was not an appropriate subject to be discussing in front of Theo. He would go and find her the moment he was finished and apologise for disturbing her breakfast.

Linda was already there in Jerry's room when she arrived and saw the shadow of concern darken Orlagh's face.

"There's nothing to worry about," Linda reassured her. "I couldn't sleep so thought I'd make an early start. Did you manage to eat something?"

"How is he?" Orlagh ignored her question and moved up beside his bed. She touched his hand gently; he felt warm and was looking much better.

"He's fine. I'm going to start the process of waking him up. As we reduce his medication he should gradually start to regain consciousness."

"I'm sorry," Orlagh said. "I didn't mean to sound so rude. I've just met the most nauseating man in the world and it completely put me off my breakfast."

Linda frowned and wondered to whom she was referring, then moving towards the monitors she began to make adjustments and after a few moments stood back.

"I'll ask for some coffee and cookies to be sent in." She said and turning towards Orlagh thought, she still looks pale and drawn, but she decided to keep her observations to herself.

"Don't expect too much at first," she began and glancing towards Jerry continued. "He's likely to be confused and groggy for a while, he'll probably go back to sleep but this time it will be natural and not drug induced."

"Will he be in any pain?"

"We'll monitor that and administer pain relief as required. I intend to do some more X-Rays; I want a clearer picture of what's going on with his shattered shoulder blade. I also want to scan his skull fracture again. Now the swelling has been reduced we'll have to decide how to proceed."

"What do you expect to find?" Orlagh sounded strained.

"There's nothing to worry about I assure you of that. These tests are routine, it's nothing more than I would do with a depressed skull fracture. A fracture in healthy bone indicates that a substantial amount of force has been applied, this increases the possibilities of associated injuries. Any significant blow to the head results in concussion, I merely want to rule out the possibilities of there being any indirect complications."

"Will you have to operate?"

158

"I don't think that will be necessary. I couldn't find any evidence of broken bone displaced inwards and there was no significant damage to the underlying tissue. He's been a very lucky man, it could have been much worse."

Looking at him now, Orlagh could hardly imagine a worse scenario.

"So, no brain damage then?"

"It's unlikely that any significant damage has occurred. As I said, the tests are merely to confirm my diagnosis. In a few weeks he'll be as good as new."

Reaching out she touched her arm gently with her fingertips, and Orlagh responded. She appreciated the human contact and Linda's straight talking.

XXIV

A shudder ran through the ship as side thrusters turned the gap between the hull and the harbour wall into a mass of angry boiling water. The bow of the *Ocean Pride* swung slowly around until it was pointing into the centre of the harbour, then gradually her engines began to throb and the ship moved towards open water.

Paul and Theo were standing shoulder to shoulder on the bridge and to the casual observer it would be difficult to tell who was in charge. Theo had to remind himself that Paul was captain of this ship.

"We'll secure the ship in dry dock," he was saying, "then we can make a full survey of the damage. Once that's done we will put together a work schedule."

The force of the shells fired from the attacking aircraft had pierced the hull but Paul had no idea how badly his ship was damaged. He had reports sent from the work parties below and from the divers who had carried out the initial checks, but it would not be until they were in dry dock that decisions could be made.

Theo was full of admiration, Paul had done everything possible to save his ship after the attack, watertight doors surrounding the moon pool compartment remained sealed and pumps continued to hold the water at bay.

"Don't look so worried," Theo shot him a glance. "Everything will be fine."

"I was just wondering how long we'll be holed up." He lied.

"Well old buddy, in a few hours time we'll know."

The druid sensed the time was near as he peered blindly into the darkness. He desperately needed something to drink, his throat was burning with the strain of chanting and his mouth was as dry as sand. This was a critical time in the proceedings and he realised that he would never drink another drop, his life was almost at an end and he was about to perform a most important ceremony. His final task was crucial to the continued domination of the druids in the spirit world. Soon The Morrigan will appear beside the goddess of Hibernia and the acquisition of the woman known as Orlagh Gairne will begin. Together they will rage war against the Phoenix Legion and the druids will be free of domination.

160

At first, the sound was faint, wings fluttering gently like gossamer against a velvet sky, and as the druid searched the darkness, he began his final chant. The wings of the Crow Goddess beat louder as The Morrigan appeared, and as his life force began to fade, The Morrigan rejoiced.

Jerry began to stir and moaned loudly as he tried to move but it was as if his limbs were made of lead. His throat was coarse and felt as if it were on fire, each time he tried to swallow it rasped like sandpaper.

The vision intensified and he drew back in alarm as the nightmare threatened to overwhelm him. Jerry had never been so anxious; fear permeated his every fibre leaving him trembling uncontrollably. His stomach tightened, turning to fire that raged throughout his body, it was then he gasped for breath.

The air around him was stirring, it was as if a heavy cloud was moving slowly from across his vision, and as it cleared light began to flood in. He could sense someone or something beside him but still he could do nothing to get away, he was paralysed, unable to move.

Shadows began to lighten and the image of a woman stirred at the edge of his vision. At first, he thought it was Orlagh, but sitting on her shoulder was a huge black bird. Black eyes that were evil flashed as it stared at him, then stretching its wings it flew up into the darkness, uttering the cry of a crow as it went.

Jerry, straining his muscles did his best to move but pain shot through his body. The shock of it made him groan and the sound drew the attention of the woman. He was sure it was Orlagh, but there was something strange about her. She moved towards him and smiled, her emerald green eyes gleaming and her lush red hair swirling around her head like flames. Dark clouds closing in around her did nothing to hide her beauty, her skin was fair and glowing; she was as pale as freshly laid snow. Jerry sighed with relief, Orlagh was safe, she was there beside him and her sweet smile saved him from his darkest thoughts.

He smiled and tried to speak but still his throat refused to work. He wanted to reach out and touch her face, but he was paralysed, a prisoner trapped inside his own body and he wondered if he would ever be able to move again.

The air around her began to clear and he stared as she came closer. Strangely, although the crow had gone he could still feel its presence, an evil atmosphere surrounding them, but suddenly the vision began to change and her beautiful green eyes filled with rage.

161

"I am the goddess of Hibernia," she began to speak. The sound of her voice invading his mind chilled him to the bone.

"Together with The Morrigan we will unite with the woman you call Orlagh Gairne and become one with the spirits of the Otherworld. You and your kind will pay homage to us for all eternity."

Drawing back into the darkness he tried to block out her image, the woman he thought was Orlagh was a charlatan, an evil presence sent to unhinge his mind. Suddenly lights flashed inside his head and white pain seared deep into his brain. He tried to turn away but was held in a vicelike grip and there was nothing he could do to save himself.

The woman's voice was still there inside his head and as he stopped to listen he realised that this time it was different. Gone were the frozen words of loathing, now her voice was soft and filled with warmth. He felt her fingers caress his skin and it was good. Now with the searing light gone, he could see more clearly and there was someone else in the room. At first he could not make out if she were real or merely his imagination, perhaps she was a ghost sent from the Otherworld to torment him.

Jerry cried out.

Orlagh watched as he opened his eyes, he screwed his face up against the light and tried to turn his head away, but then his eyes began to focus and his expression changed; his mouth twisted in terror and he cried out.

"Jerry, can you hear me?" Linda stepped quickly up beside him.

The heart monitor beside his bed was racing and an alarm began to buzz loudly.

"Jerry, my name is Dr Linda Pritchard, you are in hospital."

Orlagh was beside herself, she did not expect him to react like this.

"Talk to him." Linda urged and standing back began to prepare a syringe with a powerful sedative. Inserting the point into the canula in the back of his hand, she began to introduce the mixture into his blood stream and immediately Jerry began to calm down.

"Why does he look so scared?" Orlagh almost cried. She was horrified to see him like this, the expression on his face the moment he saw her was not what she had expected.

"He's probably been having nightmares," Linda explained. "It seems to be a common occurrence with coma patients. He'll be fine in a few moments."

She avoided telling Orlagh that with some patients it had taken years of therapy to overcome the terrible things they had experienced whilst in an induced coma. Researchers still had not worked out why this happens to some people; perhaps it was the drugs used during the procedure.

"I'm so thirsty." Jerry croaked as he became fully awake.

It was the first thing he said and as his dreams began to fade, he looked up and attempted a smile.

"Thank God." Orlagh cried, and wiping tears from her face, she hugged him carefully.

Linda raised the bed using a control pad and as the motor whirred Jerry became more comfortable, then she leaned towards him holding a beaker of cool water.

It was heavenly, the water cooled his throat and quenched his thirst, and with every sip, his strength began to return. When he was finished, he rested his head back against the pillow and started to take stock. His right arm was strapped tightly across his chest and he felt light headed. Every time he moved pain shot through his chest and at one point, he thought he was having a heart attack. His head was throbbing mercilessly and he felt exhausted.

"What happened, where am I?"

"Jerry, my name is Dr Linda Pritchard," she told him again. "You have been involved in an accident." She glanced at Orlagh before going on. "How are you feeling?"

"Like I've been run over by a steam roller. What happened?"

"Don't worry about that right now. You are in hospital on board the *Ocean Pride.*" Linda watched him carefully, gauging his reactions as she fed him information.

"Oh yes," he frowned. "Wasn't the ship damaged, is that how I came to be in here?"

"Not exactly," she told him. "Listen Jerry, I want to carry out a few tests, you have suffered a head injury and I want to see how your brain is functioning."

"Well, best of luck with that." He managed a grin this time. "Is that why I have such a raging headache?"

"Yes, I'm afraid it is. As soon as I've completed my tests I'll arrange for some stronger pain relief. You'll feel better soon I promise."

"Okay Dr Pritchard, whatever you say."

Jack was on the bridge with Paul when the call came in from the hospital.

"Hi Jack it's Linda."

"Hello Doc, what news?"

"Jerry has come round, he's confused and sore but early indications are encouraging."

"That's great news," he said. "How is Orlagh taking it?"

"Very well, I think she is marvellous given the circumstances."

"I'm glad to hear that." Turning towards Paul, he nodded. "Okay Doc, thanks for letting us know, you take care now."

He returned the telephone to its stand before looking up. "Jerry is awake and he's not a dribbling idiot."

"You have such a way with words." Paul replied dryly. He knew that Jack was fond of Jerry and was just as worried as any of them.

As soon as they arrived at the dry dock, the entrance closed behind them and was sealed before a series of hydraulic arms gripped the ship and held it secure. Huge blocks were positioned beneath the keel and when Theo was satisfied, a giant pump house beside the dock began flushing out the water. This was a slow process that would take the rest of the day.

When the hull was finally revealed, the daylight had faded leaving the sky dark. Theo had arranged for powerful spotlights to be positioned around the ship and when they were turned on, he began his survey. The hull had been breached in five places, twice close to the moon pool chamber and the rest towards the bow. Fortunately, the mechanism that operated the moon pool doors was not damaged, the hull not completely breached. Further forward was a different story. Here plates were buckled and cracks ran like spiders webs from the twisted steel. A hole large enough to crawl through had allowed water to flood into the ship, but luckily, Paul was quick enough to order this section to be sealed before the deluge could sweep through the rest of the lower compartments.

With that part of the ship now dry, they were able to access the damage from inside. This area was used for storage and everything was ruined either by the exploding shell or by floodwater. Jack had his men deep clean before the repairs could begin.

"It's not so bad." Theo was telling Paul. "I expected to see more destruction; your ship is very well built."

"Yeah, but it's not designed to withstand exploding cannon shells, there's no armour plating below the waterline."

"As I said before, you worry too much." Theo punched him lightly on the shoulder and chuckled.

Jack joined them on the bridge.

"I'm taking the Sikorsky up with Wings. We're going to Bodrum to see Lewis and collect the fishing boat."

"Okay Jack." Paul replied.

"We'll also be taking a three man crew, they will bring the boat back here," turning to Theo, he asked. "When will your transport be arriving?"

"Fifteen hundred hours tomorrow."

"That's perfect we should be back by then."

Jack was determined to get into the Sea of Azov as soon as possible. He was aware that time was passing them by and with Jerry out of action, his hotline to the Brothers of the Sacred Whisper was temporarily unavailable. He felt sure that Jerry would discover more if only he could get onto the internet, but for now that would have to wait.

"We'll leave for the wreck as soon as modifications to the fishing boat have been made. Dave Fox has some men standing by; I intend to have the sub installed within twenty four hours of its arrival." He discussed his schedule in more detail and Theo made a few recommendations.

It would take Razor and his team a few days to arrive. Jack had no idea yet what role they would play, but of one thing he was certain, they would have to be ready for anything at a moment's notice.

Orlagh was fussing around Jerry.

"Are you comfortable, do you need more pain relief?"

"I'm fine," he told her for the hundredth time. "I feel a little light headed so definitely don't need more drugs."

He had decided not to tell her about his terrible dreams or that he had seen her portrayed as the goddess of Hibernia. She would take it all too seriously and worry about the implications. Her beliefs regarding all things spiritual annoyed him, besides he needed time to work it out for himself. At least now, when he slept, ogres from the Otherworld did not haunt him.

Jack had called in before he left for Bodrum, and Linda had been there to oversee the visit. She did not want him taking advantage by pressing Jerry into service; he required complete rest, besides she had not yet completed all her tests, she knew how persuasive Jack could be.

"As soon as Jerry is able I'll let you know." She promised, and Jack had to be content with that.

Jack flew with Wings and his small team of men into Bodrum Milas airport then they drove the thirty five kilometres to meet with Lewis Philpot at the Institute of Nautical Archaeology.

"Hello and welcome." He said as soon as Jack and his men arrived.

"Lewis." Jack gripped him firmly by the hand. "I sure didn't expect to see you again so soon."

"Quite old boy, do please come in and make yourselves comfortable whilst I order us some tea."

Jack introduced Wings and the others before they sat down.

"So," Lewis began. "I understand you've had something of an adventure."

Jack was certain that Lewis knew nothing about what had happened and he was careful with what he said. He knew that Paul had skirted around the issue regarding the need for a small boat when they had spoken the previous day.

"We have a problem with the ship," Jack began. "Nothing serious, just a few teething problems, but we had to abandon our expedition in the Sea of Azov and make for Istanbul."

"You did locate the wreck?" Lewis was eager to know if they had managed to look inside the container.

"Oh yeah, we sure did. We sent down an eyeball ROV to take a look, that's why we need a small boat. With the *Ocean Pride* out of action for a couple of weeks, a little fishing boat would be perfect. I could of course bring one in from the States, but it's much more convenient to hire one locally."

"I understand Jack."

Paul had been explicit regarding their requirements during their telephone conversation, he insisted on a twin-hulled boat and Lewis knew Jack well enough not to ask too many questions.

"You won't be able to raise the container with such a small boat." He said eyeing Jack suspiciously.

"No of course not. What we aim to do is dive on the wreck and make an attempt to gain access using cutting equipment."

"I see." Now Lewis looked worried.

"We'll take every precaution to protect whatever is inside." Jack didn't want to say any more.

"Well, I have a craft in mind that might suit your purposes. One of my contacts has a 'Workcat' available and I'm sure we can negotiate a sensible hire fee."

Lewis slipped a piece of paper across the table with all the details neatly typed up. There was even a small colour photograph of the boat. Jerry picked it up and studied it.

The 'Workcat' was a twin-hulled craft converted to be used as a fishing boat. It was ten metres long with a displacement of seven tonnes. Its engines produced three hundred and thirty horsepower and the boat was capable of thirty knots. With its long-range capabilities, it suited Jacks purposes admirably.

"We'll need to make certain modifications," Jack told him. "Of course any changes made will be put right before the boat is returned." He pulled a file from his bag.

"If by any chance it's damaged or lost, I will pay a handsome compensation package. I have included all the details."

"My word, you have thought of everything."

"In my business it pays to be organised."

"Tea?" Lewis asked the moment the tea trolley arrived.

"You English and your tea!" Jack grinned.

Wings was intrigued, he loved the sound of Lewis' accent and listened to every word. He watched as he poured tea from a dainty pot into bone china cups sitting in saucers on a silver tray.

Jack was expecting the ritual but it was the first time Wings had experienced anything quite so English. Laid out on a stand was a selection of fancy cakes and the men watched as Lewis helped himself. It did not take them long to dig in, the cakes might look a little 'pink and fluffy', but they made a delicious accompaniment to their tea.

When they were finished, it was time to go to the marina, it was a short distance away so the men piled into the car. There was no room for Lewis so he jumped into his own car and led the way.

"The owner of the boat is away," Lewis told them when they arrived. "The keys are in the package I gave you and he told me to help ourselves."

"He's trusting." Jack remarked.

"It's not a problem; he's a good friend of mine. Tony and I go back a long way, he's also an ex-pat."

Lewis took them along a floating pontoon and at the end they found the boat.

"Yilmaz?" Jack said eyeing the name painted across the bow.

"It means Dauntless." Lewis translated.

"Dauntless sounds good." Wings nodded, admiring the craft.

"Sure looks well maintained." Jack liked what he saw.

The *Dauntless* was spotless, her blue and white paint gleamed in the sunlight and the lifting gear, used to lower the nets into the water, was well oiled. Everything necessary to carry out fishing was stowed in its place.

Wings and the men went all over the boat checking out the systems, ensuring that everything was ready for a voyage.

"The fuel tank is full," Lewis told them. "I insisted that Tony top it up."

"Thanks Lewis." Jack said as he accompanied him back along the pontoon. "We'll let you know what we find the moment we have any news."

He looked over his shoulder and thought for a moment that his co-pilot was going to insist on returning home by sea.

Jerry managed to eat a light lunch, he was still groggy and catnapped constantly, Orlagh would often find herself having a one-way conversation as he dozed off mid sentence.

He was gaining in strength as the drugs used to keep him in a deep sleep wore off and flushed from his system. Linda monitored his progress closely, carrying out her tests until she was satisfied that further surgery would not be necessary. He would begin physiotherapy for his shoulder injury in a few days time, it was important to get the joint moving.

"That's great news," Orlagh said when Linda told her. "I have to admit, he's a lot better than I expected."

"I know," Linda glanced at her sympathetically. "It always looks worse when patients are in a coma and wired up to all sorts of machinery."

Orlagh was looking much better herself; the strain of the last few days had left her drained. At least now, she could sleep.

"I'm so relieved that he has no brain damage, I don't know how we would have coped if that were the case."

"You would have found a way," Linda assured her. "You do realise that Jack will have Jerry working as soon as he's able."

"I know that," Orlagh made a face. "He needs Jerry to do some research using the computer. It's no use me offering to help because I don't have knowledge of the subject he's interested in."

"Well, at least Jack will be away for a while. He's heading back into The Sea of Azov. That at least will give Jerry some time to recover before he starts working again."

Orlagh nodded, she had forgotten all about the container on the sunken ship and had not given the Amber Chamber another thought. For her nothing else mattered but Jerry, she was completely focussed on his welfare and recovery.

She would have to contact Janet at the National Museum, her boss Peter O'Reilly would need to be kept informed. It was unlikely that they would be returning to Ireland at the end of their two week holiday, Jerry's injuries would delay them for the foreseeable future, it would be a while yet before they could consider moving him.

"I would like to keep him here for at least a week," Linda said, reading her thoughts. "I've been assured that the repairs to the ship will not affect us in any way, so we'll assess Jerry after that. If all is well, we can make arrangements to have him transferred to a convalescent hospital in Ireland."

"I must admit, I'm in no hurry to leave," Orlagh said turning towards Linda. "I was a couple of days ago, but now after everything that's happened I feel safe here aboard *The Ocean Pride*."

"Well, it may be just as well," Linda nodded. "Whatever's going on regarding the two of you will probably have blown over by the time Jerry's well enough to leave."

Orlagh hoped that were true. She could not help thinking that trouble was brewing. She could feel the heat rising from the Stave of Yew in her pocket and occasionally when her guard was down, she could feel the druids closing in. She was convinced they were trying to get inside her head and influence her thoughts.

By mid afternoon the following day, Theo's ship carrying the submersible arrived. Modifications to the *Dauntless* had already begun, but she was not yet ready for the sub. All the equipment that Jack and his men would need had been loaded and stowed out of sight, but the only thing holding them up was the ongoing work between the hulls.

"We'll transfer the sub tomorrow," Jack told Theo. "The modifications should be complete by first thing in the morning."

Theo had his ship anchor out in the bay. He wanted it to remain unnoticed, there were a number of freighters lined up waiting to be unloaded, it would not look out of place. Having another ship hanging around the dry dock was not a good idea.

The repairs to the *Ocean Pride* were going well; new plates had been shaped and were being welded into place. Once that was done protective layers of paint had to be applied to the new sections of hull and the ship made ready to put to sea, but that would not take place for at least another ten days.

Theo and Jack made their way towards the Wardroom. They had cleaned themselves up and were both changed for dinner, now they were looking forward to sinking a few beers. At that same moment, Orlagh was in her cabin putting the final touches to her make-up. She had managed to sleep for a couple of hours and was now feeling refreshed. She realised that she was famished, she had not eaten a proper meal for days and was sure that she must have lost weight, the waistband of her skirt felt loose. Studying herself in the mirror, she was finally satisfied then, opening the cabin door, she stepped out into the corridor.

The Wardroom was noisy with men eating and drinking merrily, the atmosphere was relaxed and Orlagh did not feel in the slightest self-conscious as she stepped in amongst them. Tables had been set in sociable groups but there were a few set aside for those who would rather eat alone. During the day, the room was laid out differently with games tables and soft furnishings; it was a place where the men could relax, it was also the only area on board where alcohol was permitted.

Orlagh slipped in unnoticed and picking up a tray she headed towards the counter where chefs waited to carve joints of meat or load plates with mouth watering vegetables. She ordered a vegetarian dish and putting the plate carefully onto her tray went in search of a table. Jack spotted her from across the room and standing up he waved his hand in the air to attract her attention. He gestured madly for her to join him and as she approached his table, she realised too late that he was with Theo Grimaldi.

Groaning inwardly, she arranged a smile on her face before resigning herself to endure his company. There was something about him that she disliked, from the moment they met she had felt it.

"Orlagh," Jack said as the men climbed to their feet. "How is Jerry?" He asked the moment she arrived.

"He continues to do well," she told him guardedly. Linda had warned her to play down Jerry's marvellous recovery rate, especially where Jack was concerned.

"Orlagh," Theo said turning towards her as soon as she had taken her place at the table. "Our introduction the other day was a little formal and I didn't catch your first name."

A waiter arrived with a basket of bread rolls and turning her attention away from Theo, she selected one.

"So, tell me Orlagh, what's the origin of your name?"

She frowned and glanced up at Jack, but he failed to notice her discomfort, so she had no alternative but to reply.

"Orlagh means golden prince or princess. It can be spelt in many different ways and in some countries is used as a boy's name."

"Is that so?" Theo was surprised.

"How are the repairs going?" She asked turning towards Jack. She had no interest in such things but could think of nothing else to say. She was hoping it would draw Theo's interest away from her and reaching for her glass of white wine, sat back in her chair and crossed her legs under the table.

"Everything is progressing well," he said. "This vessel is very well built, so it shouldn't be long before she is ready to go back to sea."

He began eating again, clearly finished with what he was saying, but she was not satisfied.

"I hear that you intend returning to the Sea of Azov."

"That's right," he nodded and swallowed noisily before continuing. "We'll probably be ready to leave sometime late tomorrow evening."

"As soon as that?" She studied him through narrowed eyes. She couldn't help admiring his rugged good looks, he was one of those men who no matter what the situation always looked stylish and in control.

"How long will you be away?" She asked before taking another sip from her glass.

"About a week I guess." He shrugged his shoulders and placed his fork down beside his plate before going on. "The boat we have is quite small so this won't be a salvage operation, more like a reconnaissance mission. There are a number of things I want to check out before deciding how to proceed."

Orlagh nodded and thought about Ed Potterton. He had spent time checking out the wreck so why did Jack need more information?

"So, when will Jerry be back on his feet?"

Orlagh realised that he was fishing for news. Linda had given him a progress report but clearly, he wanted to know more.

"Not for a while yet I'm afraid. It will be a couple of weeks before we can even think about leaving."

Putting down her glass, she leaned forward and picked up her cutlery. She had ignored her plate for long enough and the delicious aromas filling the air was making her feel hungrier than before.

"I will of course have to phone home, I should speak with my boss at the museum. Obviously, I'm going to need some extended leave, I'm certainly not leaving here without Jerry."

"I haven't met Jerry yet," Theo cut in on their conversation. "I've heard a lot about him though."

Orlagh began to eat hoping that he would get the message, but that was too much to hope for.

"How long have you two been together?"

"I've known Jerry for almost two years." She replied, offering no more information than that.

"Two years and no ring on your finger."

"Our relationship is no business of yours." Orlagh glared at him.

Theo could see she was annoyed, her reaction amused him and he couldn't help himself.

"Surely the fellow should make a commitment; he sure would be sore if someone came along and snatched you away."

"I don't think that's likely to happen." She did her best to remain calm; she didn't want him to see that his comment was hurtful.

"Stranger things happen at sea," he continued and reaching for her hand, patted it and shuffled closer.

Orlagh could feel her anger rising. She couldn't believe where this conversation was going and having him in such close proximity appalled her. Taking a deep breath, she moved away from him.

"Jerry is a fine young man," Jack said. He could see that she was upset and did his best to ease the situation. "I'm sure he's well aware of how lucky he is to have someone like Orlagh."

Jack checked Theo's plate. They had just about finished their meal and now was probably a good idea to get Theo back to work. He felt guilty about having to leave, Orlagh looked as if she could do with some company right now, but Theo was obviously not what she needed.

"I'm sure he does, the fortunate young fool."

Orlagh's eyes flashed, she was nearing her limit and Jack, desperate to avoid a confrontation stood up.

"Ah Linda," he said his face filling with relief.

She saw him and moved towards their table. She was surprised to see Orlagh there, but was pleased to see a plate of food in front of her.

"Dr Pritchard." Theo said rising to his feet. His body language was welcoming and Jack knew that he would love to remain and entertain both women.

Seeing an opportunity to steer him away, Jack slipped his hand under his elbow and made their excuses and reluctantly Theo allowed himself to be steered away.

"Thank you for that." Orlagh sighed with relief. "I don't like that man."

"I know what you mean," Linda replied as she slipped into the chair that Jack had just vacated. "He does seem a little creepy but he's very popular amongst the crew."

They waited in silence as a steward approached their table and efficiently cleared away the empty plates.

"He's so blunt and rude he doesn't seem to care what he says." Orlagh continued the moment he was gone. "I wonder if he's like that with all women."

"I get the impression that he's a typical chauvinistic pig," Linda nodded. "I sure wouldn't want to find myself alone with him."

Orlagh shuddered at the thought and changed the subject. "Are you starting physio with Jerry tomorrow?"

They began to relax and chatted easily. Linda ordered her meal as a waiter stopped by their table, and she was happy to see that Orlagh had managed to eat something. The last thing she wanted right now was another patient alongside Jerry in her small hospital.

A man dressed in the uniform of a harbour security guard stepped out of the shadows. He wandered along the dry dock and had a perfect view of the repairs that were going on. Taking his time, he acted like a man bored with his duty, but all the while, his mind was alert as he began to estimate the size of the work party. He was surprised at how efficient the engineers were, it was almost midnight and still work was continuing.

He decided they must be working shifts and it was his responsibility to observe their patterns, he would have to estimate the size of the operation and report back to Schiffer.

Jerry found the first session of physio exhausting. Linda started gently and releasing his arm from its sling, manipulated his shoulder. As his arm moved, it seemed as if the bones were grating together and Linda, probing with her fingertips, pushed fragments back into place.

Jerry grimaced each time she moved his arm and Orlagh, standing helplessly beside his bed did her best to encourage him. She wished that Linda would increase his pain relief, but she knew he hated taking medication.

"That's good." Linda said encouragingly as she released her grip. She gauged his willingness to move his arm unaided before folding it back across his chest then Jerry breathed a sigh of relief.

"That's it for now," she smiled. "There's more movement there than I anticipated. I want to change the dressing on your chest wound then I think we're done here."

Snapping on a pair of surgical gloves, Linda pulled a trolley loaded with supplies closer to the bed.

"There's still no sign of infection," she told him once the dressing had been removed and, cleaning dried blood from around the wound, she applied another sterile dressing. "I'll reduce your intake of antibiotics; once you've completed the course I don't see the need for more."

"Good." Jerry grunted.

His face was pale and pinched and Linda noticed Orlagh's expression.

"Don't worry," she touched her arm gently. "He's much stronger than you give him credit for."

"But his injuries are..."

"Not as bad as they look." Linda interrupted.

"I'm glad you think so Doc." Jerry groaned theatrically.

"Get some rest and we'll have another go later. It's important that we get some movement going through your shoulder."

"Whatever you say Doctor Pritchard." Jerry looked at her and grimaced. He realised that he was going to have to endure a lot more pain before he would feel the benefits, he also knew that he was very lucky to be alive.

The modifications to the *Dauntless* were almost complete and the submersible was being transferred from Theo's supply ship. A docking system had been fitted between the hulls where the sub would sit, and a hatch situated under cover in the forward cabin would allow access. Anyone watching the fishing boat would be completely unaware of the submersible or the men coming and going. They would of course have to be cautious, a four man crew was necessary to run the boat and with Jerry and Wings Wallace on board, only four men could be seen on the deck at any one time.

Jack was under no illusions, even though they were acting as a legitimate fishing vessel, he was sure they would come under surveillance the moment they arrived in the area where the wreck was situated.

His plan was to fish a grid pattern that would take them close to the wreck. The *Dauntless* would innocently turn away and fish in the opposite direction, returning every hour to begin the pattern all over again.

Jack felt sure this would be enough to cover their tracks. As soon as they arrived, he intended to launch the submersible. He would have the opportunity to rendezvous with the fishing boat each time it completed its run, and if anyone intercepted them all they would see is a fishing boat going about its business.

Jack was happy with his plan it was simple and seemed watertight, now all he had to do was get the submersible coupled up between the hulls then carry out a few tests before getting underway. Supplies had been loaded and having thought of all eventualities, extra equipment was stowed into every available space.

That night Orlagh was unable to sleep. Images of druids found their way into her dreams and at times, she was convinced they were actually in the room with her. She could feel the goddess of Hibernia nearby, but she was yet to show herself. Orlagh put that down to Madb and her animal allies, she was certain they were looking out for her, protecting her from the evils of the spirit world.

Madb was often there beside her and sometimes Orlagh caught a glimpse of her, but each time she turned her head Madb was gone. She had only ever seen them clearly once, Madb the young woman with Madadh-allaidh the wolf and Sailetheach the magnificent stag. That had been during a sacrificial ceremony on the island of Gog. The goddess of Hibernia had been there waiting for the moment of her death, and it was then that Orlagh had felt the full force of the Belgae Torc.

The Stave of Yew remained at her bedside. It was such a beautiful thing, carved with mysterious Ogham characters that she had not yet been able to decipher. She thought it was maybe a symbol of evil and nothing good would come of it, but she could not bring herself to part with it. It should have been tossed overboard the moment she discovered it, but she was curious to know how its magic worked. It was a direct link with the druids, and by learning more about it perhaps she could turn its power against them.

She had done what she could to protect herself using charms and chants she had learnt during her dream quest. Cernunnos, lord of the forest, had guided her and the shaman had shared his knowledge. Her only regret was not being able to spend more time there and discover more about the wisdom of that enchanted place.

Rolling over she sighed and closing her eyes tried to clear her mind of such thoughts, but it was no good, she was beyond sleep and her mind refused to rest. Turning on the bedside lamp, she groaned and screwed up her face against the light then sliding her legs over the side of the mattress, searched for her clothes. The only way to exercise the demons inside her head was to go and get some fresh air.

The world was still and warm as she stepped out onto the afterdeck and looking up she gasped with wonder. The sky was a mass of sparkling gems, and stumbling towards the rail, she looked out towards the horizon. The moon remained hidden behind a glittering curtain of midnight blue, but it hardly mattered, the glow from the stars was sufficient to cast a stunningly ethereal light over the world. Orlagh tried to count the galaxies, but there were not enough numbers in the world to tally the balance.

When at last she was able to look away, she realised how strange it was to be standing on the deck of a ship that was surrounded by land. The huge doors holding back the sea sealed the dry dock and although unable to see it, she knew the ocean was there. Leaning against the rail, she allowed her thoughts to run riot, going over in her mind what they had done since their arrival. Their holiday had not turned out as she expected. She could never have imagined that it would be like this; two weeks exploring the ancient cities of Anatolia seemed harmless enough, but then she had not anticipated running into Jack Harrington. From that moment, their holiday had been turned on its head.

"Good evening golden princess."

A voice startled her and turning towards the sound, she discovered Theo Grimaldi standing beside her. The rail dug into her back as she pushed against it and she realised with annoyance that she was trying to get away from him, so standing her ground she refused to move.

"Good evening to you." She said after composing herself.

"What brings you out this night?" He asked, and balancing his elbows on the rail, exhaled noisily.

He was so close that she could smell the drink on his breath; he had also been smoking a cigar.

"I couldn't sleep," she told him, "how about you?" She didn't really want to know, but could think of nothing else to say.

"Oh, just out doing my rounds." He glanced down over the side but the curve of the hull obscured his view.

They could hear the sounds of men working in the pit beneath the ship, but they could see nothing of them.

"I always have a stroll before turning in." He was aware of her standing beside him; the scent of her skin was driving him wild. He thought her a very beautiful woman.

Orlagh realised he was scrutinising her and it made her feel uneasy. Gripping at the rail, she could detect movement at the edge of her vision and thought that she could hear someone whispering her name, but she couldn't be sure. Was it real or just her overactive imagination? She resisted the urge to look.

"It sure is a fine night."

Once again, the sound of his voice unnerved her, it drove away her thoughts and forced her to look up at the stars.

"It reminds me of Ireland," she said, surprised at the way she was willing to confide in him. "When you go up into the mountains surrounding Dublin you rise above the light pollution from the city, then you can see all the stars in the sky. Jerry and I sometimes go up there at night to look down on the River Liffey. It appears like a darkened thread running through the city, broken only by the bridges, and occasionally you can see lights from the municipal building reflecting in the water. If you look closely, you can even see aircraft coming in and out of the airport."

Listening intently, he found the sound of her accent fascinating.

"You make it all sound idyllic." Theo, moved by her description was drawn even closer to her. "Listen," he said his voice barely a whisper. "Perhaps whilst your man is laid low I might help you out, you know, a little male company." Reaching out he laid his hand on her arm.

Orlagh was appalled by his touch, the meaning of his words were clear and she could hardly believe that he would have the nerve to suggest such a thing.

"I think you must have had a little too much to drink."

"That might be so," he replied, "but it's never been a problem."

Orlagh was speechless, she had never been spoken to like this before and cursed herself for being so open with him. She should never have mentioned stargazing with Jerry.

"I think I'll go in now, it's very late."

"I'll accompany you to your cabin."

"That won't be necessary," she told him firmly. "I'm more than capable of finding my own way."

For a moment, she was sure he was going to insist, he was a huge man and she would be defenceless against him if he chose to become violent, but fortunately the lust light faded from his eyes and he removed his hand from her arm.

"As you wish." He said and turning away stared out into the darkness.

Orlagh's heart was racing, she wanted to run across the deck, get away from him as fast as possible, but resisting the urge, she walked as calmly as she could towards the steel door and pulling it open slipped into the corridor beyond.

Once inside her cabin she stood with her back against the door and looking up at the ceiling, wished that Jerry were there with her. She felt so alone and vulnerable, and now that Grimaldi had made such a blatant pass at her, all she wanted to do was to go home.

Later the voices returned. At first, they were merely whispers but soon gained in intensity. With her confidence levels low, she had let her guard down and now the druids had found a way in. She would have to be more careful, remain alert, use her strength to keep them out, but their magic was strong. The goddess of Hibernia was behind them, she had given them her full support and there was little Orlagh could do against them.

Schiffer received the report from his agent posing as a security guard and having studied the information was able to decide what to do next. He would have to be more careful this time, his previous attempts to grab the girl had ended in failure, but at least he was in possession of the Belgae Torc.

His men on the ground in Istanbul had failed him, it had been unwise to engage in a street battle and killing the druid had definitely been the wrong thing to do, there was bound to be repercussions.

Bringing his hand down sharply on his desktop, he stood up. He knew exactly what to do and was determined to put his plan into action immediately.

Just over twenty four hours later the *Dauntless* arrived at its destination. The Sea of Azov was mill pool calm and three men on deck were preparing to begin a day's fishing. In no time at all they had their nets ready to go over the side and the boat was set on a course that would bring them close to the wreck. In the space between the hulls, Jack and Wings were already in the submersible.

"Stand by Jack." The man in the cockpit spoke calmly into a tiny microphone fixed to the peak of his cap.

The *Dauntless* did not have a traditional wheelhouse; the cockpit was high tech and resembled the flight deck of an aircraft. Where the wheel should have been was a tiny joystick, and beside that, a sonar screen. Beneath the joystick was a panel that linked directly to the engine and overhead was the communication and navigation equipment.

The sonar was used for spotting and tracking shoals of fish, but on this trip, it would prove useful for locating the precise position of the wreck. A powerful computer linked all these systems together and from a single control panel, the skipper could monitor everything simultaneously. The computer could also monitor the system that controlled the boat and, once everything was set, it worked like an autopilot.

The man in the cockpit began speaking clearly into his microphone counting down from five, his eyes fixed on the computer screen as his hand hovered over the release mechanism. Once operated this would launch the submersible, setting it free from its cradle between the hulls.

"Okay Jack, Bon Voyage!" He said as he pulled the lever. "Be sure to send us a postcard."

"Roger that control," he replied.

On board the submersible, Jack and Wings were strapped into their seats and every bit of space around them was packed with equipment. The instrument panel glowed dimly and the whole thing resembled the cockpit of a space shuttle.

Pushing the little joystick forward, Wings steered the sub into a shallow dive and as soon as they cleared the twin hulls, he checked the depth gauge. There was just under fifteen metres beneath them and, controlling their rate of descent, he glanced at Jack.

"Forty two feet," he said doing a mathematical conversion, then turning his attention to the sonar screen in front of him he made a course correction.

He was amazed at how responsive the little sub was; he did not expect it to react so well. It was just like an aircraft and the similarities were comforting. Apart from the display systems, the world beyond the cockpit was three-dimensional, the depth of water similar to flying at altitude. He was aware of the attitude of the sub; it would pitch, roll and yaw just like an aircraft and he liked the feel of it. The pump jet propulsion system relied on water forced at high pressure through turbine-like engines and it was proving to be a very effective drive unit. The grin on his face was as wide as it could go and as he surveyed the instrument panel, he could hardly stop himself from laughing.

Jack knew that Wings would appreciate taking the controls. He had designated him pilot of the sub and insisted he study the manual before climbing into the pilot's seat.

Gradually as they went deeper, the colour of the water began to change. The light was fading fast but powerful spotlights situated on the nose of the sub illuminated the way ahead, although visibility was good with the lights on low power, Wings relied on his instruments to guide him.

As the bottom came up, he levelled off and peered through the canopy that domed above their heads. Here they could see only a few metres ahead so Jack increased the power of the spotlights and suddenly they had a perfect view of the smooth sandy bottom. The water temperature was holding steady at twenty four degrees Celsius, it was only two degrees lower than the air temperature at the surface. Because of the shallow character of the sea, the temperature usually lowers only by a few degrees with depth.

Wings stared through the canopy in wonder. He had never experienced anything like this before. Usually when diving, it was into a very cold and dark environment. He had once snorkelled in tropical waters and this reminded him of that.

Natural light permeated the strange world around them, this encouraged algae and plankton to cloud the water. Because of this low transparency, it was unable to sustain much in the way of plant life and bottom development was poor, very little would grow, hence more algae and plankton. Despite this, it still reminded him of a lagoon, aquatic life was abundant and because of the food available, it was a perfect place for fish.

"What have we here?"

The sound of Jack's voice disturbed his thoughts.

"Look at the way the sea bed has been disturbed."

The Sea of Azov is uncomplicated with sand covering most of its bottom. It is like a huge bowl, shallow around the edges gradually becoming deeper towards the middle. Tides and the gentle movement of the water rippled the profile they were following, but Jack had noticed a changing aspect. It was as if a storm had disturbed the bottom and the further they went the worse it became.

"Look at the way the sand has been churned up," he said. "Bring her up a little and turn the spotlights onto full power."

The submersible rose up and as the beam of light increased in intensity, they were able to get a panoramic view of the disturbed area. It seemed to be radiating out from a central point which lay somewhere ahead.

"It reminds me of a huge moon crater," Wings said. "Something pretty big must have hit the bottom."

Jack shot him a sideways glance. "Just like ripples on the surface of a lake."

"I like that analogy Jack." Wings nodded appreciatively.

Jack knew exactly what they were looking at and the moment they came upon the wreck his suspicions were confirmed. The container was gone and in its place was a gaping hole. The wreck had been blasted in two by the force of an explosion and debris lay in every direction.

"That must have been some blast." Wings said.

"Yeah," Jack agreed. "Lewis was wrong though, the container couldn't have held the Amber Chamber. There's no evidence of that in the debris field, in fact there's not much left of anything."

Wings brought the submersible to a standstill and hovering above the wreck, the spotlight directed over the hole left in the seabed.

"Someone has gone to great lengths to prevent us from discovering what was inside that container."

Wings had studied the film taken by the Eyeball ROV, he had seen the way the container was sealed to the deck of the ship. Something very interesting was going on here and he could hardly wait to solve the mystery, but now it seemed they were too late and all the effort had been for nothing.

"What's that?" Jack said moving his face closer to the canopy. "We'll need to get out there and take a closer look."

The submersible was fitted with an emergency escape hatch that could be used as an air lock allowing divers to come and go. The small chamber would accommodate one man at a time; it prevented water from entering the sub once the hatch was open. They were already wearing diving suits; Jack had anticipated some extra vehicular activity and had air tanks stowed for the occasion.

"I'll just park this thing and set the computer to babysit mode."

Wings was as excited as a schoolboy and began feeding commands into the computer.

XXVIII

Schiffer, accompanied by two of his men, walked up the ramp leading from the edge of the dry dock and strode onto the deck of the *Ocean Pride*. Their movements were relaxed and full of confidence and dressed like members of the crew it was as if they were returning from an extended shore leave. Once on board they put their bags down and made their way towards the rail to peer over the side. Their interest in what was happening over the side was staged, an act for those who might be watching.

Each man was familiar with the layout of the ship, having studied plans they could find their way around in the dark. They knew exactly what was expected of them, nothing could be allowed to go wrong, besides, Schiffer himself was amongst them.

Orlagh left her cabin and made her way directly to the hospital. She had not slept well again and was now feeling exhausted. Her mind gave her no peace, it kept on going over events and she found it impossible to relax.

Jerry seemed much stronger today; he was out of bed and on his feet and when she arrived Orlagh was surprised to see him up and about.

"Jerry, what are you doing out of bed?" She said standing in the doorway.

"Linda is a slave driver," he sighed and glanced towards her seeking sympathy.

"Don't be such a baby," Orlagh smiled. She was overjoyed that his sense of humour had returned. Moving towards him, she kissed his cheek gently. "I'm sure she knows what she's doing."

Jerry grunted and easing himself down into a chair, studied her. She had made an effort to conceal the dark rings around her eyes, but it did not fool him.

"You're not sleeping very well." He said after a while.

"No, I'm afraid not."

"Why is that?"

"There's too much going on inside my head, I don't get a moments peace." Touching the side of her head with her fingertips, she screwed up her face.

184

Jerry was concerned. Little by little, his memory was returning and he was beginning to fill in the gaps. He remembered about how worried she was about the druids being aboard the ship. He could also remember talking to Jack about her concerns, but he had no idea what happened after that.

"When I was unconscious," he began, "I had the most horrendous nightmare."

She looked at him and could see that he was struggling to find the right words. Linda had already warned her about this, she said this was common, coma patients often reported experiencing nightmares.

"I seemed to lurch from one dreadful experience to another; it was a never ending round of torment. It was by far the worst thing I've ever experienced."

Moving towards him, she covered his hand with her own, and squeezing his fingers softly urged him to continue. He looked so miserable and all she wanted to do was wrap him up in her arms and soothe him, but with his arm strapped tightly across his chest and his head bandaged with what looked like a turban she thought it wise not to be so physical.

"One moment I was in a cave where a druid was chanting, the darkness was complete; it was as if I were blind. I was so cold and all the time I could feel the wings of something huge flapping soundlessly around my head."

Orlagh held onto his hand doing her best to ground him in the present.

"I think that I received a warning of some kind," he continued, turning his head so he could see her better, "but I can't remember what it was about." His brow furrowed deeply as he screwed up his face. "I'm pretty sure it must have been important, all I have to do now is work out what it was."

Closing his eyes, he became silent then, opening them wide he stared at her.

"It was a horned shaman, he came from the Otherworld."

Orlagh was surprised at his outburst, Jerry did not believe in that kind of thing and was always ridiculing her for her beliefs.

"Why would he appear to you?" she asked. "You don't believe in all that spiritual stuff."

Ignoring her comment, he went on. "I saw Madb and she was exactly as you described her."

"Don't you think that is why she looked the way she did, surely my

185

description was lodged away in your brain somewhere and you simply remembered what I told you."

"I also saw the goddess of Hibernia." He said in a small voice. "At first I thought it was you."

She stared at him and resisted the urge to shudder. His mentioning the goddess brought back unwelcome memories that she would rather forget. Her animal allies began to stir, she could feel them drawing in around her, and taking comfort from their presence, she listened to what Jerry had to say.

"She looked exactly like you, the same lovable face, beautiful green eyes and flame red hair." A smile crossed his face and he closed his eyes as if to hold onto the memory.

"She moved so provocatively and she completely took me in. I was convinced that it was you but after a while, I began to feel uneasy. I could sense evil surrounding her and as it became more intense, I was suddenly aware that people had died to give her strength." Jerry paused and his breathing became ragged. Orlagh could feel the stress rising from him.

"She is like some kind of parasite feeding off the lives of others and the more she takes, the stronger she becomes," he continued. "I could feel her trying to get inside my head; she wanted to feed off me, like a vampire sucking the blood from the living."

"That's what it feels like to have the torc around your neck." Orlagh whispered.

The atmosphere inside the room changed, fear and uncertainty filled them with some kind of archaic belief. Talk of the goddess and the torc left them both feeling uneasy and despite herself, Orlagh began to believe that Jerry had really experienced these things, even though logic told her that it was simply a fantasy fuelled nightmare brought on by the drugs used to keep him in a coma.

Linda breezed into the room.

"My word," she exclaimed. "You two look as if you have just been to a funeral, why the sad faces?"

Orlagh stood up and running her hands over her arms attempted to banish the chill that had seeped into her bones.

"We have just been discussing what to do next."

Linda shrugged her shoulders and moved across the room, she didn't believe a word of it.

"You look awful," she told Orlagh bluntly. "Are you sure you're okay?" Reaching out she touched her shoulder with her fingertips.

"I'm not sleeping very well."

"Would you like me to prescribe something to help with that?"

"No," Orlagh shook her head and glanced towards Jerry. "How is he doing?"

"Well, as you see, we have just finished a gruelling physio session," she grinned, "and he didn't stop moaning throughout."

"Jerry doesn't like going to the gym, he would rather go to the library instead." Orlagh smiled and Linda was happy to lighten the mood.

"I can hear you both," Jerry butted in. "I hope you are not conspiring to join forces and gang up on me."

"Now why would we do that?" Linda laughed.

"Well, you know, a defenceless fellow like me."

"Oh you poor thing, are you feeling vulnerable in the presence of two glamorous creatures like us?"

They laughed together and Orlagh appreciated what Linda was doing.

"Jerry," Linda said becoming serious. "If you need more pain relief you must let me know. I'm going to change your dressings now then you must rest. I'm also planning some more physio later, but don't worry, this time I will focus on light muscle stretching. Think of it as a yoga session."

Jerry closed his eyes and tried to imagine the scene, he was about to make a comment but then thought better of it.

The women left the room and went next door into the little pharmacy.

"He really is doing well," Linda insisted. "I'm very pleased with his progress, he is responding to treatment and his physical injuries are healing nicely."

Linda pulled a box of sterile dressings from a shelf and transferred them to a tray.

"My main concern was the state of his wounds; a body fighting infection takes a lot longer to heal."

"Your main concern," Orlagh said, picking up on Linda's statement.

"Well," Linda turned to look at her. "The other thing is his mental health. With a brain injury all kinds of complications can occur. Jerry has been very lucky, there doesn't appear to be any long term issues, but I'm a little worried about his state of mind."

"What do you mean?" Orlagh frowned.

"He's going to be confused and will probably display a loss of memory, but some patients who have been placed in an induced coma can suffer from very deep psychological problems during the weeks following recovery."

Orlagh stared at her and thought about what Jerry had said earlier. She knew he was not himself, but given the circumstances that was hardly surprising.

"Of course, I expect him to be a little depressed," Linda continued. "It's a natural reaction to the injuries he's suffered. All I'm saying is be aware of his moods, he will be very low at times and will need our help with keeping his spirit up."

Orlagh nodded but remained silent.

"I'm also a little concerned about you." Linda's expression softened.

"Oh, don't worry about me, I'm okay really. I just want Jerry to get better so we can go home."

"Of course you do and that will happen soon. Just focus on keeping him occupied, but don't forget about what I said, I really can give you something to help you sleep."

"Thank you Linda, you are so kind."

They hugged then Linda gathered up what she needed and went to make Jerry more comfortable.

Jack and Wings left the submersible and pushed away from the airlock. They made their way slowly towards the remains of the wreck and with some basic tools began to excavate a hole in the centre of the crater.

"There's some kind of tunnel down here," Wings said as he brushed more of the sand away.

They were soon moving lumps of rock and, digging deeper, the water around them became thick with silt. It was like working in a fog and after a while it became impossible to see so they were forced to take a break, allow it to settle before they could continue.

Jack was certain the tunnel they had found was not natural, the walls were too smooth, its shape too regular. It was obviously man made and he could make a pretty good guess as to who had dug it.

From the mouth of the tunnel, it disappeared into the seabed at an angle of about thirty degrees then after a short distance, they encountered a barrier.

"It's been sealed," Jack said. "There must be a dry tunnel on the other side. I knew that container was a docking system of some kind."

Wings, squeezing up beside him, was amazed to see a steel door materialising out of the gloom, and running his hand over it he brushed away a few remaining pockets of sand.

188

"Whoever destroyed the container didn't want to completely ruin everything. I wonder what's behind that door."

"I can't help thinking the same," Jack said.

Checking it out thoroughly he took particular interest in the seal that ran between the wall of the tunnel and the edge of the door. Passing his hand over the smooth surface, he studied the wall and wondered what kind of equipment had been used to bore into the rock. Whilst he worked, he thought about how they were going to get beyond the door. An idea was beginning to formulate in his head but first he wanted to check something else.

One of Schiffer's men stationed himself outside Orlagh's cabin. In his hand, he held a short wave radio and was in communication with his colleagues. He also carried a small laptop computer. It was his job to report when Orlagh returned to her cabin; this would set off a chain reaction of events that should result in a successful mission.

In the Sea of Azov, Jack and Wings returned to the *Dauntless*. They had to wait for it to complete its fishing run, turn, then make its way back before they could rendezvous. A couple of hours later they were back in the submersible waiting to be released once again over another section of the ocean.

The depth beneath them was no more than thirty metres and their target was towards the end of its run. As the boat was about to make its turn, the skipper spoke into the tiny microphone.

"Release in five, good luck Jack."

Inside the submersible Jack and Wings listened as the seconds counted down then with a sudden lurch the sub was cut loose.

"I have control," Wings said calmly as his fingers tightened round the joystick.

Pushing the power thrusters forward, he angled the nose down into a shallow dive and the sub slipped easily into the depths. After a few seconds, he levelled off and using the instruments, steered towards their target.

"I'm sure looking forward to seeing this." He glanced at Jack who was checking the sonar screen.

Wings had seen the video footage of the FW190 attack, but he had not seen them for real. At the time of the attack, he had been in the workshop fighting the fire that swept through the Sikorsky hangar. If it was not for his quick thinking and bravery the damage to that part of the ship would have been much worse, they may even have lost the helicopter.

"What's this?" Jack said suddenly.

Like before the smooth sand, which made up the seabed, had been disturbed. This far out from their target the disturbance was minimal but as they drew nearer it became progressively worse.

"Coming up on co-ordinates now," Wings told him and Jack activated the spotlights.

Shedding their forward motion, Wings reversed the flow of the thrusters until they were at a standstill, then hovering over the spot where the FW190 had crashed they stared down in disbelief.

"Just like the container," he whispered his voice laced with disappointment. "There's not even a souvenir large enough to hang on my wall. Now why would they do that?"

"By destroying the evidence there's nothing left to incriminate them." Jack told him. "We could probably have measured the fuel tank, work out how much fuel it carried, that would have given us an idea of its range. From that we could have discovered how far away their base was."

"Even if it had used drop tanks to get here, there would have been sufficient fuel to get it home." Wings nodded.

"Exactly, but now we have nothing."

Jack sent out a coded message alerting the *Dauntless* that they would be waiting at the rendezvous point and Wings, turning the sub sharply, steered a course back towards the surface.

Orlagh remained with Jerry, talking quietly until he drifted off to sleep. He did this at least three times a day and she was getting used to his routine. He seemed to be exhausted all the time and the physio sessions were making it worse, she also suspected the drugs that Linda was giving him were partly to blame.

"It won't be long before Jerry feels less tired," Linda assured her as they left the hospital. "For now sleep is good for him, it's a great healer, you should try it yourself. Why don't you try to nap during the day; that might be the answer especially if you are having trouble sleeping at night."

"I think I'll give it a go." Orlagh agreed. "I'm going back to my cabin now."

"I've got to go and track down Paul. I haven't seen him around for a few days now."

"I guess he's busy what with the repairs going on." Orlagh shot Linda a glance as they turned yet another corner. "I bumped into that slime ball Grimaldi the other evening." She confessed.

"You don't like him much, I can tell." Linda smiled. She stopped walking and turned towards Orlagh before going on. "Neither do I as it happens, he gives me the creeps."

"He made a pass at me."

"What, when?" Linda reached out towards Orlagh.

191

"It was the other night. I couldn't sleep so I went out on deck for some fresh air."

"What did he say?" Linda looked shocked but wanted to know all the details.

"Well," Orlagh made a dismissive gesture in an attempt to play it down. "He offered me his services seeing as Jerry is out of action."

"No, really?" Linda gasped. "Damn cheek, what did you say? I guess you gave him a hard time."

"No, not really, I just told him in no uncertain terms that I wasn't interested."

"Poor you," Linda made a face. "I would have been mortified if he'd come onto me like that. I would have a word with Paul if I were you."

"No, I don't want to make a fuss, I've caused enough trouble already, besides, I can handle it."

"None of this is your fault." Linda told her. "You have enough to worry about without having to fend off unwanted attention."

"He had been drinking and was obviously feeling amorous; I was probably in the wrong place at the wrong time. Maybe I shouldn't have been out on my own at that time of night."

"Don't you dare think like that," Linda was annoyed. "This is a safe ship and you definitely should not have to restrict your movements because of someone like him."

Orlagh nodded, she did not want to think about Theo Grimaldi anymore, and Linda saw her expression change.

"Okay, you just take care and get some sleep."

They went their separate ways and Orlagh made her way back to her cabin.

The man on surveillance duty radioed a message to Schiffer the moment Orlagh appeared and their plan was put into action. The third man in their team was on his way to the hospital and when he arrived, he found Jerry sleeping. Setting up his webcam, he linked it into his mini laptop before turning the camera towards Jerry. When he was satisfied, and he had a clear image, he whispered a codeword into the microphone clipped to his lapel then in another part of the ship Schiffer knocked on the cabin door.

Orlagh opened it and almost collapsed with shock, Schiffer was the last person she expected to see standing there.

"It's nice to see you again Dr Gairne, may I come in?" Stepping forward he forced his way into her room.

"What do you want?" She managed as she pulled herself together. "What are you doing here?"

The other man accompanying Schiffer closed the door behind them and ignoring her began to set up his laptop on her bed.

"How dare you barge in here, what do you think you are doing?" Her initial shock was turning to anger.

"That will become apparent in a moment." Schiffer replied coldly, eyeing her with distain.

His frosty stare and guttural accent unsettled her and slowly she backed away. The laptop on the bed came to life and the man made some adjustments using the keyboard. An image of Jerry appeared on the screen and Orlagh gasped with disbelief, then moving closer she could see him more clearly.

"You will do as you are told or I will have Mr Knowles killed."

The tone of his voice left her in no doubt that this was no idle threat and as she watched, a man appeared beside Jerry brandishing a syringe.

"As you can see," Schiffer continued calmly. "If you don't do precisely as I say I will order his death."

Orlagh felt her legs go weak and staggering backwards fell against the wall. Reaching out she placed her hand on the bedside table for support and could hardly believe what was happening.

"What do you want?" She managed, her voice sounding strange to her ears.

"You," Schiffer simply said. "We are going to leave now and in exactly five minutes you will join us behind warehouse number three on the quayside beside the ship. You will speak to no one and you will come alone. Is that clear?"

Orlagh remained speechless; her brain hardly had time to comprehend the implications of what he had just said.

"Is that clear?" He said louder this time.

Orlagh, startled into reality nodded but remained silent.

"Good." Schiffer said. "See you in five minutes." Glancing at his watch, he nodded to his companion then they turned and left the room.

Orlagh remained frozen to the spot. Her first reaction was to rush down to the hospital and check on Jerry. None of this seemed real, but as her brain began to function, she realised that it was. Schiffer was unlikely to be bluffing, she knew how ruthless he could be. He would not hesitate to kill Jerry if he did not get what he wanted and the only way she could save his life was to do as he said.

Glancing round the room, she wondered what to do next. It was then she realised that she would have to alert someone. There was no time to telephone or make contact with a member of the crew; her five minutes were ticking away at an alarming rate. Snatching up her notebook, she rummaged in her bag for a pen and tearing out a page scribbled a note. Looking round she searched for a place to leave it. Her make-up bag was standing on the dressing table so moving quickly towards it she tucked the note under one corner, then glancing at her watch realised she would have to go, there was no time to lose. Rushing from her cabin, she dashed along the corridor leading to the deck, and sweeping down the ramp she looked around for warehouse number three.

Orlagh was angry and frustrated. How on earth had Schiffer managed to get to her, she thought it was safe aboard Jack's ship. There was supposed to be security in and around the harbour.

Stumbling, she almost fell as she hurried down the ramp and putting her hand out she grabbed at the rail to steady herself. At the bottom, she stopped to catch her breath. There had been no one along the way to question her and she was thankful for that. Schiffer's instructions were clear and she was in no mood to explain why she was leaving in such a hurry. Jerry's life was at stake and he was more important to her than anything else.

Orlagh eyed the buildings that lined the quay. She had no idea where warehouse number three was, all the buildings in this part of the harbour looked the same. They were dull and industrial and would not look out of place on a Victorian film set.

Moving away from the ramp, she swept past the area where the men were working on the ship. Fluorescent tape strung out between plastic safety cones fluttered in the breeze, these marked the spot where materials and equipment was stored. Supplies from Theo Grimaldi's ship delivered earlier that day were piled up neatly ready to be used.

Crossing to where the pathway became wider, she turned the corner of the nearest building and ahead she could see warehouse number one. A huge number displayed on the wall had once been painted in brilliant white, but now eroded by time, it looked as sad as the building itself. A few hundred metres away stood the building she was looking for. Part of its number was missing because a huge hole had been knocked in the brickwork. This building was in a sorry state and Orlagh shuddered as she made her way reluctantly towards it. Dodging around a hole in the pavement, she pushed her way into a narrow alley running beside the building and when she reached the other end she came across a car parked in the shadows. Hesitating, she stepped out from between the buildings. Her heart was beating wildly and she had a very bad feeling about this.

The moment she appeared a man got out of the car and opened the rear door. She had no choice but to do as he wanted and sliding onto the seat, the door slammed shut behind her.

Schiffer was sitting in the front beside the driver and as soon as she had settled, he turned his head to face her.

"Nice of you to join us, you are just in time."

Holding a small transmitter up to his face, he spoke in German and when he was finished, he nodded towards the driver and the car pulled smoothly away. As they turned the corner, Orlagh saw a man running from the ship. He was carrying a mini laptop in his hand and drawing level with the car, he snatched open the door and threw himself in beside her. As soon as the door was shut, the car sped away.

A druid concealed in the shadows watched as the car drove past. He would have to move quickly if he did not want to lose them. Dashing from his hiding place, he made his way towards one of the fishermen's huts, and throwing open the doors he knew there was a motorcycle stored inside. Tearing off a side panel, he traced the ignition wires from the battery and after fumbling for a moment he touched two bare wires together. The engine roared into life and throwing his leg over the seat, he manoeuvred the powerful machine out of the hut. Revving the engine, he toed the gear lever and the machine shot forward and as he passed the gate the druid raised his hand and waved at the security men, then he roared after the rapidly receding car.

The car drove inland for about twenty minutes before pulling off the road and disappearing into a fenced compound surrounding a private airfield. A light aircraft was parked up at the end of a short grass runway and a row of hangars surrounded the car parking area. Schiffer had the car stop beside the clubhouse.

The druid on the motorcycle arrived as the occupants of the car were entering the building. Cutting the engine, he freewheeled to a stop just outside the gates and watched before deciding what to do next. Ensuring the coast was clear he pushed the bike towards the nearest building and parked it out of sight, then pulling off his crash helmet, he wondered what was going on. He decided to wait in the shadows and consider his next move. He could sense Orlagh's distress, she was carrying the Stave of Yew and he could feel its power. Placing it inside her cabin had been a stroke of genius; he knew she would not be able to resist its charm.

The light aircraft suddenly roared into life and a cloud of grey smoke spewed from its exhausts. The engine revved for a second before settling down into a steady rhythm and the propeller idled. Currents of air disturbed by the sudden movement sent grass cuttings and gravel into the air.

The druid no longer had the luxury of time, he had to act now and as the door to the clubhouse opened, Schiffer appeared. Turning towards Orlagh, who was following behind, he said something.

The druid, acting casually, made his way towards the aircraft and ducked under the tail section. Through the side window, he could see the pilot in the left hand seat and as he watched, the co-pilot hauled himself up into the seat beside him. Behind them, the compartment was empty, the interior the size of a family saloon car. The druid nodded as he opened the rear door and climbed in. Both pilots glanced over their shoulders but made no comment, the noise inside the aircraft was far too loud for them to be heard and after a moment, they lost interest and continued with their pre flight checks.

Orlagh and her guard approached the aircraft; Schiffer was no longer with them, and as they drew level, the guard reached for the door handle and the druid slipped a thin long bladed knife from his sleeve. He concealed it beneath his arm then shuffling across the seat waited for the door to open. Orlagh climbed in behind the pilot and barely looked at him. The guard opened the door beside the druid and stood back mistaking him for some kind of maintenance engineer. The druid nodded and climbing out pushed past the guard before slipping the point of his blade in under his ribs. Piercing his diaphragm, it went up through his lungs and found his heart then, the man slumped to the floor with hardly a sound. The druid rolled his body under the aircraft before climbing back in. He slammed the door shut then nodded to the pilot who released the brake and they started to roll forward.

Gathering speed quickly, the aircraft bounced along the grass strip before lurching into the air and Orlagh felt her stomach drop with the sensation. As the nose of the aircraft angled skyward, she was pushed down into the seat and grasping at the door handle held onto it tightly until her heart stopped palpitating. Out of the side window, she could see buildings falling away below them.

She knew the man beside her was a druid, she could feel his power. It was like an electric current washing over her and her hair stood on end as her skin prickled. The Stave of Yew concealed in her pocket came alive; she could feel the warmth radiating from its core as it vibrated against her skin.

With the aircraft now level, they reached the limit of their climb and now with the engine beating more regularly, she shuffled into the corner leaving a space between them. She knew this man was dangerous, she had just seen him kill a man. Schiffer must realise by now that the aircraft had been hijacked and at any moment, she expected the pilots to receive a message over their radio, but they continued calmly, unaware that a druid was in the aircraft with them.

She tried to work out what was happening; the last time she was in a situation like this the druids and the Phoenix Legion were working together. She wondered if that were still the case or could they be at loggerheads. Perhaps this man was working alone, but why would he do that? So many unanswered questions filled her head and all the while, she wondered why he was there beside her.

Suddenly he leaned forward and with a gesture demanded a headset. The noise inside the aircraft was sufficient to make talking impossible and the only way to communicate was over the intercom system. The co-pilot passed him a head set and sliding it over his head, the druid adjusted the earpieces before talking into the microphone.

Orlagh had no idea what they were saying to each other but the atmosphere inside the cabin changed. The druid seemed to be making demands and the men began arguing. She was frightened, trapped inside a tiny cabin with three men who were becoming increasingly hostile towards each other. From where she was sitting, the only way to go was down and she did not like the sound of that.

Clearly, negotiations were not going well so the druid reached inside his jacket and pulled out a pistol. Orlagh's eyes widened and her stomach lurched as he pointed the weapon towards the co-pilot. The man had nowhere to go and the force from the blast was sufficient to throw him against the control column.

The aircraft lurched violently to one side as the port wing dipped and the noise from the engine increased. Orlagh was thrown back in her seat as the cabin rolled, and clawing at the door handle she squealed but the noise drowned out her terror.

The side window shattered and the door was splashed with blood but fortunately, the cabin was not pressurised so there was no danger of exploding decompression. The icy blast rushing in convinced her that they were about to die and as the pilot fought to stabilise the aircraft, the druid reached forward. Grabbing the dead co-pilot, he pulled him back into the seat and now with his weight off the control column the pilot was able to bring the aircraft back under control.

Orlagh could feel her heart pounding against her ribs, the sensation of falling was gone and now she could breathe again. Opening her eyes, she glanced at the druid beside her; he was pointing his gun at the pilot and speaking calmly into the intercom. The aircraft began to change course, and as the horizon crept up the windscreen, the pilot put the aircraft into a shallow dive. Leaning forward, the druid checked the instruments and after a moment was satisfied that his orders had been carried out. He kept the pistol trained on the pilot but Orlagh was convinced he would not use it. Who would fly the aircraft if he shot the pilot?

Closing her eyes against the horror, she tried unsuccessfully to think of something else. The smell of blood and fear filled her nostrils and her stomach churned uncomfortably. She knew she must slow her galloping heart, she was feeling light headed and inside this enclosed space the last thing she wanted to do was vomit.

She had no idea how long they had been in the air, her body clock had stopped functioning, but she realised it could not have been more than an hour. Slowly the aircraft pitched forward and opening her eyes all she could see through the windscreen was water. She was holding her breath and her chest was becoming tight, so forcing herself to breathe her mind began to function again.

The pilot was in control, and levelling off he steered to the right, then she could see a peninsula jutting out into the sea dotted with mountains and draped in dense forest.

Sweeping over clear blue water, they cleared a tiny inlet with not much altitude to spare and the pilot nudged the aircraft lower until Orlagh was convinced they were about to land in the sea. They were flying parallel to the gradually rising land, the sea remained under their port wing and Orlagh continued to be amazed at how low they were. Gripping the door handle even tighter, she shuffled lower in her seat and began preparing for a crash landing.

Suddenly the engine lost revs and the aircraft settled but thankfully, it remained level. At first, the wheels grazed the sand but as the weight increased, vibrations began to run through the airframe, it was as if the aircraft was threatening to shake itself to bits.

The pilot was instructed to land on the beach, the tide was low and a strip of damp hard packed sand seemed the perfect place to put down, but as soon as the aircraft settled, the pilot knew it was a mistake. The sand was not as solid as it appeared and glutinous jelly-like mud drew them down until the pressure on the landing gear was too great and tore them away. The aircraft slammed onto its belly and the noise of crumpling sheet metal was like thunder. A loud crack sounded as something shattered then suddenly they were back in the air. They did not remain airborne for long, pitching forward the windscreen splintered as the nose tried to bury itself in the mud then filthy water spewed into the cabin. Finally, the aircraft flipped over onto its back before spinning around, then one of the wings sheared off.

It seemed an eternity before the aircraft stopped then after the terrifying noise there was nothing but silence.

Jack and Wings were back aboard the *Dauntless,* which maintained its pretence of fishing.

"I want to get onto a computer and do some research." Jack said turning towards Wings who was busy shutting down and securing the submersible.

Jack was desperate to discover where the FW190s had come from. He had to find out where the Phoenix Legion had set up base, he also needed some technical information.

Climbing up through the hatch that coupled the submersible to the boat, he settled in the cabin and logged onto his laptop. Typing FW190 into a search engine, he was soon sorting through a list, then selecting a likely looking site he began to scan a list of specifications. There was much more information than he could have hoped for, and reading the closely typed paragraphs, he soon discovered that many variants had been tested during the early part of the 1940s. The production run spanned four years and the FW190 proved to be one of Hitler's most successful fighters.

Checking out the latest version, he learnt that its operational range was a little over five hundred miles and turning to a map, he began to study the coast of Ukraine. Allowing for modifications he decided to be generous and using the spot in the Sea of Azov where the aircraft had come down as a starting point he measured out a distance of just over two hundred and fifty miles.

Jack thought for a moment but decided not to look any further. This he considered was a fair range for the fighters, allowing for time over the target and burning fuel in the attack, even with modern day tuning, the engines would not be significantly more economical.

It was of course possible that he was looking in the wrong place completely. The aircraft may not have flown directly from their base; they could have made a series of doglegs in order to conceal their intentions. This would cause anyone trying to track them some confusion in working out their original location.

His eyes flicked over the coastline as he considered other likely sites, but after a moment, he realised that it was impossible to guess. He would have to run with his gut instinct. Left to him he would hide his base away from the coast, further inland it would be more remote and there would be less chance of being discovered. There were plenty of abandoned castles and mining towns in Ukraine, this seemed the most likely place to hide an army.

Sitting back in his chair, he thought for a moment. He had to be sure of his reasoning, filter out all the garbage and make use of his more logical ideas. The Phoenix Legion would need water so this would put them close to a river; it would be an effective highway for delivering men and provisions. Reaching for a pen and paper, he scribbled some notes and when he was finished, he sat back.

He wished that Jerry could help, with his contacts he would be able to provide him with crucial information.

"Here boss." Wings said as he squeezed into a space beside him. Handing him a mug of coffee he nodded at the laptop. "This looks interesting."

"Thanks," Jack grunted and laying down his notebook, took the mug. "Can you get onto Paul; see if Razor and his team have arrived yet."

"Sure Jack, I'll get onto it right away."

Wings settled into a computer chair beside the communication console.

On board the *Ocean Pride* Linda was talking to Paul over the ships intercom system.

"Have you seen Orlagh recently?"

"No, I'm afraid not. Why do you ask?" The tension in her voice alerted him.

"She's not been down to the hospital this morning which is most unlike her. I've tried phoning her cabin but there's no answer and her cell phone goes straight to voicemail."

"Okay Linda, leave it with me. I'll go along to her cabin myself; see if I can find her."

"Thanks Paul, keep me informed will you, Jerry is beginning to wonder where she's is."

Paul frowned as he replaced the receiver. Orlagh was always at the hospital early, she never missed an opportunity to be there when Jerry woke up. Calling to the officers who were stationed close by he began to issue orders.

"One of you go to the library, the other check out the gym. See if you can locate Dr Gairne. I'm going to see if she's in her cabin."

The men went their separate ways and twenty minutes later were back on the bridge. Orlagh was nowhere to be found, even a general announcement over the ships intercom failed to produce results.

"It seems she's not on board sir." One of the officers reported.

Paul had been to her cabin and found the door locked. He had a bad feeling about this. She would never have gone ashore without telling him first and the fact that they could not raise her on her cell phone bothered him even more.

"Get a man from maintenance to meet me at her cabin," Paul said. "Ask him to bring an overriding password for the lock on the door."

Each cabin on board ship relied on an entry keyboard for access. These were operated by an electronic card reader that had to be set up by the master computer or by punching in a security number chosen by the occupant of the room.

Paul decided that Linda should be there when he went into Orlagh's cabin. He had no idea what he would find, besides, if she was in there she might be in need of medical attention.

Fifteen minutes later Paul joined Linda and with a maintenance engineer, they soon had the door open, but once inside they discovered the cabin was empty.

"Where the hell is she?" Linda exclaimed and pushing open the door, she checked out the wet room.

"Obviously not here." Paul replied wishing he could have thought of a more original response.

Glancing around he could find no clues as to what might have happened to Orlagh. Nothing seemed out of place, the book she was reading was still on the bedside cabinet and her bed was neatly made.

Linda was methodically going through cupboards and drawers checking clothes and belongings. Her make-up bag was still on the shelf that served as a dressing table, if she was going someplace she would have at least taken that, Linda thought.

"What's this?" She said, reaching for a note that was partially concealed beneath the makeup bag.

Scanning it quickly she gasped audibly before passing it to Paul.

"This can't be true." He shook his head in disbelief.

The note told how Schiffer's men had come on board and forced their way into her cabin. They had also infiltrated the hospital and threatened to kill Jerry if she refused to go with them.

"There was no evidence to suggest that anyone had been in the hospital." Linda told him.

"We have to assume this is genuine and Dr Gairne is now a prisoner of the Phoenix Legion." Paul said.

"But I don't understand," Linda looked at him furiously. "How did they manage to get on board and kidnap her?"

"We are supposed to be in a secure harbour," Paul reminded her. "We are in a dry dock for goodness sake."

"Well that's no excuse to relax security." She snapped.

Paul had no answer but she did have a point and it made him feel even more responsible. He paced the room wondering what to do next. Of one thing he was certain, Jack would not be very happy when he told him.

Wings spoke to one of the officers on the bridge. Captain Seymour was not on station, he was busy dealing with a situation of some kind, but as soon as Wings told him he was enquiring on Jack's behalf the man became a lot more helpful.

"Razor and his team are expected to arrive sometime tomorrow," he began, "they are travelling separately from different locations so will not all be arriving at the same time."

Wings relayed this message to Jack. "Something is going on," he told him. "I was unable to speak with Captain Seymour himself."

Jack looked up from what he was doing and frowned. "I wonder what he is up to."

A plan was beginning to formulate inside his head. He had already sent Razor an e-mail detailing his preliminary ideas, but Razor would have to do the legwork if he was going to discover the location of the Phoenix Legion. He was sure that once Big Mac was briefed, he would do a little prospecting; he was after all an IT specialist and was bound to have contacts. His network was far reaching; there wasn't much that happened without him knowing about it.

Orlagh was stiff and sore when finally she woke up. Carefully she opened her eyes but a bright light assaulted her senses. Groaning, she closed them again and fought off a wave of nausea that threatened to overcome her. Her head was spinning mercilessly and there was a dull ache in the small of her back. After a while, she summoned the strength to check herself over and reaching out with her mind, visited each part of her body in turn. When she was satisfied, she gingerly opened her eyes again and this time was able to cope with the light.

The first thing she saw was a huge stone mullioned window. This was the source of light and as the sun shone through the tiny leaded glass panels, it danced merrily from all the polished surfaces in the room.

Looking away, she discovered an enormous open fireplace against the opposite wall. Corinthian columns standing either side of the inglenook supported a mantle made of solid oak; the wood looked ancient and blackened by time.

On the next wall hung a tapestry made from richly coloured thread. The medieval scene complicated by intricate detail, it would take her days to work it out.

Sitting up in bed, she pulled her knees stiffly up to her chin and wrapped her arms around them tightly. Beneath the sheets, she was naked, she had no recollection of arriving in this place and looking around could find no sign of her clothes. She had no idea where she was, the last thing she remembered was being inside the aircraft. Her terror returned and with a shudder, she re-lived the moment it had turned over and tried to bury itself in the mud. She wondered what had become of the pilot and the druid.

Suddenly there was a noise and a door beside the tapestry opened. A young woman entered hesitantly and as her eyes swept the room, she approached the bed where Orlagh was sitting.

"My Lady, you are awake." Her voice was heavy with accent.

"Where am I?" Orlagh croaked. She was unaware that her throat was so dry.

"You have no need to be concerned. You are uninjured and you are safe."

Closing her eyes, Orlagh breathed deeply as another wave of nausea swept over her.

"You will be quite drowsy for a while yet," the young woman told her. She moved forward taking small paces. "We had to administer medication when you arrived; it was just a mild sedative to help with your discomfort."

"Well that's just grand, so I've been drugged." Orlagh opened her eyes and fixed the woman with a stare. "Where are my clothes?"

She withered under the weight of Orlaghs stare and her confidence plummeted as she backed slowly away.

"They were ruined in the crash," she stammered. "You were covered in mud and dirty water. There was also a fuel leak from a ruptured pipe." She swallowed noisily and looking down at the floor clasped her hands awkwardly in front of her.

Orlagh sighed, then, eyeing the woman more closely noticed that her fingers were chaffed red. She obviously worked hard at whatever it was she did here.

"So where am I," she asked in a much softer tone. "Am I a prisoner?"

"Oh no my Lady, you are not a prisoner, you are an esteemed guest." Peering at Orlagh through lowered lashes, she continued. "You are in Maina, the central peninsula of the Peloponnese."

Orlagh stared at her. She was finding it difficult to understand her thick accent and needed time to unravel what she had just said. "And where is that exactly?" She had no idea where Maina was.

"Maina is a region of Southern Greece," she explained, and taking the initiative, moved closer. She was aware of Orlagh's inability to understand, so this time she spoke more clearly.

Orlagh frowned; she was still none the wiser. She had no idea where the aircraft was taking her, it was then she remembered the druid, how he had murdered the co-pilot. She could still see the expression of shock on his face followed by agony as he died. Orlagh shuddered and the woman mistook her sudden movement for something else.

"Are you cold my Lady; would you like me to light a fire?"

"No," Orlagh opened her eyes and gazed at her. "That won't be necessary."

Standing close beside her bed, she reminded Orlagh of a nun dressed in a habit dyed the colour of the sky. It swept the floor as she moved and covering her hair, she wore a wimple of pure white silk. She resembled one of the figures in the tapestry. Turning away from the girl, Orlagh studied it. At first, she thought it depicted a typical medieval scene, but as she looked closer, she could see that the figures represented druids involved in some kind of ritual. It was then she realised the woman was a druid or priestess.

Razor was the first to arrive in Istanbul and as soon as he set foot on the *Ocean Pride,* he found himself surrounded by security guards and was escorted to the bridge.

"Paul old chum, how the devil are you?"

Captain Seymour was standing in his customary place and as soon as he heard his old friend's voice, he turned to face him.

"Razor, welcome aboard." Striding confidently across the space that separated them, he took a firm grip of Razor's hand and shook it vigorously.

"Sorry about all the security," he frowned comically. "We've had a few problems around here."

Razor nodded in agreement, surveying the damage to the bridge.

"Looks like you've had a rare old time of it. How's Jack?"

"He's fine," Paul's frown turned into a wide grin. "He's not here at the moment, you know Jack."

"Oh yes, he won't stay in one place for long especially if there is no action."

Razor knew that Jack was in the Sea of Azov; Paul was obviously unaware of the exchange of e-mails that had gone on between them.

"So," Razor said glancing out of the window, "where is the gorgeous Dr Gairne? Jack told me she was onboard, I haven't seen her in a long while."

"Ah," Paul's expression became pained at the mention of her name. "Therein lies the problem." He rolled his eyeballs theatrically up into his head.

"Problem," Razor said looking puzzled, "what do you mean?"

"We seem to have lost Dr Gairne."

Paul began to explain what had happened earlier and reaching for a file, he extracted her note.

"Does Jack know?"

"Not yet but he's sure going to be mad when he finds out."

Razor nodded. He knew how angry Jack could get.

"You will have to tell him soon."

"You don't have to remind me. I've delayed telling him in the hope that she might turn up or we discover a lead, anything to give us a clue as to what happened to her."

At that moment Linda appeared.

"Dr Pritchard," Razor exclaimed with genuine joy. "You are a welcome sight for weary eyes. Tell me, what does a fellow have to do to get you to agree to meet him for supper?"

"You fool," she smiled sweetly at him. "You had better watch yourself because one of these days I might just accept your offer."

Stepping forward she leaned in affectionately and wrapped her arms around him. Lifting her off her feet, Razor planted a kiss on top of her head then as she looked up, he kissed her cheeks before setting her down again.

"How's your patient?"

"Which one?" she eyed him mischievously. "I do have more than one just now, but I assume you are referring to Jerry Knowles."

"Yes I am, like me he's another fine young Englishman."

Beaming at him she tried not to snort, she was about to make a suggestive comment but then thought better of it.

"He's doing very well, or at least he was until Orlagh disappeared."

"He didn't take the news well then?"

"What do you think?" Moving away from him, she recovered her business like composure and clasped her hands behind her back. "He's convinced she's been kidnapped by druids."

"Could he be right?" Raising his eyebrows, Razor waited for her to reply.

"I guess he might be, but her note clearly states that it was Schiffer of the Phoenix Legion who abducted her."

Razor nodded and thought for a moment.

"She may have been forced to write that in order to throw us off the scent."

"I don't know," she said pacing the floor. "I feel sure it's genuine and the Phoenix Legion have her."

"And why do you think that when Jerry seems convinced otherwise?"

"Oh I don't know," she stopped pacing and looked up at him. "Call it women's intuition."

"Whilst you two argue the toss," Paul cut in. "I've got to go and make a phone call. It's high time Jack knew about this."

On board the *Dauntless* Jack was outlining his plan. He was determined to get a look inside the tunnel on the bottom of the sea before the day was out.

"I plan to seal the mouth of the tunnel with a bung then pump the water out." He told them. "Once that's done we'll cut a hole in that steel door and gain access to the tunnel beyond."

Wings stared at him in amazement, he could hardly believe what Jack was saying but he did not have the nerve to question him. He was in no doubt that Jack would make it happen.

"We'll cut through the door using a battery operated grinder and cutting disc." He explained, filling him in with the details he made it sound simple.

"How do we effectively seal off the tunnel? The water pressure down there must be tremendous."

"We'll use a rubber coated lifting bag. We can inflate it using water from inside the tunnel and once it's sealed against the walls, excess water can be pumped out through a tube."

Wings was warming to the idea. He had seen rubber coated lifting bags in use before and knew how effective they could be, but he had never seen one used as a bung; however he knew it was possible.

Jack, as if to underpin his theory, typed a command on the keyboard of his laptop and stock photographs of lifting bags used to bung up huge oil pipes appeared on the screen.

"Here," he said spinning the laptop round so Wings could see more clearly.

"Okay," Wings said, "the evidence speaks for itself. When do we get started?"

"We'll go in a few hours. First, we need to get loaded up, find something to eat then get some rest. It won't be an easy task getting inside that tunnel. I also have to organise Razor and his team."

The communications system alerted them to an incoming message and one of the men picked up the receiver. Listening for a few seconds, he frowned.

"It's Captain Seymour." He said before handing it over to Jack.

"Hi Paul."

"Jack, we have a problem."

Orlagh dressed quickly in the clothes she was given and then she managed to eat something. Her thoughts took her back to the last time she was held captive by the druids, the food and drink they had given her then had been drugged. Of course, she had no way of knowing, but if it was the same now it was too bad, she was ravenous and in desperate need of something to drink.

The only thing left of her belongings was the Stave of Yew. It was sitting on a small table beside the bed and reaching for it, she ran her fingers lightly over the runes carved so beautifully into the wood. She could feel the force running through it and knew that it was both precious and menacing. The druids had made it from sacred wood. In ancient times, yew trees would have surrounded sacred groves; this was a tree they revered. The yew could also be found on nodes or beside springs. These were powerful locations, where druids and those from the spirit world would meet to communicate or cast spells. Here they felt closer to their gods; the yew tree was some kind of link bonding the worlds together. For generations staves of yew had been used as votive offerings. Staves just like hers would be carved during ceremonies, then, cast into the spring water that formed in pools around the base of the trees. Water is probably the most important element of life; it is also a barrier separating our world from the Otherworld.

Pushing these thoughts from her mind, Orlagh made her way across the room, stopped in front of the window, and stared out at the garden. She knew there would be yew trees; these were situated in the corners of the garden where the shade was most intense. They were magnificent specimens having stood like guardians for centuries. She smiled, perhaps they were old druids who had died and been transformed, remaining there in the garden for ever keeping them safe from evil. Turning away from the window, her thoughts drifted back to what she had read on the internet. The wood was sacred to Hecate and the Crone aspect of the Triple Goddess; both are guardians of the Underworld, death and the afterlife.

Orlagh shuddered and pushing her hand into her pocket moved towards the door and opened it. Standing outside in a narrow alleyway were two women.

"Hello," Orlagh said cheerfully. "Do you mind if I take a walk in the garden?"

"Of course my Lady." One of them replied. Her accent was not so heavy, it had a different ring to it.

They stepped aside as Orlagh moved towards the door leading to the garden.

Orlagh wondered why they insisted on calling her 'my Lady'. She didn't dislike the idea, it was rather grand and made her feel important. Looking back over her shoulder, she watched as the women fell in behind, they followed at a respectful distance. It was just like before when held captive with Roz Stacey on the island of Gog. They had an entourage then accompanying them wherever they went.

The heat of the garden came as a shock after the cool interior of her room and keeping to the shade, Orlagh followed the neat little footpaths that wound their way around the flower borders. Many of the flowers and plants she could identify but equally there were those she had never seen before. The colour and form were pleasing to the eye and occasionally a breeze would send a magnificent scent wafting through the air, it was then she would have to stop and enjoy the fleeting moment.

Moving further away from the house, she made her way slowly towards the boundary wall. She wanted to see beyond the garden, she had to find some kind of landmark, anything that might offer a clue as to her whereabouts. She had been told earlier that this was Maina, on the central Peloponnese Peninsula, but this meant nothing to her at all.

"What do you mean she's disappeared?" Jack bellowed. "Where has she disappeared to?"

"Well, if we knew that Jack I would send a team out to get her back."

Jack grilled Paul about security on the ship and asked some very awkward questions. Paul remained calm and did his best to answer them all.

"If Schiffer does have her, it's now become a priority that we discover the location of his hideout."

Paul agreed. "I wonder why he wants her, what use is she to the Phoenix Legion?"

"Last time it was the druids who showed more of an interest in her." Jack reminded him. "You know how we found her after one of their rituals."

Paul shuddered at the memory. They had discovered both Roz and Orlagh left for dead, laid out on altar stones within a huge stone circle.

Jack continued. "From what we know about the druids, it's my guess they must have something Schiffer wants. Maybe he intends using Orlagh as a bargaining chip. I have a distinct feeling that the druids and the Phoenix Legion are not quite so chummy as they were a year ago."

"That could be true," Paul replied. "If what Jerry said is correct about there being druids on board, then they too must want her."

"Possibly," Jack said. "It was all about the Belgae Torc last time. I wonder what they are after this time."

"Orlagh told us about the deaths in the mountain village in Turkey." Paul began thoughtfully. "Wasn't that about the torc?"

"Yeah, it was."

"Druids or Schiffer's men?"

"If I had to guess, I'd say Schiffer. That village was pretty close to where the Junkers went down. Maybe it was carrying the torc and the girl from the village found it on the mountainside. As soon as word got out that there was treasure, he would have dispatched his goons to recover it by any means."

Paul nodded, then he realised that Jack could not see him. "Yeah, you could be right. It's something we didn't consider at the time, hell, we didn't need to until now."

"Listen buddy," Jack said. "I've had an idea about those FW190s that attacked us. I've been doing a bit of digging and reckon they came from somewhere in the Ukraine."

Paul listened but remained silent.

"It's my guess," Jack continued, "that the Phoenix Legion are holed up in a castle. There are plenty of abandoned places like that in Ukraine. With their sense of history and from what we've seen before, where else would they be?"

"I can see where you're coming from Jack."

"I also think they will be found near a major river. That's how they must provision themselves; I imagine that remote places in Ukraine are a little light on highway access."

Paul was amazed at his theories. Jack always managed to come up with the bright ideas.

"Get Razor onto it will you. Tell him to research a river called Dnieper." He spelled it out and Paul wrote it down. "I realise this is a long river, but the Phoenix Legion must be holed up along it somewhere."

"Why this river Jack?"

"Because it's the only major river in Ukraine and its well within the range of the fighters."

"Okay I'll get onto it right away. E-mail me everything you have." He felt sure that Jack would have done his homework thoroughly before suggesting this plan of action.

"Sure pal and in the meantime Wings and I are planning to get inside that tunnel. I'll tell you all about it in a day or two."

"You take good care of the boy Jack. I don't want to be writing to his mother telling her how brave he was."

"I'll look after him, don't worry about that. You're beginning to sound like his mother yourself."

Paul laughed as he shut down the communication unit.

Orlagh completed her tour of the garden and was still none the wiser. She had no idea where she was. The house seemed to be in the grounds of a much larger estate, she knew it was situated on the coast because of the sea birds wheeling overhead and mixed in with the heady scents from the garden she could smell the sea.

Sighing deeply she thought about Jerry. What was he doing at that very moment? Perhaps he was undergoing another painful physio with Linda or maybe he was worrying about her? Suddenly a thought that was so unthinkable stopped her in her tracks.

"Are you alright my Lady?" The women were beside her in a flash.

"Yes, I'm fine." Orlagh told them as she pressed her hand against her thudding heart.

Glancing at the flint stones built into the wall, she thought about the man she had seen standing over Jerry with a syringe full of poison. Schiffer's threat had been clear, she was left in no doubt that he would have ordered Jerry's death if she did not comply with his demands. Her stomach lurched at the thought, but she was convinced that Jerry was safe. She would know if anything had happened to him, she felt sure of it.

Wings was loading equipment into the submersible. Lockers located on the hull were now full of flexible lifting bags and wiping his hands with a towel, he was eager to see how Jack's plan would unfold. Plugging the entrance of the tunnel then draining it of seawater was an outrageous idea and the more he thought about it the madder it seemed, but of one thing he was certain, if anyone could pull it off then Jack was that man.

Other equipment like pumps, hoses, grinding and cutting gear were stowed inside the sub until it resembled an untidy workshop stuffed full of tools. There was barely enough room left for himself and Jack.

Extra cylinders of breathing gas were fixed to the hull using brackets and heavy duty cable ties. This would be essential to provide an atmosphere inside the tunnel once the water was pumped out.

At last, everything was ready and the sub was standing by for its next mission. Wings was eager to get going but realised they would have to wait until the *Dauntless* was in position.

"Twenty minutes." Came the reply when Wings asked the question.

"Better get settled in," Jack told him and calmly followed him down the short ladder leading between the hatch and the hull.

Slamming the hatch shut behind them, Jack turned the handle sealing them into their own little world and Wings made himself comfortable in the pilot's seat. His eyes swept over the control panel as he began his pre-flight checks, now all they had to do was wait for the order to cast off.

Razor, Kylie and Mac were sitting round a table in the Wardroom studying a map of Ukraine. A laptop was open, it's screen decorated by a colour diagram of the Dnieper River. They discovered that it was in fact one of the largest in Europe.

Rising near Smolensk, it flowed for 2,145 kilometres to the Black Sea.

"What's that in miles?" Kylie asked

213

"About 1350," Mac told him.

"Jack wants us to search it?"

"Not all of it," Razor said, "just the bit that runs through Ukraine."

"That narrows it down to 680 miles," Mac added.

"Yeah but that's well beyond the range of those fighters." Kylie reminded them.

"Then our job gets easier," Mac grinned. "Now all we have to do is search 200 miles of river."

Kylie whistled and rolled his eyes.

"No one said it would be easy." Razor growled, and rising from his chair, stretched his arms above his head as he arched his back.

"Maybe it's not the river we should be studying." Mac said, his eyes narrowing.

Kylie and Razor looked at him.

"We should check out the traffic. Jack told us he thinks the Legion is using the river as a highway, so we should study the boats."

"Good idea," Kylie grinned. "With a bit of luck one of them will lead us right up to their front door."

"I wonder how busy the river is." Reaching for the laptop, Razor tapped away at the keys and as the screen changed, he began reading from the text that appeared.

"There are dozens of cities and towns dotted along our stretch of river," he informed them. "There are also a number of tributaries running off the Dnieper. We'll need to locate them all and check out the likely ones. There are also a few reservoirs dotted along the river with ship locks allowing vessels of up to 270 by 18 metres access as far as Kiev."

"What's that in English?" Kylie asked again.

"890 by 59 feet," Mac did the maths.

"Pretty big then," he said glancing up at both Razor and Mac. "How far along the river is Kiev?"

"Too far up, it's well out of the range of our fighters."

The printer began to chatter as Razor printed off another map. Picking up a pencil and plastic rule, he plotted an arc that covered 200 miles from the centre of The Sea of Azov.

"This is about 50 miles short of their optimum range, so we have to focus on the river up to and possibly just beyond this mark."

Leaning forward for a better view, they studied this new piece of information.

"Right," Kylie began, "I have an idea. We need to get on top of this, so what we do is survey it from the air."

214

"Go on," Razor nodded and sitting back folded his arms across his chest.

"I have a drone we could use as a spy in the sky. We fly it up and down the river using its camera to search out likely looking ships."

"Sounds like a plan," Razor agreed.

"This baby of mine works on a combination of battery cell and solar energy. It harvests power during daylight hours then as darkness falls it switches to batteries."

"What about cameras?"

"It has a high magnification, high resolution spy camera mounted up front. It also has an infrared for night time use. Everything it sees it records and we can access that data using my laptop. We can also see in real time, as its happening."

"How long before this drone arrives?" Mac asked. He had remained silent but now he stepped forward.

"I have one with me. I never travel without one or two of my little friends; you never know when you might need one."

"We'll be able to launch it from the Sikorsky once we arrive over the mouth of the river."

"No need," Kylie said. "I'll launch it from here and within a few hours it will arrive on station to begin its run up river."

They stared at him and he felt compelled to explain further.

"It has a cruising speed of just over 100 mph."

"Incredible," Mac snorted. "I can't wait to see this thing."

"It's one of my own creations," Kylie boasted. "Don't ask me how high it will go because you won't believe it."

"Go on, try me."

"A couple of months ago I took one up to just over 60,000 feet. I wanted to try out a new miniature satellite camera and the view was just incredible."

Mac stared at him opened mouthed.

"It will stay in the air for months. The batteries are good for about two years."

"Two years?" Mac laughed.

"I knew you wouldn't believe me."

"With you around I'd believe anything." Razor said slapping him on the back. "Let's get this bug of yours airborne."

XXXIII

"When is Orlagh coming down to see me?" Jerry asked for the hundredth time.

"I've told you before," Linda explained again. "Schiffer has abducted her."

It was like talking to a child and she hated having to tell him, but he had a right to know.

Jerry would remain like this until the shock wore off, then she was hoping he would begin to function normally again.

"How do you know he has her?" Jerry frowned.

"We found a note in your cabin; luckily she was able to alert us."

She decided to leave out the bit about him being in danger too.

"It's the druids who have her not the Phoenix Legion. They need Orlagh to help them bring the Goddess of Hibernia and The Morrigan from the Otherworld."

Linda stopped what she was doing and turned towards him.

"What do you mean Jerry; you've never mentioned anything like this before."

"It was in my dream," he explained, "one of my nightmares."

The blood drained from his face and the memory of it left him pale. Linda moved to his bedside and laid a hand on his shoulder.

"Look Jerry," she began, "they were nothing more than bad dreams. The Phoenix Legion have Orlagh and Jack has already taken steps to get her back. Just be patient and I'm sure things will turn out just fine."

"Jack needs my help," Jerry sat up straighter. "I must do what I can to help him find Orlagh."

"You are in no fit state," she told him gently. "You must concentrate your energies on your own recovery."

"I'm fine; I just wish I could remember things. My mind is all over the place at the moment."

"What do you expect Jerry. You've just received a shock on top of a serious head trauma. You are very lucky to have retained all your faculties. You do realise you could have been paralysed or worse."

"I'm sorry Dr Pritchard, I know you are right, but if I could have my laptop I might be able to be of some help."

She didn't like the sound of that. Although he was improving significantly and gaining in strength daily, he still required complete rest.

"Let me think about it," she said, realising that if she did not give in he was likely to get out of bed and go to the library where he could log onto a computer.

"The moment I consider you fit enough for duty I won't hesitate to allow you to help."

Schiffer was furious. He could not believe they had lost Dr Gairne. He would have some awkward explaining to do when he returned to headquarters. He knew the druids were responsible and he was determined to make them pay. In fact, he had already decided on a course of action having radioed his intentions ahead. Sitting back in his chair, he was smug in the knowledge that preparations for retribution were already underway.

Kylie was on deck preparing his drone for flight. Kneeling down beside the tiny aircraft, he was talking to it softly as if it were a pet, but the moment he heard Razor and Mac approaching he stopped his affectionate narrative.

"I'm impressed," Razor said as soon as he spotted the drone. "It looks just like the real thing."

"This is the real thing," Kylie replied with a lopsided grin. "Why re-invent the wheel, if the concept works..."

"Plagiarise you mean," Razor teased and Kylie looked hurt. "I expected to see a bug eyed critter."

"Well, this mission is different. No one is going to notice this little bird so it doesn't have to look like a dragonfly. Stealth is what this baby does best."

The drone was almost a perfect replica of a stealth bomber only in miniature, its delta wing and fuselage were perfect in every detail.

"This is where the camera is situated," Kylie pointed to the cockpit area where two window-like openings looked out over the nose. "This one on the right is the lens for the camera and behind the left window sits the infra-red. The avionics are in the nose section just like any other aircraft. We have GPS, Flight Recorder, Laser Guidance system and everything this baby needs packed away in micro size. She is a marvel of modelling." He continued boasting and his chest swelled with pride.

"The delta wing is made up of solar panels and underneath where the undercarriage would normally sit are lightweight battery cells. Its brain is right up here on top." He ran his finger along its back until he reached the raised section above the cockpit.

217

"This little bird has the ability to think for itself. For example, if it runs into a storm it will automatically change course to avoid it. If it's attacked it will take evasive action, it will fly somersaults if that's what it takes to remain in one piece. I can override the system at any time and fly it manually using my laptop."

"You seem to have thought of everything," Mac said.

A small red light on top of the drone flashed three times then went out.

"That's the tracking system activated," Kylie explained and turning to his laptop, a GPS reference appeared on the screen.

"Right," he said climbing to his feet, "it's time this baby went wheels up."

Picking the drone up from where it was sitting on the deck, he carried it to the rail and launched it over the side. Razor and Mac held their breaths as they watched it tumble out of control towards the concrete below.

Kylie remained unconcerned and turning back to his laptop, he knew that with increasing airspeed the drone would respond automatically. The onboard computer began to calculate orientation and thrust and as the tiny motors burst into life, the nose lifted and pointing skyward the drone climbed at an impressive rate.

Kylie, with a smug grin on his face, made a few tiny adjustments on his keyboard then began tracking the drone's progress as it headed out of the bay.

Razor and Mac crowded in beside him, the drone was already out of sight and they watched on the screen as it changed course and began following the coastline. Steadily it gained altitude before turning away from land, then, swooping out over the Black Sea, it was gone. It would be at least six hours before the little aircraft arrived on station to begin tracking over the estuary of the Dnieper River.

In the Sea of Azov, the *Dauntless* made its turn close to the wreck, and inside the submersible slung between the hulls, Wings listened intently for the order to go. On the mark, he punched the release handle.

"I have control," he spoke calmly into the microphone then pushing the thrusters forward the submersible dived smoothly towards the seabed.

In his earphones, Wings could hear the sound of propellers overhead. The rhythm faded as the *Dauntless* motored out of earshot then they began to track her progress on the sonar.

218

Bleeding off speed from their rapid descent, Wings eased the nose up a few degrees and as the bottom came into view, he levelled off. Flaring out like an aircraft, the submersible became stationary in the water, then easing the throttle forward a notch, it began to creep along the bottom. After a few minutes, the wreck appeared on their instruments and turning on the powerful spotlights it was not long before they had it in view.

Peering through the canopy Wings manoeuvred closer, then when he was satisfied, he settled the sub gently on the bottom.

"Nicely done Wings," Jack said as he unbuckled himself from his seat.

He wanted to get started right away. He was worried about Orlagh and once this part of the mission was over, he was determined to help Razor and the team rescue her from the clutches of the Phoenix Legion.

XXXIV

A large unidentified helicopter rose majestically into the air. On board were twenty crack storm troopers, impeccably turned out in authentic Second World War uniforms. Each man carried an original Schmiesser MP40 machine pistol and a 9mm Luger.

As the machine gained altitude over the improvised airfield, more of the medieval castle came into view and when the men on board looked down, they could see five FW190s parked beside their temporary hangers. There was space for a sixth aircraft but this remained empty, a stark reminded that the game of war was a dangerous one.

Each aircraft had been fitted with additional fuel tanks. Slung beneath the wings, these resembled huge bombs, their sleek cylindrical bodies painted the same shade of sky blue to match the underside of the fighters. These were drop tanks and could be released at anytime during flight. They more than doubled the range of the aircraft, but on this occasion this still would not be enough, a re-fuelling stop would be necessary if the pilots were to bring their aircraft home safely. Luckily, Schiffer had an ally in a neighbouring country where no questions would be asked, five Second World War fighter planes could drop in for fuel and rouse little suspicion.

With the helicopter, it was quite different. A re-fuelling stop would cause no problems; no one would raise an eyebrow if a conventional helicopter dropped in.

Two druids accompanied by a small group of women came to Orlagh's room.

"You are to come with us." One of the men rudely informed her.

"And where do you think you are taking me?" She asked, planting herself firmly in the centre of the room.

An awkward silence followed as the women stared from Orlagh to the druid.

"My Lady," the other man began more respectfully. "We would be most grateful if you would do as we ask. As you see," he gestured towards the women, "your safety is assured."

One of the women stepped forward and said. "No harm or offence is intended."

Orlagh remained defiant and wondered why they kept on referring to her safety. She was about to ask but stopped herself, maybe it would be just as well not to know.

"Very well," she heard herself say. "Lead on."

They did not go out through the gardens as she expected but remained inside the house. Moving in single file, they went along a darkened corridor and Orlagh could feel the ground beneath her feet sloping downwards. After a while, the air became cooler and stale, it reminded her of a damp cellar.

One of the men went on ahead and pulling on a ring fixed to a huge wooden door, slowly it creaked open and they passed through into a large gloomy chamber. There was no hesitation from the women surrounding her, they bustled her along with hardly a change in stride and before long they passed through another door and out into an open courtyard.

Orlagh, squinting in the bright light, saw what looked like an over-sized golf trolley standing alone in the middle of the yard. The men climbed into the front seats and the women crowded into the back, and as soon as they were all on board it moved smoothly away. After a short distance, they entered a tunnel and it reminded Orlagh of the Metro system in Paris. They had not gone far when they came to a halt; ahead was another huge door, this time it swung open automatically and they were off again. Coming out of the tunnel, Orlagh had to shield her eyes once again then she discovered they were in another courtyard.

Stone walls crowded in on all sides and the sound of the trolley on the uneven surface echoed as they rattled along the uncomfortably narrow pathway. Soon they arrived at a much larger place. Here was a huge grassed area where she could see people going about their business. Some of them stopped to stare as the trolley passed them by and Orlagh was surprised when a man in the crowd made a sign with his hand against evil. The expression on his face was grim and Orlagh shuddered. She could feel the Stave of Yew vibrating in her pocket. It was hot against her skin and she was convinced the women pressed in around her could feel it too. What was it about this strange object that made her feel obliged to carry it around with her?

Jack and Wings worked together unloading equipment from the submersible and placing it inside the tunnel entrance. This was both time consuming and heavy work but at last, they had everything in position.

Clearing away the last of the sand, they heaved the package containing the lifting bag into place. Made from high resistance fabrics and coated with a synthetic rubber, it was perfect for these underwater conditions. It remained folded inside a bale-like package, but once they started the inflating process, it would balloon into shape and mould itself to the sides of the tunnel.

Jack hooked up a second pipe to the battery operated pump and laid it out along the base of the wall. It stretched to the end of the tunnel, its mouth positioned beneath the lifting bag, it would be used to channel excess water from the tunnel once it had been sealed.

Everything they needed was packed into the space around them and Jack began a final check. As soon as they started the process, they would be cut off from the submersible.

They were going to use water from the tunnel to fill the bag and now with the pump working it was beginning to inflate. Wings watched intently and could hardly believe that he was involved in Jack's crazy plan.

Rearing up like a beast, the bag began to unfurl in front of them and it was not long before it filled the space blocking out much of the natural light. Jack lit the lamps and as the bag pressed tightly against the sides of the tunnel, he shone a light at Wings who was studying the pressure gauge. This was a critical moment, too much pressure could damage the bag and too little, it would not seal effectively. Jack had already done the maths; he had set a cut off valve on the pump to activate as soon as the bag had sealed sufficiently against the tunnel walls.

Wings flicked a switch and water began to race along the evacuation tube. This discharged water from inside the tunnel out into the ocean and as soon as the level dropped significantly, a vacuum began to form around them. The pressure needed to be equalised so as the water level dropped Jack operated a valve on a bank of cylinders allowing breathing gas to pour into the void. They would have to continue wearing their breathing equipment because the artificial atmosphere forming around them was heavily laden with moisture.

As the pressure equalised they began to feel more comfortable, but with the water level dropping steadily, the temperature inside the void began to rise. Wings was tempted to remove his mask, he was becoming increasingly uncomfortable with the cylinder strapped to his back. Even if they could breathe the atmosphere they had created, it would soon become stale as they used up the oxygen. Jack was relying on the air beyond the steel door to be sufficient for their needs; only then would they be able to remove their diving equipment.

At last, the water level reached their ankles and they were able to start work. The bag was holding fast, having sealed perfectly, and now all they had to do was to cut through the steel door. Plugging their ears against the noise and donning the correct safety equipment, Wings started the grinder and soon had a shower of sparks bouncing around the walls. Smoke and fumes filled the work area and sweat stung his eyes, misting up his goggles. He could feel his heart racing against his ribs; this was partly to do with his exertions and partly from the excitement generated by what they might find.

It took more effort than he anticipated to cut through the door, the steel was much thicker than he thought possible and now the muscles across his shoulders were beginning to complain. At last he felt the disc penetrate and he soon had a hole large enough for them to squeeze through. Powering down the grinder, he let it drop to the ground and with his chest heaving, he pulled off his goggles and wiped a hand across his face.

The air was thick with fumes and he could almost taste it through his mouthpiece. Standing back, he allowed Jack to swing his hammer and with a single blow the cut section gave way and it clattered to the ground on the other side of the door.

Like gentlemen explorers crowding around the opening of a long forgotten tomb they peered into the darkness. It was as black as night, even with their torches all they could see was an empty space shrouded in gloom.

Jack went first climbing through the hole, careful to avoid snagging his breathing equipment on the rough edges. Wings followed close behind. He was still hardly able to believe they had managed to carry out Jack's seemingly impossible idea. Struggling to contain his excitement, he followed Jack along the tunnel breathing deeply in an attempt to control his raging emotions.

After a while, Jack stopped and flashing his torchlight scanned the way ahead. The ground underfoot slopped gently downward and where the tunnel began to narrow the air grew cooler. The sweat clinging to his skin evaporated leaving him chilled, then suddenly he removed his mouthpiece and tentatively sniffed at the air. After an experimental breath, he turned to Wings.

"It's fine."

Wings tore the cylinder off his back and flexed his aching muscles. It was a relief to be rid of the weight and now he was able to breathe more easily.

"There must be an air purification unit around here somewhere." Jack said.

223

Wings looked around, his eyes following the beam of his torch. The walls were of rough-hewn rock that was grey and drab. Here and there he could see flint stones sticking out, it all looked old and natural, hardly a place in which to find high tech equipment.

The trolley stopped beside a magnificent crenulated keep. Arrow slits decorated the stone walls and a portcullis guarded the entrance. As they climbed out, Orlagh was ushered over a narrow wooden drawbridge that spanned a deep dry moat and passing through the entrance, she looked up. High above her head she could see murder holes. These were once used as chutes through which boiling oil could be poured onto the heads of the unsuspecting enemy attacking the gate. She shuddered.

"Wait here." One of the men said and with her entourage of women, Orlagh was made comfortable in an ancient guardroom.

It was not long before the men returned with an old fellow whose face was as wrinkled as an un-ironed shirt. His white hair spilled over his shoulders and hung down his back like wire, but his eyes were sharp and pure.

"Welcome," he said, his voice more powerful than he looked. "You, the woman who resembles the Goddess of Hibernia will be honoured at a ceremony where the goddess and The Morrigan will appear." He paused for breath. "You will become as one, the triple goddesses in human form."

Orlagh stepped back, she could sense the power resonating from this man and it made her feel uncomfortable. She had no idea what was expected of her and in an attempt to control her racing heart, she remained silent.

From the respectful attitude of those around her, she realised that he was either a druid or priest of some high order.

"Take her to the inner sanctum and prepare her for what will be done." With that, he turned and vanished into the darkness.

For a moment no one moved. The tension amongst them remained high but as soon as the spell holding them was broken, they did as he had said.

"You heard the priest."

Drawing in around her to form a protective circle, the women conveyed her along another sloping corridor until they came to a winding stone staircase. In single file they made their way deeper into the earth and, with a shudder, Orlagh wondered if she would ever see sunlight again.

Finally, they arrived at a series of richly furnished chambers, each one lit by candles and lamps. The light given off was soft and warm; it enhanced the atmosphere and helped to ease Orlagh's apprehension.

The air was sweetened by burning incense. At first, she was convinced that she could smell apple and cinnamon, but the scents were much more complex. They seemed to change as she moved and finally she gave up trying to identify them.

She was taken into a small ante-chamber where standing on a heavily ornate table was wine and goblets. One of the women poured a measure and offered it to her. Orlagh suspected that like before it was drugged, but she could not help herself. It was as if she had been conditioned to accept her fate and lifting the goblet to her lips, she took a sip. The others sensing her unease took up their goblets and filling them with wine drank merrily, then one of the woman beside her turned and said.

"Let me explain what will happen," she smiled excitedly.

Orlagh watched her closely and as she spoke, it was as if she was seeing the woman for the first time. Her eyes were huge and shone with an unusual clarity and her olive coloured skin glowed with youth.

"You will be refreshed, then we will cleanse your body and re vitalise your skin with oils. Your hair will be washed, dried and perfumed and when you are ready you will assemble amongst the goddesses." She almost danced with joy. "It will not be an unpleasant experience I can assure you of that."

The Stave of Yew remained inert inside her pocket. There were no vibrations or waves of heat pouring from its wooden heart, it was as if this far underground it had lost its powers.

The helicopter made its first fuel stop in Bulgaria. The storm troopers remained inside, out of sight of prying eyes. To the casual observer, the aircraft was simply full of cargo, the pilots having made a short stop before continuing on their way. In a few hours time they would be making their return journey and would need to stop again, they should then be carrying one extra passenger.

Almost seven hundred miles away, five FW190 fighter aircraft streaked down the short grass runway. With engines on maximum boost, they clawed their way into the sky just clearing the perimeter fence, and once safely airborne they assembled over the hydro-electric power station. Checking out their systems, the pilots set a southwesterly direction and began to follow the Dnieper River.

As soon as they were over the estuary, they turned and continued along the coast for a few miles before steering out over the Black Sea.

The first two hundred miles of their journey would be over water; this was the most dangerous part of the mission, if anything were to fail whilst over the sea, the chance of rescue was very slim.

Jack and Wings continued along the passageway leading from the cavern.

"This would make an ideal storage area," Jack said, his voice producing a strange echo, "with supplies coming in through the container on the sea bed."

"You think that was the point of entry?" Wings said glancing at him sideways.

"I'm convinced of it. The coast is more than fifty miles away, so whatever was going on here would have had a reliable supply chain."

"I guess you're right."

"What do we have here?" Jack said as he flashed his light towards the wall.

An industrial switch the size of his fist was recessed into the wall and as they approached, Jack could see no signs explaining its use.

"What do you think it does?" Wings asked.

Jack remained silent; he examined it carefully before curling his fingers around it.

"Let's find out."

Bulkhead lights set at intervals along the curved roof suddenly came to life bathing them in a bright glow, and as the lamps warmed up the light became more intense.

"Wow," Wings exclaimed, "I wonder what's powering them." Turning off his torch, he pushed it into his pocket.

"Battery cells," Jack answered. "Or maybe a generator of some kind."

The tunnel remained in total silence; there was no indication of a generator or other power unit rumbling away behind a closed door nearby.

"The power source must be substantial." Wings agreed.

"Well whatever it is I'm please we found the light switch," Jack grinned, "at least now we can see where we're going."

They made their way further along the tunnel and soon came up against another steel door. It was a perfect fit hugging the curved shape of the walls and Wings was reminded of the entrance to a Hobbit house. He would never admit this to Jack.

Going to the door, Jack pushed up against it but it did not give, even by working the handle it still did not want to move. The hinges were stiff but with a bit of effort from them both, they soon had the heavy door groaning inwards slowly.

"Wow!" Wings exclaimed again.

They stepped into an area that had clearly been used as a laboratory of some kind. Benches were lined up against the walls and cabinets filled the gaps in between. Some of these were for storage, a few still bore signs revealing their contents. The information was technical and printed in German so Jack could only understand the occasional word.

"We'll need to photograph these." He told Wings, who was inspecting a sealed fume cupboard.

Huge filters were housed in ducting that ran from the top of the cupboard and disappeared into a wall on the opposite side of the room.

"Must have been used for something serious." He murmured, thinking out aloud.

Instruments and empty containers littered the workbenches and moving closer he discovered a Dewar flask.

"Don't open that!" Jack said as he dashed across the room.

"What do you think went on here?" Wings glanced at him. "They were obviously testing something, but what, and why here on the bottom of the sea?"

"I think they were manufacturing something," Jack told him, "and more importantly they didn't want the rest of the world to know about it."

On another workbench, they found vials neatly laid out in a rack. Each container held a carefully measured amount of clear liquid.

"These are presumably for hypodermic syringes." Wings said, and picking one up he weighed it in his hand.

There was no evidence of what they contained, no label or notes to give away their secrets.

"We had better collect samples for Linda to test. We need to discover what's been going on here."

Jack had a fair idea but he kept it to himself. The Dewar flask they had found on the mountainside had contained a modified version of the deadly nerve gas Sarin. Perhaps this is where they developed the gas, he thought.

"Do you think this is some form of vaccination against the effects of Sarin gas?"

It was as if Wings could read his mind and Jack was amazed that he had come up with such an idea.

"Could be," he replied, "Linda had some idea that something like this was being developed."

He moved to where Wings was standing.

"This would be as safer place as any to mess around with something as deadly as this. If anything went wrong it could hardly annoy the neighbours."

Wings began collecting samples, placing them carefully into polystyrene lined aluminium cases that he pulled from his rucksack. He added the Dewar flask and when he was finished, he photographed every label and poster that he could find.

"What's through here?" Jack muttered to himself and going through an open doorway discovered an ante-chamber.

This area was much smaller than the laboratory; there were no benches or cabinets lining the walls. At first, he thought it was just another storage space, but then something attracted his attention.

Fixed against the back wall was a stainless steel panel containing six perfectly round tennis ball sized holes. Moving quickly across the room his skin began to crawl with apprehension. There was something sinister about this panel. From their carefully arranged openings, the holes ran deep into the seabed and a residue of dust, left over from the boring process, covered the ground around his feet. Jack found more evidence of dust just inside each hole and pulling his torch from his pocket, directed its beam into the first hole; but it was no good, it was unable to penetrate very far into the darkness. He checked out the others but came up with the same result.

"What have you found Jack?" Wings asked, moving up beside him. "They look just like miniature tunnels," he said, confirming Jack's thoughts.

"I wonder where they go," Jack said, "what could have made them and why?" So many questions filled his head.

"I think I can answer one of your questions Jack." Wings turned and pointed to a strange looking cylindrical object that had been abandoned on a shelf.

Reaching for it, Wings lifted it down and studied it closely. It was much lighter than he expected and on one end, he could see a red reflective panel.

"Let me see that thing." Jack said as he moved towards him.

Turning it over in his hands, he discovered a spring catch, which operated a small sliding panel. Opening the panel, he found the aperture behind was empty.

"This looks as if it was designed to carry a Dewar flask." Jack continued to study the object carefully then he focussed his attention on the red-capped nose cone.

"I'm sure this is a laser."

Moving towards the holes in the wall, he offered the object up; it was a perfect fit.

"These have not been mechanically bored," Wings said as he ran his fingers over the smooth surface, "they must have been laser cut."

"So this little critter is a mole. It must have been used to cut these tunnels." Jack frowned, going over everything they had discovered. It was all beginning to make sense.

"It's my guess that Sarin gas was modified here and then sealed in these flasks. Each flask was then placed into one of these moles which have been used as vehicles to deliver their deadly cargo."

"You could be right Jack, but where have they gone?"

Jack paced the room hardly daring to voice his conclusion. With the mole gripped tightly in his hand it was as if he could stop it from achieving its objective.

"You've seen firsthand what that gas is capable of. If it's deadly on the side of a windblown mountain just think how effective it would be in a heavily populated area."

"Surely you're not suggesting that this is a weapon designed to be used in some kind of terrorist attack."

Suddenly Jack had a flashback. He could see the huge atomic missile standing in its silo on the island of Gog. The Phoenix Legion had another missile stationed on a neighbouring island; both were aimed at significant cities; Washington and London.

"I'm afraid we may have stumbled upon another deadly attempt at world domination."

Wings was appalled. If it was anyone else but Jack suggesting this he would have discounted it out of hand, but he knew that Jack had seen this kind of thing before.

"Are we too late to stop it?"

"We probably are," Jack nodded gravely. "That's why our ship was attacked. The Phoenix Legion didn't want us getting too close to the container. I suspected all along that it was a docking station, but I had no idea this was going on."

"We have no way of knowing where these things were sent."

"They can only have been gone for a few days so maybe they haven't yet reached their targets. The Phoenix Legion must have been making their final preparations when the *Ocean Pride* sailed right up to their front door."

They remained silent for a moment both lost in the enormity of their discovery, then Wings exhaled noisily.

"How do we stop it?"

"I've no idea," Jack replied grimly, "we need to get this lot back to the ship where Linda can work on the contents of the vials. Maybe they will give us some answers. I also want to get inside this thing." He waved the mole in the air. "Perhaps it's got its own secrets to reveal."

XXXVI

Following the coastline where Ukraine spilled out into the Black Sea, the drone banked to port. Below the estuary, the Dnieper River spread its fingers delta-like across the landscape. If the drone had arrived thirty minutes earlier and five thousand feet higher, it would have met five FW190 fighters coming in the opposite direction.

The little onboard computer was recording every movement; it activated the camera, which now scanned the way ahead, it also picked up and recorded every ship moving along the deep channel far below.

On his screen, Kylie could see the estuary was made up of lagoons and marshy flood plains spreading haphazardly along the coast. From the air, the thick vegetation covering the landscape appeared well managed. He was surprised, he expected this region to be wild and untamed and following the drone's progress, he studied his laptop with increasing interest.

"Nothing stands out as belonging to the Phoenix Legion." He remarked.

"What do you expect," Mac said looking over Kylie's shoulder. "They are hardly likely to fly a flag advertising the fact."

"I suppose you are right, Schiffer is lower than a snake in the grass."

Mac grinned at Kylie's analogy.

"Does this drone of yours have radar?"

Kylie looked up before answering. "Yes it does have a basic system. It works a bit like ACAS, aircraft avoidance system."

Mac nodded his understanding and Kylie continued.

"It operates over a fairly short distance. Why do you ask?"

"I thought that as the Phoenix Legion has fighters they may also have other aircraft at their disposal. Perhaps if your drone could pick up and monitor air traffic..."

"I see what you're saying. It would have to be fairly slow moving though for the drone to have any chance of following it."

"Of course," Mac nodded, "I was thinking of aircraft taking off or coming into land. The place we are looking for must be close to an airfield."

"Good idea Mac, I'll get onto it right away."

Turning towards his laptop, Kylie typed in a command and after a few moments, he sat back in his chair.

"The drone is making its first sweep of the river. It's programmed to fly approximately three hundred miles upriver, then turn and make its way back. The round trip should take about six hours."

"Where is the turning point?"

"A place called," leaning forward he checked his notes, "Kremenchuk."

Mac turned back to where Kylie was sitting and studied the map himself.

"That's about the ultimate range of the FW190s. There's not much point in searching beyond that."

Following the river with his fingertip, he could see that above Kremenchuk it opened up into another reservoir. There were a number of hydro-electric power stations situated along the river so he guessed another dam would be found there.

Orlagh was feeling a little lightheaded. This must be due to the alcohol she thought, or maybe the wine had been drugged after all. Either way she didn't much care, she felt relaxed and a warm glow was spreading throughout her body.

"It's time for you to bathe my Lady."

Before she had a chance to object, the women moved in and slipped the robe from her shoulders. Standing naked in the middle of the floor, she glanced round to ensure the men had gone.

"You are quite safe with us." The woman beside her said. She could sense Orlagh's discomfort and taking her hand, led her towards the pool. Tiny lights were glowing beneath the surface of the water, it looked inviting and tiles set around the edge gave the impression of permanence. Orlagh stepped into the warm water and slowly lowered herself in. The perfumed water tingled against her skin just like champagne against her tongue. The sensation was subtle and not in the slightest unpleasant and as she lay back she closed her eyes and began to enjoy the sensation.

Two of the women followed her in and as one applied soap to her body, the other washed her hair. At first, it seemed strange to be pampered in this way, but there was little she could do about it. The sweet oils and the warmth from the water was like silk against her skin, it washed away her cares but in no time at all, or so it seemed, she was being raised from the bath. Soft towels were used to dry her body then she was laid down on a raised section where deep rugs had been arranged. Here oils were applied to her skin and her muscles gently massaged until she felt totally relaxed.

When they were finished, the women dressed her in a robe of purest white. Gold thread adorned the hem and the decorated neckline glowed in the light from the lamps. On her feet, they placed sandals of the softest leather.

Her hair was brushed until it resembled silk of the deepest red, and on top of her head, they placed a garland of tiny white flowers. Orlagh felt marvellous, and looking into the faces of the smiling women, she could feel their adoration and excitement.

Her Stave of Yew was resting on a small table and reaching for it, Orlagh held it tightly in her hand. It felt good against her palm, like a living thing she could feel its energy pulsing through her fingers. She sighed contentedly then suddenly she thought about Jerry. It was a fleeting half thought that was gone almost as quickly as it arrived. Jerry represented a life that she was about to leave behind and the more she struggled to hold onto his memory, the quicker it slipped away.

"It's time to go my Lady." Someone whispered, and Orlagh allowed them to lead her away.

Peering at her entourage as they made their way along the corridor, Orlagh realised that it was becoming difficult to see them clearly. Perhaps the oils they had rubbed into her skin were beginning to affect her mind. She was relaxed and a soft glow permeated her body until it filled her completely, she was not in the slightest concerned for she could sense no evil.

From up ahead she could hear the sound of chanting. At first, it was soft but as they drew closer, it became more intense until it sounded like monks chanting in a monastery. The pitch of human voices rising and falling was hypnotic, but there was something haunting about the tune. She had never heard anything like it before, it played with her emotions until finally it moved her very soul.

She was led into a huge cavern lit by flaming torches, and although she couldn't see them, she knew that many people were gathered here. The air was charged with anticipation and as she was drawn in, a druid appeared out of the darkness. He was chanting, his voice louder than the others as he moved steadily towards her.

Orlagh faced him alone; her entourage gone, swallowed up by the darkness.

"Come into the Triquetra."

A voice sounded inside her head, the instructions were clear, but she didn't know what to do. Relying on her instincts to guide her she spotted three interlinking circles laid out at her feet and stepping over the carefully measured line, she moved into the first circle. The druid remained in the centre where the three circles converged.

He was a magnificent man, tall and thin, he was dressed in a rich robe that swept the floor. Although his face was obscured by darkness, she could feel him staring at her.

Looking at the Triquetra laid out at her feet, Orlagh realised its significance. This religious symbol was three fold, the other circles reserved for the Goddess of Hibernia and The Morrigan, who were yet to show themselves.

Orlagh stood rooted to the spot, the druid continued to chant and as she focussed on the sound, she could feel her soul begin to stir. It was as if his magic was her jailor and instinctively she knew that she would never leave this place.

The Stave of Yew clasped tightly in her hand came alive, it began vibrating softly against her skin. It was as if the forces surrounding it were waiting in rapt anticipation, it would not be long now before the others appeared, they would join the circle and the knot would be complete.

The druid moved into the second stage of the ceremony and from somewhere in the darkness Orlagh could feel the presence of the goddess. She had experienced her once before in a ceremony on the island of Gog, but then it was Madb and her animal allies who were there to keep her safe. They had plucked her from the jaws of death and she wondered if they would appear again this time.

It was dusk, the sun had already bled into the western horizon and the remains of the day were fading fast. Sweeping out over the sea five FW190s lost altitude, and hidden by the darkening sky they turned to approach their target. Hauptmann was the call sign for the leading aircraft and the pilot, thumbing a button on the control column, spoke calmly into his microphone.

"Heinrich, radio check."

Heinrich receiving." Came the reply and in turn each pilot checked in using his call sign.

Gustav, Emil, Friedrich and Heinrich remained circling whilst Hauptmann made his bombing run.

Rising up above the cliff top, the FW190 climbed high into the sky before flipping over onto its back then the pilot lined the nose of his aircraft up on its target. This was a role the aircraft had been designed for and ground attack was its speciality.

With a solid fuel missile slung under each wing, it was a deadly platform and letting the nose drop a few degrees, the pilot fingered the firing button. The ground came up at an alarming rate but he waited until the very last second before easing back on the yoke, at the same moment, he stabbed the button, then the magnificent bird began to climb away.

There were no explosions as the missiles found their mark; these weapons were carrying something far more deadly than explosives. Gustav came next screaming out of the sky to deliver death, then the others followed at thirty-second intervals.

With their mission almost complete, they regrouped, but before setting a course for Macedonia, where they were to refuel, Heinrich dropped a flare in the centre of their target area.

Ten minutes later the helicopter carrying stormtroopers made its final approach. Lining up on the coloured flare burning brightly below, it began a steep descent and at the same time Hauptmann, in the lead fighter delivered his report over the radio.

The target had been softened so they were to expect little resistance.

"Stand by," the pilot announced over the intercom, "jump in sixty seconds."

He touched a button on the control panel and a red light appeared above the door in the cargo hold, it flashed three times before staying on. This was the signal for the stormtroopers to stand and check their kit before leaving the aircraft. The door slipped open and the men at the head of the line stood, waiting for the green light to flash.

The pilot, easing off their descent, brought the helicopter to a hover just a few feet above the ground. The downdraft from the rotor blades caused a mini hurricane that drove smoke from the flare to circle crazily around the undercarriage.

On the green light, the men jumped and as soon as their feet touched the ground, they rolled, coming up into the kneeling position. Covering with their weapons, they were ready to shoot at anything that moved and within seconds, the whole troop had gathered in a tight formation. The empty helicopter lifted away and circled out to sea, it would remain on station on a pre-determined flight path until instructed to return.

The druids were drawn to this place by the ancient cave systems running beneath the headland. The castle ruins were a bonus; the less damaged buildings used to store machinery and equipment.

The Stormtroopers filed into a small courtyard and working their way through the buildings, searched for the entrance to the tunnel system.

"Check the buildings thoroughly," Peter Huber, the officer in charge, issued his orders. "Don't bother with the ruins."

The number of bodies lying around the courtyard surprised him; he was amazed by the effectiveness of the gas. The pilots had done a sterling job and he was proud to be part of such an efficient team.

"Over here." One of the men shouted as he appeared at the door leading to a tower.

A spiral staircase made of stone ascended as expected, but it also descended into the rock floor to continue down under the foundations. They had found what they were looking for and charging down the steps they gathered at the bottom before pressing on in single file along a narrow passageway. The tunnel took them into a chamber but in front of them, cut into the back wall, they were faced with two entrances.

"Scouts," Huber called, he was going to send men in to explore the tunnels.

Suddenly a druid appeared but before he had time to duck back into the tunnel the Stormtroopers reacted. The first rank dropped to their knees, shouldering their weapons as the second rank closed up, filling the gaps between them.

The druid stood frozen with shock. Facing him in the semi-darkness was a troop of men dressed authentically in Second World War German army uniforms. He could hardly believe that Schiffer's men had discovered their hideout.

He had no idea of the fate of his comrades on the surface; the gas had not penetrated this far into the tunnels. His fight or flight reactions kicked in but before he had managed to turn and run, bullets ripped his body apart. The noise inside the confinement of the chamber was like thunder and the air became thick with cordite. Empty cartridge cases ejected from the breeches of their rifles pinged from the walls and bounced across the stone floor.

Before the sounds had dissipated, the Stormtroopers moved out. Kicking the body of the druid to one side, they filed into the tunnel he had emerged from and the deeper they went, the thicker the air became. The atmosphere became damp with cold and the light dimmed further, but soon they found tiny oil lamps set into niches along the walls. Flames danced like imps and as they passed eerie shadows crept along the stonework. Following the trail, they soon encountered a huge open space. Here the darkness was almost complete; it filled the chamber with an oppressive weight that pressed down amongst them. Although the men could sense the vastness of the place, it was not clear how far it extended.

The sound of a druid chanting somewhere in the shadows alerted them and as their night vision improved they could see a circle of tiny lights set out on the floor. Pale candlelight reflecting from a white robe gave a ghost like impression and suddenly Huber realised they had found Dr Orlagh Gairne. Now all they had to do was extract her from this unholy place.

Raising his right arm, he made some rapid hand signals. His men knew exactly what to do, fanning out they merged with the darkness and waited for the order to attack. First, Huber had his part to play and reaching into his pocket his fingers closed around a slim silver case. Inside was a syringe filled with the serum that would keep her safe from the Sarin gas. Moving silently forward, he crept up behind Orlagh and slipped the fine needle into her exposed flesh. She felt nothing as he injected her with the clear liquid. Focussed on the druid and in some kind of trance she had no idea what was going on around her.

On his signal, the troopers reacted without remorse tossing small grenade like devices into the darkness. They knew that death was a certainty and as the weapons clattered nosily across the stones, they began discharging their deadly load. Invisible clouds of gas rose up into the air and people began to die. Like a scythe cutting ears of corn, the gas went to work and people collapsed forcing others around them to panic. Pushing forward in a futile attempt to escape, it was not long before they too met the same fate as their colleagues.

Huber grabbed Orlagh and pulled her backwards. No longer could she hear chanting, the druids rhythmic mantra was replaced by the sound of panic and death from the people around her. Her eyes flew open, her link with the spirit world broken, and staring nervously into the darkness she cried out.

The Stormtroopers had taken a huge risk, they had disturbed the druid's ceremony and this was a hazardous thing to do. Spirits from the Otherworld would be present so withdrawing along the tunnel they did not look back. All they had to do now was return to their rendezvous and get away with their prize.

Orlagh was in shock, her awakening had been swift, the drugs and the power of the ceremony left her disorientated. She was aware that people had died and as they emerged from the tunnel, she could see at least a dozen bodies scattered around the courtyard. Men and women had collapsed along the path, but there was no time to stop and help. There was no indication of how this disaster had happened and it did not occur to her that the men beside her could have caused it.

Suddenly she was forced down onto the grass in the centre of the courtyard and the men closed in around her as they waited for their colleagues to appear. In the distance, she could hear the sound of rotor blades chopping through the air and as the sound became louder, a huge machine emerged out of the darkness overhead. It hovered just inches above the ground sending a hurricane of downdraft that almost knocked them off their feet.

A huge door in the side of the helicopter opened and men began to leap up into it. When it was her turn, the man behind unceremoniously boosted her up into the entrance and as soon as she was inside, someone pushed her down onto a hard bench and men began to crowd in around her. They were breathing heavily, the scent of sweat and fear filling the cramped space made her feel nauseous, and as the machine began to vibrate the noise inside became sickening. The pitch of the engine continued to rise until Orlagh thought her eardrums would burst then the helicopter reared up and she almost blacked out.

Jack and Wings were back inside the space between the steel door and the lifting bag. They were both wearing their breathing equipment and Wings was patching up the hole he had cut in the door earlier with a type of resin, and glass re-enforced plastic matting. Once applied, this material would become as rigid as the door itself and was more than sufficient to prevent the tunnel from flooding.

Whilst he was working on the door, Jack started the pump and reversing the flow, allowed water to pour back into the space. It would be impossible to collapse the rubber bung that sealed the entrance because water under such pressure would rush into the tunnel and crush them instantly. The chamber would have to fill slowly, the atmosphere inside bled away until the pressures were equalised, only then would they be able to swim back to the submersible.

"We'll leave all the equipment here," Jack said, "I have a feeling we will need it again very soon."

Wings was relieved, he was not looking forward to lugging the heavy tools back to the submersible. Leaving the tunnel, they swam steadily towards it and before entering the air lock, stowed the aluminium box containing the Dewar flask and the mole into a storage locker situated on the hull. Jack was not prepared to share the confined space inside the sub with a box containing deadly Sarin gas.

Once inside they helped each other to pull off their diving equipment and now breathing more easily, Wings settled into the pilot's seat. He began to carry out the usual checks, scanning the dials and controls on the panel in front of him.

"The Dauntless won't be on station for another twenty minutes." Jack reminded him.

It would only take a few minutes to rendezvous with the boat and dock between its hulls, so Wings busied himself with a few housekeeping chores.

Jack's head was filling up with questions to which he had no answers. He was certain that once Linda tested the contents of the vial she would discover that it had something to do with the Sarin gas. Obviously, the mole was a sophisticated delivery system, but he could not understand why the Phoenix Legion would go to such lengths if it were their intention to deploy the gas in some kind of terrorist attack. Why not use a more conventional delivery method.

The holes in the wall bothered him; six holes meant at least six moles, six destinations that would suffer the effects of a deadly gas attack. If these moles were allowed to reach their intended targets then the death toll could be catastrophic. He had to find a way to track them down, put them out of action before they were able to wreak destruction. A plan was beginning to form inside his head.

"Two minutes Jack." Wings glanced back over his shoulder.

"Roger that." Jack buckled on his safety harness and lifting the communication set, made contact with the *Dauntless.*

"They are on schedule," he informed Wings. "You are clear to go".

Wings nodded and pushing the throttles slowly forward, eased back on the joystick and the submersible began to rise from the seabed.

Jack realised that their business was unfinished and looking back out of the small porthole he watched as the tunnel disappeared behind the remains of the wreck. He could not shrug off a feeling of doom that threatened to engulf him, so turning away he focussed on returning to the *Ocean Pride* and putting his plan into action.

The helicopter stopped to refuel in Macedonia. The moment it touched down Orlagh peered out of the side window. Until now, there had been nothing to see but thick clouds. Occasionally she had caught sight of a clear night sky dotted with stars but now all she could see were a few random buildings under bright spotlights.

This was no commercial airport; there were no passenger jets or busy terminals, nothing to offer an opportunity for escape. This place was as desolate as her mood and now her spirit sank even lower.

The men beside her remained where they were, they did not intend to leave the cabin so Orlagh assumed they would not be staying on the ground for long. She sighed and moved into a more comfortable position.

The helicopter was still moving slowly along the runway and from beyond the window; she could see a number of small aircraft parked up beside one of the buildings. They were strange looking machines painted a drab grey with what looked like some kind of camouflage markings. She shuddered as the last in line disappeared from view then the helicopter turned sharply to the right and stopped. The rotor blades wound down and as the vibrations running through the airframe subsided, she could hear another sound coming from outside.

A fuelling rig was being attached to the helicopter and although she could not see it, a huge tanker had parked up beside them and was preparing to discharge fuel into the helicopters tanks. Suddenly the sounds were drowned out by another noise. At first, it was like a throaty cough, which soon developed into a stuttering roar before settling down into a steady beat. Instinctively she knew that one of the small aircraft had started its engine. Others joined in and after a few minutes, they began to roll along the runway close to the buildings. Small flashing lights on their wingtips caught her eye and she was unable to draw away from the window. It was fascinating to watch these deadly looking aircraft as they made their way towards the end of the runway. Puffs of blue smoke and flames stuttered from exhaust pods situated along the side of their sleek noses and the propellers disappeared into blurred discs of light as the engine revs increased. The aircraft seemed to come alive, they represented a deadly force and even though she found them frightening, Orlagh was fascinated by their presence. These were lords of their element and picking up speed, they roared along the runway until they lifted off and climbed effortlessly into the black sky. She watched until their flashing lights disappeared from view then all that was left were the sounds of the helicopter and fuel rushing into its tanks.

Half an hour later, the tanker recovered its fuel pipes then started its engine. It pulled away without her ever seeing it then suddenly the helicopter began to move, they were about to start the next leg of her journey.

The drone swept out over the estuary and turned gracefully before making its way back along the river. It had completed one pre-programmed circuit, turning somewhere near Dniprodzerzhyns'k and now it was preparing to repeat the journey.

Using a small joystick linked to his laptop, Kylie flew the drone manually taking it lower, and as it lost altitude, it remained hidden against the darkened sky. Using the infrared camera, he scoured the shipping lanes searching for ships that may be displaying the livery of the Phoenix Legion. A flag or banner would have done, but he realised that it would probably not be quite so simple. The Phoenix Legion would never advertise that fact that ships of its fleet were operating in the area.

It was tedious work tracking the drone, so they took it in turns to watch the monitor. It would be just his luck, Kylie thought, to fall asleep at the crucial moment and miss an opportunity, so reaching for his coffee mug he took a mouthful and kept his eyes firmly open.

Several hours later and the estuary was bathed in sunlight. The FW190s, sweeping in from over the Black Sea, began the final leg of their journey and with the river ten thousand feet below it appeared like a ribbon of silver against an olive green background.

Villages and small towns were dotted at intervals along its route, and from their vantage point, the pilots looked down on what seemed to be a landscape arranged with some purpose, but that was far from the truth. History had dictated the emergence of these settlements with farming at the centre of things, fields planted with crops merged with the forests, but further up river heavy industry had changed the face of the countryside forever.

Where once only the smallest boats could navigate huge dams had been built to supply hydro-electric power to the expanding population. Rapids and rocks that were once a hazard now lay underwater in manmade lakes and huge ships could now safely bring their trade into the interior of Ukraine.

The leading aircraft began to lose altitude slowly, and throttling back, the exhausted pilot led the others into a descent that would bring them home. Theirs had been a marathon mission, probably the longest ever undertaken by a group of Second World War fighters. These machines were not designed for long haul flights. They would have been stationed in makeshift airfields close to the battle zone; it was their job to intercept enemy targets both on the ground and in the air. This would have entailed short hops of one or two hour duration.

They had covered almost two thousand miles and the little aircraft had performed faultlessly. They were a testament to German engineering, having been restored and carefully maintained.

Spaced at ten-minute intervals and in line astern, the leader broke radio silence. He sent out an identification code before making his intentions known. Speaking clearly in German, he alerted the airfield of their imminent arrival, then, giving his final orders to the other pilots, he checked to see that his undercarriage had locked in the lowered position before making his final approach. It wasn't unknown for an exhausted pilot to attempt a disastrous landing without lowering his undercarriage.

Several miles away the drone was maintaining an altitude of two thousand feet. It had already made its turn and was now on its way back down river, completely unaware that five FW190 fighter planes belonging to the Phoenix Legion were settling on a short grass runway.

Within minutes, the aircraft taxied to their individual sheds, and surrounded by ground crew were pushed in under cover before the doors closed on the outside world.

Jerry was furious, he was not going to be treated like a child anymore, if he had to stay in bed for a moment longer, he would go completely insane.

At first, the shock of losing Orlagh was almost too much to bear, but now able to think more clearly he was determined to help Jack in any way he could.

"Good morning Jerry," Linda said as she appeared in the doorway of his room, "how are you feeling today?"

"I'm fine," he responded.

He sounded distant because thoughts whirled uncontrollably inside his head, he was desperate to grasp them and work out an effective plan.

Linda, moving up beside him studied thoughtfully. She could sense his frustration and checking his pulse and temperature, made adjustments to the graph in his notes.

"I'll change your dressings in a moment then arrange for some breakfast and coffee to be sent in."

"Can I have my laptop?" he fixed her with a determined stare.

Linda was expecting him to ask, she realised that she could not deny him for a moment longer. His strength was returning more rapidly than she expected and he hardly slept during the day now. It was obvious that he was beside himself with worry and would do anything to help get Orlagh back, but he remained her responsibility, she would allow him to do nothing that would undermine his recovery.

"Okay, but there are conditions," standing back she fixed him with a steely gaze.

The weight of her stare surprised him and he realised he would have to agree to her demands. "Whatever you say Doc."

"This is the deal." She folded her arms across her chest before going on. "You may have your laptop, but the moment I think you are overdoing it I will pull the plug. Is that clear?"

Silence hung between them and Jerry looked at her defiantly. He resented being spoken to like that, but then his expression softened as he realised that she only had his interests at heart.

"Okay, agreed. Do we have to shake on it like gentlemen?"

Linda laughed and the atmosphere in the room lightened. At least Jerry had lost none of his sense of humour.

Once his dressings were changed and he was more comfortable, Jerry eased himself out of bed and into a chair. This was the first time he had left his bed since arriving at hospital and he was delighted at this new development.

Propped up by cushions and with a small table positioned across his knees, his laptop was set up in front of him. A power lead trailed across the floor to a socket in the wall and beside his laptop was a notebook and pen.

Linda arranged for a fresh pot of coffee to be brought in and when it arrived, the aroma filling the room lifted his spirit.

He wasted no time and as soon as his laptop had booted up he went straight to the Brothers of the Sacred Whisper website. If anyone had any news, it would be Mad Max.

The forum page opened up and as the screen came to life, Jerry scanned the list of names that appeared. These were people who were currently logged on and like a social networking page; he could simply click on a name and begin a conversation. There was no one that he recognised so moving the cursor to a search box, he typed in Mad Max. The search program initiated but came up with nothing, clearly Max was not on line. Jerry sighed; he desperately needed to speak with him. He rarely made contact with anyone else on the site apart from joining in with various conversations, so he could not resist spending a few moments scanning the list of current topics. None of them looked remotely interesting, there was nothing relating to the Phoenix Legion or the druids.

He was about to log out when a headline caught his attention. Like a news flash, a box appeared on a tool bar at the top of the screen and clicking on it, he opened it up.

'Druids lair in southern Greece at*tacked by Phoenix Legion Stormtroopers.*' He began reading the article and soon discovered that a poisonous nerve gas had been used to slaughter hundreds of druids. The news item was succinct and heavily edited by censorship, but reading between the lines the message was clear.

Sitting back in his chair Jerry turned what he had learnt over in his head. This piece of information raised many questions. Why had the Phoenix Legion attacked the druids, he thought they were allies. His eyes darted back to the screen but he was unable to learn more.

XXXVIII

Kylie studied the screen on his laptop as the drone flew over the reservoir near Nikopol. He checked the information coming in from the tiny onboard computer and it confirmed the drone's position, speed and altitude. It was maintaining just over ninety miles per hour at a height of five thousand feet and looking at the picture on the screen it was clear that nothing much was happening.

He was bored with his constant vigil and tapping the pen he was holding against the side of his coffee mug he turned away from the screen. Stretching his arms luxuriously above his head, he stood up and paced the room only then did he begin to feel a little better.

Snatching up his empty mug he turned towards the coffee machine and was about to pour when an alarm sounded on his laptop. The radar system on board the drone had picked up a fast moving object converging onto its course. Abandoning his mug, Kylie returned to the keyboard and began pressing keys.

An indicator flashing on the screen was moving from a southwesterly direction, it was not yet close enough for the camera to provide a clear visual, so making a few calculations, he discovered that the target was travelling at one hundred and fifty miles per hour. Its current altitude was eight thousand feet and at that speed, it would not be long before it overshot the drone.

Kylie sent out instructions, increasing speed to maximum and making a slight course correction, he realised that still put the drone almost fifty miles per hour slower than the approaching aircraft.

He continued to study the screen and as he watched, it became clear that the aircraft was losing altitude. It was now one thousand feet lower but maintaining its course and speed.

The aircraft overtook the drone, passing two thousand feet above and some way off to port. Kylie made another course correction, activated the forward-looking camera and as the drone came round it locked onto the co-ordinates that he had provided. The camera zoomed in and picked up the image of a helicopter. It was huge, large enough to be carrying a cargo, but it displayed no logos or emblems. The only identification mark was a number stencilled onto its side but he felt sure that would reveal nothing.

The helicopter was drawing away swiftly and there was nothing he could do but watch it go. The radar system was short range and soon the contact would be lost, but from the attitude of the helicopter, it was obvious that it was following an approach course and would soon be landing somewhere. Kylie's heart began to beat faster and his stress levels soared; they had been waiting for this development. His fingers skipped over the keyboard as he fed information into his computer, he was using a program to predict a possible landing site. This would at least provide them with a viable search area.

The helicopter was soon dozens of miles ahead steering an easterly course as it ducked under five thousand feet. The drone was flying at maximum speed, Kylie could put it into a dive, increase its pace and help reduce the ever-increasing gap between them, but it would be a futile act. It was imperative to maintain contact with the helicopter for as long as possible, with every extra minute their chances of predicting an accurate landing zone improved.

Mac wandered into the control room. It was almost time for him to relieve Kylie, but first he would have to top up his caffeine levels.

"We have a contact." Kylie told him.

Forgetting his coffee, Mac moved across the room and looked at the computer screen.

""It's now beyond our camera range and our maximum speed," Kylie explained, "but we do have a predicted LZ."

Mac remained silent as he took in the information. Kylie had set the laptop screen so it was split into four equal sections with each quarter displaying different technical data. One was devoted to the radar system and was constantly updating, another quarter showed the view from the onboard camera. The sky in front of the drone appeared empty and clear, but as he looked closely, he could just make out a speck in the distance. The camera could be zoomed into a higher magnification, but there was no point, the helicopter was ordinary enough displaying no outstanding features. The third section was devoted to vector, speed and altitude, with the final part continuing to predict a landing zone.

This information was being updated constantly and all they could do was watch and wait. Of one thing they were certain, the helicopter would be well out of range by the time it landed.

Orlagh felt her stomach lurch as the helicopter suddenly lost altitude. It hit a pocket of rising air and the turbulence turned their gradual approach into something more uncomfortable.

Resisting the urge to cry out, she gripped the bench either side of her legs and held on tightly as she waited for the sensation to pass.

Her heart was beating rapidly and her mouth was dry. They had been in the air for hours and she was hot, thirsty and exhausted. Her energy levels had hit rock bottom and the further she travelled from the druids, their influence over her seemed to wane leaving her feeling deflated.

There was no longer any sensation from the Stave of Yew in her pocket and her spirit sank even lower as she studied the men pressed in around her. She was appalled at the way they had attacked the druids' stronghold. There had been so many people killed, the women attending her were callously murdered along with the druid carrying out the ceremony and she was sure there had been countless others watching in the darkness. She had no idea how many had perished.

The drug administered by the druids was beginning to wear off and now she could see things more clearly. The Phoenix Legion had mounted the attack, that much was clear, but she could not understand why. She thought they were working together, so why would they be fighting each other? Thoughts whirled around inside her head as she remembered the faces of the dead.

At last, the helicopter touched down and she was thankful to be back on solid ground. The noise from the rotors winding down left her ears ringing and when the door was finally thrown open, a rush of warm air washed into the cabin. The men began to move and as soon as there was more space, she was urged to stand. She hardly had time to steady herself before being pushed towards the door.

Orders were issued in a language that she did not understand, then an officer dressed in a black uniform approached.

"You are to come with me." He said, addressing her curtly in English, but his accent was thick and difficult to understand.

Orlagh was ushered across the landing area towards a large building, which doubled up as a workshop and aircraft hangar. One of the fighter planes she had seen earlier occupied the space at one end, and men dressed in grey boiler suits were in attendance.

"Wait here." The officer said, pushing her roughly down onto an upturned crate.

She did not have to wait long, an army lorry squealed to a stop outside the open door and men began to scramble up and over the tailgate,

"Let's go."

Orlagh stumbled towards the lorry and looked up. It was obvious that she was expected to climb up, but she hesitated. There was no way she could do it dressed in her long robe and soft slippers.

"Schnell." Came a gruff order from somewhere behind her, but before she had time to move, rough hands lifted her off her feet and she was dumped unceremoniously onto the hard wooden floorboards. One of the men sitting on the bench running the length of the lorry took hold of her collar and hauled her up beside him.

It was more than an hour before the drone arrived at the co-ordinates set by Kylie. Although narrowed somewhat, the search area was still huge, but circling at three thousand feet he used the camera to scan the landscape below. The light was fading fast and shadows were lengthening across the valley floor. Soon it would be completely dark and he would be forced to use the infrared camera, but first he was going to make good use of what light remained. He wanted to get an idea of the landscape; he figured that what they were looking for would be situated not far from the river.

The drone levelled off and maintained altitude then throttling back, Kylie reduced its airspeed by twenty five percent. With the aircraft trimmed, he began to program the on-board computer and once that was done, the drone would start flying a circuit.

Their search was based on an overlapping grid pattern that relied on the cameras mapping out the terrain. The radar system would record any movement, and he calculated that it would take five hours to cover the whole area. He was convinced the landing zone was down there somewhere, even if the helicopter had departed they were sure to find evidence of its base.

Sitting back in his chair, Kylie watched the screen with interest. A canal of some kind cut through cultivated fields as it made its way towards the Dnieper River. From above it looked nothing more than a narrow irrigation channel, but he realised it was more than that; it must be several metres wide. A wooded hillside sloped down towards the river, the trees so densely planted that it made a natural barrier against those intending to gain access to the valley.

The *Dauntless* cruised into harbour and using powerful searchlights to illuminate the basin, made its way towards the wall on the far side. A man appeared on the harbour wall, Wings, standing at the bow, threw a line up to him and the man tied it off.

As soon as the boat was secure, they disembarked and went

towards the dry dock in search of the *Ocean Pride*. Jack was carrying the aluminium box containing the Dewar flask and mole, and Wings following on behind, held onto the briefcase full of notes.

"Hi Jack, welcome home." Paul greeted him with an outstretched hand.

"I have a present for Linda," Jack said the moment he stepped aboard. "I must get it to her right away, there's not a moment to lose. How is Jerry?"

"He's fine, he might have some news for you," Paul explained, "he's been working on his laptop for most of the day."

Jack raised his eyebrows and looked surprised.

"Razor and the guys are in the Wardroom, or in what they call The Control room."

"I'll catch up with them later, I must see Linda first. I'm afraid she's going to be working late."

Ducking along the corridor, he left Paul to deal with Wings.

"Did you have fun?" he asked turning towards the young man.

"Awesome Captain Seymour sir, it was truly awesome."

Paul grinned at his youthful enthusiasm; he could see a lot of himself in the lad.

"You just watch yourself; a man like Jack Harrington can lead you into a whole lot of trouble."

"Sure thing sir, I'll take your word for that."

He knew that Jack and Paul went back a long way and had heard tales of their exploits. He was full of respect for both men but he idolised Jack.

"We sure did have some fun," he continued as he began to relate their adventure.

XXXIX

Jerry thought that as it was evening he would have better luck speaking with Mad Max. He wasted no time in browsing, going straight to the Brothers of the Sacred Whisper website, he began a search for his contact, but it was no use, Max was still not there. Jerry sighed with disappointment and checking the open forum again, he looked for an update regarding the attack on the druids' base, but there was nothing new. The article he had read earlier remained unchanged.

He was about to give up and log off when unexpectedly a message popped up on the screen in front of him.

'Hi Caradoc.'

It was Pixie Lee using his identification name.

'Hello there, how are you?' Jerry typed as quickly as he could using one hand.

'Oh not so bad, yourself?'

They exchanged pleasantries before Jerry steered their conversation to a more serious subject.

'What do you know about the attack on the druids?'

There was a pause before he got his answer.

'Well, it was definitely carried out by the Phoenix Legion.' She told him.

'Why did they do it? I thought they worked together.'

'That is true; however, it seems the druids had something the Legion wanted.' Again, she paused; it was as if she was reluctant to continue.

'Is it something to do with the Belgae Torc?' Jerry asked.

'You could say that, but the Legion already has it.'

'So what is it the druids had if it wasn't the torc?'

'Power for one thing,' she told him before going on. 'The Legion are worried that the druids will become too powerful through their magic and beliefs,'

'But surely the Legion could use the druids' power to their own advantage.'

'True,' Pixie Lee typed. 'Word has it that if the druids become too powerful they will withdraw their support from the Phoenix Legion. The druids were coming to the end of a sustained program of ceremonies designed to unite three mighty elements. You have to realise that a coalition between goddesses is pretty serious stuff.'

'Why would they want to do that?' Jerry remained sceptical; he did not share her Celtic beliefs.

'Well, it's partly to do with unfinished business in the spirit world. A hugely important ceremony went wrong about a year ago with almost catastrophic effects. The druids and the Phoenix Legion had to disappear for a while but now they are back with a vengeance.'

Jerry knew a lot more about what she was referring to, but he chose to keep this information to himself.

'By bringing these three elements together,' she continued, 'the Goddess of Hibernia will breathe with life once again. The Morrigan, the goddess and the woman with red hair will become a mighty force.'

'The red haired woman?' Jerry typed frantically.

'Yes, it seems she was captured recently and is the living likeness of the Goddess of Hibernia.'

Jerry was stunned by this new development. He was also amazed at Pixie-Lee's knowledge, he had never told her about Orlagh or her connection with the druids.

'The Phoenix Legion also wants this woman. Once they realised the druids were holding her, they had no option but to attack. Word has it the raid was a success and now the woman is being held by the Phoenix Legion.'

Jerry was unable to reply, the news hit him hard and left him reeling, he needed a few moments to gather his thoughts.

'Why does the Phoenix Legion want this woman?' He could not remember if he had already asked this question.

'I think it has something to do with her being a key figure in the ceremony to bring the goddess back to life. Without her, the druids are powerless; this is exactly what the Legion want. They now hold all the cards and the druids will do anything to get this woman and the Belgae Torc back. Max was close to discovering the truth but I haven't heard anything from him in days. I'm really worried.'

'What was it he thought he knew?'

'I don't know, he didn't share his knowledge with anyone, he simply disappeared before he had a chance to say anything.'

This was another piece of disturbing news.

'You had better take care Caradoc, I've already told you more than I should.'

'Do you think something has happened to Max?'

'It's not been confirmed yet but I believe so. Knowing a little about what he is mixed up in frightens me more than anything. Nothing good will come of this Caradoc, you should be worried too.'

Jack appeared at the door. "Jerry, how are you?"

Jerry was staring at his computer screen going over what Pixie Lee had just told him when Jack walked in.

"Jack, what are you doing here?"

He explained briefly what had taken place over the last few days, and as Jerry listened, he arranged his thoughts into some kind of logical order. The last week had been confusing enough but now with this latest development he felt as if he were tumbling once again into the abyss. He glanced at his computer screen but Pixie Lee was gone, the chat room deserted and her name missing from the list of those left online.

Jerry logged out and shut down his computer before looking up at Jack.

"I have some news for you," he began. "I've just received confirmation that the Phoenix Legion have Orlagh."

"I see," Jack nodded. He was not surprised and was in no doubt that the information Jerry had was correct.

"My contact also told me that the druids had Orlagh, this was why they were attacked."

"When was this Jerry?"

"Earlier today, first thing this morning I think."

A deep frown creased Jack's forehead as he thought about what Jerry had just said. He was confused; he had been told that Orlagh was taken from the ship by Schiffer and his men, so how had the druids ended up with her?

"Look Jerry, it's great to see you looking so well but try not to worry, it's important that you take care of yourself. I don't want Dr Pritchard blaming me for tiring you out. I've got to go now to see Razor and the guys but I'll swing by again in the morning. You should get some rest, you've done good today."

The Wardroom was full of the sounds of men relaxing and as Jack stepped into the room, the noise hit him like the blast from a furnace. Most of the men were familiar faces and they acknowledged him as soon as he appeared.

Razor and Mac were sitting by themselves at a table.

"Jack," Razor called out and standing up raised his hand above his head.

Laid out on the table in front of them was a map of Ukraine and Jack could see a series of lines and notes pencilled in.

"Am I glad to see you," Razor said, "We have a development."

He brought Jack up to speed with what had been happening.

"So, you tracked a helicopter using one of Kylie's drones and you say it landed somewhere in this area." Leaning over the table Jack pointed at a section of the map.

"Yes, as you see it's within the range of the fighters. We think this is where the Phoenix Legion is holed up. It's only a matter of time before we flush them out."

Jack filled them in with details of the attack on the druids' camp and that Orlagh had been airlifted out.

"Do you think it's possible that the Legion dispatched their men from this location? It's a heck of a long way from Greece." Razor said glancing at Jack.

"I know it's a long haul, but with the right helicopter and a well planned supply line I think it's possible."

"The helicopter we saw was certainly big enough to carry a small taskforce; where else could the Phoenix Legion be operating from?" Mac said adding his own thoughts.

"We've had no intel regarding their whereabouts and it seems unlikely that they could be anywhere closer to Greece. You would have thought that Turkey would be a likely place to set up base, but they would be spotted flying from there."

Jack rubbed his fingers across his stubble and leaning forward studied the map.

"No I think your men are right, they must have a base somewhere in Ukraine, it's where the fighters appeared from in the first place."

"What do they want with Orlagh?" Razor asked.

"According to Jerry the answer to your question is twofold. Firstly, they must prevent the druids from becoming too powerful. Apparently Orlagh is a crucial element to their ritualistic ceremonies and through her they appear to gain strength."

Mac shot Razor a glance but it did not stop Jack from continuing.

"Secondly, the Phoenix Legion want Orlagh for reasons unknown," he paused to study their faces. "We must find out where they are holding her and what they intend to do next."

Then he told them about what he had discovered in the laboratory beneath the Sea of Azov.

"I need to see Kylie, he must have something, a bug of some kind that we can send into those tunnels. We need to find out where those moles have gone."

Kylie was busy watching the screen on his laptop when Mac went in to relieve him. He should have taken over hours ago but Kylie insisted on doing a double shift especially now things had become more interesting.

"Jack wants to run something past you." Mac told him and Kylie finally relinquished his post. Tearing his eyes from the screen, he got to his feet.

"Be sure to let me know the moment something happens."

"Of course, you'll be the first." Mac assured him.

Turning away, Kylie left the room. He needed a break, he had been staring at the screen for hours and now his eyes were complaining. Caffeine had sustained him throughout his vigil, but suddenly he was feeling the effects of fatigue.

"Hello Jack, welcome home." He shook hands with his friend.

"I hear you've been busy."

"Only these last few hours," Kylie grinned, "you know what surveillance is like, hours of boredom followed by a few seconds of action."

"I can imagine."

With the friendly banter over Jack got down to business, he told Kylie about what they had found.

"Where do you think these tunnels go?" He asked.

"I have no idea, they seemed pretty deep. What have you got that we could send down to track those moles?"

Kylie studied the photograph that Wings had taken and after a few moments said. "I think I have just the thing. I had better put a call through to base, get them to send out some of my little friends."

It was now completely dark outside and shadows were dancing eerily around the stonework. The lorry began to slow down but before it stopped, men began leaping out over the back like paratroopers. One of them made a joke about a tailgate jump, but Orlagh did not understand his humour.

She waited for the lorry to stop before getting to her feet and once the tailgate was lowered, she stood on the edge and peered nervously down. Someone whistled and the men laughed. Orlagh could feel their eyes feasting on her, but ignoring them and their lewd comments; she hitched up her robe and began to climb down.

As soon as she was safely on the ground, the men gathered around her and she was marched quickly through an open gothic doorway leading into a huge medieval hall. Giant wall hangings adorned the walls and at one end above a magnificent fireplace hung a full length red, white and black banner. She had seen this kind of thing before in old photographs but had never imagined that she would see one for real. A huge swastika, a symbol of Nazi dictatorship made her shudder. It dominated the end of the hall and Orlagh felt dwarfed under the weight of its symbolism. For thousands of years this had been a symbol of peace and good fortune, but all that had been destroyed. Now the Swastika had come to represent occupation, depravity and death.

"Ah, Dr Gairne," a man's voice echoed amongst the heavy oak beams overhead and Schiffer stepped into view. "How kind of you to join us again, I trust you had an agreeable journey."

"Why did you have to murder all those people?" her voice trembled.

"Murder, what can you mean?" he frowned as he eyed her curiously. "I simply ordered the slaying of a few peasant priests, but murder, you must be mistaken."

"There were women and children amongst the druids and you killed them mercilessly."

"Sub humans like druids deserve no mercy," he began and standing up straighter, he oozed arrogance. "As far as women and children are concerned they were lebensunwartes leben, life unworthy of life, whores and filthy spawn who have no place on god's earth."

Orlagh was speechless; she could hardly believe that he could be so callous. Surely, these beliefs belong to a time past.

256

"You are shocked I think by my ideology of racial hygiene. Those who are corrupted by an infusion of degenerate elements must be removed, they cannot be allowed to breed and pass on their deformities, besides we have no more use for the druids."

Orlagh was aware of his outlandish Nazi beliefs. Adolf Hitler had championed racial purity and actively drove out and eradicated those deemed unworthy, but how could these abominably archaic ideas have any relevance today?

"Why are we having this conversation?" she demanded. "I have been dragged here against my will and ill treated by your men."

"Let me remind you Dr Gairne, it was you who brought the subject up. As for the matter of your being ill treated, I doubt that very much. You are our guest here and will be afforded every consideration and comfort."

"I have been dragged here against my will," she insisted, "so therefore I am your prisoner."

"As you choose to believe, however whilst you are under my care you will receive the hospitality you deserve."

She looked up at his stony face and shuddered. His words hung in the air between them like an executioner's axe and she realised that she would have to be very careful indeed. Schiffer could make her incarceration as unpleasant as he pleased.

"I'm very tired and thirsty after my journey, could I please be shown to my room and have some refreshments?"

"Of course, you may indeed." Schiffer grinned as he eyed her. "I will also have something more appropriate for you to wear sent in."

She was still dressed in her white ceremonial gown; it was now soiled and stained and a little threadbare.

Orlagh was shown to a surprisingly well appointed room situated at the top of one of the towers. A magnificent four-poster bed dominated it and heavy curtains hanging from bolsters were tied back with thick golden cords. Where the garderobe would have been was a narrow doorway leading onto a basic but functional bathroom. It had a flushing toilet, a tiny hand basin and the smallest shower cubicle she had ever seen. There was even a double glazed unit set into the gothic stone mullioned window, but the scene beyond was shrouded in darkness. There was not yet sufficient starlight for her to see out.

Orlagh had no idea where she was, she had been cooped up in a helicopter for most of the day and even with a couple of stops, it was impossible to tell which direction they had been travelling. The only people

257

she had seen since arriving were uniformed military men who spoke with thick German accents.

Once she had freshened up, she moved back into her bedroom and wondered what she should do. Her surroundings appeared formidable, escape would need careful thought and planning, but what she needed most was rest. She must build up her strength and courage before attempting any kind of breakout. She had no idea what Schiffer had in mind for her, but based on her previous experiences she could hazard a guess.

Razor joined Jack and Wings in one of the engineering workshops on the after deck. Wings was standing over the mole; it was laid out on a workbench like a corpse on a mortuary slab. Tools had been arranged on benches around him and moving in, he began the operation of dismantling it.

Jack wanted to know how it worked, only then would he begin to understand its full capabilities.

"Obviously it was designed to carry the flask," Wings began, "and we can assume a Dewar flask containing a deadly nerve gas." He glanced up at the others before continuing. "We think the business end contains a laser of some kind that is capable of cutting through solid rock."

He had no idea how much Jack had told Razor, but for his benefit he carried on talking as he worked.

"We need to discover what powers this thing, how it manages to find its way and how far it's designed to go." He paused again before selecting a tool from the bench.

"You had better proceed with caution," Jack said. "I don't anticipate any danger apart from the obvious risks associated with a job of this kind, but you can never be sure."

They were all dressed in grey boiler suits and safety glasses that were compulsory when working in the engineering workshops.

Wings picked up a screwdriver and began dismantling the outer case. Access panels sat at intervals along the metal structure and these came away easily exposing a complexity of electrical wiring and computer circuits.

"This must be the power source," he pointed at a series of tiny battery cells, "but I've never seen anything like this before."

"The Phoenix Legion are experts in technical development. Their scientists probably designed and built these to order."

"I think you may be right," Wings glanced up at Jack. "This must be the

258

mini computer system that runs the show." He probed carefully with an electrician's screwdriver. "Can we hook it up to one of ours, see if we can mess with its brain?"

"That would be a good idea," Jack confirmed, "be aware of booby traps. I seem to recall an eyeball ROV linking up with a computer system in a rogue submarine. The computer self destructed before any information got through."

"What happened to the eyeball?"

"It was turned into scrap metal along with the control room inside the sub."

"Some booby trap," Razor grunted as he took a step backwards.

Wings, undeterred began connecting up a laptop computer to the jumble of electrical units inside the mole. He worked confidently and when everything was ready, he powered up the unit and lights began to flash on the computer screen. He had programmed it to run through a series of complicated searches, scanning for bugs in the system.

"All good so far," he reported with a satisfied grin. "Ah, we have a radiation count that's rising." Pausing, he waited for the details to appear on the screen. "It's nothing to worry about, but I think we've found our primary power source." Turning towards the computer, he typed in a command. "We have ourselves an RTG."

Peering closely to where the mid section had been exposed, there were no more removable panels, the rest of the body was sealed.

"This is where the radioisotope thermoelectric generator must be located. An RTG is an array of thermocouples used to convert heat released by the decay of a suitable radioactive material into a usable power source." Wings sounded like an expert.

"These are used to power satellites and space probes," Razor said. "The Soviets also used them to power remote facilities in the Arctic Circle. These things remain active for years and that suggests that these moles have been designed for a long term purpose." He moved slowly around the workbench as he continued.

"They must be targeting some far off locations," he stopped beside Wings.

"They could, I guess, be capable of boring a hole right across the globe."

"And carrying a highly toxic cargo," Jack added.

"So we can assume the targets are not necessarily close by then." Razor continued with his train of thought. "These could be long term weapons, designed to reach their target then lay dormant, waiting for a command to activate. It would take some time to reach say New York, Washington or London, for example. If we are looking at a synchronised attack then moles that don't have so far to travel would have to wait for the others to get into position."

"It wouldn't take much to bounce an activation command off a satellite." Wings cut in. "This little fellow could be sitting pretty just waiting for the party to begin."

They remained silent, each man lost in his own thoughts. The enormity of their deductions were frightening, this was a significant breakthrough.

"Of course this could all be pure conjecture." Razor said glancing up at both Jack and Wings in turn.

"An educated guess I agree," Jack responded, "but I think we're not far from the truth. We have to assume the worst, but there's one thing we have to know."

"The intended targets," both Razor and Wings said in unison.

Jack had an idea that maybe this was something Jerry could help them with.

XLI

The following day Kylie drove out to Ataturic airport just outside Istanbul. He had arranged for a consignment of micro drones to be sent out from their headquarters in New York, and now he was on his way to collect them.

The hour might be early but still Jack went to see Jerry, he wanted to fill him in on what was happening.

"Do you think you could use your online contacts, see if there is any word out there about the moles?"

"I'll do my best Jack." Jerry was pleased at the prospect of doing something useful.

"We really need to find out where they might surface." He continued before telling him about their theories.

"Do you really think these moles are capable of biological attacks on cities around the world?"

"Given the evidence I'm afraid so."

"To what end? Surely, the murder of thousands of people would be a pointless exercise."

"I guess it's a display of dominance and power. Last time they had atomic weapons directed at both London and Washington."

"True, but then their grudge was with the powers that defeated and humiliated them at the end of the Second World War."

Jack nodded. "But this time it's different, now we are looking at six targets at least."

They remained silent for a moment then Jerry asked. "Any news from the drone yet?"

"No, Mac's been monitoring its progress for much of the night, but nothing as yet."

"It can only be a matter of time; we know they are out there somewhere."

Jack was amazed at his optimism. It wasn't so long ago that Jerry was in a deep coma. The injuries he had suffered were life threatening but here he was, sitting upright in his chair, willing to do anything to help find Orlagh.

"Ah, Jack," Linda appeared at the door. "I have the results you wanted."

"That's great," Jack grinned, "can you do a presentation in say," he glanced at his watch, "twenty minutes?"

"Give me half an hour and I'll be pleased to. Your office?"

"Yeah that would be good. I'll muster the others."

Jack assembled Razor, Mac, Wings and Paul. Kylie was still somewhere between the ship and the airport. An officer had been recruited to watch the drone, with strict instructions to disturb the meeting if there were any significant developments.

"Right gentlemen," taking a sip from her water bottle, Linda eyed her audience. "Let us begin."

She had set up her laptop and was going to use the overhead projector with diagrams to underpin her delivery.

"The contents of the Dewar flask were practically the same as you found on the mountainside. Without doubt, this biological weapon attacks the nervous system and it's been modified to kill instantly, conventional Sarin gas would take at least a few minutes if not longer to be effective. It would of course depend on the health of the victim, but this stuff is infinitely more deadly."

"The flask is designed to fit inside the mole. How much chemical would there be in the container and what damage could it do?" Paul asked the question that concerned them most.

"That depends on a number of factors. Release it in an enclosed space and the effect would be catastrophic," she paused, "let's say for example a crowded underground train station, or a shopping mall. Anyone within a half-mile radius would be killed instantly and beyond that, depending on the rate of dilution into the atmosphere, I would estimate that no one within a mile and a half radius would be safe."

"What do you mean by that Doc, what kind of effect would it have on people at that distance?"

"The elderly, sick and very young would probably die pretty quickly from some kind of respiratory failure. Heart attacks and strokes would be a common form of death with others experiencing some degree of seizure. The emergency services would be inundated and unable to cope with the volume of casualties."

"I guess depending on the weather, wind speed and such; out in the open air the effects would be reduced." Mac added.

"I would imagine so," she turned to face him, "but these weapons have been designed to be used in enclosed and busy places."

"If for example one of these moles was to release its gas in a metro station, could it be possible for the poisonous cloud to be dispersed along the track and affect other stations miles away. You know how air is pushed through tunnels in front of trains."

"This is true and very feasible. It's my guess that the moles have been programmed to target metro stations and other tunnel systems like sewers and gullies."

"Can you imagine gas clouds rising up out of the drainage system along New York Main Street? During rush hour, hundreds of thousands of people would be cut down and it wouldn't stop there. In the panic that would follow, many more people would be killed under the weight of the stampede."

"What about the vials?" Jack asked before anyone else could add to the speculation.

"Yes, now that was very interesting. It's a countermeasure against the effects of the gas."

"An antidote?"

"Not as such," she typed a command into her laptop and a diagram appeared on the screen. "The serum seems to have been developed as a barrier against the effects of the gas. It would be administered before exposure, to reduce if not negate altogether the effects."

"So an army could be rendered immune?" Jack asked.

"Yes, that's true. They could in theory take the drug then walk into a poisonous cloud and survive."

Jack thought about what Linda had said. He knew that experiments like this were carried out during the Second World War. Nerve gas like Sarin had been developed as weapons of mass destruction with countermeasures and antidotes being high on the list of scientific priority all over the world. Unfortunately, this had resulted in human experimentation. Prisoners in Europe had suffered extensively in concentration camps, used as guinea pigs for all kinds of tests many of which resulted in death or disfigurement. Hazardous experiments designed to help military personnel injured in combat situations had taken place, with those unfortunate enough to be involved exposed to new weapons such as nerve gas and the drugs used to counteract the effects. All this was undertaken to further medical understanding and to measure the amount of suffering military personnel could take on the battlefield with the results being used to help develop recovery and welfare.

"Jack," Paul said for the fourth time. "You have an important message."

An officer from the watch had come down to the Wardroom with an urgent communiqué.

"Okay, sorry Paul, I was miles away."

Making his apologies, he left his place at the table and followed the man to the communications station where he could take his incoming call.

The men listened as Linda began her summing up, each one struggling with their own fears and theories, and when she was finished, she left them seated around the table.

They were left in no doubts, they must focus their efforts on discovering where the moles had been sent, but as yet they had no idea how they were going to stop them from achieving their goal.

Finally, with the meeting over Paul made his way back towards the bridge and on the way he ran into Jack.

"I've had some bad news," Jack began, "I must return to the States immediately."

"Why, what's happened?" Paul stopped and looked at his friend.

"It's a personal matter. My mother has collapsed and I have to go to her right away."

"I'm sorry to hear that." Paul said his face a mask of concern.

"It's serious," Jack continued, "I just spoke with her doctor, even if I leave now I will probably be too late."

"Then you must go Jack, leave everything to me, I'll organise the men, you don't have to worry about a thing."

He could see the hurt etched into his friend's face. Paul knew that Jack would never leave a task half finished, and it was clear that he was torn between an obligation to the job and loyalty towards his mother.

"Let's go to my office, we need to make plans."

As soon as they arrived, Paul got them both a strong mug of coffee, then sitting down in comfortable chairs they began.

"Okay Jack, how do you want us to proceed?" Paul wanted Jack to feel in command; clearly, he was in shock and needed guiding back onto familiar territory.

"Get Wings to take Kylie back into the Sea of Azov. They must get those drones into the tunnels and find out where the moles have gone. Wings knows the procedures, but make sure he understands that he's not to take any unnecessary risks. He's got to get in and out of there as quickly as possible."

"Okay Jack." Paul was making notes as his friend relayed his orders.

"Tell Razor to assemble his taskforce. The moment the drone has located the Phoenix Legion, they must be ready to go in. Their main objective is to recover Orlagh, but there may be further information to be had. I'm guessing there is some kind of control room deep in the heart of their hideout."

There was no doubt in his mind that his men could carry out the job.

"When did you say the ship would be ready to sail?"

264

"Theo tells me within the next seventy two hours."

"Good," Jack nodded, "that gives you three days to make ready. I want you up there in the Dnieper River in support of our guys. I appreciate the dangers, but sending the ship in as close as possible might be the only way we can get our people out."

"Okay Jack, leave it to me will you. Now you must be going."

XLII

he *Dauntless* was prepared for the return journey across the Black Sea and into the Sea of Azov. Kylie had his micro-drones and support systems safely stowed on board, and Wings was overjoyed at the prospect of leading him into the tunnels and underwater laboratory. He still found it hard to believe that he had been there himself, Jack had turned a seeming impossible task into reality and now he was going to do it all again.

The journey out was uneventful and tedious. They could hardly motor at top speed, the boat was capable of over thirty knots, but a fishing vessel would never exceed its most economical cruising speed.

Mac kept watch over the drone and shared a twenty four hour vigil with Razor. They planned for every scenario and Mac, using his own computer, fed information into a program based on the intelligence they had gathered. He had a clear picture of the terrain and by using maps downloaded from the internet was able to study the area in minute detail.

He always did this, very little was left to chance; he would plan every raid minutely, calculating the odds of success. He would never agree to a manoeuvre without first putting it to the test against some computer model.

Their taskforce was made up of thirty six highly qualified men, all ex-military, drawn from both the British and American Special Forces. Each man was handpicked by Jack and Razor and employed as security enforcers for the company. It was not unusual for them to find themselves in some very unstable parts of the world. In the kind of work Jack was often involved in a private well trained army was an essential asset.

"What do you make of that?" Mac asked Razor who was sitting at a table on the other side of the room.

The drone was soaring at two thousand feet and on the screen, they could see the usual heavily wooded valley rolling down towards the Dnieper River, but this time there was something different. On the right bank about half a mile ahead were the ruins of an ancient castle. Perched up on a rocky outcrop it peeped out above the treetops with a commanding view across the valley. At first, it was hard to see as the eroded stonework had taken on the colour of its surroundings blending in perfectly with the environment. It was only as the drone corrected its course that the edge of a tower stood out against the sky.

Mac set the co-ordinates using the laptop keypad and the drone adopted an elliptical orbit above the area, then using the camera he zoomed in for a closer look. Under high magnification, details began to emerge. At first, it looked innocent enough, just another romantic ruin abandoned long ago, but as he studied the surrounding area, he began to think otherwise.

The landward side of the hill had been cleared and the lower parts of the castle looked as if they had undergone some degree of restoration. Some of the buildings surrounding the castle were obviously new additions, and the scars in the landscape suggested occupation by more than just a rich developer or eccentric inhabitant.

"It seems this place has been the focus of some interest recently." Mac said to himself as he zoomed in even closer.

The drone turned lazily over the spot and with more of the secret landscape being revealed Mac became convinced they had found what they were looking for.

"Is that a landing strip?" Razor asked pointing with his fingertip at what appeared to be light aircraft landing area.

A row of buildings cleverly disguised to blend in was arranged along one side of the short runway and there were clear indications that this place had seen action recently. Marks in the ground made by heavy vehicles stood out and as Mac flew the drone closer, he confirmed his suspicions.

"Something has used this place not long ago," he said pointing to where aircraft had obviously landed and taxied across the grass. Tyre marks stopped at the sheds.

"Second World War fighters," Razor mused, "I would hazard a guess those buildings are hangars."

"Could be," Mac agreed. "This is where the helicopter must have landed. It's bang in the centre of our predicted landing zone."

"Where is everyone, the place looks deserted?"

Mac set the drone on a course that would allow them to look at the bigger picture.

"Maybe we'll find the Phoenix Legion camped up on the hill."

The following day Orlagh was moved to another room. She was marched briskly along a gloomy corridor by Heidenrech, one of Schiffer's S.S.Officers.

"Halt." He said loudly once they had climbed a stone staircase that spiralled upwards for several floors.

Stepping past her, he inserted a huge key into a lock then pushing the ornately carved door open, led her into a pleasantly furnished room.

"You will find everything you require here." He told her, his accent guttural and his manner curt.

"Am I to be locked in like a prisoner?" Orlagh snapped, her eyes blazing fiercely.

Heidenrech eyed her with disdain.

"We are civilised people here Dr Gairne, you will be under house arrest, nothing more."

"Why am I to be locked away?" She persisted, angry at the thought of being imprisoned yet again.

"For your own safety," he began, "you must realise that you are vulnerable. We have many," he paused searching for the right words, "frustrated men here most of whom have not been home for a long while. So as you might appreciate, it would be unwise for you to be wandering around unchaperoned." He eyed her distastefully again as he took in her thin heathen robe.

"You will find a wardrobe of more suitable clothing and a bathroom through there." He nodded towards another door.

Orlagh was furious, the way he looked at her made her feel dirty and she was about to launch into a tirade of abuse, but changing her mind she clamped her lips together and remained silent. What good would it do, she asked herself. He had obviously made up his mind about her and she would have to live with it.

Clicking his heels smartly together he nodded stiffly then, performing a perfect about turn, he marched out through the open doorway leaving her standing there alone in the middle of the room.

The heavy door banged shut behind him and she heard the key turning in the lock, then nothing moved, the room becoming heavy with silence. Taking a deep breath, she could feel her heart racing and she became light headed, she must remain calm, she thought, and looking around began to take stock of her surroundings.

It was comfortable enough with solid stone walls curving slightly as they followed the shape of the tower. A stone mullioned window over-looked the valley below and there was a stone window seat. Worn by time, it formed part of the wall that was at least a metre thick. This was an original feature and she wondered how many others over the generations had sat and mused in this very spot.

Taking her place on the cold stone, she glanced out of the dusty window. The view across the valley was breathtaking, trees growing side by side formed an unbroken carpet that rolled down to the water's edge, and far below, she could see the river. It twisted and turned as it made its way through the valley meandering like a drunken fool, and in the distance, she could see where it joined the main river.

She had no idea how long she had sat there, time stood still as she contemplated her fate. It was not like before when held prisoner on the island of Gog. Then the Phoenix Legion and the druids worked together and she had a purpose. The druids needed her to help celebrate the power of the Belgae Torc, and bring life to the goddess of Hibernia. The Phoenix Legion had benefitted, but here it all felt wrong. Something must have happened to drive them apart, and the horror of the attack played on her mind. Forcing it away, she had no wish to dwell on what she had seen.

The light outside was fading and a chill began to emerge from the stones, so turning away from the window she went to find some warmer clothes.

The drone began another circle as it orbited high over the castle ruins. Soon it would be dark and they would have to use the infrared camera. Razor realised the chances of spotting anything was slim and effectively they would have to wait until daylight.

"I say we brief the men," Mac said. "This is the place, I feel sure of it. It's right where we predicted the helicopter would land and it's well within the range of the fighters."

Razor knew he was right but he would feel better if they had some tangible evidence. Sending in a taskforce based on such slim intelligence could turn out to be a complete waste of time and if they were wrong, a mistake like that could cost Orlagh her life.

"Okay Mac," he said after a few moments. "Let's get our men assembled in the Wardroom and start the ball rolling."

"Wait, what's that?"

On the screen in front of them, something on the ground was moving.

"Zoom in quickly." Mac said and the resolution sharpened as the camera focussed on the target.

"Well I'll be damned, would you just look at that!"

Marching between the buildings were two columns of men dressed in World War Two German army uniforms.

"It's uncanny," Mac said, "just like watching an old war movie. Those uniforms look perfect."

"Look at those 'piss pot' helmets!"

"Right Mac, we'll muster the men and get this show on the road."

This was the evidence they had been waiting for and now there was not a moment to lose.

In the Wardroom, men were sitting around every available table. The tables had been arranged so the men could see a smart board, and now an aerial view of the castle complex including the landing strip was projected upon it.

"The best way in is by Sikorsky," Razor began. "We'll land on the perimeter of the grass runway, this way we should attract little or no attention from those inside the castle. Anyone seeing us land will probably assume we are a scheduled visit." He paused to look at the men.

"It must be at least two miles from the castle so we'll have a little trek." Mac took up the narrative.

"Yeah, time enough to get our bearings and decide how best to get inside that fortress." One of the men said.

"We'll have the drone circle above the ruins as soon as its daylight, then we'll have a better picture of the layout. I'll also see what I can discover on the internet, there's sure to be photographs of this place."

Razor and Mac took it in turns to brief the men and as they discussed their plans they all agreed on one thing, more intelligence would be helpful if they were to make an effective battle plan. The layout of the castle would be a crucial element; they needed to know what they were up against.

"How many troops are stationed there?"

The answer to this question was what the men wanted most.

"We have no idea at this time." Razor replied.

"Where are they keeping Dr Gairne?"

"Again, we have no idea."

Murmurs washed around the room like a Mexican Wave and Mac spoke up before the disquiet turned into a riot.

"We are working on the scenarios. The computer is crunching numbers as we speak; it's just a case of feeding in the intelligence as it becomes available. As Razor said, the drone is sending back valuable information all the time and we have other resources to study."

This quietened the men down and they began to discuss weapons and firepower, then after about half an hour Paul and Theo arrived. They slipped quietly into the room and took their places at a table, listening to the conversations, becoming acquainted with what was going on.

270

Although they were not part of the taskforce they wanted to be in on the briefing, but events regarding the ship repairs had detained them.

"I'll fly the Sikorsky." Theo said when there was a lull in the noise of the briefing.

"You're not part of the team." Razor reminded him.

"I'm aware of that, but with Jack gone and Wings out on a mission, I figure you'll be needing a helicopter pilot."

"I can fly the Sikorsky." Razor said.

"I know that, but you will have your hands full commanding men on the ground." Theo continued to put his case forward and the men listened.

"I can get you in there, take off and remain on station until you need me to pick you up."

"It makes sense." Paul broke the silence that followed Theo's speech. "Besides, it's not as if you're going in under fire, it should be safe enough."

"Well, I can't guarantee that will be the case for the evac." Still Razor was not convinced.

"We'll just have to deal with that at the time," Theo nodded. He didn't need to be reminded of the dangers. "Paul should have the *Ocean Pride* in position by then anyway, so a few holes in the helicopter shouldn't be too much of a problem, it's not as if we'll be facing a long distance flight.

XLIII

Twenty hours later the *Dauntless* was making her first run over the wreck in the Sea of Azov.

"Stand by to launch." A command sounded in Wings headphones and he replied as he tightened his grip on the controls.

Glancing across at Kylie who was strapped into the co-pilots seat he grinned.

"Are you ready?"

"Yeah, let's get going."

Kylie had never experienced anything like this before and sitting in the cockpit of the submersible, he could easily imagine that he was about to be launched into space. In his lap, he was cradling the box containing the micro-drones. It should have been stowed with the rest of the equipment but he could not bring himself to part with his little toys.

"Ten seconds to separation." Came the voice again and Wings began the countdown to zero. The moment he was ready he nodded his head and Kylie pressed the button, cutting them loose.

The submersible lurched forward and nosed dived crazily as Wings applied the throttle and as soon as they were clear of the twin hulls, he eased back on the little joystick until the sub was level and just a few metres off the bottom.

"Hit the spotlights," he said and Kylie, doing as he was told, lit up the seabed with powerful beams of light.

Peering through the dome overhead, Kylie could hardly believe his eyes. The wreck was now nothing but a collection of scrap metal parts and the container had disappeared completely.

Wings brought the sub down with hardly a bump.

"We'll have to walk from here I'm afraid." His voice was heavily laden with excitement as he began shutting down the systems, then he unbuckled his safety strap and climbed out of his seat.

As soon as they had pulled on their diving gear, they exited the sub through the escape hatch, and still clutching his box of drones, Kylie followed Wings who was making his way steadily towards the narrow tunnel entrance. Kylie was a competent scuba diver but this was not his natural habitat, he much preferred to be on land, feeling the wind against his skin.

The narrow entrance opened up into a small cavern with a steel door located at one end, the first thing Kylie noticed was the patch that Wings had used to secure the door. Tools and equipment lay scattered under a thin covering of sand and turning towards the pump, Wings activated it and soon the bag lying at the entrance began to inflate.

It was not long before the lifting bag filled the entrance completely, then the water level began to drop. As soon as it was below the patch on the door, Wings used a grinder to reveal the hole he had cut previously.

The cavern beyond was pitch black but this did not deter Kylie from peering in. Wings, moving up behind him used his torch but it was no use, he knew the thin shaft of light was impossibly inadequate to penetrate the darkness but he did it to show Kylie the extent of the problem. Without hesitation, he climbed through carefully easing his breathing equipment over the jagged edges.

Kylie followed and stumbled awkwardly into the tunnel. It was uncomfortable wearing a diving suit complete with breathing equipment in such a confined space and he soon began to sweat, but once they had gone a safe distance Wings stopped and pulled off his facemask.

"This is amazing." Kylie said, shrugging the cylinders from his back.

"It's not far now." Wings told him and a few minutes later, they were ready to move on.

Wings soon found the light switch they had located before and turning the industrial sized switch, the bulkhead lights came on.

"Wow, what's powering those?"

"Jack thinks it must be a battery of some kind linked to a generator."

Kylie switched on his hand held computer and waited for it to boot up. He would use this to programme the micro-drones and track their initial progress, but once they were back on the ship he intended to use a satellite link to do the job.

Waving the device around in front of them, he frowned.

"I'm picking up a strong radiation reading."

"As in nuclear?" Wings glanced at him.

"Yeah, it could be our power source. Let's get the drones on their way then check it out."

The micro-drones were perfectly made mechanical insects. They each had two pairs of wings protruding from pear shaped bodies. These allowed them to perform like tiny dragonflies and on their underside were situated three pairs of legs. Tiny cameras were mounted like eyes up front and antennae like sensors protruded forward just like the real thing.

Each drone was about the size of a hornet and powered by a tiny battery.

"These little chaps will remain active for about six months. They can fly at twenty miles an hour and move along the ground at a brisk walking pace. They are virtually indestructible."

Wings was fascinated as he balanced one on the palm of his hand.

"Right," Kylie said, "where are they going?"

Wings led the way into the chamber where the six holes were located and Kylie powered up each micro-drone in turn. He allowed them to fly around as he tested their circuits and once he was satisfied, he flew them towards the wall and perched them at the entrance of each hole.

"Let's get these little babies going." He pressed a key on the tiny keyboard and little red lights began to glow on each drone then after a second or two they took off and were gone.

Wings pressed his face up against one of the small tunnels but he couldn't see a thing. The drones had disappeared and the only way to track them was electronically. On Kylie's hand held computer, six little red lights were flashing rhythmically and he grinned with satisfaction. He set in motion the command that would link them to the satellite, the information would then transfer automatically to his laptop located onboard the *Ocean Pride*.

"That's it," Kylie announced. "Let's go and find the source of that radiation."

Using the Geiger counter facility on his tiny computer, Kylie led the way. Wings had not been inside this tunnel before; leading off at right angles from the laboratory it was much smaller than the main tunnel. He had to crouch lower in order to avoid banging his head on jagged rocks that protruded from overhead.

"Here we go." Kylie said as he came up against another steel door.

The tunnel widened just enough for them to crouch side by side and reaching out his hand, Wings pushed against the door but it did not budge.

"It must be locked or jammed." He said, stating the obvious. "We'll have to use a crow bar and force it open."

A warning sign had been posted on the door, but it held no meaning for them as it was in a language they did not understand.

Reaching into his pack, Wings pulled out what looked like a folded walking stick. Made from the strongest carbon fibre he used it as a lever to splinter the wooden frame then the door sprung open. Inside they found a nuclear power plant.

Squeezing into the cramped chamber, they stared at the device. It was a mass of pipe work and electrical circuitry and in what looked like a huge golf ball was the assembly that held a nuclear isotope.

"This thing could probably run for hundreds of years."

"Yeah, for as long as it remains stable." Wings replied eyeing the poor condition of the walls and floor.

"There's no reason why it shouldn't even in these conditions." Kylie said, running his hand over the pipe work.

The main device was about three metres long and one and a half metres in diameter. Spaced along the outer casing were pressure release valves and a cooling manifold, this in turn was connected to a power generator where the heat from the isotope was converted into electricity.

"What have we got here?" Kylie said his voice filling with alarm.

Wings looked up and moved quickly to where he was standing. In the gloom, he could see a device flashing and a set of numbers counting down at an alarming rate.

"This is a timing device."

"For what?" Kylie asked.

"A type like this is usually reserved for sophisticated explosive devices. We had better get out of here and fast."

Wings wasted no time in explaining further and shot out through the door. Moving as fast as he could, he made it to the end of the tunnel before he was able to stand upright, then turning to Kylie, he helped him to his feet before racing back the way they had come.

Reaching the spot where they had left their diving equipment they began pulling it on. Kylie stuffed his hand held computer into a water-proof bag, and working as quickly as they could, they made their way towards the steel door.

Climbing through the hole, they pulled on their masks before hitting the switch that would begin flooding the chamber. They did not bother to make a new plug for the hole in the door, Wings simply held up the glass fibre panel he had made previously and using silicone mastic sealed it into place. This was only a temporary fix, water would flood into the tunnels eventually but that was not their primary concern. They had to get as far away from here as possible before the explosive device went up.

"How long was left on that counter?" Kylie asked.

"I have no idea; I didn't have time to look. Why use the power source as a bomb?"

"That chamber must have been booby trapped. Perhaps by forcing the door we activated the detonating device."

They stared helplessly at each other and waited for the water level to reach a sufficient level before they could break the seal and equalise the pressure.

After what seemed a lifetime, the water had reached the marker and Wings activated the valve that would synchronise the pressure inside the tunnel with that pushing against the lifting bag.

On the surface, the *Dauntless* had just completed another turn and was heading back towards the spot where they had released the submersible. It would take just over half an hour for the fishing boat to complete the distance and all the while, a radio operator was on station waiting for a message from the men they had sent to the bottom. When the message came through it would mean the sub was nearing the surface, only then could they resume communications. If Wings and Kylie were not ready for the rendezvous, it would mean another hour would pass and another sweep of the fishing beds as the *Dauntless* maintained the pretence of a working boat.

Suddenly a huge explosion shook the air turning night into day and soon after the percussion wave hit the *Dauntless* almost stopping her in the water.

"Change course," the skipper instructed the helmsman. "Turn the bow into that wave."

Before the sound had cleared the heavens, there came another even more alarming noise. On the horizon, a heaving tidal wave rose up like a monster from the deep and with the force of a runaway train, rushed towards them like a tsunami. It could easily capsize them, reduce them to fragments, but by meeting it head on, the boat would have the best chance of surviving its destructive force.

The man at the helm disengaged the autopilot and wasting no time gunned the engine as he began the manoeuvre. The little boat responded faultlessly and he was left in no doubt they would be safe enough even if it proved to be a rough ride.

The *Dauntless* dropped into the depression that preceded the wall of water, then like a terrifying fairground ride, she rose up an almost vertical cliff of grey angry sea.

The men on board tied themselves to whatever was solid enough to survive the onslaught and this simple act saved them from being dragged into the maelstrom of foam that swirled around them. With twin hulls slicing through the water, the engines struggled against the opposing force and when they reached the top, the helmsman cut the throttles and they toppled over the edge. The *Dauntless* went into freefall tumbling down a vertical cliff.

The boat smashed into the concrete-like water at the bottom and the crew gasped, the wind driven out of them by the sickening impact. The *Dauntless* was left wallowing in stunned misery, but a split second later the helmsman pushed the throttles forward and brought her back under control. The little fishing boat steered onto course almost undamaged and continued her journey towards the source of the explosion.

"Get a message out to the sub." The skipper said turning towards the man on the radio.

Instinctively he knew the submersible could not have survived an explosion of such force, and he realised there was little or no chance of finding Wings and Kylie alive. Something had gone terribly wrong, the explosion had undoubtedly originated from the tunnels on the seabed and now he would have to inform Paul of the tragedy.

As soon as they arrived over the spot where the sub had been cut loose, they activated the sonar equipment and began to scan the bottom, but it was no use. There was nothing left to see, the explosion had transformed the ocean floor into something quite different, there was nothing left of the tunnels or the laboratory. The remains of the wreck had completely disappeared, like the submersible it no longer existed.

"Prepare a team to go over the side." The skipper ordered. It was a futile act, but he had to confirm what he knew to be true.

XLIV

Orlagh had spent hours locked inside her room occasionally visited by attendants who brought food and drink. Sometimes they would stay for a while chatting merrily as if all was well with the world.

Her headaches had returned with a vengeance. Thor's hammer beat a rhythm inside her head until she felt nauseous and sitting down on the edge of her bed she reached for the Stave of Yew. This was an unconscious move that she found herself doing more often lately. The wood felt smooth and cool as her fingertips brushed over it, then, lifting it up she pressed it against her forehead. It was heavenly against her skin, and closing her eyes she laid back as soothing waves of comfort washed over her.

What was it about this strange talisman that held her fascination? She asked herself again but still could find no answer. In moments of boredom during her incarceration, she had attempted to travel back to her dream world. She wanted to seek the wisdom of the Shaman, but it was impossible, the doors to the spirit world were firmly closed to her. It was as if she had never been there at all, it had simply been a dream, the result of her overactive imagination. That is what Jerry would say whenever they discussed her experiences.

She sighed again, emotion catching at the back of her throat as she thought about Jerry. She missed him so much and ached to be near him. When with the druids her feelings for him had somehow become subdued, she hardly gave him a thought, but now things were different and she thought about him all the time.

She wondered how he was coping with both his physical injuries on top of worrying about her. She knew he would be beside himself not knowing where she was, then a sob caught at the back of her throat and she wished more than anything to be with him, nurse him through his recovery. Turning over, she buried her face in the pillow and rode out the emotions that surged through her body.

After a while, she managed to compose herself and with an effort focussed her mind on other things. She chose not to dwell on the horrors of the attack or the ruined stronghold but thought about the ceremony itself. She wondered what the druids were trying to achieve now they were clearly no longer partners with the Phoenix Legion. What had

278

become of the Belgae Torc after the murders in the mountain village in Turkey? That was another unsolved mystery. Questions filled her head, taunting her mercilessly, and with them came renewed anxiety then, suddenly her headache returned. Groaning aloud, she hauled herself up off the bed and staggered towards the bathroom where she dry retched into the pan.

After a while, she leaned drunkenly against the sink and splashed cold water over her face before peering at herself in the mirror. She was horrified by what she had become. Her face was pinched and pale, but what shocked her most was the state of her lifeless red hair.

The following day the *Dauntless* returned to harbour and making its way towards the wall, tied up close to the dry dock.

Theo had doubled the workforce in an attempt to complete the repairs to the *Ocean Pride* and now they were almost ready to start re-floating the ship. On board, preparations were being made to get underway and as soon as the water level was high enough and the huge lock gates opened, the crew would take up their duties again.

The *Dauntless* was shut down and secured before the men began hauling their gear onto the *Ocean Pride*. Their hearts were heavy with loss; both Wings and Kylie were popular members of the team.

"We searched the ocean floor," the skipper reported directly to Paul, "but there was nothing left to see."

He handed over a file containing a digital recording of their dive and a written account of everything that had taken place.

"There was nothing you could have done." Paul consoled the man as he took the file. "'They must have disturbed something or the Phoenix Legion knew we had discovered the laboratory. Perhaps our boys were simply in the wrong place at the wrong time."

This was no consolation; the deaths weighed heavily on them all and worst of all they may never know what caused the explosion that killed them.

"At least they achieved their objective. We've managed to get inside Kylie's computer and the micro-drones are sending signals back to the satellite."

"Well that is good news," the skipper smiled. "I was beginning to think the drones had been destroyed in the explosion."

Jack would be devastated by the news. Paul had been unable to reach him but left messages urging him to make contact immediately.

Jerry could feel vibrations running through the ship the moment the engines started. Linda had told him that the repairs were coming to an end and they would soon be returning to the Black Sea, their destination the Dnieper River, a journey that would take about thirty hours. He was also aware that a task force was scheduled to leave the ship in twenty four hours. A drone, searching for the Phoenix Legion headquarters had apparently located a possible site.

Turning on his computer, Jerry wanted to know if anyone had information about Orlagh. He would speak with Mad Max first, so typing in a password he logged onto the Brothers of the Sacred Whisper website and went straight onto the forum. Not much was happening, there were only a few visitors to the page and as Jerry scanned the names, he realised that Max was not there. He was about to abandon his search when a message flashed up on the screen.

'Hello Caradoc'

'Pixie-Lee, how are you?' They exchanged pleasantries before Jerry began to ask awkward questions.

'Have you had any contact with Mad Max?' He typed as quickly as one hand would allow.

'Let's go into a private room,' came the response. Pixie-Lee was as paranoid as ever.

'What news have you?' He urged, anxious to get their conversation underway.

'I have some sad news.' She began. 'I've been waiting for you to log on. I didn't want to leave you a message, I must tell you this myself.'

'What's happened?'

'Max has been murdered.'

Jerry was stunned by the news that appeared on his screen.

'What do you mean, when?'

'It happened about a week ago, that's why you have not been able to reach him. I didn't find out myself until a couple of days ago.'

'Do you know who killed him?'

'It was almost certainly the Phoenix Legion.'

Silence stretched out between them as Jerry took in what she had just told him.

'I can't believe it.' He typed. 'Are you certain?'

'Oh yes, it's true alright. Max was silenced, he knew too much. What he was involved in is really dangerous so you need to be very careful.'

He knew just how treacherous it was, he had the scars to prove it, but the shock of knowing that the Phoenix Legion had murdered Max was almost too much to take in.

'*Where was Max when he was killed?*'

'*Berlin, that's where he lived. My sources tell me he was interrogated before being beaten to death. It's horrid just thinking about it.*'

'*Do you know what he was working on?*'

'*No and I don't want to know. I want nothing to do with the Phoenix Legion or the druids. It's just too dangerous. Whatever is going on with you needs to stop or you will be killed too.*'

Pixie-Lee didn't know the half of it. Jerry had told her very little about his involvement in all of this and as far as she was aware, he was researching for his university degree.

'*I know there is more to your involvement than you are telling me.*' She typed. It was as if she had psychic powers and could read his thoughts but then she explained.

'*I hear things, I make connections. I'm not stupid you know.*'

'*I'm sure you're not.*' He responded.

Words continued to appear across his screen.

'*Max was my friend. We never met in person, but came to know each other very well over that last three years.*'

Jerry didn't know how to respond. She was obviously devastated and scared out of her wits. She had helped him out before, her knowledge was invaluable and he wondered if she was holding back vital information.

'*Is there anything you can tell me, anything at all that might help bring his murderers to justice?*'

There was no reply and he wondered if he had overstepped the mark. He waited for a long time just staring at the computer screen willing her to reply then suddenly a series of numbers began to appear.

Jerry stared at the screen and frowned then reaching for a pencil, he copied them down on a piece of paper.

601015

245607

Pixie-Lee had left no explanation and now she was gone. Holding the paper between his fingers he frowned, what was she trying to tell him?

He studied the numbers closely; they were not long enough to be telephone numbers and could not be dates of birth or any other significant calendar dates either. He didn't know enough about mathematical formulae to identify them as such, so pushing away the stand holding his laptop he eased himself up out of his chair. Holding his hand to his head, he sighed deeply. He needed time to think, work it all out, but then he had an idea. Two heads were better than one and three would probably solve the problem.

Eventually he found Razor and Mac in their little control room that was located just off the Wardroom.

"Jerry, what are you doing up here?" Razor said the moment he appeared in the doorway.

Ushering him in quickly he checked the corridor to make sure he was alone. He guessed that Linda had no idea Jerry had escaped from the hospital ward.

"Here pal, have a seat." Mac stood up and offered him the computer chair he was sitting in.

"How's it going? Jerry asked as he lowered himself carefully into the chair.

"As you see, busy, busy, busy." Razor grinned, indicating to the heap of files and papers spread out over the table.

"I need your help," Jerry began dragging a folded piece of paper from his pocket. "I've just been given these numbers, they may have some significant meaning but unfortunately I can't work it out on my own."

Mac stepped closer and taking the paper, studied it for a moment. His face showed no emotion as he passed it to Razor.

"Where did you get this?" he asked.

"As I said," Jerry looked up at Razor. "One of my internet contacts gave it to me but I'm completely stumped. I've no idea what those numbers mean."

Going to the computer, Mac typed in a command before turning back to face Jerry.

"These numbers are coordinates from the WGS. The World Geodetic System is used in mapping and navigation; this also includes GPS Satellite Navigation System."

"Okay," Jerry frowned, "so to what do these coordinates refer to?"

Mac looked towards his computer.

"60° 10' 14" N is a Latitude reference and 24° 56' 07" is Longitude and according to the computer this is the GPS Coordinates for Helsinki, Finland."

Jerry remained silent as he considered what Mac had just told him, both Razor and Mac stared at him waiting for an explanation.

"I'm sorry chaps, I still have no idea what this means."

He went on to explain how he came by the numbers and what Pixie-Lee had said about Max.

"So, your contact is convinced that Max was murdered by the Phoenix Legion."

"Yes," Jerry nodded, "and I'm inclined to agree with her."

He explained further about the Brothers of the Sacred Whisper website and the forum.

"I have used this forum before and find it to be invaluable."

"Okay," Razor began pacing the room. "These people may have been useful in the past but why are they being so guarded now?"

"Well, for two reasons I guess. Firstly, Max disappeared over a week ago and because of this there is not a lot of information going around. I imagine his murder has put a dampener on discussions that involve the Phoenix Legion. Unfortunately I didn't get an opportunity to speak with him myself so I'm relying on others to pass information on."

"Where did Max get these coordinates from?"

"Again, I have no idea, but they must be significant. I imagine that is what got him killed."

"Is there anyone out there who would be willing to shed some light on this?"

"No," Jerry shook his head, "my contact is terrified. I got the distinct impression that she knows nothing about these numbers. Max must have simply sent them to her in desperation before he was killed."

"There you are Jeremy Knowles." Linda suddenly appeared at the door and she was furious.

"You men should be ashamed of yourselves. Can't you see this man is in no fit state to be interrogated?"

Razor opened his mouth as if to defend them both, but thinking better of it closed it again.

"I'm far too busy to be chasing around after you," she glared at Jerry. "If you won't stay in your room I'll have no alternative but put a lock on the door."

Breathlessly she stared around the room, it resembled a pigsty and she wondered how they could work in such a mess.

"Come on," her voice softened a little. "Let's get you back to the hospital. You're not well enough to be up yet."

Razor and Mac remained rooted to the spot. They offered no help as Jerry was led away, but they were relieved to see the back of the ferocious Dr Linda Pritchard.

XLV

Schiffer's office was full of men. Heidenrech had assembled the group for a meeting with his superior at precisely the appointed time and now they were deep in conversation. Standing apart from the others, he leaned back against the wall and made no attempt to join in with the discussion.

"You will carry out the ceremony this afternoon?" Schiffer addressed the longhaired druid.

"Yes." The man nodded slowly. "It will last for several hours and will take place in the crypt below the Christian altar." He grinned with pleasure at the prospect of a Pagan ceremony so close to consecrated ground and the others in the group added their appreciation.

These were rogue druids, seduced by Schiffer's promises. They were prepared to carry out a ceremony that would deliver ultimate power to the Phoenix Legion. Schiffer himself would be present; he was going to be granted ancient rights and have access to all their secrets.

"Then go and make your preparations, Heidenrech will ensure you have everything you require including the Belgae Torc."

"My Lady, you are to come with us."

Orlagh was surprised to see the attendants. Four women dressed in robes filed into her room and immediately the atmosphere began to thicken. Something was wrong she could sense it.

"Why should I come with you?" Rising from where she had been sitting by the window, she reached unconsciously for the Stave of Yew.

"The druids require an audience with you."

Orlagh knew this was a lie, and the stave came alive in her hand. Vibrations began to course through her fingers and the cold wood became warm.

"If they want to see me then they can come here."

The woman facing her hesitated and the colour drained from her face.

"Please do not make this even more difficult," she hissed, "you must come with us."

"I will not." Orlagh stamped her feet, her voice rising as she stood her ground.

None of the women dared to move, they just stared at her in disbelief. They had not expected her to defy the word of the druids.

Orlagh's eyes flashed and drawing strength from the Stave of Yew, she stared back at them. She had never considered it an ally, in her mind it had always been a talisman of evil, but still she did not have the strength to dispose of it.

Suddenly the women parted as a giant of a man pushed between them. He towered menacingly above her.

"You have been instructed to come with us." His deep voice was gruff and it filled the room.

"I will not." Orlagh stood with her hands on her hips.

The man, wearing the cloak of a warrior, was used to women doing as he bid. He sighed deeply and Orlagh sensing his fierce temper stepped away from him. He was a powerful man who could quite easily overpower her, but time stood still as she waited for something to happen. Slowly he lifted his arm and placed his hand on her shoulder. His touch was as light as a butterfly as his fingers grazed her skin and she shuddered. She wanted to move, get away from him but her legs refused to work. Suddenly he gripped her by the neck and lifted her off her feet. Orlagh attempted to scream, but his fingers were strong and as he applied pressure to her throat, darkness began to cloud her vision. Panic rose up inside her but she was powerless to react, still her body would not obey her commands. The last thing she was aware of was the Stave of Yew vibrating vigorously in her clenched fist.

The warrior carried Orlagh from her room and the attendant women followed on behind shocked by the violence. They had expected Orlagh to accompany them without fuss, and glancing at each other nervously, they could do no more but remain at a respectful distance.

Orlagh was laid on an ancient stone in the crypt deep below the ruins of the castle then the warrior stepped back.

"Prepare her," he said glaring at the frightened women. "She will remain unconscious for a while then recover with no ill effects."

He turned to leave and the women rushed to Orlagh's side. Stripping her of her clothes, they cleansed her body with sweet smelling oils before brushing and braiding her hair with tiny flowers. Once that was done, they dressed her in a brilliant white robe trimmed with gold and soft leather slippers were placed on her feet, and when finally she came to her senses, she was still holding onto the Stave of Yew.

XLVI

The *Ocean Pride* was making steady progress and in the Wardroom Razor and Mac were briefing the men.

"In a few hours time we will be leaving the ship in the Sikorsky. Our destination is half way up the Dnieper River in the Ukraine." He paused to look at the men who were studying the map he had set up on the interactive whiteboard, then using the remote, he zoomed in on an area.

"This castle ruin is where we believe the Phoenix Legion to be holed up. Don't be deceived, these may look like old ruins, but be assured there will be an extensive system of tunnels running beneath this whole area."

"What about defences?" one of the men asked.

"We have run a number of computer programs to predict the logical positions for conventional weapons." Mac answered the question, and using a laser pointer began to make his way around the diagram.

"We are likely to encounter machine gun emplacements here, here and here." He pointed out positions of strategic value and backing them up with coloured gridlines, predicted the crossfire. "We don't expect mines or heavy equipment such as tanks."

Memories of their encounter with Stormtroopers on the island of Gog filled his head. They had been very lucky to survive an attack by a Tiger Tank and he was hoping there would not be a repeat performance.

"The environment doesn't allow for the use of heavy equipment," he said reassuringly. "However, there are a number of Second World War fighter planes located nearby. We will of course do our best to ensure they don't get off the ground."

It was his plan to disable these on their way in, but because of time restraints and the need for stealth, that would probably have to be shelved.

"We are going to set the Sikorsky down on the light aircraft landing area just here." Using the laser pointer, he highlighted the position on the screen before going on. "It's about two miles from the castle so we shouldn't arouse too much suspicion on the way in."

"What about airfield defence?"

"There are no indications of that." Mac looked directly at the man who had asked the question and was reminded of Kylie. Both Wings and Kylie were sorely missed as too was Jack, but nobody mentioned that.

"We have studied the area extensively using a drone and there seems to be no airfield defences in place," pausing, he waited for the screen to change. "Once on the ground, we split up into two groups and perform a classic pincer movement. We will assault the castle from two sides." He glanced at the men, giving them chance to make a comment, but they remained silent.

"I don't anticipate much resistance at this stage, they won't be expecting us, but stay alert at all times. I guess the lookout posts will be manned, they have heavy machine guns covering the countryside so our first objective will be to take them out. We'll stage covert attacks on these two positions."

Images of a grass covered pillbox like structure appeared, then they were shown a view of the only standing tower, it had a machine gun post on top. Mac went on to give details about how these raids should be carried out and he answered all their questions.

"Snipers with .50 cal's will be set up around the airfield. Their job is to take care of any fighter movement and to give covering fire if we need it."

"Where do you suppose Dr Gairne is located?"

Both Razor and Mac looked up, this was the question they had been waiting for, and were surprised it had taken so long to be asked.

"Frankly we have no idea; the computers have failed to come up with any suggestions. The problem we have is a complete lack of Intel regarding this stronghold."

Mac continued with the reply. "We'll just have to see what comes our way. I know it's not ideal, but between our two groups we'll sweep the place clean."

"What about numbers? We represent a small force; there must be dozens of troops stationed there."

"We don't anticipate huge numbers. We have been studying the place for some time now but have only seen a few troops. I agree, we will be facing a crack force, drilled and disciplined, but we are more than a match for them."

The Taskforce remained silent, each man content to make up his own mind regarding Mac's reply.

"The moment we locate Dr Gairne, we withdraw." Mac gave them details of the code words they would use over the battlefield radios.

"There are to be no unnecessary heroics." He didn't need to say more.

"Right gentlemen, if there are no more questions, I suggest you all eat a hearty meal and get some rest. Wheels up at 16:00 hours."

At first, the sounds around her were confusing. Noises floated in and out of range and she didn't know what to make of them. Suddenly the volume increased, and holding it inside her head in an effort to analyse it she realised it was the sound of a druid chanting.

Forcing her eyes open, she glanced around but there was nothing to see, the darkness was complete so focussing her other senses, she tested the air, it was stale and damp. Her arms were pinned to her side and she realised that she was being held upright. Someone was pressed up behind her, his arms circling her waist she could feel the warmth from his body. Holding herself rigid she dared not move, her heart was beating uncomfortably against her ribs but she had to remain calm. Shuffling slightly she planted her feet firmly on the ground and standing upright she felt the arms around her relax a little. Now with her body responding to her commands she made tiny experimental movements. She was not restrained, that was a good thing and after a moment, the man released his hold completely and stepped away.

She was left alone in the darkness and although she could sense people around her, it was too dark to see them, it was just like before and memories of the attack on the druids began to fill her head. Pushing these thoughts away, she focussed on the chanting that she could hear, it was an eerie sound full of menace and she shuddered. A dull ache at the base of her neck was a reminder of the events leading up to this moment, she had been in a situation like this before and nothing good had come of it then.

More druids joined in, their voices rising and falling with a rhythm that seemed to pulse from within her skull. This made her head ache even more and in desperation, she attempted to block it out completely.

Her eyes were adjusting all the time and now she could see tiny lights from candles dancing at her feet. Peering further into the darkness, she realised that she could see Schiffer. He was sitting on an upright chair on a slightly raised area and seemed to be staring straight ahead. Druids were moving around him, flitting in and out of the darkness, and as she watched, they performed some kind of ritualistic dance. This was a good sign; with Schiffer in attendance, the people in the crowd must be safe. Again, unwelcome thoughts of the attack on the druid's lair filled her head and desperately she tried to block them out.

Orlagh's attendants were standing a short distance behind her, four young women watching the performance. One of them was wringing her hands nervously and gripped by fear she knew this was wrong. The druids had not prepared thoroughly enough for this ritual and she was certain that something was going to go terribly wrong. They were not sufficiently elevated in the order to be carrying out a ceremony as important as this.

"This is not right," she murmured. "The ceremony states that the woman with red hair must come of her own free will. We have forced her to be here and nothing good will come of this."

No one heard her warning.

The helicopter, sweeping out over the peninsula, was on a course that would take it away from the main river. Theo Grimaldi was at the controls with Razor occupying the co-pilot's seat and both men remained silent, lost in their own thoughts.

The atmosphere inside the Sikorsky was charged with anticipation; it was always like this before a mission with each man anticipating the battle to come.

"Three minutes to the landing zone." Theo spoke calmly into the intercom and the men became alert.

Above the doors situated on either side of the cabin, little red lights began to flash, when they turned green the doors would open and the men would go.

At one thousand feet, the Sikorsky hung in the air like a huge dragonfly then Theo, coaxing it into a sudden turn, lined up on the grass runway below. Anyone tracking their progress would think they were simply passing overhead.

The ground came up at an alarming rate as they lost altitude then at the last second, Theo pulled back on the controls and the helicopter touched down with hardly a bump. Men tumbled out as fluidly as water pouring over rocks and as soon as their feet hit the ground, they disappeared into the undergrowth. Seconds later Theo piled on the power and a tornado-like draft flattened the grass around the landing zone. With its engines howling madly the helicopter rose up into the air and was gone.

On the ground, the taskforce split into two groups then began their assault on the castle. Checking the hangars, they spread out across the airfield but found nothing, the ground crews were nowhere to be seen.

Snipers went to ground as planned and setting up their weapons made good use of the environment. Digging in, they prepared to wait for further orders.

Razor was in command of one group with Mac leading the other. Between them, they numbered twenty eight, two groups of fourteen highly trained men. Mac took his men off to the right in a flanking manoeuvre that would bring them out in front of the tower, leaving Razor to approach the castle head on.

Razor had his men stop and dig in amongst a clump of bushes; he wanted to check the way ahead. He was sure there was a command post around here somewhere and using a hand held computer, he brought the drone in low over their heads and made a sweep of the area. Studying the tiny screen, he had a perfect view and soon found what he was looking for. On a slightly elevated position, a pillbox type structure was built into the ground. It seemed to be reinforced with concrete and steel and camouflaged with clumps of grass and foliage. Calling his men around him, Razor began to issue orders.

Mac and his team had further to go; their first objective was to take out the machine gun post located on top of the remaining tower. Mac studied it through his binoculars and could see that recent restoration had been carried out. Fresh mortar filled the gaps eroded away by harsh winters and glass panels were set into gothic windows. This replaced old wooden shutters once used to keep out the worst of the weather and he could see ancient metal brackets fixed either side of the stone mullions that held them in place. Mac took all this in but could find no way into the tower.

From the top, the soldiers operating the machine gun had a magnificent view across the countryside. Mac was relying on them being careless and not too focussed on their task. He knew how tedious it could be manning a position like this especially when an attack was most unlikely.

Holding position, Mac kept his troop out of sight. He considered using the snipers set up on the airfield to take the men out, but that would give away their position and could affect their escape plan. He would have to deal with the problem himself.

"Set up two sharp shooters," he made his decision. Indicating to where he wanted his assault rifles positioned, he checked the range to the top of the tower. There were two men situated up there and it was imperative to take them both out at once. He did not want one to survive and call for reinforcements.

"As soon as both men appear, deal with them."

Earlier they had used the drone to check the machine gun post and discovered that both men were smokers. They would regularly stand and take in the views as they enjoyed a cigarette, this would be the ideal time to attack.

XLVII

O rlagh was pushed forward until she was standing inside a hastily drawn circle marked on the uneven floor. Glancing nervously around she wondered what was going to happen next but all she could see were candles glowing like tiny stars against a blackened sky. Locating Schiffer, she wondered what part he was playing, this was the second time she had seen him at a druid ceremony.

Druids were dancing in and out of the pale circle of light and as she watched, one shuffled along on legs that were old and tired. Long silver hair hung down his back and his shoulders stooped under the weight of a lifetime, in his outstretched arms, he carried something. Orlagh could not see what it was, he was too far away and the shadows helped to keep his secret, but as he drew near, she could hear him chanting. His voice rising and falling with a rhythm that remained rich and clear was by far the most vibrant thing about him.

Something flashed as it caught the light and she took a sharp intake of breath, she had seen this before. On top of a cushion rested the Belgae Torc. It was not clear at first but as he moved closer, she could sense its power. She was hardly aware of the Stave of Yew that she was clutching, but suddenly it began to vibrate. She did not even notice the spirits stirring around her, but as they crowded in the air became thick with their presence.

Forcing herself to breathe evenly she watched as the druid moved ever closer. She could see the torc clearly now, it was magnificent, its golden surface reflecting and amplifying the feeble light from the candles. Wrought by Madb in her uncle's forge so many lifetimes ago, Orlagh could see the twisted strands of white gold plaited into rope as thick as a man's thumb, beautifully carved finials were fashioned to represent the rising sun and the moon. She knew that one end was dedicated to Belenos, the Sun God and the opposing end was carved with a hare. This was to honour Eostra, the Goddess symbolising abundance and good fortune.

A horse's head devoted to the Goddess Epona sat at the end of a short chain, and when fastened, Epona sat between Eostra and Belenos. This was strong magic indeed and Orlagh staggered under the weight of its spiritual implications.

The druid stopped in front of her and bending forward placed the cushion at her feet. The torc, now in the light of the candles glistened like a serpent coiled, ready to strike.

Orlagh was held in rapture, frozen to the spot she could hardly move. Her throat ached and her mouth went dry as her blood pressure began to soar. She knew exactly what would happen when the torc was placed around her neck and she was unable to react.

The druid began chanting again but this time the sounds were different. Raising his arms above his head, he turned towards the darkness and invited the spirits to cross from the Otherworld. They were welcome to enter the world of the living, and as they shuffled forward, Orlagh could feel them brushing against her skin as they jostled for position.

Raising the torc up from its resting place, the druid held it aloft before making a descending arc, and as he lowered it slowly, it touched the top of her head. Candlelight seemed to intensify and the torc glowed like a halo, it reflected gold against the red of her hair, and as he brought it down his twisted knuckles brushed against her ears. Slipping it over her head, it weighed heavily against her skin and the spirits wailed with excitement as the warmth of its splendour splashed from her body.

The druid withdrew leaving her standing alone and everyone watching held their breaths in anticipation of the glory to come.

Razor crept silently up behind the gun emplacement and locating the entrance could see two men lounging against the concrete walls. A third man was positioned behind the deadly weapon that was covering the trees where his men were holed up.

Using hand signals, he silently gave instructions to the men accompanying him, then, creeping forward like cats stalking a mouse, they withdrew their knives and prepared to spill blood.

Unfortunately, as Razors men were about to pounce, gunshots rang out alerting the guards but they had no time to react. Their deaths were not as clean as Razor would have hoped; two of the men went down but the other was only wounded. Jerking and crying out he reaching for his weapon, but Razor was too quick, grasping his head he twisted, snapping his neck and with a final spasm the air wheezed from his body and he lay still.

With the job complete, they were now able to move on. Razor signalled to his men before making contact with Mac. He chose not to mention the ill-timed attack on the tower by his snipers.

Moving towards the semi derelict castle, Mac led his men into the first open doorway he could find. Luckily, this took them to the interior of the underground complex and not into a dead end. His luck continued to hold out, they encountered no resistance.

Razor was not so fortunate, the sound of gunshots alerted some of the uniformed guards and now they were filing out of their hiding places brandishing weapons. These were elite S.S. Officers and caught in the open, Razor and his men had no option but to find what cover they could and open fire. The first shots rang out and men did their best to cover each other, but the German soldiers were good, ducking out of sight, they returned fire at an alarming rate.

"How many are there?" Razor called out.

He was sure he had counted only four men but the gun battle was so intense that they must number more.

"Three left," someone cheered as he scored a hit.

Razor organised his men, he could not afford to be pinned down for long. More troops were sure to be alerted by the sound of gunfire and he did not want to hang around.

Three of his men slipped away to one side and began working their way around the ruins as the remaining troop drew the enemy fire. They were soon in position and on the signal fired their weapons, then there was silence.

They had to move quickly, it was imperative to find Dr Gairne and evacuate as soon as possible, so moving forward they went towards the safety of a wall and out of the line of fire.

At first Orlagh could feel nothing, the torc around her neck remained inert but the Stave of Yew in her hand was burning into her skin. The druids were chanting with ever more intensity now and the air around her was alive with movement.

Schiffer, from his elevated position, was grinning insanely as he stared down at her. His ice blue eyes seemed to bore right into her skin and she shuddered under the weight of their stare. From the crazy look on his face, she was certain that he had been driven mad by the might of the ceremony.

One of Orlagh's attendants screamed but the chanting of the druids concealed the sound of her cry. She could stand it no longer and turning, fled into the nearest tunnel.

The torc began to vibrate. At first it was almost imperceptible, like the touch of a butterfly's wings against her skin, Orlagh was hardly aware of it. Soon the vibrations began to grow in intensity and the fluttering became stronger as it pressed against her throat.

Slowly the torc began to awaken, it seemed to writhe like an asp around her neck and as it vibrated, it tightened until it began to restrict her breathing. Orlagh gasped as panic rose up within her breast.

Through tunnel vision, she could see movement. It was not clear at first, but she knew what it was, she had experienced this before and it was something that she was not keen to repeat.

A red haired woman with piercing green eyes smiled sweetly as she made her way towards her. Her smile radiated warmth and confidence, it was designed to put her at ease but Orlagh was not fooled. It was just like looking at herself in a mirror and she shuddered. The goddess was a perfect image, but she represented everything that Orlagh was not. Evil swirled around her like heavy clouds in a storm, and as the goddess moved closer, she gained in strength feeding off Orlagh who was growing weaker by the second.

Something fluttered in the air beside the goddess and trying desperately to focus her eyes; Orlagh struggled to understand what was going on. A huge black bird rose up out of the darkness and she knew exactly what it was. The Morrigan in the form of a Crow was the Celtic Goddess of War.

Her legs almost gave out as realisation took hold, this was serious druid magic, it could not be possible if it were not for certain elements coming together.

The torc and the goddess of Hibernia together represented a serious menace, but with support from The Morrigan, they could harness some incredible spiritual power.

XLVIII

Razor and his men entered a tunnel that slipped beneath the foundations of the castle. Here it was wide enough for three men to stand shoulder to shoulder and working their way forward they kept their assault rifles up ready to fire.

Suddenly, from out of the darkness, Stormtroopers appeared and the first rank of Razor's men dropped to their knees. The second rank closed in behind and shouldering their weapons night turned into day as muzzle flashes lit up the enclosed space. The German soldiers hardly had time to react and most of them fell on the first volley but two of Razor's men failed to get to their feet. Nothing could be done for them now, their bodies would be recovered on the return journey.

Urging his men forward, Razor sprinted along the narrowing space, and jostling for position, they charged into the open chamber. A roughly hewn wall containing three separate tunnels faced them and halting his men, Razor used a light to investigate. There were no indications that people had passed this way and ducking into each tunnel in turn, he found nothing to convince him that this was the way to go. He had three choices and it was crucial that he chose the correct one, but then something suddenly appeared in front of him and twelve automatic weapons pointed at an unsuspecting target.

The woman, wide eyed with terror skidded to a stop and collapsed into a heap on the ground. Razor, throwing himself down beside her was convinced she had died from fright, but after a few moments her eyelids fluttered and she let out a cry.

"We are not going to harm you," Razor said squeezing her hand reassuringly as he helped her to sit up.

"Who are you?" she groaned, her English thick with accent.

"Where is Dr Gairne?"

There was no response; she simply stared at them her eyes full of disbelief.

"The red haired woman," he tried again. "Do you know where she is being kept?"

This time it worked and she nodded vigorously.

"You must follow me quickly." She said, struggling to her feet. "Please, you must trust me; I will show you where the druids have taken her."

"Druids?" Razor exclaimed. That was the last thing he expected to hear.

"Yes, there is a ceremony taking place and your friend is in grave danger."

Razor had no choice but to follow her into the dark tunnel.

Mac was lost; he had no communication with Razor, the stonework surrounding them was the reason for that, so retracing his steps he took his troop back to their original position. He knew where Razor had entered the tunnel system and it seemed logical that he would eventually return this way, so digging in he had his men cover every eventuality. Wherever Razor went trouble would never be that far behind.

The Morrigan is a shape shifter who would normally take on the form of a Raven or Crow. She is also known as a protectress, having the unique ability to draw upon a person's strength and then empower that person to confront his or her own challenges, often in the face of insurmountable odds.

In the true Celtic tradition, The Morrigan has appeared in a variety of Triple Goddess trinities. The Triple Goddess can wield incredible power, and together the three aspects will become one, Orlagh as the maiden, the goddess of Hibernia, the mother and The Morrigan as the crone.

The Morrigan took her place at Schiffer's side and he could feel her power coursing through his body. She was the Goddess of War and with the support of the Triple Aspect, there would be nothing to stop him from imposing his will upon the world.

The goddess of Hibernia, drawing herself up to her full height, towered above Orlagh and looked down on her. They were identical apart from their souls, Orlagh was pure and gentle with the goddess pure evil.

The torc was tight around her neck and Orlagh was struggling to breathe. The vibrations were keeping her alive, an irritation to focus on as her life essence drained slowly away. Steadily she became weaker but then Orlagh saw movement from the corner of her eye. Characters appeared in her peripheral vision but were not clear, they remained as shadows simply refusing to materialise and although she could feel their presence, she was left frustrated. There was something familiar about this new sensation, she had experienced it before and gradually realisation took hold. Madb and her animal allies were there with her and relief began to flood through her, she tried to call out to them but her voice remained trapped at the back of her throat.

A vision of Jerry filled her head and her heart beat faster then, as she heard the sound of his laughter, her eyes pricked with tears. He was teasing her about her animal allies.

Madadh-alluidh the wolf, brushed past her, the coarseness of his hair scratching her legs and all thoughts of Jerry disappeared. The wolf did not appear in her vision but remained with Madb on the edge of her awareness.

The magnificent stag was her true ally; he appeared to her in all his majesty and with movements that were slow and deliberate he positioned himself at her left hand. His presence filled her with hope; his was a powerful force, a solid reminder of her link with the creatures from the Otherworld.

Her vision was fading fast, death was not far away and standing with her allies, she heard a voice. At first, it was a whisper and she did not understand the words, spoken in an ancient tongue, the meaning lost in time.

"Focus on the words and you will know true wisdom." The stag whispered and turning his head he looked at her with smouldering eyes.

Orlagh almost buckled under the weight of his stare but with a huge effort, she managed to lift her head. Nothing else seemed to matter, the world could end right now and she would be safe. His eyes burned red and clear and as she looked, she began to understand.

'The yew, a Stave of sacred wood holds the power of re-birth. Carved with a sacred prayer, the ancient runes contain a charm of great energy. Use this now to strike the Goddess down before she takes what remains of your strength.'

With her final breath, Orlagh bellowed out a cry then Jerry appeared. He filled her vision and nothing else seemed to matter, with him beside her, she was invincible.

Striking out at the goddess the Stave pierced her breast and a storm of hatred filled the air around her. It was like nothing Orlagh had experienced before and drawing on the support from her allies, she stood defiant in the face of evil. A maelstrom of spirits, maddened with anger, swirled around her head and the noise was deafening as they wailed with frustration and fury. Slowly the goddess began to fade and as the torc loosened its grip, the stag and the wolf howled their battle cry. This alone discouraged The Morrigan from leaving her perch, and staring down at Orlagh she screeched out a curse that was full of loathing.

Madb stepped into full view, and coming between Orlagh and The Morrigan she turned to smile before reaching out to take hold of the torc that she had wrought so long ago. Her fingers lovingly caressed the golden twists and she loosened the chain of Epona, breaking the stranglehold that gripped Orlagh so tightly.

Orlagh gasped and fell to the floor, her chest rising and falling rapidly as her lungs struggled to draw in precious air. She remained there as a battle raged overhead, then gradually the sounds became different and a strange smell tainted the air. Madb and her animal allies were gone, she could no longer feel them beside her, they had returned to the edge of her vision where they would remain frustratingly close but never in sight. She was convinced that she had felt the wings of a crow beating madly overhead but even that was gone and now she was completely alone.

Razor followed the woman along the narrowing tunnel. He could hear noises from up ahead and as the sounds of chanting became louder, the woman's fear seemed to increase and her pace began to slow.

Suddenly she stopped and pressing her body tightly against the wall was unable to go on. Raising her arm, she pointed the way then Razor and his men squeezing past disappeared into the darkness.

It was not long before they arrived at the place where the tunnel opened out into a huge black space. Tiny points of light laid out on the ground drew Razor's attention and he recognised them as candles. It was then he saw a bundle lying on the floor. At first, he did not realise that it was Orlagh, it was merely a shape half hidden in the darkness. Suddenly a shot rang out and sharp chips of stone stung his face.

Dropping to one knee, he brought his weapon up to his shoulder and returned fire. The rest of his men followed suit and soon the darkness turned into flashes of light as a battle commenced between them and an unseen enemy. The noise inside the cathedral-like place was almost unbearable as weapons fired and the smell of cordite filled the air.

The seat where Schiffer had been sitting was empty, and reaching out Razor grabbed Orlagh. Dragging her back towards him, he shouldered his weapon and bending forward scooped her up into his arms before turning to flee. His men offered covering fire, but now the resistance was lighter than before and they made it safely back into the tunnel.

Retracing their steps, they approached the entrance and Razor could hear the sounds of a raging battle.

Mac and his men were engaging a group of Stormtroopers who were well dug in just outside the tunnel entrance. The sound of stray bullets smashing into the stonework sang a melody of death that effectively held Razor and his men prisoners, it was impossible for them to emerge.

Lowering Orlagh's unconscious form to the ground, Razor moved carefully forward; he needed a plan and he needed it now.

Above the madness of the gunfight, he managed to raise Mac on his field radio and between them they agreed a course of action.

"Right men," he called back over his shoulder. "On my mark we are going to get out of here."

He told them about the Stormtroopers and the plan he had made with Mac then they moved out.

Scooping Orlagh up into his arms, Razor was the first to leave. The air was no longer thick with incoming bullets, but the sound of gunfire could still be heard from the Stormtroopers' position.

In the split second it took the men to exit the tunnel, Mac had stopped returning fire. This gave Razor the chance he needed to get out and as soon as his men had filtered left and right, the firing resumed.

Razor would do nothing to endanger Orlagh's life further but pausing, he set his men up to join the battle. The Stormtroopers stood little chance now they were under attack from two directions and in no time at all the battle was over.

Once it was safe to move out, Razor's men joined up with Mac's and merging into one fighting unit they began to make their way back slowly towards the airfield. The moment they thought they were in the clear more enemy soldiers appeared and two of Razor's men fell.

"Take cover in those trees." Mac yelled. "I want suppressing fire." He didn't need to spell it out, his men knew exactly what to do.

Suddenly dozens of Sormtroopers surrounded them, and heavily outnumbered, they were effectively pinned down. The air buzzed like crazed insects as bullets flew and it was not long before their ammunition began to run low. It was then that Razor realised their situation was becoming hopeless.

High above the battlefield Theo was at the controls of the Sikorsky. From his elevated position, he had a perfect view of the proceedings and he could see that it was not going well for Razor and Mac. The men on the ground were in grave danger and it did not take a military tactician to work out the likely outcome. He had to act now, so making a decision based on desperation and bravado; he forced the nose of the helicopter down and held the throttle wide open. If he could just distract the Stormtroopers for a few moments, it might be enough for his friends to make a run for it.

Gaining as much speed as possible, Theo waited until the very last minute before heaving back on the stick. The Sikorsky, dangerously low, skimmed the tops of the bushes as it clawed its way back up into the sky.

Dancing a drunken jig the helicopter swept between the opposing forces just a few metres above their heads. The downdraft from the spinning rotor blades along with the fearful noise of the screaming engines had the desired effect. The Stormtroopers, surprised by its sudden appearance stopped firing and kept their heads down, this gave Razor and Mac a few precious seconds in which to move out.

As soon as they realised what was going on they began firing their weapons with renewed effort, some of them aiming at the climbing Sikorsky, whilst others scored hits on Razor's men.

Theo glanced over his shoulder as he fought with the controls and could see men moving quickly out of the trees and along the slope towards the airfield. His plan had worked and now all he had to do was work out why an alarm was sounding from the control panel.

"Razor," Mac bellowed into his field radio. "On your left beside the tower, is that a mortar?"

Razor was unable to stop, with Orlagh unconscious in his arms her safety was his primary concern, but glancing over his shoulder, he could see two men setting up a tubular-like short barrelled weapon. Leaping over a low branch, he burrowed his way into the thick bushes before skidding to a stop beside Mac.

"Mac, what did you say about a mortar?" Laying Orlagh down gently between them, he snatched up a pair of binoculars and focussed the lenses on the base of the tower.

A small group of Stormtroopers had gathered around two men who were setting up a mortar. One of them was holding what looked like a Dewar flask and Razor, focussing the binoculars, took a closer look.

"Gas," he murmured. "They are preparing to launch gas on our position."

Mac stared at him in disbelief and his face paled.

"We're not equipped for an attack like that."

"No," Razor replied as he lowered his binoculars. "If it's the modified Sarin gas then we are finished."

Lifting his field radio, he barked out some orders. The snipers around the airfield responded immediately to his request and opened up with the .50 cals on the base of the tower. The effect was spectacular as lumps of stone and mortar from around the spot where the Stormtroopers were working exploded into the air.

Unfortunately, the mortar was hidden by the tower and the enemy were out of the line of fire.

"Get Theo in here fast," Mac said. "He must land at the bottom of that ridge." He pointed to where it was relatively safe for the helicopter to land. If they were lucky enough, they could defend the area whilst making an effective evacuation.

Razor, doing as Mac suggested, alerted Theo to the danger and the details of their plan.

The incoming fire churning up their position became more intense as men swarmed from their underground accommodation to join the battle. It was now far too dangerous for Theo to attempt a landing, they would never get away with it and as soon as the gas was launched, they would all be killed in seconds.

Theo listened intently over the radio whilst wrestling with the controls. Something vital had been damaged and the helicopter was vibrating madly. At least it was still in the air and responding to his input, but he wondered how long this would last.

Turning onto a course that would bring him over the landing zone, he kept the castle on his left hand side. He could see muzzle flashes swarming like silver fish beneath the surface of a pond, but he had no time to admire the view, he had to concentrate on his landing. It was going to take all his strength both mentally and physically to bring the Sikorsky in and hold it steady whilst the men clambered aboard. All this would have to be carried out under heavy fire.

Suddenly another alarm sounded and the helicopter slewed to one side. Theo swore and wrenching the joystick back, managed to stabilise the aircraft but the controls felt mushy in his hands and pushing the throttle forward he prayed for more power, then the engines began to smoke.

Theo peered out of the side window and could see the dead gunners lying beside their heavy calibre machine gun on top of the tower, then he had a clear view of the mortar crew below. They were keeping their heads down because the .50 cals were still hammering away, but this did not stop them from preparing to fire. He watched as a man dropped the Dewar flask into the barrel then the gunner began fiddling with the firing mechanism. Razor, Mac and the men were just seconds away from death.

Thoughts of Orlagh filled his mind and his nostrils flared at the memory of her scent. She was a beautiful woman and he was attracted to her from the start, he would love to run his fingers through her magnificent red hair.

Flicking the helicopter over onto its side, he held the throttle wide open and put it into a dive. It rolled onto its back seconds before slamming into the mortar position.

The ground around the tower heaved as it disappeared beneath a column of earth and fire. The sound of the explosion deafened them and burning fuel erupted high into the air. The mortar along with the crew was obliterated and now the tower began to collapse around the remains of the helicopter.

Razor and Mac looked on in disbelief, even the incoming firing had stopped as men stared at the carnage. White-hot fragments began to rain down around them, bushes caught alight as burning fuel and vapours started fires.

"Move out." The order was given and men dashing from their ground cover ran towards the airfield.

The snipers on the .50 cals could see what was happening and covered the retreating men with rapid fire. Razor, gathering Orlagh up once again followed his men as bullets snarled between them but miraculously only a few of them were hit, both Razor and Mac made it to the rendezvous point unscathed.

"We have no airlift," Mac said between gasps, "and I don't intend hanging around here for much longer."

Razor nodded in agreement. Unable to reply he struggled to gather his breath, and laying his head down in the grass beside Orlagh, he recovered sufficiently before checking her for injury. She was still unconscious but there was no sign of trauma, her vital signs were good and she was breathing steadily.

"We'll have to make our way back to the main river on foot," Razor said looking up at Mac. "We can join the ship there."

"Sounds like a plan but how do you intend making contact with the *Ocean Pride?*"

Their short range field radios were not powerful enough to raise the ship and there was no cell phone signal. Suddenly they heard the sound of engines cough into life and they watched as two FW190 fighter planes made their way along the short runway. Barely enough time had passed for their temperatures and pressures to reach safe operating windows before the engine pitches changed and the aircraft, turning into wind, prepared for takeoff.

Roaring down the runway their wheels lifted from the grass and the aircraft zoomed low overhead. Gaining altitude, they banked hard and altered course before heading towards the distant horizon.

"Schiffer and one of his henchmen," Razor shouted above the noise of their departure. "Maybe we could use the radio on one of those machines to raise the ship."

"Are you going to risk it?" Mac stared at him. "Those hangars are probably swarming with Stormtroopers."

"I guess you're right but seeing those FW190s has given me an idea."

Using his hand held computer, he located the drone that was still circling overhead, and taking control, flew it back towards the runway and made a perfect landing. Reaching into his pocket, he pulled out a pencil and a piece of paper and began scribbling a note.

"What's going on now?" Mac frowned.

"We can use the drone," Razor told him.

"What do you mean?"

"Well, it's simple, as it has no radio we revert to a more traditional method."

Still Mac did not understand; Razor might as well have been talking in riddles.

"Do I really have to spell it out for you?" Razor said rolling his eyes. "We can use the drone as a carrier pigeon."

"Brilliant, now why didn't I think of that?"

Razor tapped the note to the underside of the delta wing then grabbing the computer, flew the drone into the air. As it climbed, he changed course and headed along the river keeping parallel to the bank.

Twenty minutes later he located the *Ocean Pride* using the camera mounted in the nose of the tiny aircraft, and dropping down towards the river, changed course again and flew towards the bow of the ship. Just a few metres out he flicked the drone up over the rail and lifting its nose even higher, shed speed before lining up on the upper deck.

"You would have thought this close to civilisation we could have used our cell phones to communicate with the ship." Mac said.

"Maybe Schiffer was jamming the signal."

"Yeah, you could be right."

"Come on pal, let's get out of here."

L

The *Ocean Pride* cruised as serenely as an ocean liner up the Dnieper River, guided by the pall of smoke spreading across the horizon she made her way towards the peninsula.

Paul was standing on the bridge, his brow furrowed deeply as questions filled his head. He knew instinctively that something had gone horribly wrong. Why were the men not making their way back by helicopter? They had lost radio contact with Theo in the Sikorsky over thirty minutes ago and he did not like it one bit.

Something caught his eye as he stood between the Helmsman and the Officer on watch, a flash in the sky above the bow interrupted his thoughts and suddenly he knew what it was.

The drone turned towards the ship and seconds later crash landed on the upper deck. Paul charged out of the door and almost tripped down the steps as the drone skittered across the deck. It smashed into the railings and before toppling over the side wedged between the bars. Paul made his way more carefully across the deck, and grabbing hold of the drone found the note taped to the underside. Ripping it off, he unfolded the paper and read the neatly written words and when he had finished he looked over the bow towards the smoke filled horizon.

The river narrowed as it made its way between a granite cutting. Before the dam was built in 1932 this part of the river was shallow, fast moving and treacherous to shipping. The water had tumbled over rocks causing rapids to surge around the small islands that once dotted the river. Trade had been almost impossible, the only way that merchants could bring in goods was over land, but all that changed once the dam was built above Zaporizhia. The landscape and the fortunes of those who lived here were altered forever as water filled the valley forming a navigable reservoir. A power station was installed and heavy industry arrived but at least some things remained unscathed. Thick forestation and farmland survived along both banks of the river, here at least things were as they should be and Paul smiled.

Turning towards the bridge, he shouted a command, then bounding up the steps he entered the bridge and went straight to the chart table. Studying the chart for a few moments, he grunted then turned towards the Helmsman.

"Around the next bend we will see the power station on the right, steer towards it but keep to the left of the buoys. Just past that will be a peninsula running out from the head of a small river, steer towards it."

His finger hovered over the chart as he checked to see where the deep-water channels went, they would have to be careful not to get too close to the sand banks.

"Have the ships tenders made ready. The moment we heave to, they are to be lowered. Tell the crews to head up that side river and keep a sharp look out for Razor's signal."

"Aye, aye sir." Came the reply, then the officer issued his orders over the intercom.

The tenders left the ship and side by side began working their way into the mouth of the narrow river. The smoke that had smudged the air earlier was now gone and in the distance they could see the ruins of the castle.

There were two men on each tender, a helmsman and a man carrying an assault rifle. There was not much danger of them being fired upon but Paul was taking no chances, he would rather have kitted the boats out with rapid firing .50 cals, but there had been no time to fit the heavier firepower.

Orlagh was still unconscious and although she displayed no sign of injury, Mac was worried that the druids had drugged her.

"Heads up," Razor said. "We have the tenders in sight."

The little boats were now in communication range, so speaking quietly into his battle radio, he gave them details of their position and five minutes later the first boat was close enough for his men to wade out and clamber aboard. The second boat came in closer and bumped its side against the bank. Reversing the engine, the helmsman straightened it up and remained as close to the bank as the tide would allow.

Using lengths of wood, Razor improvised a gangplank and managed to board the tender without getting his feet wet then, Mac lifted Orlagh up and passed her to Razor before losing his balance and almost falling in.

"Steady on Mac," Razor grinned and easing Orlagh down beside him, he made sure she was comfortable before reaching out for the equipment that Mac was holding out.

As soon as everything was aboard, the order was given and the engines revved sending diesel fumes across the surface of the water. Their job was done and now all they had to do was return to the ship. Razor had his men keep watch for Stormtroopers who may have followed them and could now be hiding amongst the bushes, but the evacuation went off without a hitch.

Paul remained on the bridge watching the events through a pair of powerful binoculars. He had snipers set up along the upper deck with their weapons trained on the area where Razor and Mac had been holed up, but there was no movement and the tenders remained unmolested as they made their way back into the main river.

Thoughts continued to run through his brain but it was no use speculating, he would have to wait for Razor's report.

As soon as they joined the ship, Razor and Mac went straight to the bridge.

"Dr Gairne is on her way to see Linda." Mac made his report and Paul listened without comment.

When they were finished, he paced the deck, shocked at what he had heard. Of course, he expected there to be casualties, but he was saddened by the news.

"So we lost seven of our men including Theo." He was still feeling the loss of Wings and Kylie. "Jack is not going to like this."

"At least we recovered Dr Gairne so I'd say the mission was a success." Razor reminded him.

"Yeah, but when will it all end? We still have to deal with the moles and the poisonous gas."

"We should inform the authorities and let them take some of the responsibility." Razor said.

"Well you know Jack, he'll want to do this covertly, take care of it himself." Paul continued his pacing. "Can you imagine the panic this would cause if it got out? We still have no idea where those moles will end up and when we do, announcing news like that will create mass hysteria as people rush to evacuate their homes. The authorities would not be able to cope and civil unrest would escalate."

Razor knew that Paul was right.

"I must speak with Linda before contacting Jack." Paul said then halting in front of them he stared. Razor and Mac had only been gone for a few hours but the stress of battle left them both looking exhausted.

"You two go clean up and get some rest."

Razor stepped out of his way as Paul left the bridge. He had never seen him looking so worried before but he knew he had control of the situation. Paul was a good man to have in command at moments like this, he always thought logically and never let his emotions get in the way.

"How is Dr Gairne?" Paul asked the moment he arrived at the trauma room.

Linda was dressed in scrubs, and with her hair tied severely back she looked as if she was about to perform surgery.

"My initial assessment suggests that she is in no immediate danger. I have done a tox screen, but you will have to wait for my report." She looked up at him and could see that he didn't look too good himself.

"She seems comfortable enough for the moment." Her tone softened and she touched his arm lightly with her fingertips.

"Why is she still unconscious?"

"If I had to guess, I would say its shock related. In the event of witnessing or experiencing a traumatic event, the body sometimes shuts down. She is probably suffering from ASD." She went into lecturer mode. "Acute Stress Disorder is a variation of post-traumatic stress which is the body's natural response to the kind of treatment she has been subjected to."

Of course, he knew all this and moving closer to where Orlagh lay he looked down at her face. He skin was almost transparent and against the red of her hair, she looked pale and ghost-like.

"How long is she likely to remain like this?"

"Probably not long," Linda did not seem the slightest bit concerned, her medical assessment remained professional and matter of fact. "Everyone is different, but I would guess no more than a few hours, that is providing she hasn't been poisoned."

"I see," Paul nodded.

Suddenly vibrations ran through the ship as the engines powered up. The tenders had been shipped and now they were preparing to make their way back along the river. It would take at least forty hours to return to Bodrum, time enough Paul thought to work out what to do next.

LI

When Orlagh awoke, she knew that Jerry was close. She could feel him; his unmistakable presence filled the cabin. Feelings of love flowed through her like blood in her veins and her heart beat faster until she thought it was about to burst.

Linda had moved her to a small cabin that annexed his room and now Jerry was sitting quietly beside her bed. He had been there for hours watching over her as she slept but ironically, at the moment of her awakening he had fallen asleep.

Orlagh smiled as she watched him, he appeared so young, it was like looking at a teenager sitting there and although there was only four years between them the age gap may as well have been decades. She felt exhausted and probably looked a mess, but as she turned towards him, he stirred and opened his eyes.

Reaching out their fingertips met and he smiled.

"Hello you," she said softly.

Jerry stood up and hobbled slowly towards her then, burying his face in her hair, took a deep breath. She smelt amazing, the warmth from her body soaked into him and he was reassured, it was really her, she had come back to him.

"It's wonderful to see you again," she whispered, "but you must promise me one thing."

"And what might that be?" he said looking up into his eyes.

"That you'll never leave me again."

"As it happened," he grinned, "it was you who left me."

Her expression changed and tears filled her eyes. "Now that couldn't be avoided."

He waited a moment as she fought off the urge to weep.

"Did you miss me?" he cringed, but could think of nothing else to say.

"More than you'll ever know."

Closing her eyes she searched for his lips and their kiss was warm and full of promise. With his one good arm, he held her tight and pulling her close felt the shudders running through her body. Tears soaked his skin and patiently, he waited for her demons to disappear.

"I felt awful having to leave you," she whispered as she told him about Schiffer and his men. More tears welled up turning her eyes to deep pools of emerald green.

"I thought he was going to kill you," she sobbed. "I had no choice but to do as he said."

Rocking her gently back and forth, he stroked her hair.

"You were brave enough to do the right thing," he reassured her.

Closing her eyes tightly Orlagh struggled with her memories. She could not forgive herself for feeling distant towards him whilst under the influence of the druids. He had seemed so far away then and it was as if their feelings for each other no longer mattered. It was difficult for her to imagine why she had felt that way, her love for him was genuine and life without Jerry was unimaginable.

"They made me wear the torc," she managed to say, pushing away her unwelcome thoughts.

"Really?" Jerry eased back a little and stared at her. "Was it like before?"

"Yes," she said after a while. "The goddess appeared and this time she was determined to have me."

He felt her shudder but remained silent, allowing her to continue.

"It was Madb and my animal allies who saved me again." She did not want to say too much, she knew how it annoyed him. It was then she told him about the Stave of Yew.

"I had a feeling it had some higher purpose," Jerry said. "From the first time you found it in our cabin I knew it would play a crucial part in all this."

"I remember now," she looked up at him. "The last thing to go through my head was that I could use it as a weapon."

"Now that is strange." Jerry nodded. "The yew has always been a symbol associated with re-birth, not death."

She was about to tell him more but did not get the chance.

"When I was in the coma, I dreamt about a druid chanting in a dark and lonely place. I remember seeing a huge black bird there too." He became silent, and closing his eyes he frowned as he re-lived the moment.

"The bird was a crow or a raven, it represented evil, I could sense death and suffering."

"It must have been The Morrigan, the Goddess of War." Orlagh whispered.

There was so much that she wanted to say but was unable to. Jerry was a disbeliever, besides she did not have the strength to put it all into words. She did not want to exhaust him with worry and felt uneasy talking to him about such things.

Suddenly the laptop beside the bed chirped, Jerry had received another e-mail.

"I had better take a look at that," he said softly. "It might be a message from Jack or even one of my female admirers."

She looked up at him and he winked mischievously.

"I needn't have worried so much," she grinned. "It seems you've lost none of your impertinence."

He was overjoyed by her reply and reaching for his laptop his face twisted as pain shot across his chest.

"Are you okay?" Orlagh was filled with concern. "Here let me get it for you."

She placed the computer down in front of him and lifted the screen, then he typed in a command and the computer came to life before he double clicked on an icon. It was a message from Pixie-Lee.

"See, I told you it would be from one of my girlfriends." There was no humour in his voice.

Rows of numbers filled the screen and she had no idea what they meant, but judging by the expression on his face, she was certain that Jerry had seen something like this before. It was then that Paul entered the room and his face lit up when he saw Orlagh. He was overjoyed to have her back safely onboard.

"Here, I think this belongs to you," he continued before handing it to her. "We have received orders to clear out of here. There's political unrest brewing up and the authorities have advised all foreign citizens to leave the area. We are to return to the States via Ireland so we can drop you off."

Handing her a pizza box, he smiled before turning to leave the room.

"I would love to stop but I have so much to do. Once you have rested we'll get together with the others."

They watched him go then Orlagh turned her attention to the box. Opening the cardboard lid, she stared in disbelief. Wrapped in a soft cloth was the Belgae Torc.

Author's note

It is normal practice to end a story with everything tidied up leaving the readers satisfied. I tried to do this with Orlagh and Jerry, ensuring that all was well with two of the main characters. It did not seem right to leave them in an impossible situation, besides it suited the plot to have them re-united and reasonably happy.

The final part of The Torc Trilogy relies on there being unresolved issues at the end of The Gordian Knot. With The Belgae Torc things were different, it could very easily have been a standalone novel, but the second and third parts of the trilogy are much more closely related.

It was clear to me early on that Jack Harrington was going to temporarily leave the story. What could be serious enough to drag him away at such a crucial point in the plot? I considered many scenarios but in the end chose to use his mother as a vehicle for this; what son would deny his ailing mother? Jack will be back with us in the final part of the story.

There is also the issue with the moles and their deadly cargo of concentrated nerve gas. At the end of the book, Jerry received a strange message, will he realise its significance and act upon it or will there be a worldwide catastrophe?

We know that micro-drones were dispatched to track the moles, but did they survive the terrible explosion that destroyed the underwater laboratory and so tragically claimed the lives of Kylie and Wings?

Why have Schiffer and The Phoenix Legion turned against the druids and seemingly the rest of the world?

With so much left unresolved the third part of The Torc Trilogy should prove to be a thrilling read.

Kevin Marsh
May 2014

Acknowledgements

I would like to thank Mark Webb at Paragon Publishing for all his help and guidance in getting this novel into print. Also with the initial proof reading, Anna Christodoulou and Mark Garbutt, who did a sterling job ironing out the wrinkles, any remaining are purely down to me. Thank you to 'Dizzy' Gillespie for his technical advice and support.

Finally, a big thank you to Maria who continues to be a 'writing widow', as most of my time is spent working in a spare bedroom, which is now my study.

Biography

Kevin Marsh has lived in Whitstable with his wife Maria for thirty years; they have two adult children who are now pursuing their own careers. Kevin has worked in Manufacturing Engineering since leaving school and for the last twelve years has taught the subject in FE colleges. His hobbies include painting using acrylics, he regularly exhibits his work. His interests include history, reading historical novels and he has recently discovered the wonders of e-books.

Lightning Source UK Ltd.
Milton Keynes UK
UKOW04f1533020914

237926UK00008B/138/P